Where secrets make their home...

Stopping to help a motorist in trouble, Katie Lynch stumbles upon a mystery as elusive as the Mothman legend that haunts her hometown of Point Pleasant, West Virginia. Could the coded message she finds herald an extraterrestrial visitor? According to locals, it wouldn't be the first time. And what sense should she make of her young son's sudden spate of bizarre drawings—and his claim of a late-night visitation? Determined to uncover the truth, Katie only breaks the surface when a new threat erupts. Suddenly her long-gone ex-boyfriend is back and it's as if he's under someone else's control. Not only is he half-crazed, he's intent on murder....

As a sergeant in the sheriff's office of the famously uncanny Point Pleasant, Officer Ryan Flynn has learned to tolerate reports of puzzling paranormal events. But single mom Katie Lynch appears to be in very real danger—and somehow Ryan's own brother, Caden, is caught up in the madness, too. What the skeptical lawman discovers astounds him—and sends him into action. For stopping whatever evil forces are at play may just keep Katie and Caden alive....

Books by Mae Clair

Weathering Rock
Twelfth Sun
Myth and Magic

Point Pleasant Series
A Thousand Yesteryears
A Cold Tomorrow

Published by Kensington Publishing Corporation

A Cold Tomorrow

A Point Pleasant Novel

Mae Clair

LYRICAL PRESS
Kensington Publishing Corp.
www.kensingtonbooks.com

Lyrical Press books are published by
Kensington Publishing Corp. 119 West 40th Street New York, NY 10018

First Electronic Edition: December 2016
eISBN-13: 978-1-60183-778-3
eISBN-10: 1-60183-778-X

First Print Edition: December 2016
ISBN-13: 978-1-60183-781-3
ISBN-10: 11-60183-781-X

Printed in the United States of America

In memory of Cathy Brehm

Acknowledgements

Thank you to my fantastic critique partner, Cate Masters, for working through chapter after chapter when I was on a tight deadline. I couldn't have finished the book without you.

To my editor, Paige Christian, thank you for your hard work in making this novel shine.

To Lyrical Underground and Kensington Publishing, I'm delighted to be part of such a professional organization.

Finally, to my husband, who has been by my side through every step of my writing journey, and who listened patiently to my endless chatter about the Mothman and UFOs. Thank you for undertaking two trips with me to Point Pleasant and the TNT. There is nothing like firsthand research when penning a novel!

Author's Foreword

In 1966-67, leading up to the tragic collapse of the Silver Bridge on December 15, 1967, Point Pleasant, West Virginia experienced a number of unexplained occurrences. Among these were Mothman sightings, an unusual amount of UFO activity, and the arrival of mysterious Men-in-Black.

I've used those events to create my own account of preternatural activity in A Cold Tomorrow. Set in 1982, fifteen years after the fall of the Silver Bridge, I've employed many of the legends from Point Pleasant folklore. As someone who enjoys researching urban legends and myth, I've placed my own spin on these. It should be noted that none of the characters in this book are meant to resemble persons living or dead in any fashion.

I've also taken some liberties with Point Pleasant by adding several roads and a number of fictional businesses such as the Parrish Hotel, the River café, Doreen Sue's hair salon, and others. The TNT is an actual site, part of the McClintic Wildlife Management Area.

A small town, Point Pleasant is situated at the confluence of the Ohio and Kanawha Rivers. It's suffered great tragedy and loss, endured the spotlight of scrutiny, but preserved. If you visit, you'll discover the world's only Mothman Museum, an amazing River Museum and Learning Center, Tu-Endie-Wei State Park which commemorates the town's frontier battle days, and also Fort Randolph, the site of an American Revolutionary garrison. The town also has an amazing riverfront with amphitheater. During one visit, I passed a pleasant summer evening there with my husband listening to local musicians and taking in the river views.

I hope you enjoy my interpretation of the Mothman and other odd events from Point Pleasant folklore. Thank you for taking the journey with me.

Mae Clair
June 2016

Prologue

December 15, 1967
Point Pleasant, West Virginia

Christmas was a week and a half away, but the cheerful bustle of downtown Point Pleasant left Katie Lynch gloomy. Across the street from her mama's hair salon, a man in a Santa Claus suit rang a hand-held bell, beckoning shoppers inside G. C. Murphy's. Another time she would have been excited to peek at the festive store displays or the toys and plush stuffed animals tucked into overflowing bins. She had her heart set on a perky white dog, since Mama said a real one was too much trouble. But even the memory of the snowy pooch she wanted to name Moonbeam had lost its appeal.

It was impossible to think of anything happy since her sister had disappeared three days ago. The only gift Katie craved for Christmas was Wendy's safe return.

Plopping to a seat on the bench in front of the salon, she chewed the inside of her lip. She'd stayed inside for a while, waiting for her mama to finish, but the odor of perm solution had worked on her stomach until she'd finally wandered outside. Despite an edge of cold in the air, she didn't mind the chill. Maybe because the sun hadn't set and the street was so busy. From her vantage point, it was easy to see the string of traffic lined up to cross the Silver Bridge farther down the road. She and Wendy had made plans to go shopping across the river in Gallipolis tomorrow. Their mama was even going to let Wendy take the car, something that had surprised them both.

And then Wendy vanished. The sheriff, most people around town, and even Mama thought Katie's older sister had run away.

"The girl took off once before," Katie had overheard Mrs. Quiggly tell Pearl Kraus when she'd dropped off a clothing donation at the thrift store. Secretly, she didn't understand why her mama worried about less fortunate people, when most of the town said nasty things behind her back. Like how she stayed out too late drinking, didn't have control over her daughters, and ran around with men.

It was the way people thought of Wendy, too—trashy and cheap. Some of the boys in school, and plenty of the girls, had even called Katie those names. Most wanted nothing to do with her. The only kids who might have taken an interest were bullies and troublemakers, friends she didn't need at twelve years old.

Locking her hands on either side of the bench, she leaned forward and glanced down the street. Across the road, two girls walked side by side, chatting intently—Eve Parrish and Sarah Sherman. They usually avoided her like most of her classmates, but never called her trashy names. Eve had even let her borrow a notebook for history class after Suzanne Flemish dumped Katie's in the toilet.

Her face burned with the memory. She'd wanted to punch Suzanne, but it would have only gotten her tossed out of school. If she'd had friends—good friends like Eve and Sarah seemed to be—maybe it wouldn't have hurt so much when she'd been forced to slink away. But Eve Parrish, daughter of the family who owned Point Pleasant's famous Parrish Hotel, would never be friends with someone like her. Wendy was the only true friend she had.

A sudden flapping noise made Katie glance skyward. A dense flock of black birds—more than she'd ever seen clustered together—swooped frantically overhead. Several people paused to look up, but most kept walking, too concerned with their regular business.

Was it her imagination or did the birds seem startled?

The sudden blare of a horn erupted from the line of cars waiting to cross the Silver Bridge. The ones that had been idling hadn't moved and more piled up behind the stalled string. It was Friday night, near rush hour as her mama called it, but she'd never seen the bridge so busy. The smell of exhaust, the flash of brake lights... Somehow it felt wrong. As if there were far too many cars and trucks for the old suspension bridge to hold.

"Excuse me, little girl." A man's voice cut into her thoughts, scattering them like the birds overhead.

Turning, Katie stood. The man who faced her on the sidewalk was tall and striking, with whitish-blond hair and ink-black eyes. Dressed in a black suit and black fedora hat, he appeared unaffected by the cold weather. She knew the style of hat because Wendy had a flashy red one she'd blown half a paycheck to buy. Katie had borrowed it once, though she hadn't been brave enough to wear it out of the house.

Her gaze dropped to the stranger's gloveless hands. It was hard to overlook fingers like that. Long and slender, the last digit of each fatter than the rest, making the tips look bulbous. A deformity of some sort. Her mama taught her it was impolite to stare, but that didn't stop a chill from dancing up her spine. The icy cold had nothing to do with the man's oddly shaped fingers, but an inner sense of warning that sent gooseflesh prickling down her arms.

"I'm not supposed to talk to strangers," she blurted.

"Well, now." The man's words were carefully modulated, tinged with an accent. He performed a slight bow, bending at the waist. "You may call me Lach. There. You see now. We are no longer strangers." His mouth stretched in a smile, revealing perfect white teeth.

Katie took a step backward. "What do you want?"

"I am looking for Doreen Sue Lynch."

What did he want with her mama? Sudden hope pinged through Katie's heart. "Do you know something about Wendy?" It was hard to mask her eagerness.

Tilting his head, the man eyed her as if she were a curious puzzle. "Wendy." He did not make the name a question, nor did he say it matter-of-factly. It seemed to Katie that he rolled it around on his tongue for fit.

"Yes, Wendy." An edge of anger bridled her words. He had to know something about her sister, dressed the way he was, obviously an outsider and someone of authority. Why didn't he come out and say what he knew? Was it because she was a kid and he wanted to speak with her mother?

Her gaze darted to the small sign hanging to the right of her mama's salon— Doreen Sue's Place. Lach looked there, too, realization dawning on his face. "Ah. Mrs. Lynch is inside."

"Tell me first." She stepped into his path, blocking his entry. He had to understand how desperate she was for news of Wendy. "If you know something about Wendy, tell me. I'm her sister."

"You misconstrue why I am here. Perhaps it would be best that I address Mrs. Lynch at another time. I did not expect her to be in a place with so many others." He nodded to the salon.

Before Katie could reply, a boom pounded the air with the roar of a cannon. The sound was so deafening, so unexpected, she cried out in fear. Above her head, the birds shrieked raucously, clamoring to be heard above a wild chorus of car horns. Somewhere across the street a woman screamed, and another began to sob. The man in the Santa Claus suit dropped his bell and raced in the direction of the Silver Bridge.

Whirling, Katie looked for the towers of the old suspension bridge, normally visible in the gap between buildings on Main Street. She saw only empty sky. As if some giant hand had descended and squashed the bridge into the Ohio River.

"That's not possible." Her stomach plummeted.

Down the street, people poured from the cars lined up to cross the bridge. Most were dazed, their expressions frozen in horror. Others screamed, pointing to where the bridge had stood. Cars on Main came to a screeching stop, drivers and passengers racing for the empty space the old bridge had dominated for decades.

As if pulled by an invisible leash, Katie took three halting steps. A horrible tightness splintered through her chest. "What happened to the Silver Bridge?"

Behind her, her mama's stylists and three customers burst from the salon. Two of the women raced past, their hair done up in curlers, plastered with bleach. By now Katie could hear the wail of sirens and the horrified screams bouncing up and down the street—"The Silver Bridge is gone! Oh my God, my God, someone please help. The Silver Bridge is gone!"

A sob built in Katie's throat. "Mama."

"I'm here."

Strong arms crushed her in a protective embrace. Overcome by a heavy cloud of rose perfume, she couldn't think past pressing her face to her mama's chest and sobbing. "How, Mama? How?"

"I don't know, baby." Her mama's voice was raspy from too many years of cigarette smoke and watered-down bourbon. Tonight it carried the added taint of tears. "All those people. All those cars."

Katie shuddered. First Wendy, now this. How many of her classmates, neighbors, or teachers had been on the bridge when it fell? It was almost as if someone had placed a horrible curse on Point Pleasant.

Drawing back, she looked about for the strange man with the light hair, but he'd vanished somewhere in the crowd of gathering people. All that remained were the sobs and the terror of a traumatized town.

And the mad, swirling dance of hundreds of blackbirds overhead.

Chapter 1

October, 1982
Point Pleasant, West Virginia

"It's star shit."

Ryan Flynn didn't question how the man knew, because—as Chester Wilson had told him earlier—he was a bona fide expert on star shit.

"We had it all over the fields when I was a kid." Wilson hovered beside him as Ryan squatted and dipped a twig into a puddle of gelatinous goo. Lifting the stick closer to his nose, he sniffed the string of mucous-like substance dangling from the tip. If it was shit, it didn't stink. The weird-looking stuff had no odor at all.

"You say it's all over the field?"

Chester's head bobbed up and down on his skinny neck. "Take a look." He swept his arm to indicate the surrounding pasture. "See those globs? They're all over the place. They'll be melting soon. That's how it was when I was a kid. You could set your watch by it."

Ryan squinted against the morning sun, picking out several shiny silver-white patches on the grass. Whoever'd dumped the stuff in farmer Wilson's pasture had gone to a lot of trouble. Yeah, it was a freak fest, some whacko's idea of a joke, but it didn't rate priority one. As a sergeant with the Mason County Sheriff's department, his time could be better spent settling disputes between neighbors, hauling in the occasional drunk—or God forbid—responding to calls on Mothman sightings. Thankfully, Point Pleasant's infamous "bird" had kept a low profile over the last four months.

"Could be someone's playing a joke on you."

"No, sir." Wilson was adamant.

Ryan stood, doing his best to take the call seriously. He had the feeling a couple of teenagers were laughing their asses off somewhere. "When did you first notice the stuff?"

Wilson scratched his chin. "Just before I called to report it. I've been busy in the lower pasture and didn't find it right off. But the star shit's not the worst of it. Take a walk with me, and I'll show you why I really called."

Lucky him. It figured his first call of the morning would border on *Twilight Zone* territory. At least Wilson hadn't blamed the Mothman for dumping the goo.

As they traipsed through the field, Ryan sidestepped several globs of the silvery goop. He'd collect some and send it for analysis, but the gunk would probably end up being a harmless concoction brewed in some kid's backyard. At his side, Wilson kept up a steady monologue about how his father and the senior Wilson's friends had dubbed the mucus-like stuff star shit back in '66. Ryan had been a kid then, but vaguely recalled rumors about the gunk.

"We'd go to bed at night and the fields would be whistle-clean," Wilson said. "Come morning we'd find the shit scattered all over the place. Sometimes there was silver tinsel mixed in. My dad had a name for that too. He called it outer space grass. It always turned up in the mornings the night after we'd see a weird light in the sky."

Ryan pinched the bridge of his nose. Mothman sightings had quieted down, but lately they'd been replaced by residents reporting strange lights. He hoped Wilson wasn't going to tell him he'd spied a UFO.

"What exactly did you want to show me?" he asked, trying to keep the man on track.

"It's just over the next rise."

Thankfully, the walk wasn't far. As soon as they crested the hill, Ryan knew exactly what Wilson wanted him to see. A pattern of black-and-white splotches defined the bulk of a large farm animal lying on its side.

"Shit." His muttered exclamation had nothing to do with stars or UFOs. Blowing out a breath, Ryan approached the cow wordlessly. Wilson and several other area farmers relied on their prized Holsteins to keep their dairy operations running smoothly. All he needed was for some drunk to have gone on a joyride and put a bullet through the animal's skull. But all thoughts of tanked-up behavior fled the moment he got a closer look at the carcass.

Odd that the kill hadn't attracted turkey vultures or crows, almost as if the poor thing was too defiled for a scavenger to touch. As far as he could tell there was no visible wound, bullet or otherwise. To be certain, he walked around the animal before squatting to take a closer look at its head.

"Sick, ain't it?" Wilson asked.

Like something from a B horror movie. Ryan didn't think an animal had that much blood in its body. The gory mess that had coagulated into a dense puddle under its head had come from its ears, nose, and mouth.

Grimacing, he glanced up at Wilson. "Was this animal ill, Chester?"

"No, sir. Fit as a fiddle."

"Kind of a weird place to find her." The cow was in a field Wilson didn't use for corralling, judging by the lack of fencing. Even odder, Ryan saw no sign of bovine tracks or crushed grass in any direction. And no footprints to indicate the cow had been led there.

"How did she get here?"

"That's just it." Looking puzzled, Wilson scratched his chin. "I haven't got a clue. I put her in the barn with the others last night. That was the last I saw her until I found her this morning." He shook his head, remorse filling his eyes as he gazed down on the dead cow. "What do you think happened? All that blood... What could do that to her?"

Ryan hated to speculate. "I'll call the county veterinarian for large animals."

"You know what he's gonna say, don't you?" Wilson looked up, his eyes bulging, face drawn in the early morning light. "Nothing about it's natural. It's like her damn brain exploded."

* * * *

Doreen Sue Lynch stubbed her cigarette into an ashtray and craned her neck to glance out the kitchen window. Her grandson, Sam, had promised not to stray. He'd helped her with the dishes after dinner, then begged to go outside with Rex, a friendly mongrel mix of Australian shepherd and retriever. She'd agreed to take her boyfriend's dog while Martin's house was being fumigated for spiders, and Sam would stay overnight because Katie was off visiting a friend.

Not that she minded. She loved having Sam, and Rex was hardly any trouble. Boys and dogs were good together, both bursting with bundles of energy. Even so, she'd have to call them in soon. It was getting late in the evening for an eight-year-old, and she wanted to set a good example as his grammie.

Spying him through the window, she drew in a sharp breath. An eerie green light spilled from somewhere above, haloing him in a cone of brackish illumination. Stock-still, Sam stood as if transfixed, his head tilted back as he gazed up into the weird light. Somewhere out of her line of vision,

Rex barked furiously. The sound made the hair on the back on her neck rise, but by the time she reached the door and wrenched it open, the dog had stopped yapping.

"Sam." Doreen Sue walked onto the rear stoop just as the green light winked out. Like someone throwing a switch. The jarring abruptness left her off-kilter and lightheaded.

It isn't happening. Not again. Please God, not to Sam.

Shaking off her vertigo, she sprinted from the stoop and was across the yard in record time. "Sam." Gripping her grandson by the shoulder, she gave him a gentle shake, drawing his attention from the sky. There was nothing. Nothing she could see. "What are you looking at?"

"Huh?" He blinked as if waking from a fog. "N-nothing. Just a cloud."

Doreen Sue bit her lip. Sam sounded befuddled and, although he wore a jacket against the crisp October air, he shivered. "Look at you. You're cold to the bone. Let's get inside."

Wrapping an arm around his shoulders, she cast a worried glance at the sky. *Nothing is there. Nothing was ever there.* "Did do you see where Rex got to?"

Sam shook his head as she led him toward the house.

"All right, you go inside and get warm. I'll look for him." The dog's barking had sounded frighteningly out of control. Nothing like the gentle animal she knew. "I won't be long."

Sam hesitated when she held open the back door.

"Grammie?" His expression hadn't changed, still composed of that same odd blankness as if he moved in a haze.

"What is it, baby?"

"Do you have any paper?"

Puzzled by the question, she cocked her head to the side. "What kind of paper?"

"For drawing. I want to draw the cloud."

* * * *

Almost ten-thirty.

Katie Lynch switched on the car radio, hoping for a distraction to pass the time. The lack of streetlights and the absence of other cars on the road made it seem later. Only a few miles outside of Point Pleasant, she looked forward to getting home. Her visit with Maureen Patton, a teacher who had taken an interest in her when she was still in high school, had been enjoyable, but she was ready to call it a night.

Stifling a yawn, she jabbed buttons on the radio, cycling through three stations before settling on "Bette Davis Eyes." At least Sam was staying overnight with his grandmother. Katie's mom might not be the most reputable person on the planet, but she loved her grandson to a fault. A blessing for Katie, since Sam had no father in his life. Not that she wanted anything to do with Lyle Mason after he'd refused to take responsibility for his child.

Best not to go there. Thinking about Lyle always ticked her off. She was glad he'd packed up and left Point Pleasant over a year ago. In a small town, it was hard not to cross paths with people you knew.

The song ended as she neared the TNT. An old World War II munitions site tucked among dense woodlands, the place was eerie during the day, downright creepy at night. Spotting a car off the shoulder, she slowed to a crawl. The front end of a blue Impala was angled into a shallow ditch, head and taillights dark. A faded "Big Brother is Watching You" sticker was plastered at a lopsided angle on the rear bumper.

Jerome Kelly.

Although the interior of the car was dark, she spied the bulk of someone slumped over the steering wheel. Quickly, she maneuvered off the road and slammed the gearshift into park. A ghosting of cold air struck her in the face as she bolted from the car and raced for the disabled sedan.

"Jerome!" Frantically, Katie rapped on the window. When he gave no response, she popped open the door. A combined reek of stale cigarettes and fast food assaulted her.

With the dome light illuminating the interior, it was impossible to miss the fat beads of sweat clinging to Jerome's face. Several wire-bound notebooks and a dozen balled up burger wrappers littered the passenger's seat. He groaned and shifted.

"Jerome, what happened? Are you all right?" He had no obvious signs of injury and seemed too young for a seizure or heart attack, but what did she know? She'd heard Jerome was a heavy smoker, and tobacco habits exacted a toll.

With a hand on his shoulder, Katie guided him back against the seat. "Jerome, it's Katie Lynch." He didn't seem to recognize her. "Are you hurt?"

He shook his head, working his mouth in an attempt to speak. No blood, thank God. But in the harsh glow of the dome light, his face looked waxy. If only another car would drive past. Her knowledge of first aid was limited to the minor cuts and scrapes an eight-year-old drummed up.

"Jerome," she tried again.

He closed his eyes, one hand bunched tightly into a fist. "Cold." Drawing a breath, he pressed it to his chest.

"Are you in pain?"

He mumbled something unintelligible and rolled his head fitfully.

"I'll get help." She was going to have to drive to town, find a pay phone, and call an ambulance. She could attempt to take him to the hospital, but feared moving him in the event he had a spinal or neck injury. Especially as disoriented as he appeared. "Don't worry. I'll have someone here before you know it."

She started to turn away, but he snagged her wrist and held fast. The panicked edge to his expression terrified her.

"Jerome, I have to get help." She hadn't gotten a good look at the front end of the car but didn't think it had been damaged. Maybe something had startled him and caused him to drive off the road. Deer were common on the back byways of Point Pleasant. Far more insidious than local wildlife, the Mothman was said to lurk within the dense labyrinth of woodlands and ponds that comprised the TNT. Maybe the monster had forced Jerome into the ditch.

Worried, Katie pried her hand free. Jerome was probably in a state of shock, which would explain his confusion and the glazed look in his eyes. "I'm going to drive into town and call an ambulance. I promise I won't be long."

He reached for her again. "Cold."

"I'm sorry, Jerome. I wasn't thinking." After shrugging from her coat, Katie draped it over his shoulders. The material wasn't heavy, but it would offer some comfort until she returned. "I'll be back as fast as I can."

Before she could move, a revolving light sliced through the darkness in a welcome swath of red. Highlights blinded her briefly before the vehicle rolled to a stop behind Jerome's disabled car.

"Thank God." Katie breathed a sigh of relief at the sight of the Mason County Sheriff's emblem on the driver's door.

"Do you need help, ma'am?" the deputy asked as he stepped from the car.

She nodded. "I'm glad you're here."

"Not to worry." He pulled a heavy-duty flashlight from his belt, flicking on the beam as he approached. She had a vague impression of dark hair and a strong jaw.

"Were you involved in an accident, ma'am?"

"No. I was driving home when I came across Jerome's car. I think he's hurt." The deputy cocked his head to look into the car. "Sir, are you all right?"

Jerome turned, blinking against the flashlight. "Cold."

"That's all he keeps saying. I gave him my jacket, but—"

"I'll radio for an ambulance." Turning away from her, the deputy headed back to his cruiser.

Katie clung to Jerome's car, hovering in the open doorway. With a grunt, he pawed her jacket from his shoulders and thrust it at her. "Take this."

"But I thought you were cold." In the background, she heard the deputy requesting an ambulance. Clutching the crumpled jacket in her arms, she bit her lip.

She didn't know Jerome that well. He was a frequent eater at the River Café inside the Parrish Hotel where she worked, and she'd occasionally see him around town. He always bobbed his head and stammered a greeting, noticeably awkward. Probably because he kept his nose buried in books on UFOs or unexplained phenomenon. He'd once told her friend Eve he'd moved to Point Pleasant to be near the Mothman.

"It shouldn't be long now." The crunch of gravel announced the deputy's return. "There's no need for you to stay, ma'am. You've done all you can."

"I-I don't know." It didn't feel right to leave, almost as if she was abandoning Jerome. She cast an uncertain glance in his direction, noting he appeared to be resting peacefully now, eyes closed, almost as if he'd drifted to sleep.

"I'll stay with him until the ambulance arrives," the deputy assured her.

She couldn't leave him in better hands than a law enforcement officer. At last, she nodded. "I'm so thankful you were driving by, Deputy...."

"Brown." He smiled slightly. "I'll make sure he's looked after."

A sudden sense of well-being flooded her, banishing the last of her reserve. She was so lucky the deputy had come along. Of course he would take care of Jerome. She had absolutely nothing to worry about now that he was there. Smiling, she walked back to her vehicle, Deputy Brown's flashlight bobbing along beside her.

Her feeling of security lasted a good two miles down the road, then swiftly departed as abruptly as it had arrived. A flutter of fear skipped through her stomach and she tried to shake it away. She had nothing to worry about. Jerome was with Deputy Brown. He was safe.

Except she couldn't recall a single feature of the deputy's face.

* * * *

Jerome Kelly was still on Katie's mind as she drove to her mom's hair salon the next morning. Sam would be spending another night with her mother, since Eve Parrish and Sarah Sherman had talked Katie into a girls' sleepover at Eve's place. She couldn't remember the last time she'd done anything so frivolous. She'd almost said no, but Eve and Sarah had been insistent, so she'd eventually relented.

Katie parked at the Parrish Hotel, then walked the few short blocks to her mom's salon. It wouldn't officially open for business for another half hour, but the stylists would be setting up stations with supplies for the day. Cutting down an alleyway, she held her coat shut against the morning air, then headed for the rear door.

Whisking a hand through her hair, she swept it from her face as she stepped inside. Her mom had been after her for weeks to color or cut it, but Katie liked the simplicity of her shoulder-length, blond locks, so easy for scooping into a ponytail. The curse of being the daughter of a hair stylist was having a mother who liked to experiment with the latest trends. Katie had endured several cuts she'd hated while growing up.

"Mom?" Sidestepping a box filled with shampoos and conditioners, she closed the door behind her. The pungent scent of perm solution and hair spray lingered in the air, reminding her of the hours she'd spent here as a child. Like the antiseptic smell of a hospital, the odor was a constant fixture, just as it had been when she'd sat in the back at a small table reading. Too many of her summers had passed that way while her schoolmates were outside playing. "Mom, are you here?"

"Out front," her mother's voice directed her.

Katie wound her way through the lunch room and past the supply closet into the main salon. It wasn't overly large—three stations, including her mom's, plus a small reception desk with a few chairs for waiting—but Doreen Sue had done her best to make the salon appealing. Right down to the butterscotch paint, hardwood floor, and glossy framed pics plucked from magazines. Katie doubted there was anyone in Point Pleasant who would request one of the radically teased hairstyles sported by models with sunken cheeks and pouty lips, but her mom seemed to think they made the salon more upscale.

"I swear it looked like the sky had a tail."

Katie stepped into the room in time to hear Wanda Perry, her mom's closest friend and head stylist, voice her observation.

"A streak of fiery red, angled to a point." Wanda puffed on a cigarette before crushing the butt into an ashtray on the reception desk. "It was the weirdest thing I've ever seen. Like something from a sci-fi movie."

"Or the *Twilight Zone*." Valerie Hall arranged hair gel and mousse at her workstation. Looking over her shoulder, she whistled a few notes from the famous theme song.

"Don't poke fun." Katie's mom flitted around, arranging magazines on a side table positioned between two chairs. Frowning, she paused to fluff a wilted plant that looked like it hadn't seen water in a week. Eve, who had a love of all things green and growing, would have cringed at the neglect.

"Strange things happen around here. Have for years," Katie's mom continued, but her frown dug deeper. She seemed edgy.

"You mean like the Mothman?" Valerie dropped into her chair and twirled around with a grin. "Hi, Katie. You're just in time to hear Wanda's tale of UFOs."

"I never said I saw a UFO." Wanda lit another cigarette. "Just that the sky looked weird."

"What are you talking about?" Katie asked.

"Didn't you notice how strange the sky was last night?" Wanda exhaled a stream of smoke. "Odd colors after sunset."

"Probably was the sunset," Doreen Sue said. She shook her head dismissively. "Light refracting, that sort of thing."

"It was a colored cloud with a tail," Wanda persisted.

Valerie laughed and spun her finger in a circle beside her ear. "I think you've been inhaling too much perm solution."

Wanda lobbed a magazine at her. "Just because you didn't see it."

Still laughing, Valerie caught the magazine with both hands and dropped it into her lap. A sly grin curled her lips as she flipped through glossy pictures of layered cuts and bobs. "What do you think the preferred hair style is for extraterrestrials?"

"Cut it out, you two." Doreen Sue waggled a finger at them. "You shouldn't poke fun at people who have seen UFOs."

"You're right." Valerie sobered, sitting straighter in her chair.

An awkward moment of silence followed during which Katie shot a sharp glance at her mother. Most people knew her mom had claimed to see a UFO in the mid-sixties, back when Point Pleasant was overrun with tales of the Mothman and nightly flying objects.

"I didn't mean to be disrespectful, Doreen Sue," Valerie said.

"Forget it." Katie's mom waved a hand in the air as if to fluff aside the concern. "I guess I'm on edge. Rex took off last night, and I've been worried sick ever since."

Katie narrowed her eyes. "Martin's dog?"

Her mom nodded. "I had him overnight because Martin was having his place fumigated. I thought Sam would like having Rex there, but the darn dog took off when the two of them were outside."

A lump formed in Katie's throat. "Is Sam okay?"

"He's fine, Katie. Just upset Rex hasn't come back."

"Have you told Martin?"

"I called him last night. He drove around looking for him, but no luck. I feel horrible."

"It's not your fault," Wanda said. "Rex probably heard or saw something. You know how dogs are. He'll turn up, you'll see."

Doreen Sue nodded, but her eyes glimmered with tears. "Martin's the first decent guy I've had in my life. I don't want him to ditch me 'cause I lost his dog."

"Aw, come on now, honey. He's not like that." Wanda moved to Doreen Sue's side. Wrapping an arm around her shoulders, Wanda tugged her close and offered a peppy smile. "Martin's crazy about you. He was following you around like a puppy when you were seeing Amos. You were just too wrapped up in that loser to notice."

Katie's mom sniffled and offered a watery smile. "I hope you're right. I'm falling hard for the guy."

Interesting. Katie would have liked to know more about her mother's attachment to Martin, but her mind was preoccupied with Sam. "Mom—"

As if reading her mind, Doreen Sue spoke quickly. "Katie, I told you Sam is fine." She nodded to Wanda, indicating she was okay, and her friend moved away. "He spent last night and this morning drawing."

"Drawing?" The word settled uncomfortably in her stomach. It dredged awake a memory from childhood—sitting cross-legged on her bed, scribbling geometric shapes and patterns in a school notebook while her mom and a man whose name she couldn't remember shouted drunken insults at each other in the kitchen.

"You liked to draw," her mom reminded her. She twined her hands together, jumpy all over again.

Katie cleared her throat. "Just for a while." The intensity of sitting hunched over that notebook, fervently sketching shapes and patterns that made no sense, was like a sliver of icy air creeping down her spine. She'd conveniently forgotten that time, locking it in a shadowed corner of her memory. It bothered her for reasons she couldn't explain.

It seemed to bother her mom too.

Shaking off her unease, Katie refocused on why she'd come. "Um… Mom. Are you sure you're okay watching Sam again tonight? If Martin needs you to help him look for Rex, I can change my plans."

"Don't even think of it." Dismissing the notion, her mom returned to tidying items around the shop. "Sam and I will be fine. And you've been planning this sleepover for weeks."

"Just a few."

That wasn't entirely true. Eve and Sarah had been badgering her for over a month to do something silly and fun. It was odd to suddenly find herself part of a trio when she'd spent most of her childhood alone.

"Well, I think it's a great idea," her mom said. "It's about time you started doing things with friends. You can swing by when you get off work and have dinner with me and Sam before you join the girls. I'm making fried chicken and mashed potatoes, and won't take no for an answer."

Katie nodded. She'd half hoped her mom would renege on watching Sam. As stupid as it sounded, she'd never been to a sleepover and didn't know what to expect. How pathetic that she was only now going to experience one at twenty-seven.

"Can I bring anything for dinner?"

"It's all taken care of." Her mom paused in the process of running a feather duster over a collection of shampoo bottles. The frown lines crept back around her mouth. "But you might want to pick up a sketchbook for Sam."

Katie's mouth was dry. "What kind of stuff is he drawing?"

Her mom looked away. "Odd things. Shapes...trees." She bit her lip. "But they're all filled with tiny triangles and boxes."

Noise.

"Like a pattern," Katie whispered.

"Exactly." Her mom set the feather duster down and turned to face her. "He said it's because of the cloud."

Chapter 2

Katie sorted through the afternoon mail, setting aside several envelopes for Eve to review later. She loved working for her friend as manager of the Parrish Hotel, but found it hard to concentrate on business.

The lobby was empty; all the departing guests checked out for the day, with those remaining scouring the town. There hadn't been a reported sighting of the Mothman for months, but the mere idea of the creature's existence kept visitors flocking to the hotel.

From her position behind the check-in counter, she cast a glance out the front windows. A nest of leaves had become snarled on the covered porch, huddled in a corner where they were shaded from the sun. Soon it would be too cold to linger outdoors, the change in weather signaling the need to store the high-backed rockers loved by guests for the season. The Halloween decorations—fat orange pumpkins, Indian corn, and dried cornstalks—could remain into mid-November.

She rubbed her eyes.

Frivolous thoughts, conjured to keep her mind off Jerome and her son's sudden obsession with drawing. Maybe she couldn't put her mind at ease about Sam, but at least she could get an update on Jerome.

Picking up the handset for the phone, she punched out the number for Ryan Flynn with her free hand. She and Ryan had grown increasingly friendly ever since Eve and Ryan's older brother, Caden, started dating. If there was information to be had, Ryan would know.

The phone cycled through four rings before he answered.

"Sergeant Ryan Flynn." His voice had a calming effect on her nerves, much as his presence often did.

"Hi, Ryan. It's Katie."

"Katie?" His tone brightened noticeably, losing some of its professional edge. "Nice to hear from you. I hope everything's okay."

"Fine." She imagined a trace of concern crinkling his blue eyes. "I was hoping you could check on something for me."

"Sure. What's up?"

"It's about Jerome Kelly." Briefly, she relayed her experience of the previous night. "I feel bad leaving him the way I did, even though I'm sure Deputy Brown is more than capable. I was hoping you'd know something… that Jerome made it home okay or that Deputy Brown took him to the hospital. I hate not knowing what became of him."

"Deputy Brown?" An odd inflection colored Ryan's words.

"Yes."

"Of the Mason County Sheriff's Department?"

"Yes." Impatiently, Katie drummed her fingers on the counter. "Is there some kind of policy that won't allow you to tell me?"

Ryan exhaled into the phone. "Katie, I know every deputy and officer in this department and there is no one named Brown."

"But that's not possible. He introduced himself and told me his name."

"Maybe you heard him wrong."

"No." Pressing her fingertips to her forehead, she rubbed the spot just above her eyebrow. She'd been rattled because of Jerome, but she'd heard the deputy clearly.

"All right." Ryan's voice was softer as if he sensed her agitation. "What did he look like?"

"He…" Katie closed her eyes and concentrated, too embarrassed to admit she couldn't remember. Several times since the incident she'd tried to recall his face and each time came up empty. "It was dark," she said at last. "I didn't get a good look at him, but I saw his car with the sheriff's department seal on the side, and he told me his name."

Silence reigned on the other end.

"You don't believe me," she accused.

"I didn't say that. Maybe he's a new hire. I'll ask around." A peace offering. An attempt to pacify her.

The effort was pathetically transparent. "I think I'll call the hospital." More annoyed at herself than him, she grew increasingly irritated she couldn't recall a single feature of Brown's face.

"*I'll* call the hospital," Ryan offered. More olive branches.

"I don't mind."

"I don't, either." He was back to sounding helpful, the Ryan she liked best. During their short time as friends, she'd known him to be stubbornly opinionated, but also courteous and charming.

"You have me curious about Brown," Ryan continued. "And Jerome. I'll do some checking and I'll get back to you."

"Thanks, Ryan. I'll be here most of the afternoon; then I'm heading to my mom's place for dinner. Tonight, I'll be with Eve and Sarah."

"The sleepover." A grin crept into his voice.

"You know about it?"

"Caden told me."

A sergeant with the Mason County Sheriff's Department, Caden was scheduled to work the late shift, according to Eve. "Does he tell you everything?"

Ryan snorted. "Hardly. Anyway, I hope you girls enjoy yourselves. Do you want me to call you at Eve's if I turn up news on Jerome?"

"Sure." She'd sleep better if she knew Jerome hadn't been sidelined by anything serious. "You're a good friend, Ryan. I appreciate it."

"No problem. Maybe we can grab a bite to eat sometime."

"I'd like that."

After she'd hung up, it occurred to her that he'd asked for a date in a roundabout way. Then again, maybe he just wanted to pick her brain about Deputy Brown and find out how a faceless, unknown officer could end up driving a Mason County patrol car.

* * * *

After work, Katie drove to her mom's home, wanting to spend an hour or two with Sam before Eve's sleepover. The sound of a radio greeted her inside the door, and she followed the music to the kitchen where she found her mom busy cubing potatoes on a cutting board.

"Hi." Her mother flashed a smile. "Sam's in the living room if you want to say hello. Dinner in forty-five. I've already got gravy simmering on the stove."

"Mmm." Katie nodded, inhaling the aroma of hot chicken stock, butter, and seasonings. Despite the non-traditional manner in which she'd raised her daughters, Katie's mom had always ensured both girls had a hot cooked meal. It might have been tossed on the table as she dashed out to grab a drink with some loser in a beat-up Ford, but she'd made sure her girls had something more substantial than fast food or snacks.

"Is there anything you want me to do?" Katie dropped a green carry tote onto the floor. The bag contained a few items she'd need for the sleepover, but also a gift for Sam.

"I'm fine, hon." Another quick smile. With her bleached blond hair and blue eyes, Doreen Sue looked like an older Kim Carnes. People sometimes said as much, a comparison that never failed to earn a flirty flutter of her eyelashes, especially if the compliment came from a man. Wearing the same clingy black leggings and oversized silk shirt she'd worn to her salon, she hardly looked dressed to be mashing up potatoes or frying chicken. At least she'd traded the stiletto heels for a pair of comfortable blue jelly flats.

"Are you sure you don't need any help?"

"I have everything under control. Go see your son. He's anxious to show you what he's been drawing."

Nodding, Katie pulled a paper bag from the tote. "Yell if you need me."

She found Sam in the living room, seated on the sofa, hunched over a loose-leaf notebook. He grinned when he saw her.

"Hi, Mom." Thrusting his pad aside, he hopped off the couch and ran to give her a hug.

"Hey, my handsome man." Katie knelt, wrapping him in her arms and inhaling a mixture of autumn grass, browning leaves, and denim. "You were outside."

"I was looking for Rex." Sam had her green eyes paired with his father's floppy brown hair. Thankfully, hair color was all he'd inherited from Lyle Mason.

"Don't worry. He'll turn up." She smoothed a scattering of bangs from his forehead. "Sometimes dogs just like to roam."

"That's what Martin said."

"Then you should listen to him." Martin was the first good guy her mom had dated. It didn't surprise her he'd go out of his way to soothe Sam's fears. "Hey, look. I brought you something." Standing, she handed him the bag.

"What is it?"

"Open it and find out."

Eagerly, he tore into the package. "Wow, thanks, Mom!" His mouth split with an exuberant grin as he withdrew two sketchbooks and a pack of graphite pencils.

"Grammie said you started drawing."

"Yep. Look at this." Grasping her hand, Sam tugged her toward the couch, then handed her his notebook. "I did most of these last night."

Katie bit her lip. "There's so many." Too many, as if her son had pored over the notebook for hours. The pages were filled with random drawings, some in pencil, most in ink. The detail was astounding. Images of trees, houses, fields, even the sky, all rendered in a precision she wouldn't expect an eight-year-old could manage. Her heart beat faster as she flipped through the pages. Sam had crammed the inside of the trees and houses with all manner of geometrical shapes. Triangles, squares, lines, and diamonds. The patterns repeated over and over in mirrored perfection.

Noise.

How did she know that term?

"Do you like them?" His face held eager expectation, his eyes bright. The corners looked a little puffy, the whites pinkish.

"When did you find the time to do all of these?"

Dancing from foot to foot, he shrugged. "Last night. Today."

"Is this all you've been doing? Don't you want to go outside and play?"

"I was outside, remember? I helped Martin look for Rex."

His eyes were definitely puffy. Maybe he hadn't slept well. Maybe he'd been up all night scribbling tiny patterns in houses and trees.

"Don't you like them, Mom?" His voice carried a note of worry.

"Of course I do." She smoothed a hand over his hair. "I'm just concerned about you. You look a little tired. Your eyes—"

"They itch, that's all." As if to prove the point, Sam dug a knuckle into the corner of his eye before pointing back to the tablet. "That one's my favorite." He tapped the open page.

Katie's gaze fell to the picture. Her mother's backyard. She recognized the willow tree near the rear porch. The flowerbed, tucked beneath the kitchen window, bare now but for a scattering of dried leaves trapped by a black plastic border. Rex was in the picture, muzzle pointed skyward, mouth open as if caught in mid-bark. A fat cloud hovered over the tree, casting a wide beam to the ground. In the center of the diaphanous cloud, small pinpricks of light pulsed like dancing fireflies. Unlike Sam's other drawings, this one did not contain any geometrical shapes.

Katie tapped a fingernail against the cloud. "What's this?"

Sam angled for a better look. "The cloud."

Goose bumps prickled her arms. Not *a* cloud, but *the* cloud. She tightened her fingers on the tablet.

"It was there right before Rex disappeared," Sam continued, seemingly unaware of her distress. "It was green."

He scrubbed his eye, this time using the back of his hand. "Rex started barking at it and then took off."

Katie wet her lips. "Did Grammie see the cloud?"

Sam shook his head. "It kind of vanished."

"Maybe it was just an ordinary cloud with a plane or something behind it." Katie wasn't certain if she made the observation to pacify Sam or herself. An icy finger skipped down her spine. An attempt to resurrect something from the past. Something she couldn't remember.

"Maybe." He shrugged, seemingly disinterested in the subject. Returning to the couch, he plopped down and opened one of the new sketchbooks. Immediately, he began to draw a series of shapes and symbols.

Katie sat beside him. "Are you going to be okay here again tonight?"

"Sure." Sam tucked his tongue in the corner of his mouth as he worked. It was hard to decipher what he drew this time, the lines crisscrossing one another, settling into a repetitive pattern.

She wished he'd go outside and play. Find a ball or run around the yard. Dig for worms. Anything. "It's going to be dark soon. Why don't you go outside and play a bit before dinner? You can draw later."

"Okay." He set the sketchbook aside.

She couldn't tell if he made the concession for her or because he really wanted to be outdoors. Likely, the former. "You know where I'll be tonight, right?"

"Sure. With Eve and Sarah, at Eve's place."

"Grammie has the phone number if you need to reach me."

Sam sighed. "I know, Mom. But come on—I'm eight now. You don't have to worry about me all the time."

She fought the urge to grin. He wouldn't appreciate the tender response, thinking she didn't consider him grown up. Which, of course, she didn't. But it was hard to tell an eight-year-old he still had a lot of growing to do.

"I know. Third grade." Cupping his chin, she tilted his head up and gave him a kiss on the cheek. It wouldn't be too long before he put a stop to such overt displays of affection. "But call if you need anything, otherwise I won't feel like a mom." Now she did smile, coaxing a grin from him in return. "And I want you to give your eyes a rest, so don't spend the whole night drawing. Deal?"

"Okay." He made the word sound like he was getting the short end of the stick, but there was affection in his tone. "I'll get my coat and go outside. Maybe Rex will come back if he sees me."

"Good idea." It would be so much better to have him focused on Rex than sketching strange clouds. As she watched him bound from the room, she assured herself there was nothing to worry about.

* * * *

Caden Flynn was not prepared to find his brother, Ryan, sitting behind his desk when he arrived for duty. Assigned to night shift at the sheriff's office, he expected the daylight officers to have cleared out by now.

"Hey." He tossed his hat on his desk. Constructed from heavy wood, the monstrosity was a relic from the 1950s, in line with most of the furniture in the department. Outdated, it was nonetheless solid, and had seen countless officers through countless years of service. Butted front to front with Ryan's, the desk's positioning allowed them to sit facing each other, making it easy to converse. "I thought you were done here an hour ago."

"I was." Rapping the eraser end of a pencil against an open folder, Ryan wore an edgy expression. "It's been a weird day."

The office was quiet, manned by a junior deputy and a clerk who traded gossip by the coffee pot. Except for his brother, who looked ready to scale the walls, the atmosphere was low-key. At twenty-eight, five years younger than Caden, Ryan still carried a reckless edge. That rashness often bristled through in his work, exposing itself as impatience or agitation. Whatever currently troubled him had obviously gotten under his skin. Either that or he was operating on a caffeine-sugar high from too much coffee and the bite-size Snickers bars he stashed in his desk.

"Weird how?" Caden dropped into his chair.

His brother frowned. "Uh, let's see…cow mutilation, phantom deputy, missing resident. Does that fit the bill?"

Okay, so Ryan was in a flippant mood. Caden retrieved a few letters the clerk had left. "You're going to have to explain that."

"Chester Wilson had a Holstein turn up dead in one of his fields."

Livestock died sometimes. Disease, even age, but his brother wasn't headed there. "You said mutilation."

Ryan nodded. "Lots of blood from the ears, nose, and mouth. No visible sign of trauma."

That didn't fit disfigurement or butchering. "Could be illness."

"I called the county vet." Ryan sat forward in his chair, leaning on his desk. "He's got to do a more thorough examination, but based on initial findings, he believes the cow had a 'concussive reaction' created by an outside source."

Caden sorted through the mail. Two notices from the courthouse—probably filing updates—and a plain envelope addressed to Sgt. Caden Flynn c/o Mason County Sheriff's Department. "What does that mean?"

"That something delivered enough pressure to make her brain explode."

"Huh."

It wasn't the first time there had been animal deaths in Point Pleasant, but one dead cow—no matter how freaky her passing—didn't mean a similarity. Over a decade ago, a number of farm animals had been found butchered, likely the poor dumb victims of a satanic cult. Caden had been in high school at the time and remembered it well. In 1966, Point Pleasant had erupted with everything from Mothman sightings to nightly reports of UFOs. Animal mutilations were just one more oddity thrown into the mix. The authorities had never caught whoever committed the grisly deeds. Most believed the culprits had moved on to new hunting grounds.

"Huh?" Ryan looked rattled, ready to sprout horns. "Is that all you're going to say?"

Caden sighed. "No. I was just thinking... Chester lives near the airport. It could have something to do with low altitude flight traffic."

"I'll give you that. I thought the same thing until Doc Holden set me straight. He said the decibel level had to be extreme. We're talking supersonic military shit."

"Everyone in town would have heard the fallout from something like that." Caden's gaze dropped to the letters in his hand. When not reined in, Ryan could pick at something relentlessly. "What about the 'phantom' deputy?"

A contemptuous snort. "You mean Deputy Brown?"

"Is that his name?" Caden sliced open the plain envelope, listening while his brother relayed a phone conversation he'd had with Katie Lynch. "Maybe she got his name wrong," he suggested when Ryan was through. "It could have been Clive Broder."

"I asked. He was off duty last night. I even tried the hospital, thinking I could pick up word on Jerome."

"What'd you find out?" Hopefully, nothing serious had happened. Jerome was loopy, hung up on conspiracy theories, but he was an okay guy.

"Nothing." Ryan frowned openly. "Jerome never showed up at the hospital—with or without Deputy Brown."

Caden shrugged, slipping a sheet of paper from the envelope. "Maybe he went home."

"I tried calling. No answer."

"Could be sleeping. Especially if he's not feeling well."

"Yeah." Ryan tugged his bottom lip with a thumb and forefinger. He was quiet a moment before speaking again. "It's early yet. Maybe I should take a drive and make sure he's okay. Katie seemed pretty upset."

And Ryan wouldn't want Katie upset. He might not admit it, but Caden was sure his brother had a soft spot for Doreen Sue's daughter. "Since you're technically off duty, I'll tag along."

"You sure?" The agitation fled Ryan's voice, replaced by a thread of wariness. "You do remember Jerome bought Hank Jeffries' old place?"

"Yeah." It was time to put that ugly fiasco behind him. He'd hung up his badge for eighteen months over the mess with Jeffries and the

Kline brothers. For too long he'd believed he could have done something differently—that Hank didn't have to die, or Parker end up in a mental ward. He'd been back on the force four months now, reinstated to his old rank. Sadly, Parker Kline would never be the same.

Hank Jeffries had been a decent guy, but he'd had two well-known vices. He was petrified of the Mothman, claiming to have seen the monster once, and he liked to drink. Excessively. Unfortunately for Tim and Parker Kline, just days from high school graduation, Hank had been drunk out of his skull when they'd decided to prank him.

Two years ago on a warm June night, Tim had dressed up as the Mothman and the brothers crept onto Hank's front porch. In the dark, fueled by an alcoholic haze, Hank had thought the monster was real. He'd pumped a shotgun blast into Tim's face, killing him instantly.

By the time Caden arrived on the scene, Hank was sobbing uncontrollably, Tim's lifeless body cradled in his lap. Only later, would Caden learn the boys had borrowed their father's truck for the night, and that Parker had raced back to grab the revolver Floyd kept wedged under the seat. When he returned, his face was blank, his eyes burning with an unnaturally bright light. Before Caden could intervene, Parker put a bullet point-blank in the center of Hank's head. Caden had been forced to fire in retaliation.

The boy spent the next several weeks in the hospital fighting for his life. Eventually, he was given a hearing, deemed unfit to stand trial, and placed in the state mental ward. A shell of the outgoing teenager who'd once been a track star for the Black Knights, he spent most of his time babbling about UFOs.

Caden puffed out his cheeks. Time to suck it up. He hadn't been to Hank's place since the night Jeffries and Tim were killed. "I can handle it."

"If you say so." Standing, Ryan snatched his jacket from the back of his chair. "Hey, what's that?" He nodded to the sheet of paper in Caden's hand.

"Not sure." Wrapped up in the past, he'd almost forgotten about the letter. Unfolding the page, he discovered two sentences in black ink written in the center.

I remember her. You should too.

"A little short on whom I should remember." Frowning, he turned the paper so his brother could see.

Ryan leaned forward to read the words. "What the hell does that mean?"

Caden shrugged. There was no return address on the envelope, but the postmark read Austin, PA. "Someone from Austin, Pennsylvania who remembers someone I might have forgotten."

"That covers a lot. Freak show, if you ask me."

"Nah. Probably just someone I sent up for domestic assault or something." Tossing the letter on the desk, Caden stood. "Hopefully, the guy's found a better home in Austin. Let's go check on Jerome so you can keep Katie happy."

Ryan frowned. "I never said—"

Caden shot him a grin. "You didn't have to."

* * * *

Hank had never been an overly neat homeowner. Apparently, Jerome wasn't much better.

Caden pulled his police cruiser into a small gravel driveway, stones crunching loudly beneath the tires. Clumps of weeds, still stubbornly clinging to life before the first frost of the year, sprouted in patches among the pebbles. Beneath the front window, shrubs huddled in a snarl of raggedy branches crowned with browning leaves. Jerome's Impala was tucked beneath a carport, sheltered by a rust-pitted aluminum canopy. "Looks like he's home." Caden parked behind the sedan and killed the ignition. The property hadn't changed much since Hank owned it. Still dingy and gray, the house sported the same shuttered windows and sagging front porch. Hank had been too wrapped up in his paranoia over the Mothman to notice the neglect, and Jerome had done nothing to step up repairs. "Think I'll wait in the car."

"Huh?" Ryan shot him a surprised glance.

"The guy's obviously home. You're probably going to wake him up by pounding on the door. No need to freak him out by finding two sheriff's sergeants waiting outside."

"Yeah. Maybe." Ryan considered it. "Okay, I'll only be a minute." Popping the door on the cruiser, he slid outside and headed for the front porch.

Caden watched through the windshield. Most would have steered clear of purchasing the Jeffries house, knowing it had been the site of a double homicide, but Jerome Kelly was a strange bird. After Hank's death, the house sat vacant for a number of months before Jerome bought it sight unseen. Rumor said he'd moved to Point Pleasant because he believed it was a hotspot for supernatural activity and UFO sightings. Toss in the fact Hank's house bordered the TNT, and it was probably more appealing. Any paranormal expert worth his snot knew the TNT was the favored terrain of the Mothman.

Covered by the sleeve of his jacket, the welts on Caden's forearm tingled—three red gashes, the center slightly longer than the rest. The branded mark of the Mothman where the creature had gripped him fifteen years ago. In all that time, the wounds had never faded, never healed. Now, the mere thought of the Mothman could reawaken his connection to the creature. He hadn't seen it in four months. Not since it saved him and Eve from the man who'd murdered his sister, Maggie, and Wendy Lynch. He'd blamed himself for Maggie's death when the Silver Bridge collapsed, and most everyone in town had labeled Wendy a runaway. It had taken fifteen long years for the truth to emerge. For Roger Layton to pay the price he deserved, killed by a creature most believed didn't exist.

The brand tingled again.

Yeah. I know better. A lot better.

Exhaling, Caden scrubbed a hand over his face. He wasn't in a hurry to be anywhere, but wondered how much longer his brother was going to wait. No one had answered Ryan's knock. There hadn't been the slightest twitch of movement behind the shuttered windows. Given the night he'd had, Jerome was probably out like a light.

Caden was about to honk the horn when Ryan held up a finger indicating another few seconds. He knocked again, then shifted to the side, peering through the front window. A few moments later, he trotted back to the car.

"Well?" Caden asked when he slid into the passenger's seat.

"I think you're right. He's probably sleeping. No movement that I could see or hear."

"Is that what you're going to tell Katie?"

"I'll wait to call her. I can always ring his house again in a few hours."

"It's your show." Caden backed out the driveway. "But I think you're going to a lot of bother over this."

"It's no bother. Katie's a friend. And I want to ask Jerome about Brown."

Being at Hank's place had made him momentarily forget the elusive deputy. It was possible someone could have slapped a Mason County Sheriff's emblem on the side of a sedan, and pilfered a uniform and badge. Bottom line: they might have an imposter. "Did you tell Pete about Brown?"

"Yeah, I told him." Sheriff Pete Weston, their boss, had been a good friend to their late father, Donal, and had watched Caden and Ryan grow up. "He put out a wire, but it's hard to ID a guy without a description. Hopefully, Jerome can do a better job than Katie."

"I guess we'll find out when he wakes up."

Caden punched the gas and headed down the road, a little too anxious to put the cheerless house behind him.

* * * *

Katie took another sip of wine and sank back against the comfy sofa in Eve's living room. Why had she let Sarah talk her into a second glass? She wanted her head clear in the event Ryan called about Jerome.

But the Chardonnay was smooth, and hanging out with her friends made her realize the fun she'd missed as a kid. Opportunities to giggle over boys, share nail polish, down soda, and eat fattening things like potato chips and cheese curls. Eve and Sarah's rapid-fire gossip made her feel part of the group.

"Polly said its head exploded." With an exaggerated shudder, Sarah grabbed a handful of popcorn from a big bowl on the coffee table. "Gruesome. Like something out of a horror movie."

"I heard someone cut out its eyes and tongue." Eve swirled the pale liquid in her glass with a grimace. "When I stopped at the grocery store, the woman at the register said it had to be the work of a satanic cult."

Katie hadn't heard about farmer Wilson's dead cow until she'd arrived at Eve's house. Maybe whatever had butchered the cow had taken Rex too. She hoped not. "I think everyone's overreacting." The practical side of her wasn't easily swayed by rumors.

"What?" Eve turned sideways to face her, drawing a knee onto the sofa. "Come on, Katie. You have to admit last night was pretty strange. All those weird lights in the sky."

"And poor Chester's cow getting slaughtered." Sarah reached for another handful of their buttery snack.

"I didn't see any strange lights, and it sounds like the stuff about the cow has been exaggerated." If there was something odd going on, Ryan would have told her. Unless...

She took a slow sip of wine.

Unless he didn't want to worry her. According to Sarah, Ryan had been the one to respond to the call about the cow. And Sarah would know. Employed at the courthouse, she was often privy to scuttlebutt that filtered down from the sheriff's office.

"But you had that strange encounter with Jerome and the weird deputy," Eve protested.

Reluctantly, Katie nodded. She'd told both her friends about the encounter shortly after arriving. "Jerome was just shaken up," she clarified. "And cold. It was probably nothing. Neither one of us saw any weird lights."

"I didn't, either," Sarah chimed in, sounding almost disappointed. "But then I was in bed early. It's pathetic when you're dateless."

"What about Darrell Mason?" Eve plucked an olive from the cheese tray. "I've seen him smiling at you when he delivers mail to the courthouse."

"Darrell?" Sarah frowned. "Be serious, Eve. He was creepy when we were kids, and he's still creepy. Always watching and listening."

"I'll side with Sarah on that one." Katie helped herself to popcorn. "He might follow her around like a puppy, but if he's anything like his cousin, he's a waste of time."

Sarah eyed her openly. "I guess you're glad Lyle's gone."

Katie tamped down the instinct to scowl. "Hopefully, he'll stay gone." It was hard talking about Sam's father without bitterness tainting her voice.

"I never really understood…" Eve fidgeted as if worried she pushed too far. "I know I shouldn't ask, but Lyle was always out of the picture when we were kids. He was older, near Caden's age. How did you two…" The sentence fumbled into silence as she shifted again, taking sudden interest in her glass.

Katie laughed. "It's okay. I don't mind talking about the jerk. It's just… you know…like admitting I was a jerk too." She took a sip of Chardonnay, liberating her tongue. It felt good to have girlfriends. She and Eve had grown close in the short time since Eve had returned to Point Pleasant, and Katie was gradually coming to know Sarah better. At first she'd feared the other woman might not warm to her, but that was old prejudices and doubts getting in the way.

"Lyle said all the right things at the right time." Glancing down at her glass, she circled a finger around the edge. "As a kid, my sister was my only true friend. After Wendy vanished, it got really lonely. And it was hard listening to the things people said. How she got knocked up and took off to have an abortion, or that she ran off and ditched her family."

Sarah sniffled. "I remember saying horrible things."

Katie was surprised to see a shimmer of tears in her eyes.

"I was such a fool back then," Sarah continued. "We all were, Katie. To think what really happened to Wendy—"

It must not be easy admitting you'd contributed to slander and gossip, especially in face of the ugly truth. "It's okay." Katie smiled softly, thankful for her new friend's honesty. "We all do and say things we regret."

It was only four months ago that she, Eve, Ryan, and Caden had unearthed Wendy's grave in a thicket of woods at the edge of town. For fifteen years her bones had lain undiscovered, her murderer free to go about his daily life. Roger Layton was dead now, the official cause of his death listed as drowning. Only a select few, Katie among them, knew he'd met his fate at the hands of the Mothman.

"I regret ever having listened to Lyle." She shook her head, recalling how stupid she'd been getting sucked up in his sweet talk. "He came along at a low point in my life. My sister was gone, and my mom and I—well, we didn't have the best relationship back then. I was flattered Lyle took an interest in me."

"He was a predator." Having gotten remorse out of the way, Sarah seemed determined to defend her. Sitting straighter, she reinforced the comment with a resolute nod, sending her coppery curls bouncing. "You were what...six years younger?"

"Hey, I'm six years younger than Caden," Eve protested.

"But you weren't a teenager when he came sniffing around. Lyle was experienced, in his mid-twenties. He probably knew exactly what to say. Didn't he, Katie?"

"He did." Scooting off the sofa, Katie plopped on the floor, crossing her legs beneath her. The alcohol had given her a slight buzz. Glass in one hand, she scooped up popcorn with the other. Sarah grabbed the bowl from the coffee table and nudged it between them.

"You know the only good thing about Lyle?" Katie asked.

Sarah gave an indelicate snort and took a gulp of wine. "You mean there is one?"

Katie swallowed popcorn. "He gave me Sam."

"Aw, that's so sweet." Sarah's face took on an expression of tenderness. "Your little boy is adorable. I hope I have kids someday."

"There's still plenty of time."

"Sure." Sarah finished the remainder of her drink. "All I have to do is find a decent guy. And no, that isn't Darrell Mason," she added when Eve looked ready to comment.

Eve laughed. "I wasn't going to mention him."

"Listen to you," Sarah countered. "You've got Caden Flynn. He and Ryan are the best catches in town."

Feeling heat rise to her face at the mention of Ryan, Katie dropped her gaze. Her telltale flush didn't escape Sarah's notice.

"I forgot." Sarah's smile was wicked. "Katie has a thing for Ryan."

"I do not." The protest was automatic.

Eve rolled her eyes. "He's certainly got a thing for you."

"You're reading too much into our relationship. Just because we chat, and occasionally get together with you and Caden—*as friends,*" she was quick to stress. "Doesn't mean there's anything between us, or that there ever will be."

"Let's find out." Sarah's eyes danced with mischief.

Katie slanted a look sideways. "What?"

"Oh, this is perfect. Wait, I have to get more wine." Clambering to her feet, Sarah looked ready to explode with excitement. "And we need candles. Eve, kill the lights."

"What are you talking about?" Eve was clearly as puzzled as Katie.

"I stopped at the store today and picked up a Ouija board," Sarah explained. "I thought it would be a kick. Remember how you, Maggie, and I always used to play whenever we had a sleepover?" Spying a shopping bag she'd carried in earlier, Sarah hustled through the opening between the dining room and living room. A smile bloomed on her face as she hefted a colorful box from the package. "Look. Brand new!"

Katie exchanged a glance with Eve. "A Ouija board? Isn't that all a big hoax?"

"Well if it is, you shouldn't mind playing." Kneeling in front of the coffee table, Sarah moved the cheese tray to the floor, then eagerly placed the box on the bare surface. "This is going to be so much fun. Eve, you have candles, right?"

"Mm-hm."

Katie thought Eve looked a little apprehensive.

"Do we really need them?" her friend asked.

"We always used candles when we were kids." Sarah tore off the cellophane wrapping. "And you have to dim the lights. It would be better if you killed them altogether."

"Okay," Eve agreed. "But I'm going to need another drink for this."

"Me too." Katie stood, stretching her legs. She wondered if Eve remembered the presence they'd encountered in an abandoned weapons igloo at the TNT over the summer. The being had no form or substance, but had left them shivering in a deluge of cold. When it spoke, the entity's voice had grated in their minds, heard only inside their heads. It offered no information, but answered yes or no questions that eventually led to the discovery of Wendy's remains. To this day, Katie didn't know what they'd encountered—ghost, alien, demon—only that the memory could still make gooseflesh spring alive on her arms.

Hopefully, the Ouija board wouldn't do the same.

Chapter 3

"You should be the one who asks the questions, since it's your house," Sarah said to Eve, placing a quarter on the board.

With its sun and moon illustrations and carnival-style lettering, the board reminded Katie of something she'd see in a fortuneteller's hut. "What's the quarter for?"

"To keep evil spirits away." Sarah's lips tipped up in an impish smile. "In the old days, it would have been an offering of silver. Now it's just a token, but the idea is the same."

They'd moved the board to the dining room table, making it easier to hover around the game. Eve sat at the head, with Katie and Sarah to either side. Several candles burned at the opposite end of the table, splattering the board with halos of flickering light. Several more occupied the top of a buffet situated beneath a double window. The rest of the room, like the night outside, was dark.

Katie fidgeted in her seat, keeping her hands in her lap. "I've never played." She eyed the planchette. A heart-shaped piece of plastic with a small, clear window, the object squatted in the center of the board. She wasn't entirely sure she wanted to know the answers the thing would divulge. Even as a kid she'd shied away from anything having to do with fortunetelling or palm reading, preferring practical answers over what-if possibilities. It was only within the last few years she'd started looking elsewhere, like the igloo at the TNT, desperate for any lead on her missing sister.

"It's easy." In the candlelight, Sarah's coppery hair carried the wine-red tint of merlot. "Place your fingertips on the planchette. Lightly, like this." Sarah demonstrated and Katie and Eve followed suit. "Eve will ask one question at a time, and we each concentrate on the answer. But first we have to invite a spirit to join us." She looked expectantly at Eve.

"I remember now." Eve inhaled deeply. The look on her face hinted they were no longer kids playing with a toy, but adults venturing into an unknown realm. When she spoke, her voice was whisper-soft. "Is there a spirit here who would like to join us?"

Katie bit the inside of her cheek and stared at the planchette. Part of her wanted to giggle and part feared they were messing with something better left alone. Seconds passed, stretching longer, funneling into a minute. She fidgeted.

"Sometimes it takes a while," Sarah whispered.

Almost immediately, Katie felt movement beneath her hand. Her eyes widened as the game piece slid across the board, stopping so the word YES was displayed in the small circular window at its point. Sarah grinned, and even Eve smiled. For a moment, Katie wondered if they were toying with her, making the thing move between them, but their reactions seemed genuine.

"Okay, um…" Eve seemed to struggle to come up with the first question. After a few seconds, her grin turned playful. "Does Caden miss me?"

The planchette remained rooted to the spot, displaying the word YES.

Sarah rolled her eyes. "That's obvious."

"How about…" Eve sat straighter, speaking to the room at large. "Should Sarah go on a date with Darrell Mason?"

The heart-shaped object slid across the board. NO.

Sarah smiled broadly. "I told you."

Katie enjoyed the silliness. It was fun asking frivolous questions, and it didn't take much to concentrate on the answers. She didn't believe in spirits so much as body and mind dynamics. Her negative opinion of Lyle had probably influenced the energy of the board. The being in the igloo had been real, but this felt like a carnival trick.

At the head of the table one of the candles flickered.

"Who should Sarah date?" Eve asked.

The planchette didn't move.

"Great." Sarah frowned. "So I'm destined to become an old maid?"

Katie knew the question was rhetorical, a muttering of complaint, but the plastic playing piece inched to the center of the board where it stopped.

Eve's eyes grew wide. "I think you took control of it with that last question."

"I didn't mean—"

"I know, but it doesn't matter. Ask it something else."

"This was all your idea, anyway." Katie tossed in her two cents.

"Okay." Sarah bit her lip as if bracing for something monumental. "Am I ever going to meet the perfect guy, fall in love, and get married?"

"That's three questions in one," Eve whispered.

The planchette didn't seem to mind. It moved over the word YES.

"Who?" Sarah queried with a grin.

The last time they had prompted it to spell something, the "spirit" hadn't cooperated, but this time the plastic heart moved to the letter Q. A second later it swept backward in the alphabet to M.

"QM." Sarah was plainly stumped.

"Must be initials," Katie said.

"But I don't know anyone with those initials," Sarah protested.

"Maybe not now," Eve chimed in. "But who's to say what the future will bring?"

Sarah shook her head. "No one names their kid anything that starts with a Q. Whoever, he is, he must be a winner."

The planchette jerked a little.

"You're ticking off the spirit," Eve said, suppressing a giggle.

"Enough about me." Sarah sat straighter. "Let's find out about Katie and Ryan."

Katie shook her head vehemently. "No names."

"All right. I can do that." Sarah's smile bordered on elfin. "Spirit," she addressed the board. "Will Katie become entangled with a man in Point Pleasant?"

Katie tried to make her mind blank. She was attracted to Ryan, but didn't want the others to know. He thought of her as a friend, nothing more. Few men would want to become involved with a single mother who had an eight-year-old. And yet the more she thought of Ryan, the more she influenced the "spirit."

The planchette slid across the board to YES.

Sarah beamed a triumphant smile. "What is his name?"

Warmth flooded Katie's cheeks as the plastic heart moved to the alphabet. She braced herself, waiting to see an R in the clear plastic window. But the heart-shaped diviner skimmed away to the opposite end of the board.

"C." Sarah read the letter aloud, clearly befuddled by the results. Other letters followed before the planchette was still. O-L-D. Sarah looked directly at Katie. "C-O-L-D. Cold? What does that mean?"

A draft of air scuttled through the room, sending the candle flames flickering.

Katie shivered. "I don't know." The frivolity she'd felt moments before was replaced by a sensation of dread. "I suddenly have a bad feeling."

Sarah wet her lips. "Spirit, who is Deputy Brown?"

Katie flinched, unprepared for the question. A bubble of anxiety mushroomed in her stomach. "We shouldn't ask—" Before she could finish, the planchette slid to the bottom of the board, stopping abruptly on GOODBYE. Katie jerked her hands back as if stung. "What happened?"

Sarah gave a little laugh, but her face had paled. "It ended the session on its own."

"Is this where we whistle the theme song for the *Twilight Zone*?" Eve asked, obviously trying to lighten the tone.

Katie scuffed her hands against her arms. "It's cold in here, isn't it? That's what Jerome kept mumbling the night I found him…about being cold."

"Well, it is October." Eve walked quickly to the wall switch and flipped on the light.

Katie glanced at Sarah. The other woman nibbled on her thumbnail, her gaze glued to the Ouija board. "Did you ever have that happen before?" Katie asked. "The thing signing off like that?"

"Maybe. I can't remember." Sarah offered a smile, but it seemed false. "I haven't played since we were kids." She moved to the end of the table and blew out the candles. "It's just a bunch of creepy fun, Katie."

"What does it mean when the planchette goes to good-bye?" Katie persisted.

"That's how you end the session with a spirit." Sarah waved a hand over the smoke spiraling up from the candle wicks, dispersing the streams into the air.

"If you believe that stuff," Eve added quickly. "Like Sarah said, it's just a bunch of silly, creepy fun."

"If you want to know more about it, ask your mom." Sarah removed the game piece from the board and looked around for the box.

"Sarah." Eve sounded annoyed.

"My mom?" Katie looked between the two, perplexed. "What would she know about a Ouija board?"

"Um…" As if realizing she'd blundered, Sarah bit her lip. "It's just what I heard when I was a kid. I remember my mom talking about Doreen Sue and how she was into all that stuff about spirits and UFOs."

Katie stiffened. She'd purposefully shut her mind off to the time her mother tried everything and anything—including talking to mediums and using Ouija boards—to learn Wendy's whereabouts.

"That was a long time ago," Eve said.

"You're right." Sarah folded up the board and placed it into the box. Before she could say another word, the phone rang. All three women jumped in response.

Eve laughed nervously. "See what talking to spirits does?"

As she stepped into the kitchen to grab the phone, Katie blew out the remaining candles.

Their nerves probably had a lot to do with the setting—candlelit darkness and a séance-like atmosphere. It had to be coincidence that the very word Jerome kept mumbling when she'd found him was also the word the board had spelled tonight. As Eve pointed out, it was October. Naturally, it was cold.

"Katie." Eve returned from the kitchen, her face white and taut. "Your mom's on the phone for you. She's at the hospital with Sam."

"Hospital?" Alarm sent Katie racing for the kitchen. Clasping the phone to her ear, she spoke in a breathless rush. "Mom, what happened? What's wrong?"

"Don't panic. It's nothing serious." Her mother attempted to sound calm, but a jittery edge made her voice wobble. "We're in the ER. Sam's eyes are swollen shut."

"Oh dear God."

"He's going to be all right, honey. I'm sure of it. But you need to come as soon as you can."

Katie closed her eyes. Cold did not begin to describe the icy fear clutching her heart.

* * * *

Katie cupped her forehead in her hand. The stiff vinyl chair in the ER was anything but comfortable. The nurses had allowed her to see Sam briefly before ushering her to the waiting room, saying they needed space to work.

"Nothing to be alarmed about." The doctor, a young man who barely looked past college age, had done his best to assure her Sam would be fine. "A bad case of conjunctivitis. We've actually had several turn up lately. Your mother did the right thing in bringing your son here."

Pinkeye. Sam was in the hospital with an acute case of pinkeye.

"You should have called me sooner." Katie didn't bother to hide her displeasure when she raised her head to speak to her mother. Eve and Sarah had wanted to come to the hospital with her, but she'd overridden their pleas, promising to call when she had news. Something she'd done a few minutes ago. There was no sense in three semi-drunk women camping out in the ER.

Her mother paced a few feet away, jelly flats squeaking softly against the floor.

The waiting room was fairly busy. An older man with thinning hair sat in the far corner, flipping through a battered copy of *Newsweek*. At his side, a teenage boy concentrated on a handheld video game. Katie had seen them arrive, carrying in a young girl who'd sprained her ankle while doing cartwheels in the backyard. The girl's mother had followed her from the ER when called, leaving the man and teen to play the waiting game. A man with a bandaged hand, a middle-aged couple who'd brought in an elderly grandparent, and an obese woman complaining of back pain occupied the other chairs.

"I called as soon as we got here." Katie's mom folded her arms across her chest in a posture that said she was ready for battle.

No wonder. They were often at odds, their relationship a bumpy rollercoaster of highs and lows. It had been that way since Katie was a child. It was bad enough her mother had spent most of Katie's youth smoking, drinking, and carousing with men who treated her like garbage, but worse knowing she'd favored Wendy. As much as Katie loved her sister, she'd never measured up to Wendy's potential. There was something about a missing child that erased all faults and elevated that sibling to make-believe perfection.

"Sam was in his room drawing, and I was watching TV," her mom persisted. "It was only when he came out to tell me his eyes hurt that I saw how swollen they were. On a Friday night with no doctors available, I brought him straight here."

Her mother had done the right thing. She was the one who'd screwed up going to Eve's house when she'd seen how pink Sam's eyes were. She never should have left. "I'm sorry, Mom. I'm just worried about him."

"Oh, honey, of course you are. But he's going to be fine." Doreen Sue sat beside her and wrapped an arm around her shoulders. "Kids get pinkeye all the time. It's nothing serious."

"The doctor said they had a bunch of cases."

"Then it must be going around. A little medication, some drops, and he'll be as good as new." Hugging Katie closer, she kissed her temple. "You saw Sam in the exam room. He was far from scared, asking the nurses all kinds of questions."

She nodded, sniffling a little. "I wish they'd let me stay with him."

"They're doing an eye bath. You would've been in the way. And Sam's at that age when he's got to prove how brave he is to everyone around him."

Her stomach fluttered. He was growing up too fast. "How do you know all that?"

"I may have raised girls, but I dated plenty of men who had boys."

Katie frowned reflexively, soured by the thought of her mother's past.

As if sensing she'd said something wrong, Doreen Sue drew back and folded her hands in her lap. "As for pinkeye, you and Wendy both had it." She faltered, twining her fingers together. Her expression looked guarded, as if she feared prodding a buried memory awake. "Do you remember?"

"No." Katie imagined she'd had a lot of childhood illnesses she couldn't recall.

"You started drawing around that time," Doreen Sue continued, still studying her. "Like Sam."

She grew agitated. So what if she drew? So what if she'd had pinkeye? Her son was in the ER, and she had a headache from too much wine. How could she point her finger at her mother's past behavior when she was guilty of not looking after her only child?

"Katie?" She jerked at the intrusion of a masculine voice and glanced up to find Ryan Flynn standing in front of her.

"I thought you were spending the night with Eve and Sarah." His blue eyes darkened with concern. "Did something happen?"

"No." She shook her head, coming to her feet. "Or yes." Confusion made her trip over her thoughts. "I mean, it's Sam." Registering the shock on his face, she rushed to explain. "It's nothing serious, just a bad case of pinkeye."

He exhaled in relief. "Still, it must be pretty bad to have you both here." He looked at Doreen Sue.

"I'll let you two talk," her mom said. "I'm going outside for some air."

And a cigarette. Katie buried the instinctive criticism as she watched her mother leave.

"Sam's going to be okay," she told Ryan. "What are you doing here?"

She shuffled to the side, clearing a path when the little girl with the sprained ankle returned to the waiting room. Aided by her mother, the girl hobbled in on crutches, managing a weak smile when her father and brother rose to greet her. The girl's doctor followed, stopping to talk quietly with the family.

"I'm off shift," Ryan said. He must have only recently gone off duty, because he still wore his uniform. "I thought I'd do some poking around on Jerome."

Poor Jerome. In all the turmoil over Sam, she'd almost forgotten him.

"Caden and I went to his house earlier," Ryan said. "His car was there but he didn't answer the door."

So he'd made it home safely. "He must have been sleeping."

"Yeah, that's what Caden said too." A sliver of doubt crept into his voice. "I called the hospital earlier, and there was no record of him being brought in last night."

"That's good. He must have been able to drive home on his own."

Ryan nodded. "I thought I'd check with ER admissions to be sure. And I wanted to follow up on Deputy Brown. If he was here, someone should remember him."

"So you believe me about him?" Why couldn't she recall the man's face?

"Let's just say if someone's running around, impersonating an officer with the sheriff's department, I want to get to the bottom of it."

At least he didn't discount her story entirely. Before she could comment, her mother burst into the ER in a whirlwind of panic.

"Please! Someone help!" Doreen Sue focused on the doctor who stood speaking with the young girl's family. "Outside! Come quick!" Without waiting to see if he followed, she raced for the exit. Ryan bolted behind her.

Heart in her throat, Katie darted after him. "Mom!" She caught a fleeting impression of jelly flats and bleached blond hair before cold night air struck her in the face.

"Over here." Her mother was crouched by a form slumped against the building. "I'm not sure he's breathing."

Ryan got there first, but was quickly pushed aside by the doctor. Katie tugged her mom out of the way as two orderlies and a nurse arrived with a gurney. Several other people barreled from the ER, including most who'd been stuck in the waiting room. Even the girl on crutches hobbled outside.

"Get these people back," the doctor yelled.

Ryan took charge of the growing crowd, ushering any non-medical personnel clear. "Okay, folks. Stand back. Let the doctor do his work."

Katie found herself shuffled toward the sidewalk. Instinctively, she reached for her mom's arm. "What happened?"

There were tears on her mother's face. No one would ever accuse her of lacking heart. "I came out for a cigarette and saw him slumped over. Do you think he's dead?"

"No."

Katie's response was automatic, but her mind had latched onto an image of the Ouija board with the planchette resting on the word GOODBYE. The wine and popcorn she'd had churned in her stomach, awakening a sharp pang of nausea. Swallowing hard, she pressed a hand to her middle. It was too much—Sam, the ER, wine, the creepy game. The doctor rolled the unconscious man over and she saw his face as clearly as she'd seen it last night.

"Oh, no. It's Jerome." His eyes were closed, his skin white and ghastly under the harsh glare of outside lighting.

"I've got a pulse," the doctor said. "Let's get him into a room. Stat."

Katie choked back a cry as the orderlies lifted him onto the gurney. Jerome never so much as flinched, his body a dead weight. Swiftly, the gurney was hustled inside, leaving a befuddled crowd to murmur among themselves.

"I think I'm going to be sick," Katie said.

"Take deep breaths." Ryan appeared at her side, steadying her with a hand on her shoulder.

"But Jerome…" She couldn't get the image of his face out of her head. He'd looked lifeless, a plastic-like sheen to his skin, almost like a wax dummy. Where could he have been for the last twenty-four hours?

"I'll get to the bottom of it," Ryan promised.

Behind her, the crowd slowly broke up, most people returning inside. Cars rumbled down the street in the distance, cluttering her mind with the sound of engines, the thump of tires on asphalt. Snatches of conversation drifted on the chill air and added to the turmoil in her stomach.

Looked dead. Spooky stuff happening…end up like Chester's cow.

And then a single name that cut through all the noise. A name that brought dread bound up with a heavier sense of awe.

Mothman.

Katie looked past the dispersing crowd and made eye contact with a man who stood at the corner of the building. But for his face and hands, he was shrouded in black from head to toe. His gaze burned through her, his eyes polished onyx, eerily familiar.

"I'm so cold," she mumbled. Then promptly doubled over and threw up.

Chapter 4

Relieved to be home, Katie held a cold washcloth to her forehead and sniffled. "I feel stupid."

"There's nothing to feel stupid about. You're just not used to drinking." Ryan set a cup of black coffee in front of her, then sat next to her on the couch. Sam had collapsed in his bed ten minutes after they'd walked through the front door, exhausted after being wired on the adrenalin of the ER. The doctor had diagnosed his conjunctivitis as an allergic reaction rather than anything viral or bacterial.

"Probably an isolated event. We've had a few cases turn up, so it could be a reaction to something environmental, like a change in air quality. Even if your son has never displayed that type of sensitivity in the past, there's always a first time."

To be on the safe side, he'd prescribed an antibiotic and eye drops. Far from traumatized by the ordeal, Sam had spent the drive home explaining in vivid detail how they'd given him an eye wash in the exam room. With her stomach still roiling after her embarrassing display outside the ER, it wasn't something she'd wanted to hear. Fortunately, she hadn't disgraced herself a second time.

Her mom had followed her home and stayed until Ryan arrived with an update on Jerome. He was the one who'd suggested coffee, although her mom provided the cold compress for her throbbing head. While Katie rarely drank anything other than an occasional glass of wine—something she probably wouldn't indulge in again for a long time—her mom had a long-standing association with hangovers.

"You don't have to stay." Katie slanted a glance at Ryan. He looked tired, a little haggard around the edges as if the day had taken a toll on him too.

A lamp in the corner cast a small puddle of light behind him, leaving the underside of his cheeks slashed with shadow. He'd started his shift early that morning and probably hadn't even been home yet.

A pang of guilt sliced through her. "I'll be all right."

"Sure you will, but I don't mind staying for a while. You've had a full night between Sam and Jerome."

Her stomach knotted. Sam was safe but she couldn't say the same for Jerome. "I should have stayed with him last night. Made sure he got to the hospital."

"Katie, it's not your fault. You did what anyone would do, given the circumstances. We've put out an APB on Deputy Brown, but it would help if you could give a description."

She winced, hating that she couldn't conjure an image to match the name. "It was dark," she said lamely. "I... I couldn't see well."

Ryan nodded. His expression troubled her, as if she'd failed him. Failed Jerome.

Irked at the glaring hole in her memory, she grasped for straws. "He must have had dark hair. Average. You know—height, build. Otherwise he would have stood out in my mind."

"That's good." He probably told every potential witness the same, coaching them with cop rhetoric. "How about some coffee?" He motioned to the cup.

"No thanks." The thought of putting anything in her stomach was repulsive. Heaving a sigh, she plopped the damp washcloth beside the mug, taking care to slide a magazine beneath it. How pathetic she could remember to care for her bargain outlet furniture, but couldn't recall the face of a cop from last night.

"I can freshen that up if you'd like," Ryan offered with a nod at the washcloth.

She shook her head, flattered by his attentiveness. They'd barely spoken to each other while growing up, Ryan a fixture with the popular crowd. She'd never heard him utter a bad word about her but her childhood nemesis, Suzanne Flemish, had done her best to make Katie believe Ryan regularly dissed her. Probably because Suzanne had spent the bulk of her teen years pining for Ryan.

Katie curled her legs to the side, sinking back against the sofa cushions. Across the room, a few superhero comics lay scattered beside Sam's favorite chair. Spiderman, Batman, Flash Gordon. They certainly wouldn't have flubbed up and forgotten a man's face.

She chewed the inside of her cheek. "What do you think happened to Jerome?"

"I don't know." Ryan's shrug indicated he hadn't drawn any conclusions from the hospital. "Whatever it was, it was bad enough to put him in a coma."

Jerome in a hospital bed, tubes sticking from him, IVs pumping fluid into his veins. He deserved far better. He had no family that she knew of, at least none in the area. The hospital and sheriff's office would do their best to track down any relatives, but in the meantime, he was alone. She'd already asked if she could visit the ICU, but that privilege was reserved for immediate family.

"Caden is working on getting a search warrant for Jerome's house," Ryan said. "Not that we suspect him of being involved in anything illegal, but it might help turn up a clue about what happened. Somehow, he got to the ER under his own power."

"And then passed out." Katie scooped the hair from her face. She probably looked a wreck—hung over, half-nauseous, dressed in the comfortable baggy sweats she'd worn to Eve's sleepover. It was a good thing her relationship with Ryan didn't go past friendship. She'd made a mess of herself lately…abandoning Jerome, getting drunk when she should have been with her son, putting stock in a Ouija board. He probably thought she was a complete screw-up. At least he didn't know about the stupid planchette and the silly questions they'd asked.

The thought awakened a connected memory.

"Ryan, when I was with Jerome, he kept repeating the word 'cold.' I thought it was odd because he was sweating. I want to make sure the doctors know about that."

"I'll tell them. Maybe he had a fever or something."

She nodded, tumbling the thought around. *Or something.* The more she poked at her encounter with Jerome and Deputy Brown, the less sense it made.

"I should probably get to bed." It had grown late. Now that her headache had begun to recede, a fringe of exhaustion settled over her.

"Good idea." Ryan stood. "I'll check with you tomorrow and see how you're doing."

Katie saw him to the door, made sure it was locked behind him, then shut off the lights in the living room. She'd worry about straightening up tomorrow when her mind wasn't fogged with relief for Sam and worry for Jerome. By the time she'd changed into nightclothes and crumpled into bed, she craved nothing more than a dreamless sleep.

* * * *

"So we're good on this?" Ryan asked. "You got an all-clear to proceed?"

Head bowed, Caden thumbed through a ring of keys. "Yeah." His voice was tight, but it wasn't surprising considering he'd only caught a few hours' sleep after finishing his shift last night. With the noon sun beating down on Jerome Kelly's small ranch home, bleaching the faded siding near-white, Ryan found it easy to convince himself their trip was a waste of time. Jerome was a loner. A conspiracy theorist who spent his down hours reading about Big Brother, UFOs, and the Mothman. It was doubtful anyone wanted to harm him.

But he couldn't explain away the presence of the unknown Deputy Brown or why Jerome was in a coma. Even so, he feared the only thing he and Caden were likely to find inside was a pile of books lauding the latest alien sighting or paranormal discovery. The guy usually had his nose buried in one or the other whenever Ryan saw him at the River Café.

"Did they actually give you Jerome's keys?" Ryan asked as Caden tried one, then another, inserting them into the lock on Jerome's front door. A fluorescent green fob with AREA 51 stamped on the front dangled from the ring.

"The doctor didn't volunteer, but I didn't see any harm in borrowing them when he wasn't looking." With a sharp smile, Caden turned the lock and pushed open the door. "We've got a winner."

"I thought you were going to get a search warrant?"

"Until I got impatient. Jerome's in a coma, fighting for his life. There might be something in here to tell us why."

He stepped inside and Ryan followed. The room was dimly lit and cluttered, shuttered by blinds. Ryan crossed to the nearest window and raised the dull white covering, allowing sunlight indoors. A flurry of dust mites sprang to life in the sudden illumination.

"Not the best housekeeper, huh?" He stepped around a tower of newspapers teetering toward overspill. Most looked yellowed and old, the edges flaked and crumbling. Small particles of paper littered the floor, along with the crumbs from some forgotten snack.

"Bigfoot sighted by three hunters near Brackenville," Ryan read aloud, bending to examine the headline on the top paper. "Looks like our boy doesn't discriminate among creatures. Imagine what would happen if he ever found out about your connection to the Mothman."

"That isn't going to happen." Caden had moved to the other side of the room where an old sofa and arm chair skirted a coffee table. An overflowing ashtray, two soda cans, and a pizza box cluttered the table. He lifted the top of the box to peer inside. "Empty. Not like he left in a hurry or in the middle of dinner."

"Did you get a chance to check with his employer?"

"Yeah. He was at work the other day, same as usual. His supervisor said he was fine."

"So how come his car is here, but we find him curled up against the wall of the hospital, nearly comatose?"

"Five bucks says Deputy Brown could tell us."

"Yeah." Ryan should have paid more attention when Katie first mentioned the man. The guy was obviously an imposter, but it stumped him how Brown could have gotten his hands on a sheriff's car.

A glance around the living room showed nothing that would make Jerome a target for someone who would want to harm him—faded furniture, a console TV, some cheap artwork and posters on the walls, the latter depicting space observatories or star fields. A solar system mobile hung above the TV, its colorful array of planets suspended by wire. Magazines and newspapers covered the floor and tables, no surface spared Jerome's messy obsession.

Realizing Caden had already moved off to investigate the kitchen, Ryan took the bedroom. Unlike the living area, Jerome's bedroom was relatively orderly, the single bed neatly made, the top of the dresser bare but for some loose change, a paperback novel, and three bottles of cologne. He checked the closet, found it filled with clothes and shoes, more magazines stuffed on the top shelf.

"Hey, Ryan. You've got to see this." Caden's voice drew him down the hall.

Ryan found him inside a small bedroom that had been converted to an office.

"What the..." Words failed him as he gazed around the cramped space. Two of the walls had been plastered with maps, star charts, and photographs of the night sky—all tacked up haphazardly with pushpins. A separate wall was devoted to the Mothman, the surface covered with newspaper clippings, drawings, and maps of the TNT. Several aerial photographs captured shots of the abandoned weapons igloos built into hillsides, their domes crowned with grass and trees.

"Where the hell did he get all this garbage?" Ryan wondered aloud.

"Who knows?" Caden bent over a desk, sorting through a hodgepodge of papers scattered on the top. "Look at this stuff. Alien abductions... extraterrestrial visitors...ley lines..." He called off random titles as he flipped through the pages. "This goes way beyond the scope of a hobby. I always knew Jerome was a bit whacked, but this is crazy."

Ryan picked up a paperback book. "*UFO Sightings and Stories.*" His gaze tracked to the far wall where a pen-and-ink rendering of the Mothman held center stage. "He seems pretty gone on the ET stuff. So what's the connection to the Mothman?"

"You live in Point Pleasant and can ask that?" Caden began pulling out drawers, rummaging through the contents of each. "There's a whole faction of people who think our town is located on some sort of doorway between worlds or dimensions."

"A ley line." Ryan nodded to one of the papers Caden had left lying on the desk. "I'm not totally ignorant about this stuff. Once I found out you had a few powwows with the Mothman, I did some reading."

Caden's mouth twisted into a frown. "They were hardly powwows. But I guess I'm impressed by the effort, since you were always a skeptic." He returned to the search, opening another drawer. "Some people think the Mothman is from another world. An alien."

"Looks like Jerome agrees." Ryan flipped through the paperback. Handwritten notes lined the margins, several sections underscored. "Why else the overkill with UFOs and the Mothman? The guy probably moved here hoping to have an encounter. I remember hearing he bought this place because of its history."

Caden stiffened abruptly. "Hank?" he whispered.

"Not that." Ryan winced at the blunder, sensitive to his brother's role in Hank's death and Parker's incarceration. "Don't you remember Hank talking about the strange shit that took place here? Seeing the Mothman... lights in the skies, noises in the woods."

"Yeah." Caden relaxed marginally. "Everyone thought he was blowing smoke."

"Well, something tells me Hank and Jerome would have gotten along. Hey, look at this." Ryan pulled a slip of paper from the center of the paperback. "Jerome might have been connected to Hank in more ways than one." He passed the note to Caden.

"October 14, seven-thirty, P. Kline." Caden read the scribbled handwriting aloud. "Has to be Parker, but what would Jerome want with a guy in a mental ward?"

"The fourteenth was Thursday," Ryan observed. "When Katie found Jerome off the road."

Caden's glance was sharp. "You think he went to see Parker at the hospital?"

His brother wouldn't like the answer, but there really was only one way to find out. "How do you feel about a drive?"

"To see Parker?" Caden hesitated, the fingers of his right hand straying to the welts on his forearm.

Ryan's gaze followed the movement. For years he'd believed the marks were the result of an injury Caden sustained when the Silver Bridge fell. The night of the collapse, his brother had been trapped under water, his arm pinned in the wreckage of his car. But the disfigurement had never faded. To this day, the odd marks remained every bit as vivid and red as when Caden had been eighteen, dragged from the icy waters of the Ohio River. It was only recently Ryan learned the Mothman had made the gashes. A wound that never healed, the marks were a branded reminder of the bond between the creature and Caden.

"I haven't seen Parker since his trial two years ago," Caden said at last. "He was out of his head then."

"Probably still is." If Caden was going to face the kid, it was best to state the ugly truth. "He might be a howling lunatic for all we know. But it would be worth learning if he's connected to Jerome."

"You're right." Caden nodded and headed for the door. "Let's go. The sooner we talk to him, the sooner I can forget I'm the reason he's there."

* * * *

Located forty minutes outside of Point Pleasant, the West Central Mental Health Institute was an unappealing five-story structure with rectangular windows and an austere-looking entrance recessed under a brick arch. Caden parked in small lot marked Visitors and killed the ignition.

"You sure you're up for this?" Ryan asked.

Caden nodded but didn't move. Odd how memories floundered awake when he preferred they remain dormant.

Parker Kline's eyes had been oddly vacant the night he killed Hank, the whites glazed, the surrounding skin red and puffy as though he'd suffered some kind of burn. Caden had imagined the kid drunk or high on something, but toxicology reports later came back negative. It was the clearest memory he had of Parker, his face caught in the lamplight from Hank's porch. *A prank*, the kid had mumbled over and over. *It was just a stupid prank.*

"Let's get this over with." He popped the door and stepped from the car.

Inside the hospital, he and Ryan went through several secure check-ins before arriving on Parker's floor. The station nurse remembered Jerome and dug up the sign-in register for verification. According to the time sheet, he'd arrived at 7:33 and left at 7:47, staying just fourteen minutes.

"We don't allow visits beyond a half hour," the blond-haired woman explained. Short and muscular with a no-nonsense attitude and plain features, she wore a nametag that read L. Brenner. "With Parker, it's sometimes better people don't visit at all."

"What does that mean?" Caden asked.

"Most of our patients—we prefer not to call them inmates—exist in their own worlds." She led them to a set of double doors inset with square windows. The glass of each was double paned, reinforced with wire mesh between panels. Tugging a retractable cord hooked to her belt, she thumbed through several keys until she located the one she wanted. The action was mechanical as if performed routinely throughout the day. "Understand, Sergeant, a lot of our patients have given up on reality. We work to return them to competency, but remaining in a fantasy helps them stay ignorant of their crimes. Our worst offenders are on the upper levels."

Motioning them forward, she led them down a bleak hallway, her rubber-soled shoes screeching against squares of black-speckled vinyl tile. Doors flanked each side of the corridor, some opened, others closed. All had the same double-paned glass windows inset with wire mesh. Caden spied a middle-aged man in a wheelchair, head tilted to the side as he stared blankly into space. In another room, a man rocked back and forth in a vinyl-padded chair, arms hugged to his chest as he hummed "Dixie" over and over.

"That's Beau Hardy," Nurse Brenner said when she noted Caden's glance. "He's convinced he's a Confederate general, held in a Union prison during the Civil War. Most of these people aren't violent—not on this floor—but they have their ups and downs. Some days they're like children, others as disagreeable as billy goats."

"What about Parker?" Caden asked.

"He pretends to listen to the radio."

"Pretends?"

"No batteries," Nurse Brenner said. "Who knows what trouble he might get up to with those."

"Then why does he listen?"

"Because that's how they talk to him."

Ryan frowned. "Who?"

"See for yourself." Drawing to a stop before an open doorway, she indicated they should enter. "We have closed-circuit monitors at the desk. I'll be able to spot trouble and send an orderly to assist, though Parker rarely gives us problems. You'll find a lounge at the end of the hall if he wants to stretch his legs." She glanced at her watch. "Thirty minutes, gentlemen. Although, I suppose I could extend that limit for the sheriff's office."

Caden nodded, hoping a half hour would be plenty. He wanted to wrap the visit and get the hell out of the place. Vaguely conscious of Nurse Brenner's shoes making the same squeaking sound as she moved off down the hall, he stepped into the room.

The space was small and somber with the same off-white walls and black-speckled flooring as the hallway. Three narrow windows, each plated with heavy wire mesh, allowed light into the room. A single bed with a nightstand and a small dresser occupied the space nearest the door, a square table and padded chair closer to the window. Parker sat at the table, a transistor radio and a roll of Scotch tape at his elbow. His fingers clenched the worn-down nub of a pencil, several other well-used nubs scattered nearby. Head bowed, he worked at shading an image on a piece of loose-leaf paper.

Ryan nudged Caden in the ribs. "Look." A nod indicated the wall beside the window.

Caden followed his glance.

Similar squares of paper covered the blank wall, each block randomly shaded. The "drawings" had been taped in a disorganized fashion, some high, some low, some with only a fraction of coloring. Others were blacked end to end, not a speck of white visible on the page.

A sensation of cold trickled down Caden's back. It had been two years since he'd last seen Parker. The boy was twenty now, much leaner than before, his hair cropped close to his head. He didn't seem to notice them, his only focus the piece of paper on which he furiously scribbled. The fingernails of his right hand, chewed to a quick, were tinted black with the lead from his pencil.

Caden cleared his throat. "Parker?"

No reaction.

"Parker, it's Caden Flynn." His gut tightened. "Do you remember me?" *I put you here.*

The pencil nub continued to move back and forth, faster and faster. A half dozen other sheets of shaded squares littered the top of the table. Like those taped to the wall, they had no pattern.

"Parker, my brother Ryan is with me. We want to ask you about Jerome Kelly. He came to see you Thursday evening. Do you remember that?"

The pencil stopped abruptly, poised on the page. Parker's head remained bowed, but Caden sensed he was listening.

He took a tentative step closer. "Jerome's sick. In the hospital. We're hoping you can help us discover what happened to him."

Parker raised his head, his eyes oddly bright, a deep blue lit from within. There was something unnatural about his gaze. As if he looked but didn't see, his sight turned inward to a spot Caden couldn't reach.

"This hospital?" The whisper-thin quality of his voice was unnerving. Brittle, it made him sound years older.

"No. He's in Point Pleasant. He's very ill."

"A coma."

Caden reacted with a start. Parker couldn't possibly know. Even if someone on staff at West Central had learned about Jerome, they wouldn't share the news with an inmate-patient. "Who told you?"

Parker tore a fresh sheet of paper from his notebook. "They did."

"Who?"

"Cold." He rolled the pencil between his fingers.

Caden shifted. Talking to Parker was like having a one-sided conversation in a foreign language. Equally as frustrating. "I can ask the nurse to adjust the heat."

"Cold must return. Evening will follow." Parker started shading the new page.

Ryan shook his head. "Caden, we're not getting anywhere." Turning his back on Parker, he lowered his voice. "The kid's obviously in his own world. I don't think he understands what you're asking."

"Maybe." He glanced to the pieces of paper taped to the wall. Newspaper clippings and drawings had plastered the walls in Jerome's office, but the shaded squares Parker was so intent on producing made no sense. Judging from the collection of pencil nubs at Parker's elbow, he'd worn down several while creating his masterpieces.

Caden picked up two of the sheets. "These are important to you." Half question, half statement. Something niggled at the back of his mind. Why the drawings? Why now?

"The radio talks to me." Parker reached for a new pencil, the tip of the one he'd been using whittled to a pinhead. "Mostly at night."

Nurse Brenner had mentioned Parker's attachment to the radio. The small transistor box stood silent at his elbow. *No batteries.*

"How does it talk to you?"

Parker ignored the question. "Jerome knew. Jerome understood the puzzle. That's why he came to see me."

Caden rubbed his temple. It was hard to believe this boy, a fractured shell who spoke in riddles, had once been a rambunctious teenager, his only cares related to running track and girls.

"Was Jerome sick?" Ryan persisted.

Parker stayed silent.

Caden blew out a frustrated breath. "Parker this is important. What did Jerome want?"

The hint of a smile tugged the boy's lips at the corners. Slowly, he raised his head. "The Mothman knows."

Chapter 5

Saturday unraveled slowly for Katie. Sam fussed when she checked his eyes in the morning, but at least the swelling had gone down. Her headache departed around noon, and by evening when she and Sam joined her mom for dinner, her spirits were improved.

"Rex still hasn't come back," her mother told her as they washed dishes after the meal. Plopping a dirty plate in a sink full of sudsy water, she sniffled slightly. "Martin thinks he might have got hit by a car."

Poor Rex. "Oh, I hope not." Katie worked at drying a glass with a blue terry towel. Sam would be devastated.

"That's not all." Her mom hadn't bothered to remove her chunky bangle bracelets, and the bright plastic clacked together as she rinsed the plate. "I heard the Batemans can't find their collie. And Stu Fletcher's shepherd disappeared. It's creepy."

"Don't tell Sam." It was bad enough Rex vanished, but Katie didn't want him hearing about the other animals. He was already having bad dreams. Last night he'd woken up screaming, insisting someone had been looming over his bed. She'd gone over every inch of the room in an effort to placate his fears, even checking doors and windows so he could see each was securely locked.

Since he hadn't been troubled by his visit to the ER, she was certain the dream had to do with Rex's disappearance and the eerie rumors circulating town. Today, there'd been new gossip about peculiar lights in the sky near the TNT and renewed whispers of the Mothman. Duncan and Donnie Bradley, brothers who insisted they'd seen the giant winged creature in June, had begun to scour the old munitions site in search of the monster.

She'd tuned out the talk, but didn't doubt there would be a number of locals hacking through the overgrowth for clues. If nothing else, it made good fodder for Halloween.

Shortly after finishing the dishes, she took Sam home to get him settled for the night. They normally attended an early church service on Sundays, but given Sam's conjunctivitis, the doctor recommended she limit his contact for the next several days. If he was going to be stuck inside, she'd have to find something for him to do.

Other than draw.

When the night wound down, she curled into the corner of the couch with a cup of tea. The house was quiet, the television off, now that Sam was in bed. Stillness settled around her like the comforting folds of an old blanket. She closed her eyes, contentedly soaking in the peace. Within seconds, a loud clatter jarred her to her feet, the abrupt movement jostling hot tea onto her lap.

"Crap." Hastily setting the cup aside, she brushed at her jeans.

A loud thud-bump-thud made her freeze in mid motion. Her heart lodged in her throat as her gaze darted to the ceiling, tracking the noise. Something thumped across the roof.

"Mom?" Looking worried, Sam appeared in the hallway. "That man who was in my room must have come back. I think he's on the roof."

"No, Sam." She hurried across the room to hug him. "That was a bad dream." But she needed to make sure. The rational part of her insisted no sane person was shuffling around overhead. A tree branch must have fallen and gotten battered about in the wind. But the other part whispered the wind wasn't strong enough to send something banging against the shingles.

"Stay here." She headed for the closet, then snagged her jacket. A quick rummage through a box on the floor turned up a flashlight.

"Where are you going?" Sam appeared at her side as she tested the batteries. "You can't go out there." Her peered up at her, anxiety front and center as he twisted his hands together.

"Sam—"

Another thump-thump like something—or someone—heavy tramped about overhead. Katie swallowed her fear, refusing to let Sam see her growing alarm.

"What's that noise?" he cried.

"Listen to me." Bending, she gripped his shoulders. "It's probably just a squirrel or a raccoon that got up on the roof."

"But you don't know that." His voice cracked and his bottom lip quivered. "It's the man again. You should call the police."

"Sam, there is no man. You had a bad dream."

"What about now?"

Standing, she zipped her jacket. "I'm going outside to look, just like I looked in your room last night. I want you to lock the door behind me and don't open it until you hear me say everything's okay." She took his hand. "Can you do that?"

Wordlessly, he nodded.

"Good." Katie smiled, hoping to put him at ease. Flicking on the flashlight, she opened the door and stepped outside. Sam immediately closed it behind her and snapped the lock into place.

The air was crisp, a cold wind rattling the trees closest to the house. As she walked into the yard, Katie spied a van parked several hundred feet down the street. Odd, but not alarming. Instead, she focused on the black, sloped shingles of the house. The trees were clustered close enough that any small animal could have scaled the branches and dropped onto the roof. By the same token, a man could too. The clatter she'd heard had been too heavy for a cat or squirrel but not a human.

As she stood debating the matter, the headlights on the van flared to life. Startled by the bright intrusion, she glanced over her shoulder. The van remained parked where it was, motor idling. A slug of foreboding oozed into her stomach. She knew most of her neighbors' vehicles by sight, but this looked more like a work truck. A plain panel job like a utility company might use. In the darkness, she couldn't see past the windshield and imagined the driver watching her.

Quickly, she switched off the flashlight and ducked beneath the trees, secreting herself in shadow. Cold sweat broke out on the back of her neck. She looked from the van to the roof. Did the driver have an accomplice who prowled around, waiting to signal an all clear?

The vehicle rolled slowly forward, small stones popping and crunching beneath its tires. Katie shivered, riveted to the spot by its sluggish advance. She should have listened to Sam and called the sheriff's office.

Crouching beneath the shelter of a maple, she tried to make herself smaller. In the moonless dark, it was impossible to tell the vehicle's true color. Dark blue? Green? Work van or not, there was no reason for anyone to be out in the middle of the night, surveying the empty road in front of her house. Her nearest neighbor lived around a bend, and the closest streetlamp was too far away to shed much light.

She bit her lip, mentally berating herself for getting trapped in a vulnerable position. If she dashed into the house and called for assistance, how quickly would a deputy respond?

Two seconds later, the van rolled to a complete stop. Still a good distance away, it squatted in the street, a plain square box with blazing eyes.

Waiting.

Katie counted to five. The wind tugged at her jacket, swirling beneath her collar. Abruptly, the van's lights flicked off, plunging her into stifling darkness. Starlight barely defined the vehicle, the low rumble of the motor ominously loud in the stillness. She inhaled sharply, one hand pressed to the rough bark of the tree.

Go away. Go away.

The driver's side door opened, the interior light briefly defining the shape of a man. The door clicked shut and the light winked out as a form stepped from the vehicle.

Every nerve in her body tensed for flight. If he advanced, she'd flee and lead the stranger from the house and Sam. Her only weapon was a flashlight, her neighbors too far away to hear her scream.

Her mouth was dry, her palms damp. A low-level hum washed over her. Faint at first, it swelled to an earsplitting cacophony. Something thumped across the shingles. *Whomp! Whomp! Whomp!*

Katie gasped, craning her neck to spy the source. An enormous shape swooped from the roof, a rapid-flash glimpse of something winged and gray. An otherworldly screech pierced the air, and in that quicksilver burst of time, terror engulfed her. A loud drone built in her head, threatening to burst her eardrums. Her knees quaked as the punishing flood of terror ratcheted higher, choking off all thought, all instinct. Sprawling face-first onto the grass, she covered her head with both arms.

Go away. Go away.

Paralyzed by fear, she prayed the thing wouldn't see her.

The sudden squeal of tires sliced through her panic, wrenching her back to the present. Burning rubber and exhaust filled her nose. Blindly, she groped for the flashlight. She clamored to her feet in time to see the red-eyed wink of taillights disappear around the bend. The humming dwindled, then died altogether. Whatever she'd seen leap from the roof—whatever she *thought* she'd seen—was gone. Weak-kneed and shaken, she raced for the house.

"Sam, it's me." Her fingers closed around the doorknob in a white-knuckled grip. "Open up. Let me in!" *Away from that thing.*

Sam unlocked the door and hastily stumbled backward. Katie wasted no time in locking the barrier behind her. Her son's face was white.

"Mom?" His voice quavered.

Try as she may to conceal the terror firing along her nerves, Katie knew it was evident on her face. She'd only caught a glimpse of the creature, but that fleeting second had been more than enough.

"It's going to be okay, Sam." She hugged him close. With one arm looped around his back, she snatched the phone from the end table and used her thumb to dial the sheriff's office.

"Hello, this is Katie Lynch." Her voice tumbled out in a breathless rush before the officer even finished speaking. "Please send someone to my house on Red Hollow Road. I've just seen the Mothman."

* * * *

Ryan discovered the news the following morning when a junior officer told him about Katie's late night call. Anxious to visit and learn the details himself, he hurried through a stack of paperwork.

An hour later, he fidgeted from foot to foot on her front porch, waiting for her to answer the doorbell.

"Ryan." She seemed surprised to find him there. Dark circles lingered beneath her eyes, and her blond hair was scooped back in a messy ponytail. She wore a pale blue robe with flannel pajamas.

"Hi." He fought the urge to wrap his arms around her. "I, uh, heard what happened last night. Can I come in?"

She nodded and stepped aside. In bare feet, she was considerably shorter than he was.

"Sam still sleeping?"

Another nod, accompanied by a soft sniffle. "He was up late. We both were."

Ryan was at a loss. "Want to tell me what happened?"

Her gaze met his. Whether in gratitude or petition, he wasn't certain.

"Let me change and I'll make coffee."

Later, seated at the kitchen table, Katie relayed her story. In the short span it had taken her to change into jeans and a sweater, her composure had returned. Ryan listened without interruption, perhaps the wrong course to take given the censure that crossed her face when she was through.

"You don't believe me."

"Katie." He took her hand. "I do believe you. Are you forgetting Caden's seen the Mothman several times? He's got scars branded across his forearm from that thing's grip." Gently, he traced his thumb over her knuckles, hoping to put her at ease. "The important thing is it didn't hurt you."

"I know." Her tone softened. "But I worry about Sam. He's already having nightmares. What if it comes back?"

"That's not likely." Everything he knew about the Mothman indicated the creature was solitary, preferring the remote acres of the TNT. Several months had passed since the last flurry of Mothman sightings. Before that, the monster had lain low for a span of almost fifteen years.

"I don't think you need to worry." The statement was a shot in the dark, but Caden would tell him if there was something to be concerned about. Not for the first time, Ryan wished he better understood his brother's connection to the cryptid, but that inexplicable bond was something Caden avoided discussing.

Ryan shoved his coffee aside. "I'm more worried about the van. I wish you'd gotten a better look at it."

"I know." Katie bit her lip, anxiety crossing her face. "It was too dark to see. It might have been green or blue. Even black or dark gray. It was hard to tell."

"And you've never seen it around before?"

She shook her head, glancing briefly at her hands. When she looked at him, her gaze was clear. "Ryan, do you think there's something odd going on?"

Confused by the question, he hesitated. Afternoon sunlight streamed through an adjacent window, herald of a gorgeous autumn day. Sitting in Katie's cheerful kitchen with its whitewashed maple cupboards and ivy wallpaper, it was hard to imagine anything remotely sinister had lingered outside during the night.

"What do you mean?"

"Everything that's happened lately." She studied him closely. "Think about it. Jerome...the mysterious deputy no one seems to know about...Rex and those other animals disappearing...all the strange lights in the sky."

He'd never been one to embrace flights of fancy. "Fanned by a lot of gossip and speculation."

"Ryan, be serious."

"I am." The last thing he wanted to do was feed her fears. "Animals disappear. That's part of life in a rural community. As for the lights, a lot of those were sighted near the airport. Factor in the Air Force bases up and down the east coast, and you've got opportunity for unusual lights in the sky."

Her gaze sharpened with a defiant edge. "What about Deputy Brown?"

"I don't know." Realizing he fought a losing battle, Ryan sighed. "Look, Katie, all I'm saying is that it's easy to jump to the wrong conclusion. You should have seen Jerome's place when Caden and I were there. It's filled with conspiracy stuff. UFOs, the Mothman...things I never even heard of. Look at this." Twisting, he reached into the pocket of his jacket slung over the back of the chair. He'd taken Jerome's battered paperback copy of *UFO Sightings and Stories* on a whim, thinking he might be able to help the man if he could get inside his head. But the book was a farfetched collection of tales and speculation that made Parker Kline seem sane.

"This is the kind of stuff I'm talking about." Ryan passed her the book. "I only flipped through it, but it's crazy. People swearing they've seen UFOs or monsters, believing in other dimensions and interplanetary travel. I like *Star Wars* as much as the next guy, but this shit, uh—crap—is seriously flawed."

Katie paused in examining the book, running her finger down a page. "It looks like Jerome made a lot of notations in the margins."

"Yeah. I'm starting to think the guy is more out there than anyone realized."

"Can I keep this?"

"Why?"

"I don't know." Placing the paperback on the table, she picked up her coffee. "It might sound silly, but I feel close to Jerome since trying to help him that night. If this"—she motioned to the book—"was important to him, I'd like to glance through it."

Ryan didn't care about Katie's interest in speculative hogwash, but her attachment to Jerome bothered him. A squiggle of emotion strangely like jealousy made his reply clipped. "Whatever. Just don't go getting crazy ideas about little green men and flying saucers."

"Don't poke fun."

"I'm not." But, of course, he was. Being condescending, even arrogant, and all because of Jerome. The guy was on the scrawny side and socially inept. Could Katie be interested in someone like that, or was she simply responding with kindness for a friend in trouble? If he didn't get off the fence soon, he'd never know. "Look, I didn't mean to ridicule, but whoever was driving that van last night was flesh and blood, not an extraterrestrial."

Her eyes grew wide. "Then you do think it was someone watching the house?"

He didn't want to scare her but at the same time wanted to be truthful. "Let's put it this way. I don't think it was anyone out for a nighttime drive or looking for directions."

She paled. "And the Mothman?" Her voice trembled as she said the name.

The million-dollar question. Which, as always, lacked an answer.

Standing, Ryan picked up his jacket. "Keep the book. I'm going to talk to Caden. It's time I find out exactly what my brother's connection is to that winged freak."

* * * *

The Mothman knows.

Caden took a swig of beer, mentally recounting Parker Kline's parting words. Sunday afternoon and he was camped on Eve's sofa, the Pittsburgh Steelers and Baltimore Colts running plays on her console TV. The last he'd looked it was nearing halftime, Pittsburgh leading ten to six.

The smell of baking lasagna wafted from the kitchen where Eve was busy tossing a salad. They'd made the pasta together, but she'd shooed him into the living room afterward, telling him to enjoy the game. Any other time he would have been eager to cheer on Terry Bradshaw or lament a bad call by one of the refs, but he couldn't focus. His mind kept drifting back to Parker and his weird tidbits of information.

Why bring up the Mothman? And what about the other thing he'd said? *Cold must return. Evening will follow.*

What the hell did that mean? There was no question the kid's mind was broken, yet Jerome had gone to see him for something.

Exhaling, Caden scrubbed a hand over his face. With a rare day off, he shouldn't be worrying over a UFO fanatic laid up in the hospital. But despite all his eccentric behavior, Jerome was a decent guy. No one deserved to spend their life in a coma, and right now, it didn't seem like he was going to come out of it.

Caden took another swig of beer. The phone rang and Eve yelled from the kitchen that she would answer. The house was hers, but he'd moved in two weeks ago—right after he'd bought a ring in contemplation of asking her to marry him. He still hadn't found the right time to propose, the diamond niggling at the back of his mind.

Five minutes later as the Colts were punting, Eve strolled into the room, a dish towel slung over her shoulder, a glass of wine in hand. "That was Sarah." She sat in the chair adjacent to him. Perched on the edge, she was obviously keyed up about something. "Her mom just left Martin's gas station after getting a fill up."

"That's news." He kept the amusement in his voice to a minimum, knowing Sarah's mother liked to gossip.

"No, no. While she was there, Mrs. Sherman saw Doreen Sue, and Doreen Sue was a wreck." Eve sipped her wine, staring intently at a spot on the floor as if trying to work through a dilemma. "I wonder if I should call Katie."

"Because Doreen Sue's upset about something?"

"No." Eve's gaze flashed to his face. "Because according to Mrs. Sherman, Doreen Sue saw Lyle buying cigarettes from the vending machine."

"Lyle?" Caden knew the name should prompt a memory, but his thoughts were wrapped up in Parker, diamonds, and the last forty-five seconds of the half.

"Lyle Mason. Katie's ex."

"Oh." Now he understood. He'd gone to high school with Lyle and his sister, Lottie. A year older, Lyle had been forced to repeat tenth grade, placing him in the same classes as Lottie and Caden. During their senior year, Lottie had died tragically in a fall from a balcony. Never social to begin with, Lyle withdrew, turning increasingly bitter. It was hard to imagine how Katie had ended up in a relationship with such a downer of a guy.

"Katie should know." Eve's glance was sharp, as if she sought approval.

"Isn't Sarah going to tell her?"

"She thinks I should."

Caden drank his beer, hoping he could stay out of it. Why did women feel the need to get involved? On the TV, the game had been replaced with a commercial of Didi Conn pandering the crispiness of Tostitos. He could use some right about now. "I'm sure Doreen Sue's going to tell her."

Eve digested the thought for all of five seconds. "I think I should."

Thankfully, the doorbell chimed, saving him from committing one way or another. Somehow it didn't surprise him to find Ryan on the threshold when Eve answered. His brother wandered into the room, declining the offer of a beer from Eve, then dropping to a seat in an easy chair.

"How's the game?" he asked.

"Halftime," Caden supplied. "Steelers are winning."

Ryan nodded, looking distracted. "Smells good in here."

"We made lasagna." Eve appeared at his side. "You're welcome to stay for dinner."

"Thanks, but I just dropped by to talk to Caden about something."

"You mean about Lyle?"

Ryan stared blankly. "Lyle?"

"Mason." Caden shook his head, deciding Parker Kline would have to wait. "Apparently, Lyle Mason, Katie's ex, is back in town."

"Sonofabitch." Ryan stood, smacking his fist into his palm. "That explains the van."

"What van?" Eve asked.

"Some jerk in a panel van staked out Katie's house last night. The guy gave her a scare."

"Oh, no. Is she all right?"

"Yeah, I just left there. She's fine, but a little shaken. Why don't you call and check in? Tell her about Lyle."

"I will." Plainly worried, Eve dashed toward the kitchen and the phone.

Scowling, Caden eyed his brother. "I know you. You got her out of the room for a reason. What is it?"

"You're right." Ryan slid into the seat Eve had vacated. "I don't like the idea of Lyle back in town, and if that was him snooping around Katie's place last night, he's going to hear from me. But that's not why I'm here."

Caden swallowed the last of his beer and set the bottle aside. He had a feeling the day was about to take a downturn. "I figured that."

Ryan leaned forward, locking his fingers between his knees. "Last night at Katie's, something scared the guy in the van away before he could cause any trouble. Something that terrified her."

Caden stayed silent, certain where his brother was leading. Let Ryan drag the creature up if he wanted, but he had no intention of getting involved.

"You know what was there," his brother said.

"I'm glad she's safe."

"Damn it, Caden, it's back. You and I have both heard rumors of the Mothman over the last couple days, but Katie's a reliable witness."

"I never said she wasn't."

"Then do something."

"Like what?"

"Find out what the damn thing wants. It's connected with you in some freakish way. It's bad enough Lyle crawled back into town, but I don't want to have to worry about Katie turning into another Hank Jeffries. The thing scared her witless."

"You told me it saved her. Chased Mason, or whoever it was, away."

"That doesn't matter. I don't want it going back there." Suddenly Ryan was an expert on the Mothman.

"And you think I can change that?"

"You've seen it up close. Hell, it saved your life more than once. If anyone has a chance of communicating with the thing, you're the best shot."

Caden glanced away. The feelings dredged up by the Mothman were not ones he wanted to remember. "I'll think about it." Ironic his brother had gone from not believing the creature existed a few months ago to suggesting he seek it out.

"Caden, I need you to do this." Ryan stared at him levelly, his tone grave.

"I said I'd think about it." In fairness, his brother didn't understand how vulnerable he was when he opened his mind to the Mothman. Exposed to a deluge of fatigue and despair. It was almost like the damn monster wanted to die. Problem was, there were too many glory mongers and curiosity seekers who'd gladly help it achieve that goal.

Caden stood. "I need another beer."

"What about the Mothman?"

"It's Sunday and I'm watching the game. I told you'd I'd think about it. That's the best I can do right now."

Ryan swore softly.

"You want a beer?" Caden asked.

"No." His brother stood, his expression tight. "Even if you don't give a rat's ass about Katie's welfare, I do." He headed for the door.

"Where are you going?" Caden called.

"Where I should have gone in the first place." Ryan wrenched open the door. "To the TNT."

* * * *

"Maybe we should try someplace else," Duncan Bradley suggested to his brother.

Donnie stopped hiking and craned his neck to study the sky. At thirty-two, he was younger by a full year, but Duncan deferred to him when it came to trudging through the woods. They'd both grown up in Point Pleasant and had spent years exploring the TNT. Even so, Duncan tended to get turned around in the labyrinth of trees, ponds, and abandoned weapons igloos. Donnie had a sharper sense of location and the ability to pick out trails.

"Maybe." He tugged down on the brim of his fluorescent orange cap.

Duncan rubbed his jaw, wondering if they were wasting their time. They'd been driving around for over two hours, parking their truck in random pull-off spots, then hiking back through the trees. They'd started with the spot where they'd seen the Mothman last June, but only succeeded in rousing a couple of archery hunters who grew irked at having their territory invaded.

Duncan had originally been keyed up about looking for "the bird," but he was starting to think there were better ways of spending a Sunday afternoon. At home he'd be sprawled in front of the TV, watching the game and downing a cold one. He was getting hungry too. He and Donnie shared an apartment, but their mom invited them home for Sunday dinner each week. In another hour, she'd be serving up pot roast with brown gravy and whipped potatoes.

"Let's pack it in for the day. Mom will have dinner ready soon, and we shouldn't show up at the last minute."

"Yeah, you're right." Donnie scuffed a work boot against a gnarled root sticking up from the ground. "Looks like today's a bust. We can always pick it up again some other time. I still say the creature's out here."

Duncan breathed a sigh of relief, already anticipating a Rolling Rock and debating football plays with his dad. Not that he wasn't gung ho about the Mothman—he wanted him and Donnie to find the god-awful thing—just that sometimes football, food, and beer took priority. But as he turned back on the path, a strange whimpering sound drew him up short.

"Hey, did you hear that?"

"Hear what?" Donnie stopped beside him and shook his head. "I didn't hear anything."

"Listen." A slight breeze rustled the orange and yellow leaves of the trees clustered around them. Somewhere in the distance a crow called and another answered. Five seconds of silence followed. He frowned. "I thought—wait. There it is again." A whimper, like an animal in pain. "Do you hear it?"

"Yeah." Donnie took off in the direction of the sound, racing ahead where the path narrowed and the trees twined together.

After a few feet, the trail disappeared completely. Duncan had to wend his way through a maze of interlocked branches and roots, his brother's fluorescent orange cap bobbing ahead. The ruckus they made trampling through the woods overpowered any other noise. If there were an animal up ahead, Mothman or whatever, it had probably gone into hiding. He was about to yell for his brother to slow down when Donnie stopped and Duncan plowed into him.

"Hey, why'd you—" His mouth dropped open. "Holy shit!"

Donnie stood frozen, his face a tight mask. "What do you think happened?"

Duncan could only stare. Several dead dogs lay in a small clearing, each with a puddle of blood around its head. Fluid had pooled from their ears, noses, and mouths. Scattered nearby, globs of a white mucous-like substance gleamed in the fading sunlight.

Duncan's gut roiled. "Isn't that the Bateman's collie?" He pointed to the nearest dog.

"Yeah…Peony Girl." Donnie lifted his arm, breathing into the crook of his elbow. "What the hell happened here? We gotta tell someone, Duncan."

The whimper came again. Duncan glanced to the right, catching a faint movement among the trees. "Hey," he called. Then more gentle, as he bent his knees and extended his hand. "Hey, there. Come on out. We won't hurt you." He recognized the dog at first glance, even though it huddled in a thicket of ferns and thistle. Martin Ward had been searching for Rex for several days. "Come out here." He whistled softly.

Cautiously, the dog inched forward, head lowered, tail between its legs. It didn't appear to be hurt, just dirty and unkempt with briars and bits of leaves snagged in its coat. Another pathetic whine issued from its throat.

"That's it. Come on," Duncan encouraged, fearful of moving lest he frighten the skittish animal. Finally, the dog lifted its nose to his hand, and Duncan grabbed its collar. He did a quick visual inspection, running his hands over the animal's fur as he spoke soothingly.

"I got a bad feeling about this," Donnie said beside him. "What kind of sicko goes around butchering dogs?" He glanced about nervously as if suspecting a madman lurked among the trees. "Maybe it was some kind of satanic ritual."

"I don't think so." Satisfied Rex wasn't hurt, Duncan rubbed the dog's neck, hoping to calm him. He'd never known Martin's pet to be overly passive, but something had put a terrible fright into the animal. The same something that had killed four less-fortunate canines and left their bodies strewn in the clearing.

"Hey, I'm serious, Duncan." Donnie sounded spooked, his voice carrying a tremor. "I feel exposed out here. Like something's watching us."

"Something probably is. The same thing that killed all these dogs." He stood, and Rex pressed against his legs. The terrified animal would probably cling to his side the entire way back to the truck. Duncan narrowed his eyes. He sensed it too…something hidden, something watching. "Let's get out of here before we end up like those mutts."

Donnie needed no prodding, hustling to retrace their steps. "We come out here again, I'm bringing a gun with me."

Duncan nodded grimly, dinner and football forgotten. "Let's report this to the sheriff, give Martin back his dog, and reconnoiter. I wanna nail the sonofabitch who did this."

A few steps ahead, Donnie glanced over his shoulder, breathing hard. "So you think it's some psycho Satanist?"

"Hell, no." Duncan snorted his contempt. "Ain't it obvious? The Mothman killed 'em."

Chapter 6

Ryan was ten miles into the TNT on Potter Creek Road when he spied Duncan Bradley's truck coming from the opposite direction. Off duty, he drove his regular vehicle, a bright blue Camaro. Despite the smaller size of the sporty car, the lane was too narrow to pass Duncan's big Ford side by side. Ryan dipped his right wheels into the grass, and motioned for the other man to pass. Instead Duncan hit the brakes and hopped from his vehicle.

"Ryan! Ryan!" He waved a hand over his head as he raced for the Camaro. Almost simultaneously, Donnie burst from the passenger's side of the truck and hurried to join his brother. Martin Wade's dog, Rex, paced in the bed of the pick-up. Ryan knew from Katie the dog had been missing for several days.

He wound his window down. "What's going on?"

"You ain't gonna believe this." In a breathless rush, Duncan told him of the grisly discovery he and Donnie had made in the woods.

"Never seen anything like it." Donnie flapped his arms, using animated gestures. "Dead dogs with their heads all effed up. It looks like something out of a horror movie. We found poor Rex hiding in the trees."

Both brothers were plainly shaken, their expressions a mixture of grim excitement and fear. If what they said was true, the dogs had died in a manner similar to Chester Wilson's cow. But the Wilson farm was miles away, meaning someone—or something—had expanded their hunting territory. If he didn't get a handle on the situation soon, new rumors would fly with everything from the Mothman to satanic cults and UFOs blamed for the killings.

"Where'd you find the dogs?"

"Two to three miles east." Duncan pointed the way. "Trail on the right. It cuts back to bottomland, then a small clearing."

"I know the place." It wouldn't be long before predators set to work on the carcasses.

Donnie whirled toward the truck. "We'll show you."

"No. That's all right." The last thing he needed was two overeager civilians with a reputation for exaggeration. "I'll check it out. You two head into town and report what you found at the sheriff's office. Be clear with the facts." His gaze traveled to Rex in the back of the truck. "And let Martin know about his dog. I'm sure he'll want to get him checked over."

"Yeah, all right." Donnie spoke for both of them but neither seemed happy with the order. Noticeably sulking, they shuffled back to the Ford.

"It was the Mothman," Duncan grumbled. "I'm sure of it."

Fifteen minutes later, Ryan squatted to examine the remains of a mid-sized collie. Like the other animals nearby, fluids and blood had disgorged from every orifice in its head. He'd have to contact the county vet again, but could tell the results would likely mirror the findings of Wilson's cow—a concussive impact resulting in a massive rupture of the brain. It made no sense. He recognized two of the other dogs, pets that came from different areas around Point Pleasant. What were the odds all four would end up here, subject to the same macabre manner of death? Something or someone had lured them.

Looking for a stick, Ryan retrieved a broken branch from the ground. Over a dozen puddles of silvery goo were scattered between the carcasses. He prodded the nearest glob. A few, thinner than the others, were in the process of melting and dissolving into the soil. He didn't need a lab sample or test tube to identify the same gelatinous sludge strewn through Wilson's pasture.

Star shit.

Tilting his head, he glanced up at the sky. In another few hours it would be dark. Good thing too, because the less people who knew about these dogs, the better. When word spread, he had a feeling the TNT would be swarming with hunters. But unlike those licensed and armed with bows, they wouldn't be stalking small game or deer.

They'd be hunting the Mothman.

* * * *

Early shift at the sheriff's department was usually quiet, but the same couldn't be said for Monday morning when Caden arrived. Two clerks buzzed about the main room delivering mail and file folders while three deputies banged out reports on antiquated typewriters. Several phones kept up a continuous jangling until snatched up by a harried clerk or deputy. Wayne Rosling, a senior officer in the department, was busy taking a report from Fran Bateman and her husband, Clay. Seated in front of Rosling's desk, Fran sniffled into a lace handkerchief while Clay held her hand.

Caden didn't see Ryan, though he'd spied his brother's Camaro in the parking lot. Shrugging from his jacket, he eyed the message slips waiting on his desk. He'd caught up on calls before leaving Saturday, but several new notes had accumulated.

Easing into his chair, he picked up the assortment and rifled through. Two were from Nurse Brenner at the West Central Mental Health Institute, one from Martin Ward about a part for his car, and one from Floyd Kline, Parker's father. The message said simply *"Stay away from my kid."*

No surprise there. Floyd must have found out he'd been to see Parker. Easing back in his chair, Caden picked up the phone and punched out the number on the message slip for Nurse Brenner. "This is Sergeant Caden Flynn of the Mason County Sheriff's Office," he said when she answered. "You called yesterday."

"I did." Brenner sounded every bit as no-nonsense over the phone as she did in person. "You've probably already heard from Floyd Kline, but I thought you should know he was in to see his son yesterday. Parker told him you and your brother were here, and Mr. Kline went ballistic. I don't say that lightly, Sergeant. You'd think he was the one who needed incarcerating."

Picturing the commotion, Caden rubbed his temple. "We don't have a good history together." That was putting it mildly. What had Floyd told him at Parker's competency hearing? *I never want to see your sorry ass again, unless it's when they put you in the ground.* "I'm sorry he disrupted your hospital."

"He did more than that. We're still trying to calm half the patients. Beau Hardy is convinced the south is rising and has been screaming retaliation against Lincoln and Grant since yesterday. For the safety and well-being of our residents, I'm going to have to ask you stay away in the future."

Not in the mood to argue legalities with her, he let the comment slide. "Is that why you called?"

"No." Bluntly. "I have a message for you."

"From Floyd?" Not a promising way to start the morning.

"From Parker."

That brought him up short. Across from him, a blond-haired woman stepped into the room and glanced nervously about.

"Parker says to tell you that 'evening will come soon.'" Nurse Brenner spoke crisply. "I have no idea what it means, and I wouldn't normally bother telling you except he was so insistent. Good day, Sergeant."

The phone clicked in his ear followed by the drone of a dial tone.

Evening will come soon. He dropped the phone into its cradle.

Cold must return. Evening will follow.

Damn Parker and his crazy riddles.

"Can I help you?" he asked, approaching the woman in the doorway. Something about her seemed familiar. Her long hair was poufy and teased, and though she wore a good deal of makeup, it appeared expertly applied.

"Yes, I…" She glanced hesitantly around the bustling room. "Is Ryan here? Ryan Flynn?"

Caden was about to tell her no when his brother appeared from a hallway on the opposite side of the room. Coffee cup in one hand, he held a magazine-sized hardcover book in the other, his concentration on the book.

"Ryan," Caden called. "Someone to see you."

Stopping by his desk, Ryan set his coffee down. "Suzanne?" A frown crossed his face. "Everything okay?" He tucked the book beneath his arm and joined her.

The woman flushed. "Yes. It's… It's not Shawn this time. I got a call about our dog, Duke."

Now Caden understood why she looked familiar. She'd been involved in a domestic dispute he'd responded to last August. Of course she would ask for Ryan. Suzanne Flemish had gone to school with Caden's brother, married young, and regretted it almost immediately. He still wasn't sure why she remained with Shawn Preech, a rough-around-the-edges motorhead who'd gained local celebrity status for his skill at dirt-track racing. Preech might be good behind the wheel of a winged sprint, but he was clueless when it came to maintaining a healthy marriage. When he'd cheated on Suzanne over the summer, she'd taken a baseball bat to his restored 1970 Dodge Charger, then tried to follow that up with a crack to his head. Caden and Ryan had arrived on the scene to find the couple screaming at each other across the damaged Charger, Suzanne clutching the bat and threatening to shatter the windshield. He was surprised she wasn't mortified to see him, but had a feeling Suzanne Preech didn't do mortification. She got even. Word had it Shawn had ditched his fling and bought Suzanne a pricey ring to patch things up.

"Oh." Ryan grimaced. "You need to see Deputy Rosling about that. He's been handling most of those calls." He motioned toward Rosling's desk where Fran and Clay Bateman were in the process of withdrawing.

Fran still sniffled into her handkerchief, but Clay shook Rosling's hand as the two men exchanged a few parting words.

Suzanne's eyes grew owlishly wide. "Do you know what happened to Duke? He's been missing for two days."

If Caden hadn't seen the damage she'd done with a baseball bat, he might have believed the beseeching expression she turned on his brother.

Ryan cleared his throat and shifted the book from beneath his arm, briefly exposing the cover. "I'm sorry, Suzanne, but we found Duke along with a few other missing dogs." Ryan touched her elbow tentatively, steering her toward Rosling's desk as the Batemans departed. "Wayne will tell you about it and get some information from you."

Caden snatched the book from Ryan as his brother helped Suzanne to a seat. The cover was unmistakable.

"What are you doing with my high school yearbook?" He shot Ryan a questioning look as his brother returned to his desk. "You got this from Mom, didn't you?"

"I did." Ryan retrieved his coffee. "I was curious about Lyle Mason."

"Well, you're not going to find any dirt on him in here." Sinking into his chair, Caden flipped through the pages, reminded of friends and faces he hadn't seen since 1968. The photographs were terribly dated, taken in a time when the Beatles and the Doors ruled the airwaves and Haight-Ashbury was the city of love. He flipped to his yearbook photo and was shocked by how young he looked, his black hair cut in a cross between Paul McCartney and RFK. A few more pages and he found Lyle Mason, his sister, Lottie, directly beside him. Lyle's thick brows were drawn tightly over his eyes, his expression challenging. It was exactly how Caden remembered him. An outsider with a chip on his shoulder, Lyle had done his best to set himself apart from the rest of the class.

By contrast, Lottie was pleasant but awkward. Shy and plump, she'd only had a handful of friends, and was often a target of ridicule from the more popular girls in his class.

An ugly memory.

Caden snapped the book shut and tossed it on his desk. "You could have asked me to borrow it. There are a lot of personal messages in there."

"Don't worry." Grinning, Ryan shook his head. "I skipped the love letters from your throng of admirers."

"My throng of—" Caden stopped, knowing his brother wanted to yank his chain. He'd had more than a few girlfriends back in the day thanks to his skill at vocals and playing guitar, but wasn't going to let Ryan poke through his teen exploits. "Forget it. I want to know what's going on around here. This place is buzzing." He gave a nod for the commotion around them. "What did I miss?"

Ryan leaned forward, talking across his desk. "The Bradley brothers found our missing dogs in the TNT."

Caden's stomach soured as Ryan told him about the discovery. Any strange finding in the old munitions site was equivalent to tinder under a powder keg. Dead dogs, ruptured brains, and "star shit." It wouldn't be long before people started screaming "Mothman" and a few of them got up in arms enough to parade around the labyrinth of roads with shotguns.

"Shit." He scrubbed a hand over his jaw. "You sure Doc Holden thinks they died the same way as Chester's cow?"

Ryan nodded. "Heard it from Sheriff Weston this morning." After sorting through the papers on his desk, he tossed a single sheet across to Caden. "Read for yourself if you don't believe me. Concussive impact, resulting in severe hemorrhaging of the brain."

Caden let the paper lie. His brother had clearly memorized the veterinarian's report. "But Rex was all right?"

"Yeah. Martin picked him up last night. Doc Holden checked him over and said he was spooked, but mostly fine. A little dehydrated and hungry. When I checked in with Martin this morning, he said Rex slept like a log." Dropping his hands in his lap, he shrugged. "Could be Rex came on the scene after whatever happened...happened."

Caden cast a glance at Suzanne Preech, who was still talking to Wayne Rosling. She held her purse on her lap with a balled-up tissue clutched in her hand. Even from where he was sitting, he could see she struggled with tears. He'd obviously misjudged her. Whatever her feelings for Shawn and his Dodge, she clearly loved Duke.

"Is that all I've missed?"

"No." Ryan reached for his coffee and took a gulp. "Apparently, there was a light show last night and Point Pleasant got buzzed by a horde of glowing objects. Mostly on Route 62 and near the TNT. The department had several dozen reports, and they're still coming in."

Caden frowned, not certain he followed. "UFOs?"

"That's what people are saying. Oh, and we had a call from Chester Wilson." Ryan smiled tightly. "His pastures are covered with star shit and he's got another dead cow."

Caden groaned. This was not how he wanted to start his Monday.

* * * *

Katie breathed in the silence of the lobby, the few guests in residence at the Parrish Hotel out roaming the town. The lack of activity gave her a chance to catch up on bookwork, but her mind kept drifting to Sam. By tomorrow he would be well enough to go back to school. In the meantime, her mom had volunteered to spend the day with him, since her hair salon was closed on Mondays.

Sam was safe at home, but it was hard not to dwell on Saturday night's unsettling visitations. Katie might have imagined the Mothman, but not the van. Now that she knew about Lyle, the driver's appearance dovetailed a little too suspiciously.

Lyle hadn't wanted his baby when he'd discovered she was pregnant, so why care now? The burden of being a single mother hadn't been easy, but she wanted nothing to do with him. And, for the most part, Lyle kept his distance. When he'd moved away, she was relieved. She'd heard nightmare stories of men who returned years later, attempting to claim children they'd fathered. What if Lyle had changed his mind about Sam and suddenly decided to take him away?

The opening click of the front door interrupted her thoughts. A second later, Sarah Sherman scurried into the lobby chased by a draft of chilly air.

"Brr." Her friend ran a hand through her coppery hair, taming the wind-tousled curls with a quick swipe. "It's cold out there today."

Katie murmured agreement. It was too early for Sarah to be off work, and too late for her to stop by the River Café for lunch. "Slow day at the courthouse?"

"Brutally." Sarah tugged off her gloves and dropped them on the reception counter. "Not that I mind an occasional slow day. It gives me a chance to dig through the older records, but I decided to cut out early."

Only Sarah would enjoy poking around in dusty birth, death, and marriage certificates. Her friend had been known to spend hours poring over documents dating back to the time of the Battle of Fort Randolph when Chief Cornstalk supposedly cursed Point Pleasant with his dying breath.

"If you're looking for Eve, she headed over to Gallipolis." Deciding bookwork was a lost cause, Katie flipped her accounting register shut.

"No. I came to see how you were doing." Sarah shrugged out of her coat and dropped it onto the nearest chair. Her purse followed.

"You mean about Lyle?"

"Of course. Eve said she called you about him. He hasn't tried to contact you, has he?"

"No." She hesitated, thinking of the van. It was probably best not to spread accusations she couldn't prove. Ryan knew about her visitor. She trusted him to look into it. "I'm not sure why he would. We didn't speak even when he lived in town."

"It doesn't hurt to be careful. He's probably staying with his cousin."

Katie hadn't thought about it, but the idea made sense. Lyle's parents had sold their farm and moved east to Braxton years ago. Lyle had stayed, keeping an apartment in town until he'd lost his job as a groundskeeper with a local nursery. Not long afterward, he'd headed north in search of work. Now that he was back, he'd try to freeload with Darrell, who lived in a trailer off Route 2.

"I wouldn't be surprised if he hooked up with Darrell." Discussing her loser of an ex took Katie's mind off Sam, but made her nervous in other ways. He'd never lifted a finger against her, but she didn't doubt Lyle Mason had a temper. "If he wants to tangle, he better tangle with me and leave Sam alone."

Sarah's gaze reflected sympathy. "I'll keep my ears open. A lot of talk funnels through the courthouse. If I hear anything, I'll let you know."

"Thanks."

"It could be nothing," Sarah continued. "Maybe he came home because it's the only place he knows. He was born here. Even though his parents are gone—"

"And his sister."

Sarah's eyes widened. "Oh dear, I'd forgotten about her. What was her name? Loretta?"

"Lottie." Katie hadn't known the shy, older girl, but in some ways, could relate. From what Lyle told her about his sister, Lottie had been a social outcast.

"Didn't she fall or something?" Sarah asked.

Katie nodded. "Lyle said there was a flat section of roof outside her bedroom window. She used to crawl out and sun herself, or watch the stars at night. Sometimes Lyle would join her and they'd sit and talk for hours. That was the side of him I saw when we dated—why I was able to overlook his other faults." Lottie had been dead for several years by the time they'd met, but Lyle's love for his sister had overshadowed his gruffness. They'd bonded over their missing siblings, then taken their relationship to the next level. "Lyle was a jerk, but he adored Lottie. If he had any saving grace, it was his love for his sister."

Before Sarah could reply, a fresh draft of cold air invaded the cozy setting. Both women glanced to the door in time to see a tall man dressed in a black suit step inside. A vague sense of déjà vu swept over Katie.

"Can I help you?" she asked.

Sarah stared openly as the man approached the desk.

An obvious stranger, he stood out more than most. A black fedora crowned his short dark hair, and his shiny black shoes were thick and rubber soled. Crisply tailored and immaculately cut, his suit appeared brand new. Through the front windows, Katie spied a large black car, possibly a Cadillac. The tug of déjà vu grew stronger.

"Good day." The man spoke slowly as if the words were difficult to form. His lips curved in a wide smile, but the grin lacked emotion. "I was wondering if you could answer a few questions." The artificial smile never left his face, plastered in place.

Gooseflesh broke out on Katie's arms. "About what?"

"I heard strange things have happened here lately. They interest me."

"Strange things?" Sarah's brow drew together in a quizzical expression.

He smiled at her. Katie wondered if his expression ever changed.

"Lights in the sky. Have you seen them?"

"No."

"Do you know anyone who has?"

"Who are you?" Katie didn't like the questioning, his incessant smile, or his odd manner of talking. She thought of Jerome's theories about Big Brother and government conspiracies. This man would fit neatly into that puzzle.

His gaze swept back, his eyes pale blue, almost colorless. "A visitor."

"From where?" she persisted.

"No place nearby." He rested his hands on the reception counter.

His fingers were unnaturally long, the last digit of each slightly fatter than the rest. Bulbous. She'd seen fingers like that before. An ache bloomed against her temple as she dug through her memories.

Somewhere in the past. Somewhere long ago...a blond-haired man with black eyes. Someone who'd stepped into her world when tragedy struck.

The night the Silver Bridge collapsed.

"Have you been here before?" she blurted.

The man shuffled back a step, his face frozen with that same insincere smile. Shock ballooned behind the mask, evident in the way his whipcord body tensed, his rounded fingers tucking into his palms. "I have troubled you long enough. If you talk to others, perhaps it is best they forget the lights they have seen."

"Who are you?" Anger knifed through Katie as buried memories spilled forth in a burst of chaotic images. Not just the collapse of the Silver Bridge, but memories she'd suppressed even deeper.

Lying curled on the back seat of her mother's car as Doreen Sue drove home on a dark November night. A blinding flash of light...her mother hitting the brakes, the car screeching to a halt on the side of the road.

Like Jerome. Just like Jerome.

Dear God, why hadn't she remembered before? Her mother had dragged her along to visit a woman in Ravenswood. Madam something-or-other, who professed to be a psychic. Katie had sat on the couch with the woman's cat, a skinny, gray tabby, while Madam and her mother conversed in hushed whispers in the dining room. Another effort on her mom's part to divine how her future would unfold and if she'd ever meet a decent man.

Katie had fallen asleep on the way home, but the violent screech of the car had woken her. She remembered the light, her mother staring through the windshield in a daze, almost as if she'd been hypnotized. And then...

Nothing.

Nothing but drawing.

"Katie, are you all right?"

Sarah's voice jarred her back to the present.

For the span of several heartbeats, her breathing hung suspended. "I..." Her hands had grown clammy. The man in black had left. Sarah stared at her anxiously, her face creased with worry.

"Yes, I..." With a deliberate tug to her shirt, Katie tried to recover. "That man reminded me of someone." She glanced around the lobby, noticed the Cadillac had left too. "Where did he go?"

"He didn't say. Just repeated something about telling others not to talk about the lights. Personally, I think the guy needs help." Sarah twirled her finger in a circle next to her ear. "He sounds like Jerome, chasing after UFOs."

"Yeah." Katie managed a shaky laugh, but her stomach clenched. Maybe Jerome's theories weren't so far off base.

* * * *

Something wasn't right.

Uncertain if she should push for information, Doreen Sue nursed a cup of coffee while Katie busied around the kitchen, cleaning up after dinner. It had been nice of Katie to invite her to stay for the meal. When she'd tried to help with the dishes, her daughter had mumbled she was fine doing them alone.

Point taken.

In the living room, Sam occupied himself by watching TV and drawing, the occasional jingle from a commercial drifting to where she sat.

If only Katie would open up and talk, but she'd never been one to share. Withdrawn and serious, she held problems close and kept others at a distance. Doreen Sue had never liked the void in their relationship, but knew she was partially to blame for Katie's remoteness. She might never win Mother of the Year, but she'd loved both daughters unconditionally from the day they were born. Now she only had one left.

"Do you want to talk about it?" She spoke to Katie's back while the theme song for *Bewitched* floated from the living room.

Katie paused in the process of setting a plate in the drain board—a fraction of a second before continuing the motion. "About what?" She reached into the sink of soapy water for another plate.

Doreen Sue sighed. Wendy would have spilled her guts long before now. Katie would require prying, and even then she might not open up. A woman with a failed marriage, multiple problematic relationships, and a less-than-desirable reputation was hardly a woman to go to for advice. But what Katie didn't realize was that hard living had taught Doreen Sue a thing or two about life. She understood people and could read them every bit as well as a psychiatrist or doctor with a string of initials behind their name. Maybe she didn't have a college degree. Maybe she hadn't even graduated high school, dropping out when she was sixteen, but she was a hell of a lot smarter than people gave her credit for. And right now she was fairly certain of the calamity that had Katie out of sorts. It didn't matter what kind of woman you were; it always came back to a man.

"It's Lyle, isn't it? You're worried about Sam."

"Lyle?" Katie half-turned, dripping hands held over the sink. "Mom, Lyle gave up his rights to Sam before Sam was born. If he comes around here—" She stopped abruptly, clamping her mouth shut. "I don't want to talk about this with Sam in the next room."

"You're right." How stupid of her. Children had big ears. Sam might be listening to Samantha and Darrin Stevens banter playfully about marriage and witchcraft, but might just as well be listening to them. "I'm sorry, Katie. I can see something's bothering you. I know you'd rather talk to one of your friends, but—"

"Mom, don't." Katie dropped a dishrag in the sink. She braced her fingers against the edge. Then, as if reaching a decision, she grabbed a towel and crossed to the table. "It's not about Lyle." Drying her hands, she took the seat across from Doreen Sue.

For a time she said nothing, her expression unreadable. Fearing she would clam up again, Doreen Sue bit her tongue. Instinct made her want to coax, but that wasn't the way with Katie. Tightening her fingers around her coffee cup, she waited.

Finally, Katie drew a breath. "I need to ask you something." She lowered her voice so Sam wouldn't overhear. "And I need you to be truthful."

A fluttery laugh pushed from Doreen Sue's throat. "Truthful? Katie, honey, what else would I be?" The word wounded her, but she had it coming. How many white lies had she told in the days when she'd run around with one man after another? When she'd woken up, passed out on the couch or hung over in the morning?

Mama has the flu, baby....

Mama's going to meet an old friend from school....

Mama can't take you to the movies. She's got to visit a sick friend.

Shamed when Katie didn't answer—they both knew there was reason for the question—she lowered her gaze and nodded. "I promise."

"Back when I was a kid...the summer before the bridge fell..." Katie spoke haltingly, the inflection of her voice uncertain.

Doreen Sue glanced up, surprised by the concentration on her daughter's face. Her brows were pulled together, the damp dish towel twisted between her hands.

"You took me with you to Ravenswood when you went to see some psychic. I don't think it was about anything special, just one of those readings you liked to have done."

Doreen Sue tensed. She'd been certain her daughter had forgotten the events of that night. At the time, unable to explain the odd encounter on their drive home, Doreen Sue had assured Katie she'd been dreaming. She'd kept up the falsehood until Katie stopped talking about the incident. Like a dream that gradually fades over time, growing murkier until forgotten, Doreen Sue was convinced the encounter had faded from her daughter's memory.

But Doreen Sue had never forgotten. She'd stood in that blinding light and gazed up into the sky, mesmerized by the circular craft hovering above the tree line.

"Coming home there was a light," Katie continued. "You stopped the car, and when I woke up, there was a blinding glow."

What she wouldn't give for a cigarette. Doreen Sue swallowed hard, thinking of the Virginia Slims menthols in her purse. But Katie didn't smoke and didn't allow it in her home.

Katie leaned forward. "You told me I was dreaming."

"You were."

"Mom." She recoiled as if physically pushed. "You told me you'd be honest. Was it a UFO?"

Trapped.

Silly that it had taken all this time to admit. Doreen Sue had shared the story with others over the years, but never mentioned Katie was with her. She'd changed the date, said she was driving home alone when the incident happened. Let them ridicule her if they wanted, but not her daughter. The tale had made her friends with some, and left her scorned by others.

"I..." If only she could wiggle her nose like Samantha Stevens and rewind the scene for a better outcome. Katie watched her intently, waiting for her answer. At last, she nodded and lowered her voice. "Yeah. I think it was a UFO."

Exhaling, as if a burden had been lifted from her shoulders, Katie sat back in her chair. "I've been trying to remember all day, but can only grasp bits and pieces. Mostly, I remember the light. Will you tell me what happened?"

Doreen Sue wet her lips. She should be grateful her daughter was genuinely interested, but feared dooming Katie to the same pitfalls that had befallen her all those years ago—odd visitors who'd warned her not to speak of what she'd seen, rapping noises on the walls at night, sounds on the roof, open cupboard doors in the kitchen as if an unseen presence had rooted through her things. She hadn't felt that fear in ages, but the ripples of dread, long forgotten, awakened gooseflesh on her arms.

"You were right about the psychic," she said at last. "A few of my friends had gone to see her so I thought I'd give it a try. Kicks and giggles, that sort of thing." She shrugged. The psychic had been a bust. Worse, she'd given up a date with Heywood Fuller to go, even though he probably would have ditched her, anyway. He'd only asked her out because he was on the rebound from his ex. The two were now happily married.

"We were near the TNT when it happened. You were lying in the back seat, half asleep. I probably kept you out later than I should have." No probably about it, but at least it had been a Friday night.

She moved restlessly, conscious Katie hung on her every word. Paul Lynde's voice drifted from the living room followed by Sam's laughter. Uncle Arthur had dropped in on *Bewitched.*

"I can still see it." She tuned out the laugh track from the TV and the homey decorations of the kitchen, much like someone closing a door. An image of the sleek metallic craft grew in her mind. "It was silvery, but with an icy cast, and hovered a few feet above the trees. Round and kind of flat with a large light underneath. The light reminded me of an eye because it kept shifting about, casting a beam on the ground. There were other lights too—red and blue—on the side of the thing. I don't know what it was, but it wasn't a blimp, and it was far too low to be a plane. I hit the brakes and skidded off the road. That's when the thing saw me."

Katie watched her intently. "Saw you?"

Doreen Sue nodded. "It seemed that way. The light, or eye—whatever it was—shifted and the whole car was engulfed by a beam. The craft glided closer and hovered in front of the hood. It covered the entire roadway. I got out of the car, but don't remember much other than staring up into the light. The next thing I knew, I was behind the wheel and the sky was empty. To this day, I swear it was some kind of alien spacecraft." She rolled one shoulder, feeling self-conscious. "I know a lot of folks called me crazy and laughed when I told them, but I wasn't the only one who reported seeing things back then. Some people wouldn't talk about the stuff because they didn't want to be laughed at. The ones who did talk were warned silent."

"Warned silent? By who?"

"The Men in Black."

Katie stiffened. "Men in Black?"

"That's what we called them. I don't know who they really were." She took a sip of coffee. The liquid in the cup had started to cool, a speck of instant creamer clotted under the rim. The longing for a cigarette grew stronger. "They were all over Point Pleasant in those days—men in black suits, driving shiny black cars. Sometimes they said they were with the Air Force but no one believed it, and the Air Force denied any association. Folks were warned not to talk about the UFOs. Some even had their phones tapped. A friend of mine used to get calls the same time every night for a period of weeks. She'd hear a man talking in some weird guttural language. Words that made no sense, like she'd been hooked into a phone call in a foreign language. It was all so strange."

"I remember a man in a black suit." Katie looked at her oddly as if trying to piece the memory together as she spoke. "I was outside your salon on the night the bridge collapsed, and he asked me where he could find you."

"I don't remember talking to any of those fellas, but I think they snooped in the house a few times. It was always when you kids were asleep or at school. I'd find things disturbed, like an open cupboard door or hear a rapping sound." Doreen Sue swished her coffee in her cup. "We never found out who they were, or why they wanted everything about the UFOs kept hush-hush. Some people said the whole thing was connected to the Mothman."

"There was a man in black at the hotel today." Katie obviously didn't remember anything about nightly noises or finding items moved around, which was just as well. "He came in when Sarah and I were there, and warned us that people shouldn't talk about the lights they'd seen."

Doreen Sue tightened her fingers around the ceramic handle of the mug. "It's happening again. Back then there were so many reports of weird lights, folks called it a UFO flap."

"What does that mean?"

"It means there was a whole bunch of sightings right here in Point Pleasant." Doreen Sue liked the idea of showing off her knowledge of otherworldly events, but hoped her daughter wouldn't label her a weird conspiracy theorist like Jerome. "Back in '66 and '67, people used to hang out nightly looking for lights in the sky. I went up to Conway Road in the TNT a bunch of times, but never saw anything except for that night coming home from Ravenswood."

Katie nodded somberly, her expression distracted. Worried because she seemed focused elsewhere, Doreen Sue reached across the table and took her hand. "What are you thinking, honey?"

Katie's gaze shifted toward the living room and Sam. "I think I remember why I liked to draw."

Chapter 7

A tranquil hush clung to the corridors of West Central Mental Health Institute.

Most of the staff didn't like working night shifts, but Nurse Brenner preferred the stillness. The hallway lights had been dimmed and patient rooms were dark. An occasional murmur or whimper disrupted the quiet as a restless sleeper battled troubling dreams, but for the most part silence ruled. Doors were shut at night, all rooms carefully secured.

Nurse Brenner's rubber-soled shoes squeaked softly against the vinyl floor as she patrolled the halls. As she neared Parker Kline's room, an odd scratching sound drew her up short. She pressed her ear to the door.

Nothing. Maybe she'd imagined the noise.

Palming the keys on her belt, she located her master and slipped it into the lock. Inside, the room was dark, a sliver of light beneath the bathroom door the only brightness to pierce the shadows. A crackling sound intruded on the stillness as if someone had set a radio to the wrong frequency. The bed was empty, blankets balled at the foot.

"Parker." She rapped softly on the door to the bath.

The static came again, interspersed with clicks. Puzzled, she tracked the source to a small table by the window. Earlier in the day she'd found Parker there, a collection of shaded and partially shaded papers scattered around him. The drawings were gone, but his radio sat near the back. In the space of two heartbeats, the faceplate exploded with light, and a loud burst of static blared from the speakers.

Nurse Brenner jumped, her pulse accelerating with the speed of a freight train. Recovering quickly, she gripped the dial, but the button refused to budge, already locked in the off position. The jarring cacophony of noise and light died as abruptly as it started, plunging the room into near-black silence.

Gooseflesh pimpled her arms.

The crazy thing had to be operating off batteries. Of course. Floyd must have snuck in a few double-As during his last visit. Biting down on her bottom lip, she used her thumb to manipulate the rear compartment.

Empty.

Her heartbeat ratcheted higher, a trickle of cold sweat oozing down her neck. No power cord.

How could the radio broadcast without power? "What in heaven is going on?"

Light flared behind the dial and the tuning knob moved on its own. With a yelp of surprise, Nurse Brenner flung the radio onto the table.

"You shouldn't touch that," a man said behind her. "He wouldn't like it."

She whirled to find Parker silhouetted in the glow from the open bathroom. He'd been a docile patient the last two years, but there was something different about him tonight. A focused intensity that turned his gaze to steel.

"Who wouldn't like it?" Her voice was a hoarse whisper.

Parker pointed to the opposite wall.

Drawings. All of Parker's drawings were tacked to the stark white surface.

Blinding light burst from the paper squares, splintering outward like shockwaves from an earthquake. A dark crevice opened and swelled in the center until all that remained was sun-white nova and shadow. With a cry, Nurse Brenner flung up an arm to shield her eyes. Something moved in the heart of that fissure, an unnatural presence tainted by ice.

Nurse Brenner's breath plumed in the air.

"I'm sorry. I have to leave now." Parker stepped around her.

"No." She gripped his arm, trying to restrain him.

The darkness rushed forward, engulfing her in a frigid black cloud. Somewhere in the back of her mind, an unfamiliar voice warned her not to interfere. Still she clung to Parker, a rush of vertigo crashing over her in a chokehold. Her eyes rolled backward as the light-headedness became too much to bear. Her last conscious thought as she crumpled to the floor was that something not altogether human had entered the room.

* * * *

Katie breathed in the peaceful silence of her house. Sam was asleep in bed and darkness had fallen outside. The living room was quiet, the TV off. There was nothing to disturb her as she paged through the paperback

Ryan had left. It wasn't simply her desire to help Jerome that kept her riveted to his copy of *UFO Sightings and Stories*, but her own curiosity.

As an eyewitness, it was easy to get caught up in the mythology of unidentified flying objects. Already she'd learned people who'd had encounters sometimes experienced behavioral changes, including fervent bursts of creativity. Some took to drawing, as if their mind worked on overload, unable to contain the input. One contactee compared it to being the recipient of a memory dump in another language.

Noise.

For Katie and Sam, that funnel of information had been expelled in a series of drawings filled with geometrical shapes. The language meant nothing to them, but others believed such outpourings could hold significance for an alien culture. She was certain the cloud Sam had seen was a UFO, but unless he brought it up, she wouldn't prod for information. According to the book, some eyewitnesses preferred to forget. From personal experience, she knew the need to draw would fade, and the memory of that obsession would vanish with the desire.

It isn't uncommon for people who have seen a UFO to experience conjunctivitis afterward, she read in the book. *The reddening and inflammation of the eyes can last anywhere from a few days to a few weeks. This phenomenon has been documented in over seventy percent of the cases of those claiming to have seen a UFO.*

Yet another indication Sam had seen something. And all those people at the hospital. Sam's doctor had told her there had been a rash of outbreaks. Small wonder given the recent wave of UFO sightings.

Katie couldn't recall anything bad happening to her after the drive home from Ravenswood, but her mom said she'd had pinkeye in the past. And her mom had acted odd when she'd mentioned it in the ER. Almost as if she'd expected Katie to remember it as something out of the ordinary.

The low rumble of a car engine intruded on her thoughts.

Probably nothing, only a vehicle passing outside. But after everything that had happened, she couldn't help worrying Lyle might return to snoop around. Snapping the book shut, she stood and switched off the lights. She'd feel better if she took a look. If it really was Lyle, she'd confront him and set him straight.

Grabbing a jacket from the closet, she tossed a glance over her shoulder. No sign that Sam had heard anything. Hopefully, he'd sleep through the night. Palming a heavy-duty flashlight, she stepped onto the front porch. A short distance down the street, the headlights of an unmarked van flashed to life.

Katie muttered a curse.

The creep was back. Well, he wasn't going to toy with her.

"Hey, you." She sprinted across the yard. "You're not frightening me so you might as well cut it out." Before she could get close enough to glimpse the driver, the van sped down the road with a squeal of tires. This time, she managed to catch the license plate.

West Virginia tags, 4ZX87Q.

"Got you now." Repeating the numbers, she thrust her hands into her pockets, hoping to find something to jot them down.

A scrap of paper.

She hurried back into the house, careful not to be too noisy as she rustled through the kitchen drawer for a pen. Sam's bedroom was just down the hall. Two nights in a row the mystery van had staked out her house. It was time to do something about the repeated lurking before something happened to involve Sam. She jotted the number down, then sank into a chair and dropped her head into her hands.

Why couldn't Lyle leave her alone? Maybe she should have Sam stay with her mom temporarily. Her mother would love the company. She might have made mistakes in the past raising her own girls, but she was a doting and wonderful grandmamma to Sam. The more Katie thought about it, the more it made sense. Even better, if she tracked down Darrell Mason, she'd probably trip over Lyle in the process. Rather than run, she'd confront him and put an end to his silly games. In the meantime, she'd call Ryan and have him trace the van number as proof Lyle or one of his cronies was trying to scare her.

As she picked up the paper and headed for the phone, Katie spied unfamiliar handwriting on the back. Halting abruptly, she sucked down a breath.

The last time she'd worn the jacket was when she'd given it to Jerome to block the cold.

* * * *

Caden made West Central his first stop of the morning. Almost eight o'clock, it was clear Nurse Brenner had endured a long night. For someone he'd never seen rattled, she appeared noticeably tense.

"You should have been here last night," she accused.

He had the feeling she wouldn't appreciate hearing he hadn't been on duty, and only learned about Parker's situation an hour ago. "I understand Deputies Morris and Gardner took the call. I got the preliminary information from them."

"I wanted *you* to come." No questioning the reproach this time.

"You told me to stay away."

Mae Clair

The flinty look in her eyes spoke volumes. Caden was thankful for the counter surrounding the nurses' station, which separated them.

"I'm here now." He shouldn't have to point out the obvious. "Why don't you tell me what happened in your own words?"

"Fine. But you need to see Parker's room." Stepping away from the counter, she motioned crisply for him to follow down the hall. Unlike the first time Caden had visited, the doors to individual patient rooms were shut and secured.

"A precaution," Nurse Brenner explained, noticing his glance. Her voice softened slightly, less sour. "Anything out of the ordinary upsets the balance of the entire floor. With the officers here last night and this morning, most everyone knows something unusual has taken place. We're trying to keep the nature of that under wraps. If patients learn Parker escaped, it could cause a chain reaction with others trying to escape too."

"I understand we have video footage." That would go a long way in determining how Parker managed to pull off what should have been an impossible feat.

"Yes. The film was given to your department last night. As you can see we have cameras positioned throughout the hallways." She pointed out a few as they walked, rectangular black boxes mounted close to the ceiling. "Parker was in the bathroom when I entered his room."

"And you went in because you heard a noise?"

"I see you've read my statement. It sounded like radio static."

"Parker said the radio talks to him at night."

She bobbed her head, her expression grim. "I thought he was making it up. We allowed the transistor radio his father gave him, but it didn't have a power cord."

"What about batteries?" He seemed to recall they weren't allowed, either.

"Not permitted because of the potential harm from the acid inside." She scratched the bridge of her nose. "The radio was basically a prop for Parker's enjoyment. It kept him calm. When I heard the crackling, I thought Floyd might have smuggled in a few batteries." Pausing outside the door, she rested her hand on the knob and regarded him steadily. "I was wrong, Sergeant. I checked the compartment and it was empty. I know it sounds impossible, but the dial lit up and the tuning knob moved on its own. I don't know how Parker did it, but he must have wired it somehow. Otherwise…" She trailed off, uncertainty creeping into her gaze.

Otherwise someone really *was* communicating with Parker through radio waves.

Squaring her shoulders, Nurse Brenner took a deep breath. "That's not all that happened. I, um…blacked out for a moment." Nervousness crept into her voice. "When I came to, Parker was gone. It's a mystery how he managed to bypass the security measures in the hospital."

Caden agreed. Even if Parker had Floyd's help, which didn't seem likely, neither father nor son was skilled enough to bypass an alarm system. "What made you pass out?"

She rubbed her hands together, growing more flustered by the moment. "Perhaps I should show you." Opening the door, Nurse Brenner motioned him inside and gestured at the adjacent wall.

Caden drew up short. The shaded and partially shaded squares Parker had painstakingly drawn were now pieced together and plastered to the wall to form a life-size jigsaw puzzle. A puzzle in the shape of man.

"What the hell?" He stepped closer. What had looked like random blocks of shading the last time he was here took artistic shape when placed in conjunction with others. Bit by bit, Parker had constructed the silhouette of a grinning man. "Had you seen this before last night?"

Shaking her head, she inched slowly closer as if afraid the drawing would spring to life. "I didn't tell anyone this. Not your deputies or anyone else." She tugged the collar of her uniform, then clasped her hands together, plainly trying to work up the nerve to reveal something unsettling.

"Take your time," Caden said.

She nodded gratitude. "It's hard working in a place like this. You get cynical to the things people claim to see. Then last night…" She drew a steeling breath. "As crazy as it sounds, that whole wall lit up with light when I was in here…almost like it was burning. There was some kind of dark cavity in the center. I could sense something in there but couldn't see it. Parker said he had to leave, and then I blacked out."

Caden stepped closer to the wall. "Burning?"

The heat of her gaze was almost tangible on his back. "You don't believe me. You think I'm as insane as my residents."

"I never said that." He fingered the nearest square of paper. Clean, no residue. He bent to study the floor, then kicked the baseboard. Solid. "Did you have anything to drink last night?"

"Sergeant Flynn!"

"I don't mean alcohol." Hands on hips, he turned to face her. "Water. Tea. Soda. Is it possible someone slipped a hallucinogenic into your drink without your knowledge?"

She pressed her lips together. "No, it is not possible, and no, I didn't have anything to drink."

"All right." That thread was going nowhere. "What about this drawing?" He jabbed a thumb at Parker's life-sized puzzle. "My guess is this isn't something the average patient pieces together. Does it mean anything to you?"

Her posture was stiff. "I'm fairly certain I know who it represents."

"Who?"

"Indrid Cold."

The name meant nothing to him. He shrugged. "Someone he knows?"

"According to Parker, Indrid Cold is someone he met during a moment of great significance." Her eyes narrowed. "I'm sure you're familiar with the event, Sergeant. I'm referring to the night Parker killed Hank Jeffries, and you shot Parker in retaliation."

* * * *

Caden walked into the sheriff's office to find Ryan camped at his desk, his forehead cupped in his hands as he studied an open file folder. Overall, the room was subdued, only two deputies on duty, both engrossed in paperwork. If the quiet held, the station might eke through the morning without the usual burst of paranormal rumors stirring the pot.

"You look as disgusted as I feel." Caden looped his jacket over the back of his chair.

"Huh?" Ryan glanced up. It took a second or two for him to focus; then his mouth flattened in a grimace. "I've got a license plate with no history."

"What does that mean?"

"Remember that van I told you about? The one outside Katie's house?"

"The one you think belongs to Lyle?"

"Yeah." Ryan swiped a pencil from a cup holder at his elbow. He rapped the eraser against the folder. "It was back last night, only this time Katie got the tag number."

"And?"

Ryan waved a hand over an innocuous-looking paper. "According to the DMV, it doesn't exist."

"Maybe she was off a digit."

"I thought of that, but she seemed certain. And even if I buy that theory, there's nothing remotely close in the sequence she gave me."

"Huh." Caden dropped into his chair. "Bogus tag?"

"Looks that way. How about you?"

"I just left West Central."

"Yeah, I heard about Parker." Ryan tossed the pencil onto the folder and linked his hands over his stomach. "The guys in the lab have been going over the film from the security cameras all morning."

"Anything?"

"No go. I had a look myself. The hallway and exterior cameras didn't pick up a thing."

"What does that mean?"

"Based on what we've got, Parker never left his room."

"What about the ceiling? Or the windows?"

"The ceiling is solid, and you've seen the windows. No way to get through them. Besides, they're rigged with an alarm in the event of a breach."

"Maybe the film was tampered with."

"Possible, but it doesn't look that way. Looks like our boy vanished into thin air."

"Great." More weird shit. "Did anyone talk to Floyd?"

"Pete had him in earlier for questioning. Said he was home all night, and didn't know anything about it."

If Pete had questioned Parker's father, the interview would have been thorough. The sheriff was friendly with most everyone in town, but took his job too seriously to let camaraderie interfere.

"I kind of believe Floyd." Caden wished it weren't the case. With him out of the picture there wasn't anyone left with a motive to aid Parker.

Ryan looked surprised. "What?"

"Nothing against Floyd, but he doesn't have it together enough to break his son out of West Central. And, more than that, why now? Parker's been there for two years. According to Nurse Brenner and the doctors I spoke with today, he was a model patient. Why decide to make a run for it all of a sudden?"

Ryan tugged on his bottom lip.

Caden could see the wheels spinning in his head. It was how they worked best, bouncing thoughts back and forth in a ping-pong match of ideas.

"His life was routine," Ryan said. "Same schedule day in, day out with no complaints."

"Same visitors too. Except for me and you."

"And Jerome Kelly."

The single wild card in the scenario. "Sure wish I knew what they talked about during those fourteen minutes when Jerome visited."

"I might have something on that later today." Ryan flipped the folder closed, abandoning the DMV report.

"What do you mean?"

"Katie has something she wants me to see. Some kind of paper she found in her jacket."

"What's that have to do with Jerome?"

"She gave the jacket to Jerome the night she found him off the road. He kept complaining he was cold." Ryan paused, giving him a chance to connect the dots. "She thinks he slipped the note inside."

"Cold, huh?" Caden rubbed his forehead. His thoughts spiraled back to the odd image taped to the hospital wall. How long had it taken Parker to create that life-size drawing and why had he bothered? "Does the name Indrid Cold mean anything to you?"

"No. Should it?"

"According to Nurse Brenner, it's someone Parker talked about a lot."

Ryan leaned forward. "So let's run him through the database and see what it kicks back."

"I've got a feeling it's going to be a waste of time."

"Why?"

"Because according to Parker, Indrid Cold lives on a planet called Lanulos."

Chapter 8

Katie was delighted when Ryan accepted her spur-of-the-moment dinner invitation. She'd half expected him to blow her off when she phoned and suggested they chat about Jerome and the van over pasta. A pitiful offer, but he'd seemed pleased. Maybe Eve and Sarah were right, and there was the chance of something more than friendship between them.

Trying not to read too much into their "date," she rushed through work, then swung by a department store in Gallipolis to pick up a Halloween costume for Sam. He'd finally decided on trick-or-treating as Luke Skywalker. At home, Katie showered, changed into jeans and a sweater, then scraped her hair into a ponytail. No one would ever accuse her of being a glamour queen, but at least she didn't spend an hour in the bathroom fussing with hair gels.

By the time Ryan arrived, she had dinner almost ready. Ten minutes later, they sat down to a meal of rigatoni, tossed green salad, and Italian bread in her dining room. Ryan brought a bottle of Cabernet, but she only had a little, the memory of Eve's sleepover still too fresh.

"Have you heard anything more on Jerome?" she asked.

Ryan speared the last of his pasta with his fork. "I got an update this morning. No change. I'd pay money to know what he and Parker talked about."

Katie had heard the news about Parker's disappearance from Jack Devon at the hotel. The cook and a few others were already speculating Floyd had to be involved. Although, if you talked to one of the Bradley brothers, you were more likely to hear the Mothman was responsible. Someone had even started a rumor the "spaceman" Parker had been in communication with for the last two years had broken him out of West Central.

According to Floyd, the alien even had a name—Indrid Cold. Floyd told Shawn Preech, who'd told Martin Ward, who'd told Jack that his kid had drawn a life-size picture of the UFOnaut—what Parker called him—and taped it to his wall at the hospital. Katie had a feeling it wouldn't be long before Cold was blamed for everything from stirring up the Mothman to the dog disappearances, cattle deaths, and the glut of "star shit" in Chester Wilson's farm field.

Sighing, she rubbed two fingers against her temple. Lately, there were too many bizarre happenings to track. Toss in the fact she'd only recently remembered she'd been witness to a UFO, and what more was likely to materialize? "What about the license plate number I gave you?" At least that was something concrete.

"Sorry." Looking uncomfortable, Ryan set his fork aside. "It came back without a match."

"But I know I got it right." Her eyesight was good, and despite the darkness, she'd seen the van clearly. This time she'd even gotten the make and model.

"It's not that I don't believe you, but the DMV says it doesn't exist. The plate was probably doctored."

"Great. Now what?" Disgusted, she slumped in her chair. "If Lyle is playing games, I wish he'd quit creeping around and own up to them. I'm worried about Sam."

"I know. I am too." He hesitated a moment. "I did some fishing around today and drove over to Darrell's place."

"Oh?" A flicker of warmth passed through her. Maybe the plate was a dead end, but Ryan hadn't dropped the idea entirely. She was touched he'd go to the extra trouble. Best not to dwell on how touched. "What did Darrell say?"

Ryan frowned. "Nothing I didn't expect. He denied knowing Lyle was in town. Said he hadn't seen or heard from him."

"Do you believe him?"

He shrugged. "I don't know. He didn't seem like he was lying, but it's hard to say. I told him to get in touch with me if Lyle showed up. He seemed okay with that, then asked about the dog disappearances. He's been talking to Shawn and Suzanne Preech." He shot her a glance that seemed to suggest she might not be overly fond of Suzanne.

It was hard to warm up to someone who hadn't outgrown the high school mentality of slinging mud behind your back.

Katie kept her expression neutral. "I heard their dog, Duke, disappeared."

Ryan nodded. "Darrell said he saw some kind of weird light in the sky the night Duke took off. He seemed more interested in that than Lyle." He shook his head. "There's too much weird shi—stuff going around town these days."

His swift correction made her smile. It was sweet he tried to temper his language for her.

"I want to show you the note I found. It's pretty weird too. But first I want to clean up the kitchen." She stood, picking up her plate. "Why don't you watch TV in the living room until I'm done?"

"I'll help." Ryan began gathering the silverware.

"You don't have to do that."

"I know I don't, but I don't mind. I'm used to helping my mom."

She followed him into the kitchen, both of them carting dishware. "How is your mom doing?"

"Really good these days." Ryan set the flatware in the sink.

Mrs. Flynn lived with him in the family home, the property located beside Eve's. Last year through "conversations" Mrs. Flynn had with Ryan's dead sister, Maggie, she'd been able to tell them where to find Wendy's remains. Katie didn't know Ryan's mother well, but was forever grateful for her part in bringing Wendy's killer to justice.

"The difference in her behavior from last year to now is night and day," Ryan continued. "My mom's no longer hung up on the past and Maggie's death. I could move out and get my own place, but she says the house is too big for her."

Katie had no such issues, her two bedroom rancher just over eleven hundred square feet. On the small side, it was enough for her and Sam, and the mortgage was manageable.

They continued to chat while they cleaned up the kitchen, then retreated to the living room with coffee and apple pie. Katie waited until Ryan had finished his dessert before retrieving the scrap of paper she'd found in her jacket. Sitting next to him on the couch, she passed him the slip.

"What do you make of this? I certainly didn't write it."

Ryan took the paper, frowning at an indecipherable scrawl of numbers. He flipped it over once, then dropped the scrap on the coffee table with the writing face-up. "It looks like gibberish."

"Jerome must have written it. Probably when he was with Parker at West Central." That was important.

"Maybe." Ryan took a moment to kick the thought around. "You gave Jerome your jacket because he was cold?"

"Yes." Something niggled at the back of her mind. Swinging to face him, she bumped her knee against his. "Now that I think of it, he never actually said 'I'm cold.' He just kept repeating the word 'cold.'" She paused before leapfrogging ahead. "And he'd just come from seeing Parker...."

"Who we know talked about Indrid Cold." Ryan finished the thought.

Or course. Connecting the dots made sense. And if she dug deeper, Sarah's Ouija board had spelled out C-O-L-D the night they'd gotten together with Eve. What if the common tie between everything that happened *was* Parker's imaginary spaceman? With all of his conspiracy theories and UFO fanaticism, Jerome would have bought into anything Parker shared about Cold. Unfortunately, of the two people who might know what the scribbled message meant, one was missing and the other was in a coma.

"And you were never able to find out anything about Deputy Brown. He had to be an imposter." She was starting to sound—even think—like Jerome. "What if he was after the message?"

According to *UFO Stories and Sightings*, organizations connected to UFOs sometimes had people pose as law enforcement officers or government officials. Usually it was to track someone of interest— Jerome?—especially if they thought that person had stumbled across an element of value. Could it be Deputy Brown was one of those? Someone who'd been assigned to watch Parker and feared he'd passed something critical on to Jerome? The book said others who'd encountered mysterious "shadow" officers were rarely able to remember them. The imposters used a type of instant hypnosis that was performed on their victims without the person's awareness. Probably why she couldn't recall a single feature of Deputy Brown's face.

Her attention returned to the scrap of paper on the table. It didn't look like much, random numbers strung in a senseless order:

```
11223344556677889900223344556677889900
33445566778899004455667788990055667788
99006677889900103123415677889900889900
99000011223344556677889900223344556677
88990033445566778899004455667788990055
66778899006677889900778899008899009900
```

The more she studied the sequence, the more Katie grew convinced the digits had to mean something.

"It must be a code of some sort."

"Possibly." Ryan picked up the paper, studying the numeric jumble. Half of his face lay in shadow, making his expression grim. "But if this note originated with Parker, it might be exactly what it looks like. Garbage."

"I don't think so." Apprehension crept up her spine. If Deputy Brown had been after the code, she could have easily ended up in a coma instead of Jerome. Plagued by a shiver of vulnerability, she reminded herself Brown didn't know she had it or where she lived. "So what do we do now?"

Ryan tucked the paper into his pocket. "Let me hang on to this for a while. I'll run it by Parker's doctors at West Central. It might be some kind of made-up language only he understood."

Along with Indrid Cold.

She bit the inside of her cheek. If Parker believed Cold talked to him through the radio, then it was possible he'd created his own fantasy language to converse with the alien. In that case, it probably really was nothing. Except Jerome was in a coma, and a sheriff's deputy who didn't exist might have put him there.

Tapping a finger against her knee, she thought back to the night she'd spent with Eve and Sarah. Cold's wasn't the only identity the Ouija board had delivered. "You wouldn't happen to know anyone with the initials QM, would you?"

"QM?" Ryan gave a short laugh. "Afraid not, but then 'Q' isn't that common. I think I'd remember. Why?"

In light of everything that had happened, adding a Ouija board to the mix didn't seem so farfetched. Plunging ahead, she told him about her night with Eve and Sarah, then went further and shared the UFO experience she'd had as a child. Afterward, she held her breath, waiting for his reaction.

He didn't scoff, but a hint of skepticism lingered in his gaze. Of her small circle of friends, he'd always been the most cynical when it came to the paranormal. An odd outlook, considering his brother carried a branded mark from the Mothman.

"It's a lot to absorb, Katie."

Her heart deflated. "You don't believe me."

"Of course I believe you." He took her hand as if to cement his trust. "You think you saw something as a kid. There's no question of that. I just don't understand why you suppressed it all this time."

"I don't, either." She wrapped her fingers around his. At least he hadn't called her crazy, or belittled her for playing with a Ouija board. Eve and Sarah and their silly ideas. And yet their silly ideas had identified Cold—and QM. Whoever that turned out to be. "Thanks for listening to me."

His lips curved in a small smile. "No thanks needed." Reaching forward, he tucked a strand of hair behind her ear.

It had worked loose from her ponytail some time ago. Given the hour, her makeup had probably dulled, too, steamed away by the boiling pasta water she'd used for dinner.

"I don't know why we were never close in school." Ryan brushed his thumb over hers. "Eve and Sarah were always around in my group."

A fluttery feeling spread through her stomach. Self-consciously, she lowered her gaze. "I wasn't friends with Eve and Sarah. Not then."

"Yeah." He expelled a breath. "We were stupid kids. I'm glad that's changed."

They were sitting close enough that when he tugged on her wrist, she naturally fell against him. And when he bent his head and touched his lips to hers, she responded. The kiss was tentative at first, but when he pressed close, the movement of his lips grew bolder.

Katie's head spun.

A perfect ending to a perfect night.

* * * *

Caden stood on the screened porch, arms folded across his chest as he stared silently into the moonlit darkness of the rear yard. Eve's property swept down an embankment to a narrow creek bordered by a small strip of woods. His sister, Maggie, used to play there with Eve and Sarah Sherman when the three girls were children. For years it had been hard to think of Maggie without suffering guilt over her death, but he'd put that stranglehold of grief behind him.

Caden had been there when the Mothman crushed Roger Layton's bones and carried him, shrieking, into the sky. It wasn't the first time the Mothman had intervened on his behalf. Once before, it had saved his life, wrenching him from the icy waters of the Ohio River the night the Silver Bridge fell. For fifteen years following that tragedy, not a single sighting occurred. Then four months ago, the creature reappeared, spotted by several eyewitnesses. It was still out there, haunting the TNT, and it wanted something.

Or so Ryan thought.

His once skeptical brother expected him to hunt the thing down for a personal powwow. Stupid, except Ryan had gotten himself wrapped up with Katie Lynch and wasn't thinking straight. Women had a habit of doing that to a guy. He was a perfect example, sitting on an engagement ring he'd tucked into a drawer, waiting for the right moment to ask Eve to marry him.

What if that moment never came? Life got effed up on a regular basis. Look at Parker Kline. One day a kid playing a prank, the next booked for murder.

Cold must return. Evening will follow.

Caden exhaled and dragged a hand through his hair. Somewhere in the distance, a dog yapped, a nighttime sound that trailed into silence. He hoped it wouldn't end up in a barren field, its brain bleeding through its ears. Effed up didn't begin to cover the parade of oddities in Point Pleasant.

"Hey." The door to the house creaked open, spilling a puddle of light onto the porch. "What are you doing out here?" Arms wrapped close for warmth, Eve stepped to his side. Without a doubt, she was the best thing that had ever happened to him.

"I thought you were reading?" he asked.

"I was. I must have dozed off." She huddled more deeply into her sweater. "It's cold out here."

"Yeah." He offered his arm and she ducked beneath it, snuggling close. So much had changed in such a short time. He'd never imagined himself getting married or raising a family, but those were all things he desired. Would his kids play in the same creek Eve had, echoes of yesteryear ringing in their laughter? "It is cold. We should go back inside."

She tilted her head to look up at him, her eyes sparkling in the darkness. "The moonlight is nice. Romantic too."

"No argument." He kissed her temple, enjoying the warmth of her pressed to his side.

Cold must return. Evening will follow.

Time to set his own rules. "Let's go inside. I have something I want to ask you."

The suggestion of a smile touched her lips. "That sounds mysterious."

He kissed her lightly. "Let's hope there's nothing mysterious about your answer."

Chapter 9

Katie hummed softly as she mounted the steps to the front porch of the Parrish Hotel. Morning sunlight cut beneath the covered overhang, splashing on vibrant orange pumpkins and brightly colored gourds. The light-hearted setting matched her mood as she swept into the lobby and dropped her purse on the reception counter.

"Someone's cheerful." Eve rounded the corner from her office, carrying a cup of coffee. A mischievous smile flirted with the corners of her mouth. She glanced at her watch. "You're early too."

"I couldn't help myself. Ryan had a morning shift and I wanted to make him breakfast."

"Ryan?" Eve's perfectly tweezed brows arched higher. "Breakfast?"

Katie waved the coming interrogation aside. "It's not what you think." She disappeared into Eve's office long enough to fetch her own coffee before returning to the lobby. Her friend sat perched on a stool behind the counter, an expectant look on her face.

"Well?" Eve prodded.

Katie resisted the temptation to share a while longer, tipping her cup to her lips while she inhaled the nutty aroma of almond decaf. "Well, what?"

Eve rolled her eyes. "Don't play dumb. You can't drop 'Ryan' and 'breakfast' in the same sentence and not share."

Katie laughed. "Okay. Honestly, though, it's not what you think." Eve's imagination was probably in overdrive. Time to squash those ideas before they took flight and sprouted gossip. "Ryan came over last night and I made dinner. We talked about Jerome and I showed him a note I'd found." She explained about the coded message in her jacket. "Afterward, he stayed the night—*on the couch*—in the event Lyle returned."

"How gallant." Eve appeared to overlook the emphasis Katie placed on his sleeping arrangement. "I hope Lyle showed up and Ryan put a scare into the creep."

"No luck. The van never came back."

"Figures. Just when he would have gotten what was coming to him. What do you think the note means?"

"I don't know. Ryan was going to run it by Parker's doctors."

Eve shivered. "I hope they find him. I don't think Parker would actually hurt anyone, but the thought of him roaming around is scary. You know... all that stuff about communicating with UFOs and aliens."

Ryan was on the fence about most of that, but he'd shown another side of himself last night. He'd let her set the pace when their kisses grew heated. It had been far too long since she'd been involved with a man, and she had Sam to think about. Ryan had understood when she'd slowed things down, worried they were moving too fast. It came as no surprise their attraction was mutual and had simmered beneath the surface for a long time. Rather than act on impulse, they'd finished the night talking about UFOs, Parker, and Men in Black. This morning Ryan had kissed her good-bye and told her he wasn't interested in seeing anyone else. Only her.

Fairytale words that had left her floating on a high. By the end of the day, the late night hours would take their toll, but she'd manage the fatigue. The cost was well worth the trade-off.

Eve cleared her throat and poked her on the arm.

Shaken from her thoughts, Katie gave a guilty start. Warmth swept across her cheeks. "Um... Why are you staring at me?"

"Because you're so obvious. You're completely gone on a Flynn brother. Take it from someone who knows." She fluttered her left hand.

"We've agreed to date."

Another roll of the eyes from Eve. "You make it sound like a contract. You're lucky Sarah isn't here. You'd better invite her to lunch and tell her." She wiggled her hand again. "I've got news too."

"What news?" Katie waited. Then waited some more.

Finally, Eve huffed out a theatrical sigh. "Do I have to flash it under your nose?" Extending her left hand, she wriggled her fingers. Light bounced from a glittering square-cut diamond.

"Oh my God." Katie's mouth dropped. "Caden proposed!" With a squeal, she tugged Eve from the stool and caught her in a hug. "I am so happy for you two. Wait, wait. Let me see the ring." Overcome by a flood of warmth, she held Eve's hand and gazed at the shimmering stone in its delicate gold setting. "It's so beautiful." If there were two people meant to be together, it was Caden and Eve. "Did you set a date?"

"Not yet." Eve positively glowed. "But probably this summer, if we can arrange everything."

"I'll help. And you can have the reception here, in your own hotel. It will be perfect."

"That's what I thought too."

"Eve, I'm so happy for you." Katie hugged her friend.

The sound of a man clearing his throat pulled them abruptly apart. "Ladies, I hate to intrude."

Katie swept hair from her eyes, embarrassed she hadn't heard anyone enter the lobby. "I'm sorry. Can we help you?"

The man who stood before the reception counter was incredibly striking and oddly familiar. He wore a black suit, black tie, and crisp white shirt with gold cufflinks. Neatly trimmed hair, nearly as pale as his shirt, contrasted sharply against coal-black eyes. A tailored overcoat lay draped over one arm. Instantly, she was reminded of the strange visitor who'd warned her and Sarah to caution others not to speak of UFOs.

"Oh…Katie…" Eve moved to intervene. "This is Mr. Lach Evening. He checked in last night. He's staying in room eighteen."

No wonder she hadn't heard him enter the lobby. He'd come down the stairs, not through the front door. "Hello." Recovering quickly, she offered a smile. Between his unusual name, arresting appearance, and the tugging sense of familiarity, she tried not to stammer. "It's-it's good to meet you, Mr. Evening. I hope you enjoy your stay with us."

"I'm sure I will. Right now, however, I'd like to find a place for breakfast. I understand your café only serves lunch and dinner." He spoke in a modulated tone, his words flavored with an unidentifiable accent. "If one of you could kindly point me in the right direction."

"There's a coffee shop one street over on the right," Katie said. "Early Start. They do breakfast sandwiches, muffins, and eggs." She didn't add that it was owned by Suzanne Preech or that the prices tended to be inflated. "There's also a McDonald's on the other side of Viand." She indicated the direction, though judging by his immaculately tailored appearance, he might not find fast food to his liking.

Mr. Evening nodded. "And the sheriff's station?"

Beside her, Eve blinked. "Why would you want to go there?" As soon as she blurted the question, she shook her head. "I'm sorry. It's none of my business. It's just we're a small town…."

"No offense taken." He offered a polite smile. "It's a personal matter which I'm sure you'd find tedious."

"The sheriff's office is to your left." Katie was every bit as curious as Eve, especially with all the strangers in town, but courtesy kept her from prying. "Several blocks down, on the corner. You'll see the sign on the door."

"Thank you both." Giving a nod, he slipped into his coat. His fingers were long and thin, but the last digit of each was plump and spherical, almost bulbous. "Good day, ladies." He crowned his pale hair with an expensive-looking black fedora, then left through the front door.

"We seem to have a lot of strangers lately," Katie commented after he'd left.

"I know." Eve craned her neck to watch the man pass beyond the windows. "Do you think he's one of those Men in Black? Donnie Bradley was in the café yesterday, and said he saw one of them lurking around the hospital."

Katie stiffened, abruptly recalling where she'd seen the man.

The night her mom discovered Jerome unconscious, a man in black had been part of the crowd. He'd loitered by the corner of the building, watching from the darkness. And her mom had said Men in Black were commonly seen in town after Point Pleasant's UFO flap of the mid-60s. It couldn't be simple coincidence that Mr. Evening and others like him reappeared just as people started talking about strange lights in the sky. The recent sightings didn't come close to rivaling the flap numbers of the sixties, but the presence of the government-like men in their dark suits couldn't be chance.

"There's something odd about them," Katie agreed. "And what a name— Lach Evening. Did you notice his hands?"

"You mean his fingers? Yeah, weird."

"The guy who came in while Sarah was here had the same type of fingers. He was dressed in black too." Far too many coincidences to be mere chance.

"Maybe it's a Halloween stunt," Eve suggested. "In another two weeks we'll be overrun with kids looking for candy. It could be some kind of publicity routine for one of the stores in Gallipolis."

Katie nodded thoughtfully, but the suggestion seemed a stretch. They would have heard if that was the case. Whatever the reason, she'd be vigilant when she took Sam trick-or-treating at the end of the month. She shivered.

Lately, there were far worse things than ghosts and ghouls haunting Point Pleasant.

* * * *

"Five bucks says he has something to do with the dogs." Ryan stood by the coffee pot looking at Sheriff Pete Weston's closed office door. Ten minutes before, a crisply tailored man in a black overcoat had arrived asking to speak with the department's chief law enforcement officer. Thirtyish, with a slight accent, fair hair, and chiseled features, he carried himself in a manner that immediately turned heads. Joy, their resident clerk, had nearly tripped over herself in her haste to usher him into Weston's office.

Caden poured hot coffee into a Styrofoam cup. "I vote Wilson's cow. Doc Holden probably asked for a second opinion. The guy looks like an expert in something."

"Nah." Ryan leaned back against the break counter, crossing his legs at the ankles. "Too immaculate and stuffy-looking. A guy like that wouldn't get his hands dirty doing an autopsy on a cow. He's probably some think-head in research. If Holden called him, it was because of the dogs."

Caden raised an eyebrow. "Five bucks?"

"Five bucks."

Caden took a sip of coffee. "I proposed to Eve last night."

"What the hell?" The rapid change of topic blindsided Ryan. Jerking upright, he rounded on his brother in explosive surprise. "You're shitting me! What did she say?"

"She said yes."

"And you didn't tell me?"

"I'm telling you now."

"I mean before. We've only been in here for—oh, hell, never mind." Clasping Caden's hand, he pumped it up and down. "Congratulations. I can't believe you're freaking getting married. Does Mom know?"

"I told her over breakfast. And Eve and I haven't picked a date yet."

"You're not going to drag your feet, are you?"

"No." The word rolled from Caden's tongue with a sliver of amusement. "Eve wants a summer wedding, so probably June at the hotel."

"Do I have to ask who's going to be the best man?"

Caden raised his coffee cup to his lips. "It depends on whether or not you win that five bucks."

"Caden. Ryan." The summons burst across the room, delivered in Pete Weston's deep baritone. The sheriff stood in the doorway of his office, his expression a mixture of agitation and impatience. Whatever brainiac-science-guy had stirred up, it didn't appear to have gone over well with Mason County's head honcho.

"In here." Gruffly, Weston waved them into his office.

Ryan exchanged a glance with his brother before trailing behind Caden. He closed the door as Weston moved behind his desk. The man they'd seen earlier was seated in a chair across from the sheriff. His overcoat and a dapper black fedora occupied the seat beside him. Fully at ease with one leg crossed over the other, he looked blatantly out of place in the small, stuffy surroundings.

"Sergeants Caden Flynn and Ryan Flynn," Pete introduced them. "This is Lach Evening."

The man stood and extended his hand. "Gentlemen."

Ryan noted the odd shape of his fingers as they clasped, the man's palm cool and dry.

"Evening?" Caden narrowed his eyes. "That's an unusual name."

A polite smile. "So I've been told."

Weston motioned them to sit, but the only who bothered was their visitor, who resumed his comfortable position.

"Mr. Evening is an expert in the field of…" Blowing out a breath, Weston looked to the stranger for help. "You're going to have to jump in on that one, Evening. I've already forgotten what you called it."

"Chimeraology." The word rolled from Evening's tongue with the slight inflection of his accent. "For lack of better explanation, it's the study of supernatural creatures and objects. The organization I work for is discreet. Private and well-funded."

Ryan exchanged a glance with his brother. "Let me guess. You're here about the Mothman."

Smiling tightly, Evening inclined his head. "I won't deny your extraordinary cryptid is the root of my organization's interest, but that's not why I've come. I'm afraid my superiors and I have inadvertently created a problem that could directly impact someone in your town."

"He's here about Lyle Mason." Cutting bluntly to the point, Weston plopped into his chair. The springs squeaked as he leaned forward and planted his forearms on the desk. "Not only did Lyle find his way home, he came back with a loose screw. Mr. Evening's already produced credentials to satisfy me that what he tells you is true."

Exasperated by the double-talk, Ryan looked from Weston to Evening. At the mention of Lyle, he immediately thought of Katie and how Mason had been skulking around in a van at night. "Someone better spit out what's going on."

"It's your show," Weston said to Evening.

The man took his time explaining.

"As I mentioned, I'm employed by a private organization that holds an interest in supernatural creatures."

Ryan wished he could place the guy's accent, but it was too hard to pin down. European of some sort, maybe Dutch.

"My position requires me to conduct scientific studies with people who claim to have experienced encounters."

"You mean like ghosts?" Caden asked.

Evening waved his oddly shaped fingers. "Ghosts, aliens, werewolves. You'd be surprised what people believe they've encountered." He hesitated briefly, tapping one long finger against his chin as if pondering the idea. "Of course, it's not in my place to validate one way or another. I simply meet with the test subjects to gather information. Those behind the studies have a specific interest in the Mothman. That's how we found Mr. Mason."

"You're going to have to explain that." Ryan couldn't keep a clipped edge from his voice.

Evening regarded him steadily. "The organization required a subject who encountered the Mothman."

"Lyle?" Caden sounded incredulous.

"So he claimed. I'm not sure how the organization found him—that's not my job—but they pay their subjects well. There are several initial interviews to weed out those looking for quick cash. By the time the subject is placed under my scrutiny, they've been thoroughly vetted. Naturally, we occasionally have someone slip through that's found a way to circumvent the process, but for the most part, the cases referred are credible."

Ryan found it hard to believe Lyle had seen the Mothman. A lot of people had jumped on that bandwagon back in the sixties, but he didn't remember anything about Mason. The guy definitely seemed like the type who'd want to make a penny off the publicity. Probably how he'd ended up as a guinea pig for Evening. "What's any of this have to do with Mason returning to Point Pleasant?"

Evening cleared his throat. "Are you familiar with the term Flicker Phenomenon?"

Ryan exchanged a glance with his brother. Even Weston looked confused. Apparently, their strange visitor hadn't shared this particular part of his tale with the sheriff.

"Flicker Phenomenon is a type of hypnosis using light." Evening spoke patiently as if instructing children. "The concept behind the study is that flickering light is able to cause alterations in consciousness, even induce visual hallucinations. Subjects are manipulated through regression."

"What does that mean?" Ryan asked.

"They are mentally guided backward in time to the point of their encounter. This allows the practitioner to determine whether or not the episode is genuine or a contrived fantasy. Specific details that might otherwise be buried in a subject's subconscious can then be harvested.

In the case of Mr. Mason, he was in a deep hypnotic state when a disruption occurred."

"What kind of disruption?" Weston asked.

"A high intensity alarm was inadvertently activated at the facility. I didn't realize it at the time, but the interruption severed my connection to him. I left for a moment to pursue the nature of the alarm. When I returned, the subject was gone."

"You mean Lyle?" Ryan disliked the term "subject." Regardless of his feelings for Katie and his gut reaction to her ex, he liked Evening's haughty manner of talking even less. "Are you saying he's still under hypnosis?"

"In a manner of speaking." Evening folded one hand over the other on his lap. "Mr. Mason is fully cognizant of the present, but during our sessions, I reawakened something from his past. I'll call it a wall. I was unable to determine the cause, only that he has internalized what he perceives to be a grave wrong. In a lucid state, he would never act upon these feelings, but his mind is no longer functioning rationally and has twisted the injustice out of proportion. Mr. Mason holds extreme animosity for someone in Point Pleasant."

"Katie." Ryan's gut clenched. "Damn it! I knew he's been stalking her."

Evening's brows drew together. "Who?"

"Katie Lynch," Weston supplied. "Mason's ex-girlfriend. They have a son together. Lyle never admitted to being the father, but it's common knowledge to most everyone in town."

"I see." Evening contemplated the thought briefly. "That would appear to make sense. It's my belief Mr. Mason will return to Point Pleasant, if he hasn't already, with the intent of collecting debt on someone's past sin. It's why I'm here. I felt it prudent to share the information so appropriate measures could be taken. Naturally, I'll need to see Mr. Mason as well in order to…rewire his brain, so to speak."

Weston frowned, plainly soured by the terminology. "We haven't seen him yet."

"Doreen Sue did, according to Eve." Caden offered the information with a shrug. "I'm not sure how reliable that is. Eve heard it second or third hand. Supposedly, Doreen Sue saw Lyle buying cigarettes at the gas station."

Evening raised a pale eyebrow. "Doreen Sue?"

"Doreen Sue Lynch," Weston inserted. "She's Katie's mother and runs a hair salon here in town."

"Of course. I believe I've passed it. I'll make a point to talk to her."

"We've also seen Lyle's van," Ryan said.

Caden frowned. "With a West Virginia plate that dead-ended at the DMV. I'm not sure it was his, Ryan." He shifted his gaze to Evening. "Do you know what kind of vehicle he was driving?"

"I can't say. The facility I work for is located in Pennsylvania. Mr. Mason's car malfunctioned shortly after he arrived. He requested advance funds to have it repaired."

"Or he could have replaced it with a van and transferred his tags. Katie said the van outside her house was dark blue or green. Plain panel, like a work vehicle. He could have picked it up cheap." Mulling the thought over, Ryan tugged on his bottom lip. "But would he be skilled enough to alter the plates? Would he even think about that if his mind was warped the way you said?"

"He would if he wanted to fly under the radar." Caden looked back to Evening. "This facility you work for...you said it's in Pennsylvania. Where exactly?"

Evening pressed a fist to his lips and cleared his throat. "We don't make a habit of broadcasting our location. The area is rural, north of Pittsburgh."

Caden narrowed his eyes. "Where?"

"Who cares?" Ryan paced off a tight circle. "Katie's had some creep watching her house for two nights in a row. Mason's been seen in town and we know he's here because of a grudge." He pivoted to face the sheriff. "Pete, I'd like to put protection on her place. I'm going to have to tell her about this."

Weston nodded. "I can have a car make regular rounds. You might want to suggest she stay somewhere else for the time being. I'll put out a wire on the van and the plate. We'll bring Mason in for questioning." Standing, he steepled his fingers on his desk, shifting his attention to Evening. "Are you staying at the Parrish Hotel?"

"I am."

"Katie Lynch is the manager there."

"I believe I met her this morning."

"Then take a good look, because that woman's got an eight-year-old kid. She doesn't need some hothead with a buried grudge targeting her because you rewired his brain. Make sure you clean this up, Evening."

"Understood." Evening acknowledged the command with a thin smile bordering on arrogance.

Ryan was tempted to knock it from his face, but Caden grabbed his arm and dragged him from Weston's office.

"Did you catch that guy's name?" his brother asked.

"I caught his conceit. It stinks. Like shit."

"*Evening*, Ryan. His name is Evening."

"So?"

"Don't you remember what Parker said? *Cold must return. Evening will follow.* Too coincidental, don't you think?"

"That a guy in the looney bin happens to hit on some dipstick's name?" He'd forgotten that quirky mantra of Parker's. It wasn't like Evening's last name was Jones. How did a kid with little connection to the outside world know about a guy like Evening? "Look, the whole thing reeks if you ask me, but you're going to have to handle that arrogant bastard on your own. I need to get to Katie."

Caden nodded briskly. "I need to see someone too." He headed for his desk.

Ryan came up behind him as he hooked the jacket from the back of his chair. "Who?"

"No one you know. At least not personally."

"Should I be worried about that?"

"Grateful." Caden smiled tightly and headed for the exit. "I'll call you when I've got something."

* * * *

Caden made a quick trip to West Central for a brief discussion with Nurse Brenner. When he asked about the name "Evening," she said the only time Parker had mentioned it was in his message to Caden. She'd thought he was referring to the time of day, not a proper name. Busy with her own mini-crisis involving a patient who insisted snakes had slithered into his bathroom drain, she pointedly showed him the door. Caden had wanted to talk with Parker's doctors, or at least look at medical files, but the authorization involved paperwork, jumping through hoops, and navigating red tape.

Instead, he headed where he'd originally planned—the TNT.

Morning had given way to early afternoon by the time he arrived, the narrow roads cut through the old munitions site splattered with sunlight. Many of the trees still had their leaves, dense woodlands on either side marked by sienna, copper, and gold. Every so many yards a narrow footpath, marked by a swing-arm post at the entrance, sliced into the foliage. Dried leaves scuttled across the road, snared on the opposite side in clusters of thistles and ferns.

The TNT was the home of the Mothman. The first time he'd seen the creature, he'd been eighteen. He and his friends, along with a few girls, had come here on a Halloween night, hoping to scare up some fun. Nothing too terrifying, a harmless trick to frighten the girls. Near the igloo where the Mothman had been sighted, he'd planned to creep into the woods, then cry out as if he'd been trapped by the monster.

Instead, he'd come upon the creature in the darkness, a grayish-white bulk sheltering beneath the trees. A thing of nightmares and chaos, it was strung together by gray flesh and leathery wings. Squatting with its wings folded close to its body, it gazed at him with malignant red eyes. A splintered branch pierced the right wing, pinning it to the tree.

He should have yelled his head off. Called for Wyatt and Glen. Instead, he'd cautiously walked forward and extracted the branch. The thing had surged to its feet and burst into flight.

He should have been terrified. Anyone who'd ever encountered the Mothman reported an overwhelming sense of horror. Unlike others, Caden had seen the creature up close. Touched it, opening a channel between them. Dark emotion had poured directly into his head—confusion, melancholy, pain. A deluge of misery that left him gasping for breath.

It had been an eye-opening experience to learn emotion was the cryptid's defense. A reflex means of driving predators away. But instead of flooding Caden with fear, it had used that power to share its misery. Quiet agony that had nothing to do with its wound but something ugly and raw, buried deep inside.

Several miles into the TNT, Caden pulled off the roadway. If he drove far enough, he'd encounter shells of buildings and old ruins tumbled among the trees. The Army left its mark behind when abandoning the site, including chemicals that leeched into the soil. Now a wildlife refuge, the TNT had been placed on the government's Superfund site for clean up. In the meantime, the continued buzz over red water seepage and ground contaminants only fueled speculation about the Mothman and other strange phenomenon. As a kid, Caden had heard tales of three-headed fish in the ponds, squirrels with eight toes, and a red fox with a double snout.

He'd never seen anything out of the ordinary other than the Mothman, but Eve and Katie claimed to have spoken to an unseen entity with oracle-like powers in an abandoned weapon's igloo. According to folklore, the TNT was bisected with ley lines. Those who put stock in the supernatural believed the igloo was positioned on one of those lines, creating a doorway, or "thin spot" between worlds. There were even tales of George Washington encountering unexplained phenomenon when he'd surveyed the land preceding the Revolutionary War.

Caden wasn't entirely convinced the legends were true, but had the scars on his arm to prove the Mothman was real. Pulling off the narrow lane, he parked his car, then killed the ignition.

The air was crisp, layered with the musky scent of dried leaves and soil when he stepped outside. The primeval atmosphere never failed to amaze him, the hush of deep woods broken only by a soft sigh of wind through the tree branches or the occasional cry of a crow. Leaving the car behind, he headed down a rutted path. Within a few yards, the trail became buried beneath overgrown weeds and briars, the brown plants acting like a net to trap fallen leaves. The latter crunched under his shoes as he threaded his way deeper into the woods.

By the time he reached the igloo, second thoughts crept into his head. He didn't doubt Eve and Katie had experienced *something* inside the bunker, but to test the theory left him waffling with indecision. On one hand, he knew the Mothman was real. He even believed the ghost of his dead sister, Maggie, had communicated with their mother over the summer. Boiled down to the dregs, the supernatural was almost commonplace in Point Pleasant if you knew where to look.

Ryan wanted him to communicate with the Mothman, but he didn't have the power to summon the creature on a whim. The thing had a mind of its own. It came when it wanted, and lately hadn't bothered. Which left the oracle, as Eve and Katie had taken to calling the unseen presence in the igloo.

It took him a while to reach the spot. Once or twice he thought he heard someone moving through the woods beside him, but each time he stopped, the sound ceased. Chalking it up to his imagination, he pulled a flashlight from his belt and stepped inside the old bunker.

Like most of the igloos in the TNT, the ammunition shelter had been cut into the hillside, making it hard to spot from the air. The crown was buried beneath a dense mat of grass, brambles, and weeds. Trees grew on top of the structure and clustered around it. Barricaded by metal doors, the bunker almost seemed a natural part of the earth.

One door stood slightly ajar, offering passage for anyone brave enough to enter.

Flicking on his flashlight, Caden stepped inside. The air was considerably colder, the darkness heavy and moist with the scent of mold and decay. He played the beam of the light over the crudely hewn walls, picking out scrawls of graffiti. Names and dates, a few symbols that may have been satanic in origin. A pile of rusted containers lay heaped in the corner, old metal barrels that had once contained chemicals.

"I'm looking for the Mothman," he said aloud to the darkness.

Silence mocked him. Of course the damn thing wasn't going to answer. Nothing was there.

He walked closer to the edge of the enclosure, playing the beam of his flashlight over the graffiti. Eve said the thing would only answer yes or no.

"Do you know where the Mothman is?"

More silence, heavier this time, as if something grew and swelled within the bunker. Cold air crept down his back.

"Did the Mothman kill the missing dogs and Wilson's cow?"

A sensation of ice pebbled his exposed skin. The temperature plummeted a good ten degrees.

No, a voice said inside his head.

He spun, jerking the beam of the light behind him. Nothing there. Of course not. The thing had communicated telepathically.

He swallowed, his mouth dry. The air grew heavier as if an unseen presence shared space with him. Something foreign and wintry that couldn't exist in a normal world. He hadn't felt fear when he'd faced the Mothman, but a sliver of it washed over him now. His free hand strayed to the pistol holstered at his hip. Little good against a specter he couldn't see, but the gun instilled a measure of security.

"I need to know what's going on."

Damn. Only yes or no questions.

Caden wet his lips. "Do you know what caused the dogs and the cow to die like that?"

Yes.

"Can you tell me?"

Silence.

Did that mean it couldn't, or wouldn't?

Turning slowly, he swept the flashlight to the far corners of the igloo. One section followed by the next, until he'd covered the perimeter. The only shapes snared by the beam were the heap of rusted barrels. The air temperature plunged again, a signal the thing grew irritated, impatient.

Caden's breath plumed in the air. "Can you tell me where to find the Mothman?"

No.

Shit. Not that trying to communicate with the damn bird would do any good if it wasn't involved in the latest rash of weirdness. He considered everything that had happened recently—the dogs, Wilson's cow, reports of strange lights, Parker and his reference to Cold and Evening.

"Do you know Indrid Cold?"

Silence. Intertwined with a sense of surprise, even shock. In the darkness, something touched Caden's face. A questing brush of fingertips like suction cups.

Recoiling, he whipped the light around, met with the same empty darkness as before. What the hell was he dealing with? Aggression would do no good.

"Do you know Indrid Cold?" His voice carried a thread of anger.

Yes.

How could this entity—whatever it was—be familiar with delusions created in Parker's mind? Unless Cold wasn't a delusion.

He shook his head. More likely he fed his own thoughts into the entity and the thing bounced them back.

"What about Evening? Do you know Lach Evening?"

Yes.

It needed to tell him what he didn't know.

"Parker Kline is missing. Do you know where he is?"

Yes.

The reply drew him up short. He could spend all day asking about specific locations. Having a powwow with an invisible bogeyman was going nowhere fast. If Parker was out there, he needed help before he hurt himself or someone else.

"Is he still in Point Pleasant?"

Silence.

Tired of playing games, Caden stalked across the igloo. He swept the beam of his flashlight toward the ceiling, then down to the ground. "Come on, answer me, you freak. Ghost, demon, whatever the hell you are. I need a fucking answer!"

Cold air gusted into the bunker with the force of a small cyclone. Caught off guard, Caden raised his arms to shield his face. The tempest roared over him, pelting him in a whirlwind of leaves, twigs, and dirt. Ice engulfed him, cold and frigid as the Ohio River. The biting sensation reawakened the memory of being trapped in his car the night the Silver Bridge fell—a glut of twisted metal, dark water, and death.

Maggie. He had to save Maggie.

Staggering under the onslaught, he dropped to his knees. The flashlight slipped from his abruptly slack grip and struck the ground with a hollow thud. The beam winked out on its own, plunging the igloo into crypt-darkness. Caden covered his face with his hands.

Frigid water.

A blackness so cold it made him choke.

Maggie.

He gasped for breath, the pressure of weighted air slowly crushing his lungs.

It wasn't real. The bridge hadn't just fallen. He wasn't pinned in the wreckage of his car, his sister about to die at the hands of a murderer.

Something loomed over him. Invisible suction-cup fingers clutched his face and wrenched his head up, pinning him in place. The grip on his chin was painful.

"Parker is my mistake to fix," an accented voice warned near his ear.

Just that quickly, the thing—whatever it was—withdrew. Air flooded his lungs. A sliver of outside light pierced the doorway, driving back the shadows. The air warmed, heating the blood in his veins. He sucked down a jagged breath. His uniform was covered in dirt, the result of being pelted with leaves, stones, and soil. Other than his unkempt state, there was nothing to indicate he hadn't dreamed the whole affair.

Unsteadily, he climbed to his feet and finger-combed his hair, sweeping it free of grime.

Parker is my mistake to fix.

Those words hadn't been in his head. Someone had spoken them directly into his ear. Staggering outside, he squinted against the sun. The whole episode had given him a pounding headache. He felt like he could chug a gallon of water.

"Caden. Hey, Caden!"

A man's voice drew him around. He turned in time to see Duncan and Donnie Bradley stomp through the overgrowth.

"What are you doing out here?" Duncan jogged to his side, followed by his brother. "Man, you look a mess." His gaze flicked to the ammunitions bunker. "Were you crawling around inside the igloo?"

Caden palmed a hand over his mouth, tasting dirt. "Something like that." Hopefully, he didn't look as rattled as he felt. The entity hadn't turned hostile when conversing with Eve and Katie, but had been openly aggressive with him.

He rubbed his jaw, wincing at the sore spot where the being had gripped him. "What are you two doing out here?"

The brothers exchanged a glance. Donnie dug his hands into the pockets of his jeans and shrugged. "Nothing really." The "nothing" sounded evasive. "Just, you know…poking around."

Caden scowled, noting the rifle Donnie clutched in his hands. "You're Mothman hunting." A half dozen dead dogs had stirred up the town. "You're not packing anything other than that Winchester, are you?"

"Just the rifle." Duncan tended to be the more forthright of the two.

His brother nudged him in the ribs. "Small game's in season," he added.

As if realizing his blunder, Duncan hastily nodded agreement.

Caden didn't buy it, but there was little he could do. The Mothman had survived for almost two decades, probably far longer. If the creature lurked somewhere within the twisting labyrinth of the TNT, the thing was smart enough to outwit two local hunters. "I didn't see your truck when I got here."

"Just pulled up about ten minutes ago," Donnie said. "We saw your patrol car back that way." He hooked a thumb over his shoulder. "Thought maybe there was a problem. More dead dogs. You know."

Hence the rifle.

Caden shook his head. "Just thought I'd take a drive." Bullshit heaped upon their bullshit. The brothers plainly didn't buy his story any more than he bought theirs.

Donnie eyed the igloo. "Find anything interesting in there?"

"The usual junk and debris. Lots of graffiti. You've seen it all before." At one time or another, almost everyone in Point Pleasant had traipsed through the bunker where the Mothman had been sighted. The old dugout and the North Power Plant had been two of the cryptid's favorite haunts.

Caden's radio squawked before he could say anything further. Stepping away from the brothers, he depressed the button on his handheld mic. "Flynn, here."

"Caden, it's Ryan." His brother sounded tense, wired on something. "I'm headed to the hospital with Katie."

Alarm shot through him. "What happened?"

"Jerome's awake. I went to the hotel to tell Katie about Evening and Lyle. While I was there, I got a message that Jerome's up and talking. Like all he did was take a nap. Where are you?"

"The TNT."

"What are you doing there?" He could almost hear the frown in his brother's voice.

"I'll tell you later. I'll meet you at the hospital."

"Got it."

Maybe now they'd get answers. Jerome had been to see Parker. Had probably put the note in Katie's pocket, and might even know a thing or two about Indrid Cold or Lach Evening. So far everything seemed to tie together. If only he could make sense of how the Mothman factored into the puzzle. Parker indicated the creature was involved, and any unexplained occurrence in Point Pleasant usually found its root in the town's infamous bird.

Hooking the radio onto his belt, Caden turned back to the Bradley brothers. "Look, guys, I'm headed to town. Be careful out here, and watch what you shoot, okay?"

"Under control, Sergeant." Donnie gave him a mock salute.

Caden sprinted for his car. Duncan and Donnie were on their own. Hopefully, they wouldn't cross anything they couldn't handle.

* * * *

"I'm telling you I heard something." Duncan crouched lower, motioning his brother forward. Donnie had the rifle, after all. They'd been ready to pack it in after two hours, tired of plodding their way through knots of browning foxtails and bull thistle. Just as they'd started to head back, Duncan heard the noise. "Up ahead. A little farther."

He shuffled forward in a crab-crouch, adrenalin licking his veins. The noise had been weird. A snuffling sound, like a dog would make. Poor pets seemed to be the favorite target of the Mothman lately. At least, he was convinced the monster was responsible. The thing probably sucked their brains out, slurping the blood like syrup. No way did he want to trip over some mutt with its head half gone.

The damn monster had to go.

Over the summer, some tourist woman and her husband had snapped a partial photo of the creature. The Whitmores had been the toast of Point Pleasant for days. Reporters wanting to interview them, people fawning over them, buying them drinks and dinner. Hell, Eve Parrish even had a copy of the photo hanging in her hotel. She'd told them they could stay free any time they wanted. If some out-of-staters could snag that kind of fame with a shot that looked like a gray blob, he and Donnie would be kings if they killed the monster. Forget local stuff. They'd make world news, maybe even Johnny Carson. There'd be magazine covers, TV specials, lots of girls wanting their autographs.

He smiled as he crept forward. His thighs burned from the strain of staying in a crouch, but the pain was worth the effort. He'd heard about the thing's eyes—red like blood, able to pick up even a glimmer of movement. It was like a damn hawk. "You got that rifle loaded?"

"Course it's loaded." Donnie sounded ticked. "What do you think I am? Some kind of halfwit?"

"Shh." Duncan made a cutting motion, slicing his hand through the air. "There it was again." Coming to a standstill, he strained his ears to listen. "Did you hear it?"

Donnie sucked on his lower lip for several seconds before shaking his head. "I don't hear anything. Probably just some squirrel in the underbrush."

Standing, he let the rifle hang lax at his side. "Let's pack it in and grab some lunch. We can hit the River Café and get a beer."

"It's going to see you."

"Hell, Duncan, there's nothing out here. Caden Flynn would have been all over it if there was."

Caden had looked shaken when they'd found him outside the igloo, and he'd been covered in dirt. Maybe he'd stumbled across the monster and didn't want to admit it had gotten the best of him. Running scared would look bad for a law enforcement officer. Not that he'd been running, but *something* had put him on edge.

"Ten more minutes," Duncan bartered, tugging the rifle from his brother's grasp. If Donnie wasn't going to take things seriously, he'd make sure the weapon got put to good use. "We know it's out here. We saw it last June."

"And haven't seen it since. I'm getting hungry. I need a burger."

Crack.

The sudden sound broke the stillness on the tail of his words. Donnie immediately dropped into a crouch. "Shit. What was that?"

Duncan's heart thumped into overdrive. A shadow loomed over them, masking the sun. Inside his skull the noise of a thousand bees swarmed to life. "Ugh!" Dropping the rifle, he clamped his hands over his ears. At his side, Donnie crashed to his knees, grunting and panting, his face twisted in pain.

The noise grew louder, joined by a battering wind. Blinking, Duncan raised his head, staring up into the sky. At first he saw nothing, just a gray blot of shadow. Then a form gradually took shape. A wing opened and expanded, blocking the trees and sky. The creature launched into the air, rising straight up like a helicopter. Duncan craned his neck, repulsed and terrified, compelled to look into its face.

He screamed.

Chapter 10

Caden guessed Katie and Ryan were already with Jerome by the time he arrived at the hospital. A quick check-in with admissions revealed Jerome had been moved from ICU to a room on the fourth floor. Taking the elevator, he shared the ride with a young girl and her mother. The girl looked to be about seven years old. Clutching three foil balloons, each decorated with a bright yellow happy face, she was plainly fascinated by his soiled uniform and unkempt hair. He'd dusted the worst of the debris from his uniform before climbing into his patrol car, but still looked like he'd rolled around in a dirt pile.

"Hi." He tried to appear non-threatening.

The woman tugged her daughter to the back, but had the decency to offer a wobbly smile. When the car pinged to a stop on the third floor, she hustled them off without as much as a backward glance. Caden rode the remainder of the way by himself, immediately snaring the attention of two nurses when he stepped from the elevator.

"Sir? Sir?" The first called, rushing after him. "Do you need help?"

"No, I'm fine." He offered a reassuring grin. "Just dusty. Thanks for your concern."

Farther down the hall, he passed an orderly pushing an elderly man in a wheelchair.

"Good afternoon, Sergeant," the old man said. He might look a mess, but his uniform garnered respect.

Caden returned his greeting, then rounded the corner toward Jerome's room.

"...didn't mean to cause such an uproar."

He caught the tail end of Jerome's words as he entered the room. The smell of antiseptic and clean laundry lingered in the air, mingled with a harsh medicinal odor. Sitting up in bed, Jerome looked pale but attentive, his thinning blond hair rumpled over his ears where the clear hose of an oxygen cannula was visible.

"I keep telling everyone I feel fine." Tentatively, he fingered the tube under his nose as if assuring himself it was still in place. For a skinny man and habitual smoker, the oxygen was probably a blessing on a normal day. His gaze shifted to Caden as he stepped to the side of the bed. "Caden. Oh man, you too." The words carried a sliver of concern. "I hope I didn't do something I don't know about. Uh, not that I don't appreciate you, Ryan, and Katie visiting. You, um…" He licked his lips nervously. "Look worse than I do."

"What happened to you?" Ryan asked with obvious concern.

"I'll tell you about it later." Right now, all he wanted to do was trace Jerome's connection to Parker Kline. "Jerome, do you remember Katie stopping to help you when your car went off the road?"

"Yeah, I remember that." Jerome's brows drew together. "Can't tell you why I went off, though. Maybe a deer?" A note of appeal lingered for them to fill in the blanks. "I kind of remember something out there on the road with me." He rubbed a hand across his lips, mulling the idea over. "At least I thought there was."

"You were pretty disoriented when I found you." Katie placed a hand on his arm with an encouraging smile. "I was worried about you."

"Thanks." A hint of color rose to his cheeks. Abruptly awkward, he plucked at the blanket layered over his lap.

Caden bit away a grin. The guy might be able to rattle off endless theory about aliens and UFOs, but grew self-conscious when accepting a compliment. Especially when that compliment came from a pretty girl.

"When I left," Katie continued, "you were with Deputy Brown. Do you remember him?"

Jerome frowned. "That's the weird thing. I only remember bits and pieces of that night and how I got here." His scowl dug deeper. "I remember being afraid for some reason."

"What about cold?" Katie's prompting was gentle, almost as if she feared upsetting him. "You kept saying you were cold."

"Cold." Jerome repeated the word as if finding something familiar in the sound. For several seconds he didn't speak, his eyes hooded, his gaze turned inward. Overhead the intercom warbled a page, asking Dr. Newton to report to radiology. Blinking rapidly, Jerome sat straighter. "That's how he communicates. Over the airwaves."

Caden exchanged a glance with Ryan. "Who are you talking about?"

"Indrid Cold."

Exhaling, Ryan webbed a hand over his face. "Not him again."

Jerome's mouth dropped open. "You know about Cold?"

"We know Parker Kline believes he communicated with someone named Indrid Cold." Caden tried not to rush the conversation, but he was growing impatient, especially after his encounter with the being in the igloo. "You went to see Kline the night Katie found your car off the road."

"Yeah, I remember now." Jerome's voice lurched up an octave and he wriggled around on the bed, pressing his fists against the mattress to push higher on his pillows. "Katie, I gave you something that night. I tucked a piece of paper into your jacket pocket. Did you find it?"

Her gaze flicked to Ryan.

"Is this what you're looking for?" He withdrew a white slip from his pocket.

"What's that?" Caden had heard nothing about the paper.

"I'll show you. There—grab the table." Jerome motioned for the rollaway stand beside his bed. A box of tissues, plastic container for water, and a Styrofoam cup occupied the top. Someone had left a can of ginger ale and a pack of saltines, but both were unopened.

Caden slid the table close to the bed, repositioning it so that the surface stretched across Jerome's lap. Tugging his bottom lip between his teeth, Jerome flattened the paper on top, smoothing away the wrinkles with a swipe of his hand. "Thank God you still had it."

"What is it?" Caden stared down at a seemingly senseless jumble of numbers.

"I didn't have a chance to tell you about it." Ryan stood behind Katie, looking over her shoulder while Jerome ran a skinny index finger through the chain of digits. "Katie found it last night. I was going to run it by Parker's doctors but haven't had a chance."

"You don't need to run it by anyone." Jerome's finger paused on the third line, excitement creeping into his voice. "Here. This is it."

Caden leaned closer. "I don't see anything."

"Give me a pen. And a notepad."

Ryan beat him to it, pulling the small tablet he used for taking notes from his jacket pocket.

"Parker gave me this," Jerome explained, without looking up. "I learned about what happened to him at Hank Jeffries' place. That's why I went to see him at West Central. After Hank killed Tim, Parker raced back to their truck."

Caden winced. "I know that." To get their dad's gun.

"Parker was going for help," Jerome said. "But he saw something on the way to the truck that changed everything. It changed *him.*"

Squashing a spike of anger, Caden paced a short distance away. "I was there, Jerome."

"I know. Parker told me everything that happened. Cold was there too."

Ryan's brows crawled into the fringe of his bangs. "Indrid Cold? The guy from Lanulos?"

Jerome nodded. He plunked his finger onto the paper. "And this is when he's coming back."

"What the hell are you talking about?" There was no disguising the irritation in Caden's voice as he stalked back to the bed. So much for not upsetting the hospital patient. "Are you trying to say that muddle of numbers means something?"

"It isn't a muddle. It's *noise.*"

Standing beside Ryan, Katie flinched.

"The cluster is intended as a distraction from the hidden message. If you look closely, you'll notice all the digits repeat in sequence, one through zero. Then they begin dropping off. Two through zero, three through zero and so on. Eventually, the sequence starts over again. But the figures in the middle of the third line don't follow the same pattern."

Jerome pointed out the line, and Caden craned his neck to see.

99006677889900103123415677889900889900

It still looked like a clutter of nothing. "I don't see—"

Jerome circled a handful of numbers in the center and read them aloud. "1031234156. These don't follow the structure of the others."

"It still doesn't explain what they mean." Katie had been mostly quiet, letting Caden and Ryan carry the conversation, but the word "noise" seemed to hold special significance for her.

Jerome looked up. "Broken down it translates to October thirty-first, at 11:41:56 PM."

Halloween.

Caden was speechless. He could see it now, military time stamped with the month and day. Damn, if the stupid thing didn't make sense. He didn't buy some make-believe alien named Cold would pop into existence at that hour, but the code was clever. A little too clever for Parker Kline, if the kid was as feeble-minded as he'd been led to believe.

Ryan exhaled loudly and slumped into a chair against the wall. Caden could read the expression on his face: *This bullshit is over my head.*

If it weren't for his connection to the Mothman and what had just happened in the igloo, Caden might feel the same way. But it was hard to discount a visitor from another world while bonded to a creature with no face and red eyes. Thank God, Jerome didn't share his room with another patient or they might all end up in West Central.

"The thirty-first is a little over a week from now," Katie pointed out.

Jerome glanced between them. "Look, I know you probably think I'm whacked, and maybe I am a bit gone on the conspiracy stuff and UFOs, but this is for real." He slapped the paper emphatically. "I don't remember what happened after I left Parker, but I think someone followed me. Someone who wanted this information." Another tap to the paper. "I think maybe I was scared and driving too fast. That's why I went off the road. And that Deputy Brown guy?" He rubbed a bony hand over the back of his neck, his Adam's apple bobbing up and down. "I think he was one of them. When he realized I didn't have what he wanted, he let me go."

"But you ended up here. In a coma," Katie protested.

"I think they messed with my head, then dumped me somewhere nearby."

"They?" The story was sounding crazier by the minute, but Caden couldn't let it go.

As if sensing he'd reeled them in, Jerome continued fervently. "You don't think there aren't guys out there monitoring the skies and airwaves, wanting to make sure all this UFO stuff is kept hush-hush? Not just government types, but others too. Shadow organizations. They've got the resources and know-how to pose as law enforcement or military. A lot of them are even connected to the military, working under the radar. Think of the panic that would set in if people knew aliens could breach our air space. Can't have that, can we? What do you think the Mothman is?"

"Jerome, enough." Caden held up a hand to stop the torrent of information. Jerome was breathing heavily even with the plastic hose supplying a steady stream of oxygen. All they needed was to get kicked out of the hospital for agitating a patient or causing him to have a setback. "Take it easy. Getting uptight can't be good for your condition."

"But I don't *have* a condition." Jerome's eyes bulged as he tried to stress the point. "I'm telling you, those guys did something to my head. Maybe they gave me a drug you can't trace. Then they dumped me here because they didn't need me anymore. Parker's going to be a lot harder to get, but they'll go after him next."

"Parker's not in West Central." Caden hated admitting the truth. "He escaped."

Jerome's face drained of color. His mouth opened and closed like a fish gulping air. Then with a great bark of laughter, he collapsed against his pillows. "And you don't believe in Indrid Cold? How the hell do you think he got out of there? Cold took him away."

"We're done here." Ryan stood up.

"Wait." Caden motioned for his brother to stay where he was. Jerome looked immensely pleased with himself. The scrawny man's shoulders shook with silent laughter. Caden didn't believe Cold had zapped to Earth and snatched Parker from his hospital room, but Jerome clearly had an inside track to Parker's mindset. It was possible he knew even more that could prove beneficial. "Do you know someone named Lach Evening?"

"No."

"Did you ever hear Parker mention that name?"

"No."

"Jerome." Katie coiled her fingers around his arm where it rested on the rollaway table. While Caden was frustrated, and Ryan appeared ready to write the whole thing off as lunacy, she seemed willing to give Jerome the benefit of the doubt. "Even if we believe you about the message, it's incomplete." She indicated the slip of paper. "It gives a date and a time, but not a place."

"I know." He seemed to deflate with the words. "Cold did something to Parker that made him the way he is now. Parker believed he was coming back to set things right. He created an opening for him with those blocks of paper he was always drawing—kind of like a beacon so Cold could find him."

"So you want us to believe he stepped through a drawing into Parker's room and took the kid with him to Lanulos?" Ryan's voice dripped with sarcasm.

Jerome's face turned red. "Mock if you will, but Parker opened a bridge. Cold can only manifest in physical form when alignments between dimensions are precise. Parker found a way to reach him outside of that boundary using the noise in his head."

"Then what you're saying is that Parker is no longer on Earth?" Unlike Ryan, Katie did not appear judgmental.

Jerome nodded.

"Then why the code?" Caden asked. "Why the date Cold is supposed to return?"

"Because that's when he *can* materialize. It has something to do with ley lines and the folds between worlds. Cold gave the message to Parker over his radio."

Ryan rolled his eyes.

"Parker's radio doesn't work," Caden said bluntly.

"It doesn't have to. Not for someone like Cold. He can manipulate frequencies. Most UFOnauts can. People like Parker call it *chatter*."

Caden hated getting caught up in Jerome's delusions, but there was no logical explanation for how Parker had vanished from his room at West Central. He rubbed his temple. "Why would Indrid Cold come back on October thirty-first? If his goal was to reach Parker, and Parker is gone...."

Jerome squirmed. "Yeah, I know. But there's some kind of obligation Cold has to fulfill. Parker said it had to do with his past and something he left unfinished. Because I believed Parker and wanted to see Cold for myself, Parker gave me the message. I think other people have been watching Parker too."

"The Deputy Browns of the world?" Ryan challenged. "The shadow organizations?"

Jerome shrugged. "I wasn't the only one who saw Brown." He looked at Katie.

"All right." Caden wanted to wrap things up. His head was pounding, and the nonsense Jerome dumped on them did nothing to mute the ache. "Is there anything else you want to tell us?"

"I want to get out of here. I want to track down Cold on Halloween."

"Where would you look?" Katie asked.

"I don't know. The TNT maybe, or on the road to my place. That's where Parker saw Cold the first time."

"You're going to have to talk to your doctors about getting out of here." It was the perfect chance for Caden to bow out of the conversation.

"Yeah. Here." Jerome extended the slip of paper on which he'd scribbled the date and time of Cold's arrival. "Maybe you don't believe me, but hang on to this, anyway. You've still got time to make up your mind."

Caden hesitated. He took the sheet, folded it in half, and slipped it into his pocket.

"Ryan, I need to talk to you." He motioned for his brother to follow and walked out the door.

* * * *

"So you want me to believe some invisible oracle tossed you around in a windstorm?" Ryan took a long pull from his beer. The talk Caden had wanted to have with him didn't occur until that night when they were both off duty. In the end, Katie and Eve joined them too, all four of them settled in a booth at the River Café.

The place was fairly busy for a Thursday night, over half the seats at the bar taken, several of the tables filled. Eve had reserved a booth for them in the back corner, the perks of owning the place. Away from the crowd, they could talk quietly without worrying about overeager ears that might zone in on their conversation.

"You must have upset the thing somehow." Seated beside Caden, Eve looked worried, her brows creased in concern. "It wasn't hostile when Katie and I talked to it."

"Leave it to my brother to piss off the bogeyman." Ryan's lips quirked upward in a good-natured smirk.

"Caden, I'm worried." Eve gripped his arm, her diamond engagement ring glinting in the glow of the brass wall lanterns. "It might have hurt you."

"I think I pushed too hard." Caden placed his hand over hers. "It turned violent when I pressed about Parker. But it answered with something besides 'yes' or 'no.'"

"Oh?" Seated across from him, Ryan leaned forward, resting his forearms on the table. Everything he'd ever heard about the entity indicated it only spoke two words, a negative or a positive affirmation.

"It said 'Parker is my mistake to fix,'" Caden explained.

"Back to Parker again." Ryan had to admit the kid's name was on everyone's tongue these days. Between his escape from West Central, worry about what he might do, and Floyd damning the whole system anytime someone got near him, it was hard not to have an opinion about Point Pleasant's tragic murderer. Ryan had even been stopped by a belligerent Shawn Preech when he'd entered the café. Seated at the bar, several empties of Rolling Rock at his elbow, Preech had demanded to know why he and Caden weren't out looking for "that lunatic kid."

"Maybe we could talk about something else." Sounding tired, Katie massaged the back of her neck.

Earlier that day, Ryan had told her about Lach Evening and Lyle, suggesting she stay at the hotel for a while, or with her mom. He'd thought it a reasonable request, but she'd stubbornly refused. At least she'd conceded to having Sam stay with Doreen Sue until they were able to get a track on Lyle.

"I agree with Katie." No surprise that Eve sided with her friend. "You guys need to give all this stuff a rest. Let's have a toast before our food gets here." She smiled broadly. "I'm getting married."

It was the perfect opening for the girls to start gushing, sharing ideas about wedding gowns, dinner menus, and flowers. Caden rolled his eyes, but there was no disguising his pleasure at being engaged. After a while, Ryan lowered his voice and spoke solely to Caden.

"You remember that star shit stuff I told you about?"

His brother nodded.

"I sent some off for analysis and got the report back today."

Caden took a swig from his bottle of Michelob. "And?"

"Nothing."

"They couldn't determine what it was?"

"There was nothing there to determine. By the time the lab got the container, everything inside had disappeared. Not a trace of residue left. It's like the stuff evaporated or vanished into thin air."

"Chester Wilson seems to think it came from a UFO."

"Yeah, I've been thinking about that." Ryan glanced across the café. Someone opened the front door, allowing a draft of cold air inside. It wasn't quite seven o'clock, but twilight had already claimed the sky, coating the windows overlooking the street with a chrome-like sheen. At the bar someone laughed loudly, and Shawn Preech added his guffaws to the hilarity. Ryan wondered how he and Suzanne were coping after losing Duke. Apparently, the dog's death hadn't stopped Shawn from downing his usual six-pack before staggering home. "If there really was a UFO, maybe it was responsible for moving that cow and dropping it in the other pasture. It could have gotten caught up in a beam or something, and that's what made its brain explode."

Caden grinned into his bottle. "It sounds like you've been reading spaceman comics."

Ryan gave him a swift kick under the table. "You got a better idea, wise ass?"

"What are you two going on about now?" Eve had apparently picked up that their conversation switched back to the taboo subject of UFOs. Before either could answer, she refocused, her gaze flicking across the room. "Uh-oh. Look who just came in."

Ryan glanced over his shoulder. Seated across from him, Eve and Caden had a view of the connecting hallway to the hotel. Patrons of the café entered from the street through the front door, or meandered down from their rooms and crossed the lobby. One of them, an obvious guest of the hotel, had chosen the latter.

"Guy likes black, doesn't he?" Caden observed.

Ryan grunted.

Dressed in his customary dark suit, this time with a black button-down shirt and tie, Evening took a table near the hallway. While looking around the room, he set a folded newspaper beside his plate. In the subdued light of the wall lanterns, his whitish-blond hair reflected threads of gold. Nancy Arnold, Eve's part-time waitress, rushed to wait on him before he even had time to open a menu.

"He certainly knows how to dress," Eve commented.

Caden scowled. "He looks like an undertaker."

"Jealous?"

A snort. "Hardly."

"He's...different." Katie's voice was thin, barely a whisper. "It's like I know him from somewhere. A long time ago."

Ryan looked at her sharply. "You've seen that guy before?"

"I don't know." Katie turned her attention to the glass of ginger ale in her hand. She was the only one who hadn't selected an alcoholic beverage when Nancy took their order. "I think he was outside the hospital the night we found Jerome. And there's something about him that reminds me of—" She stopped abruptly, sucking down a sharp breath. "I remember now. The night the bridge fell."

"What are you talking about?" Caden's eyes narrowed.

Ryan tensed involuntarily. The collapse of the Silver Bridge was a tragic subject for everyone in Point Pleasant, but not everyone had suffered the death of a loved one. He and Caden had lost their younger sister, Maggie, and Eve had lost her father.

"I was outside of my mom's hair salon." Katie kept her gaze lowered as if watching the memory unfold in her glass. "I remember there were a lot of birds in the air, like something upset them. Eve and Sarah were walking across the street toward the Crowne Theater. It made me think how nice it would be to have a close friend like that."

Eve reached across the table and squeezed her hand.

Katie smiled faintly, looking at her friend. "A man asked where he could find my mom. I thought he was there about Wendy, because he looked so official, dressed all in black. And he had, he had..." She drew in a shaky breath.

Ryan slid his arm around her shoulder. "Katie, what's wrong?"

"He had weird fingers." She looked at each of them in turn. "Slender, but kind of fat at the end."

"Just like Evening." Caden's expression was grim.

"He told me his name was Lach. He had blond hair."

"Bingo." Ryan glanced over his shoulder to find Evening staring directly at him. "I need to have a talk with our man over there."

He started to stand, but Katie gripped his hand. Her eyes were wide when she gazed up at him. "Ryan, don't. There's something else."

He eased back into his seat. "What?"

"He hasn't aged. He looks exactly the same."

"But that was fifteen years ago," Eve protested. "How is that possible?"

"Dinners should be up in ten." Nancy appeared at their table with a cheerful smile. Energy rolled off her in waves and bubbled over in social charm. "Would you like another round of drinks while you're waiting?"

Seemingly flustered by the interruption, Katie lowered her head. "I'm good."

"Me too," Eve said.

Caden motioned to his bottle. "I'll take another Michelob."

"Same here." Ryan slid his empty to the end of the table where Nancy scooped it up. "Hey, uh, the guy you just waited on…there behind us with the blond hair."

"Oh, him." Nancy's voice escaped in a breathy rush, her gaze darting momentarily to Evening. "Yes?" To Ryan she looked like a love-struck schoolgirl.

Had to be the clothes. Either that or the accent, if he could ever place the damn thing.

"Did he say anything odd to you?" He didn't know why he asked, only that the guy was starting to give him the creeps. He'd never bought the whole expert-on-supernatural-creatures story, or whatever Evening had termed his pseudo-science. But with every moment that passed, he grew convinced everything Evening said was a lie.

"Weird you should ask." Nancy tucked a pencil behind her ear. "He wanted to know if you and Katie were a couple."

"Shit." Ryan bolted to his feet.

"Ryan, please." Katie grabbed his hand. "He might remember me. Maybe he's worried what I've told you about him."

"Hey, if you know something, spill the beans." Nancy's voice was bouncy. "I'm too embarrassed to ask him about his accent, but I'd love to know where he's from. He's gorgeous."

"Nancy." Eve's glance and tone carried the censure of a boss. "Drinks, please."

"Oh, yeah. Sure." The girl bobbed her head. "And food in ten, like I said."

She'd no sooner hustled away then the door to the street burst open with an explosive bang. Donnie Bradley rushed inside, followed closely by a breathless Duncan.

"Hey, listen up!" Donnie thrust his fist into the air, his face a ruddy mask of excitement. "Break out the booze. We nailed that bastard."

"What are you squawking about?" Shawn Preech swung around on his bar stool. "What bastard?"

"The only one that matters." Duncan pushed past his brother. "I shot the Mothman. I think I damn near killed the fucking thing."

Chapter 11

Caden waited only long enough for Duncan and Donnie to tell their tale before heading to Eve's office and grabbing the phone. He called Weston at home, catching the sheriff in the middle of his dinner. "We're going to need patrols in the TNT."

"Lyle?" Weston huffed a guess.

"No." Caden turned his back on the window behind Eve's desk, blocking a view of the Ohio River. Fifteen years ago, the tall towers of the Silver Bridge had commanded that vantage point. "The Bradley brothers just came into the River Café, going on about the Mothman."

"Aren't they always?"

"This is different. Duncan says he shot the thing. Might have even injured it enough to kill it."

A loud clatter echoed over the line. Small wonder if Weston dropped something. "He's certain?"

Caden scrubbed a hand over the back of his neck. "As certain as he can be." An excited babble of voices drifted beneath the closed door, alerting him a crowd gathered in the lobby. Apparently, word had spread from the café to the hotel. "Duncan said he and Donnie were scouting in the woods when the thing burst out of nowhere. He put a bullet in it when it soared over their heads."

Weston spat a curse. "Let me guess. They're getting everyone fired up to go into the woods with them."

"Something like that. I'm still at the hotel. I left Ryan in the café trying to keep a lid on things. A lot of it's just swagger, but some of these guys are going to be piling into their cars and trucks with guns to go Mothman hunting."

"I hear you." Weston exhaled noisily. "Rosling's at the station. I'll call in and have him put a patrol together. With any luck, this whole thing will blow over in one night. If we're going to have a lot of idiots running around with guns, we need to be visible."

"I'm headed there as soon as I hang up."

"Good." Weston paused, and Caden had the sense he was mulling something over. "What do you think? Did Duncan really hit the thing?"

"Hard to say." The thought lay like a rock in his gut. The Mothman had saved his life more than once. How did you wish death on a being like that? His gaze dropped to his forearm where the marks the creature branded him with peeked from beneath his sleeve. "I'll radio if I find anything."

"Do that." Weston's voice was gruff. "We don't need this turning into a circus. If the media gets wind of it—"

"I hear you. Gotta run." Caden hung up the phone as Eve stepped into the office. A din of voices rose behind her before she muffled them into silence by closing the door.

"Word's spreading." She moved closer to the desk, absently twisting the diamond ring on her finger. Her eyes appeared overly bright, the corners of her mouth stretched in an anxious line. "I'm worried, Caden. What are you going to do?"

"My job." There was no time to go back for a patrol car, but he kept a .38 locked in his glove box. If the thing was dying, then he needed to end it humanely before some half-assed hit squad splattered the TNT with the creature's innards.

"Tell Ryan where I'm headed." Rounding the desk, he gave her a quick kiss, then headed for the door. "Do me a favor and keep an eye on Evening. Something about that guy doesn't add up."

"He already left."

"What?" Caden stopped in his tracks.

"He left the café not long after you did." Eve twisted the ring again, worrying it back and forth. "It's crazy out there. There's a crowd growing in the lobby. Mostly guests, but people are starting to wander in from the street. And Duncan and Donnie are trying to round up a hunting party to go into the TNT."

"Great."

"Ryan read them the riot act and told them to keep away from the place, that the sheriff's office would handle it. Some of the guys aren't buying it, and Shawn Preech is telling everyone whoever finds the Mothman is going to be famous. Mr. Evening left right before things got hectic."

"Ryan's going to have to deal with it. If he has to, he can call city police." Caden needed to get to the TNT and find the damn creature before someone else did. If word spread through town, it wouldn't only be hunters headed to the old munitions site, but reporters too. Weston didn't want a circus, but there wasn't much they could do to stop the frenzy. "I'll be back as soon as I can."

He opened the door and stepped into the lobby—directly into the chaos of rumormongers and camera flashes.

* * * *

It took a good hour for the lobby to clear out. Katie was thankful when most everyone who remained congregated in the café. The majority of the curiosity seekers had left, a few snapping pictures of the famous Mothman photo that hung in the lobby. It would be interesting to know what Glenda and George Whitmore thought of the latest uproar. Eve had told them they could stay free whenever they wanted thanks to the business their photo brought the hotel. It had certainly drawn a lot of attention tonight, even if Katie did think it looked like an indiscernible gray blob. Enough papers and science-fiction journals had splashed it on their front page, that everyone from fanatics to the mildly curious viewed it as the holy grail of Mothman evidence.

A muffled din of conversation drifted from the River, as she busied herself straightening up the lobby. Donnie and Duncan had left with eight to ten others, all of them hyped up on the idea of tracking down the Mothman.

"There's gotta be a blood trail," Donnie had said. Others agreed.

Ryan left a little before they did, headed for the TNT to rendezvous with Weston's patrols. Most who remained simply wanted to coast on the wave of lingering excitement. When she'd popped her head in the eatery a few minutes ago, some of the older patrons were sharing tales from the '66 and '67 sightings. Mothman fever was back, and it looked like it was going to be a while before the flurry died down.

The sound of the front doors opening drew her attention from the magazines she was arranging on a table by the window. She straightened in time to see Suzanne Preech step inside and sweep a hand through her hair, taming her platinum curls.

"Hi, Suzanne." Katie picked up several outdated magazines, cradling them in the crook of her arm. "If you're looking for Shawn, I think he's in the café."

"You mean he didn't go with the others?" She flattened a hand against her stomach, sounding relieved. "I got wind Duncan and Donnie were telling everyone they shot the Mothman."

Katie nodded. "Things have mostly calmed down since then. Duncan and Donnie went to the TNT and took a bunch of the guys with them."

"I was sure Shawn would go." Biting her lip, Suzanne took a hesitant step forward. A mixture of pride and jumpiness warred in her gaze. She was obviously flustered by something.

"He wanted to, but Ryan Flynn talked him out of it." Katie didn't add it was because Shawn had downed too much beer to be traipsing around in the woods with a loaded gun. If he didn't fall flat on his face, he'd likely shoot himself.

Suzanne closed her eyes. "Thank God." She flattened her hand against her stomach a second time before seeming to realize her voice betrayed too much. Straightening her shoulders, she lifted her chin. "I mean… That's nice."

Katie experienced a moment of sympathy. "I'm sorry about Duke. Ryan told me what happened."

"Thanks. I miss that big smelly dog." A faint smile touched Suzanne's lips before her gaze drifted in the direction of the café. "I should probably go round up Shawn. It's getting late for a work night. If he wants to kick back with a few cold ones, he can do it tomorrow on a Friday." Having said her piece, she started past Katie. She was halfway across the lobby when she halted. "I heard Ryan's been visiting you a lot."

Katie stiffened, immediately defensive. It was no one's business if Ryan came to see her. She was about to blurt something about small town gossip when Suzanne's face softened with a smile.

"You know how people change when they get older?' She tucked a strand of hair behind her ear. "Ryan's the same kind-hearted, decent guy he was when he was a kid. If I were you, I'd hang on to him."

There was nothing smug or threatening in the observation, not even a challenge he might still be fair game. Before Katie could say anything in return, Suzanne left and headed down the short hallway to the café. Bewildered, Katie listened to the door swing open. The din of voices grew louder with the barrier removed, one rising above all the others.

"Look who it is," Shawn Preech slurred. "My lovely wife. And mother-to-be."

* * * *

Caden reached the TNT before anyone else. Starting with the empty shell of the old north power plant off Fairgrounds Road, he explored the crumbling interior, using a flashlight to guide his way through the dark. The beam sent some small creature scurrying deeper into shadow, but he discovered nothing to suggest the winged humanoid had been there.

Later, he checked the igloo where he'd run afoul of the oracle-like being who lurked inside. Nothing.

He attempted to communicate with the thing, hoping to discover where the Mothman was hidden, but the igloo was empty, silent as a tomb. It would only be a matter of time before Duncan and Donnie returned with a lynch-mentality search party. Legally, there was nothing he could do to stop them from roaming the grounds, but the situation felt primed for disaster. Hopefully, the patrols Weston promised would arrive first, the police presence enough to keep any thrill-seekers in order.

After driving for some time, randomly pulling off here and there to investigate trails cut between the trees, he decided he was going about it all wrong. Once or twice, he heard the distant rumble of a car engine or caught a flash of light deep in the woods, alerting him others had arrived. If the Mothman was out there, he wasn't going to find the cryptid playing needle in a haystack. In every encounter he'd had—except the first, when he'd helped the creature—it had come to him. Maybe it would do the same again.

Caden drove farther down the road, then pulled off in an area void of trails. An owl hooted somewhere off to his right. Leaving the vehicle behind, he wound his way through a knotted tangle of pine, firs, and oaks, heading deeper into the endless labyrinth of trees. The air was heavy with the scent of dried leaves and dark loam, the wind rustling branches overhead. Old wood clacked together with the sound of hollow bones. A full moon helped guide his way, and the beam of his flashlight sliced a trail through the dark.

Careful to note his path, he headed in a southwesterly direction for about five minutes. It was easy to get turned around in the woods, especially at night. Depending on how far you ventured, the ground could quickly turn into marshy soil or boggy wetlands. Eventually, he paused, waiting for any unusual noise. When nothing came, he flicked off the flashlight and waited.

You've got to be out there somewhere.

Most people who'd seen the Mothman claimed to have spotted it more than once. A few eyewitnesses from the sixties adamantly maintained the cryptid had been trying to communicate with them. Some believed it had attempted to warn the town of the Silver Bridge disaster before the collapse. Others insisted the monster was a harbinger of evil and had caused the tragedy.

Duncan and Donnie had spotted the Mothman last June. How ironic if the thing returned in an attempt to communicate with them and the idiots had shot it instead. For all he knew, the creature had secreted itself away in isolation to die. Caden's life had been in danger every time the creature appeared. Is that why he couldn't find it now…because there was no threat of harm?

The hum started as a low vibration.

It rolled over Caden, awakening a memory of sulfur and chaos, a being born of nightmare. The sound pulsed and thrummed, growing louder. A second later it exploded in a shrill burst that drove him to his knees. Dropping the flashlight, he clamped his hands over his ears. Anger pummeled him, raw and beet-red. Not his emotion, but the intrusion of something alien. A disorganized mind locked with his, battering him beneath a blizzard of fury and pain. Wind howled through the trees, the branches chattering like the dead. He clamped his jaw, grinding his teeth.

Stop! I can't—

And just that quickly, the wind died and the conduit of emotion snapped. Something crouched five feet away. The hum remained, a muted drone at the back of his skull.

Slowly, he stood. The glowing eyes of the Mothman tracked his movement.

It was hard to look at the creature, its face a mere suggestion of form. There was nothing where the head should be, just two enormous eyes, red as scarlet wine. Much like a human, it had two arms and two legs, but its feet were three-toed, ending in long, lethal claws. Talons took the place of fingers, and two massive gray wings sprouted from its back. Half humanoid, half bird-like, it was wholly demonic and nightmarish in appearance.

Caden wet his lips, unsure how to communicate. The thing seemed able to project emotion, so he tried to do the same. In the dark, he couldn't tell if the Mothman was injured, but did his best to mentally convey concern.

Instantly, he was blasted by rage. Staggering beneath the violent onslaught, he took two steps backward. The Mothman rose to its full height, towering well over seven feet. The tips of its wings arched above its back. Caden flicked on his flashlight, passing the beam over the creature. It didn't as much as flinch, but he spied a bullet hole near the top of its right wing. Duncan *had* shot the thing. Far from mortally wounding the creature, he'd only served in ticking it off. Royally.

Another surge of rage pummeled Caden. No words, only a pulsing need for retribution.

"Don't." This time he spoke the word aloud. "They were afraid. They reacted like anyone would. You can't—"

The hum swelled in savage retaliation.

He grunted, doubling over. His fingers clamped down on the flashlight, and the beam wobbled over the ground. Mercifully, the loud vibration retreated. He breathed raggedly through his mouth, anger mushrooming within. His own.

"These are my friends. My town. You will not terrorize them."

The Mothman shrieked. With a burst of motion, it launched straight up into the sky. The thunder of its wings was almost as painfully loud as the humming synonymous with its presence. It hovered only seconds. Long enough to drill Caden's mind with a primeval need for vengeance.

He raised an arm to shield his face when a gale-like wind buffeted him. He didn't have to look to know the creature was gone.

Or that Point Pleasant was its target.

Chapter 12

Katie was happy to take a lunchtime break when noon rolled around. She'd snagged a booth at the River Café for her and Sarah. Eve was unable to join them, but Sarah wanted to get together, and Katie agreed it would be nice to chat about something other than the Mothman. For three days, the monster had terrorized the town. It stampeded cows in several farm fields, chased a carload of teenagers on Route 2 more than a mile, and buzzed Warren Gardner in his backyard—or so the stories went. True or not, the reports had everyone on edge, Point Pleasant plagued by the same heightened sense of fear that overshadowed it in the mid-sixties.

Ryan and Caden, along with a number of deputies, had been working double shifts, frightened residents calling if they heard so much as an unusual rustle at night. Duncan and Donnie, having recruited a few followers, still tromped around the igloos hoping to spot the creature, but so far, the cryptid had proven elusive. Duncan was disappointed he hadn't killed it or gained overnight fame, but several reporters had shown up to talk to him. Thrilled by the attention, he and Donnie made the most of the limelight.

Business at the hotel boomed with curiosity seekers arriving daily, requesting directions to the TNT. A few claimed to have experienced their own encounters, but many simply wanted to soak up the atmosphere of Mothman fever. As a result, the café was busier than normal for a Monday. Everyone seemed to be chatting about Point Pleasant's famous "bird." UFOs were forgotten, and Katie hadn't heard of anyone spying a man in black clothing for days. With the exception of one, the mysterious strangers had gone low profile.

Lach Evening strolled into the café from the lobby, halting just inside the door. His black eyes swept the room before pausing on her. A strikingly handsome man, there was something unsettling about him.

Katie glanced at her watch, hoping Sarah would arrive. Lach made her uncomfortable despite being nothing but polite each time they spoke.

"Good afternoon, Ms. Lynch." Evening appeared on the opposite side of the booth, looking woefully out of place in a tailored black suit with crisp white shirt.

Who walked around like that during the day?

"I wonder if I could speak with you?" His voice was almost melodic.

She took a sip of the soda Nancy had brought earlier. "I'm meeting someone."

"It will only take a moment, I assure you." Inviting himself, he slid into the seat across from her. His smile was staged to perfection as he rested one long-fingered hand on the table.

She tried not to stare at his oddly shaped fingertips.

"I'd like to ask you about Lyle Mason," Evening said.

"Like you asked me about my mother fifteen years ago?"

His smile faltered. "I beg your pardon?"

"The night the Silver Bridge fell." She could be wrong, but wouldn't know without pressing. "You were looking for my mother, Doreen Sue Lynch. I was outside of her hair salon and you asked where you could find her."

"I'm afraid you're mistaken. It must have been someone who looked like me."

"I don't think so." She gazed pointedly at his fingertips.

Evening cleared his throat. Withdrawing his hand, he laced his fingers in his lap. "I don't believe I've ever visited Point Pleasant before."

She didn't buy it. "You look the same."

He chuckled. "There, you see? I would have aged a great deal after fifteen years. I do not want to take up your time, Ms. Lynch, only ask you about Lyle Mason. I believe he might try to contact you."

"Ryan told me about him."

The hand reappeared, two fingertips tapping the table. "Ryan?"

"Flynn. From the sheriff's department."

"Oh, yes." Evening looked thoughtful. "Did Sergeant Flynn explain the entire situation?"

"Thoroughly." She'd been shocked to hear it, more to learn of Lyle's claim of encountering the Mothman in the past. In all the time they'd been together, he'd never mentioned anything to her. Knowing her ex, he'd probably invented the tale, hoping to ride a gravy train as far as it would take him. That mentality was in line with the Lyle she knew. "I haven't seen him, Mr. Evening."

"Lach." He inclined his head cordially. "Please."

She ignored the solicitude. "Ryan told you about the van outside of my house?"

"He did."

"That's all I know."

"Very well." He withdrew from the booth, then stood at her side. "If you do encounter Mr. Mason, please contact me the moment you see him. It's imperative I take him back to my facility in Pennsylvania in order to restore his mind. I plan to stay at the hotel for however long is necessary."

She wasn't sure if she should be impressed or bothered by his dedication. He bid her good day, then left through the front entrance, holding the door for Sarah as she hurried inside. Katie's friend beamed her gratitude with a fetching smile, but Lach merely nodded politely and continued on his way. Sarah hurried to the booth and peeled off her coat. She scooted in across from Katie.

"Be still my heart. He held the door for me."

Any man with manners would do the same.

"Lach Evening?" Katie had no idea her friend was so infatuated.

"Who else? I've been trying to find an excuse to talk to him."

How ironic considering Katie wanted nothing of the sort. "Tell him you've seen Lyle, and you won't be able to get rid of him."

"Your ex?" Sarah set her purse aside. "What does he have to do with anything?"

Katie gave her the run down on Lyle, Evening, and the facility Evening supposedly worked for.

"So our distinguished gentleman is some kind of head doctor?" Sarah waved for Nancy, calling out an order for a Coke. "Freaky that he does hypnosis, but consider me under his spell." She wriggled her eyebrows. "Even if he does dress like one of those weird Men in Black, it looks good on him."

Katie sipped soda through a straw. "I think he's one of them."

"He can question me any time he wants. Hey—speaking of questions— did you hear about Suzanne Preech?"

"What about her?" Katie tried to keep pace with the swift change.

"I heard from Jenny at the drugstore she's pregnant."

Katie thought back to the night Suzanne had shown up at the hotel looking for Shawn and the words he'd slurred when she'd walked into the café: *Look who it is. My lovely wife. And mother-to-be.* "I thought she might be. Shawn blurted something when he was in here the other night."

"I don't think she's happy about it."

Nancy arrived with Sarah's soda and asked if they were ready to order. They both settled on grilled cheese sandwiches with tomato soup.

"Suzanne asked me to dig up some old records on Shawn's family," Sarah explained after Nancy had left.

Aside from working in the records division at the courthouse, Sarah counted genealogy among her hobbies.

"Well, Shawn's always bragged his ancestors go back to the time of Fort Randolph." Katie had no such illustrious forebears. As far as she knew, her grandmother had been the first of her family to arrive in Point Pleasant, brought by her husband when she was a young bride of sixteen. By contrast, Shawn claimed his forebears were original settlers, descended through Obadiah Preech, who'd been stationed at the Revolutionary War fort. Maybe Suzanne wanted to determine if Obadiah was real.

"Are you going to help her?"

Sarah nodded. "You know how I like digging around in old documents. Besides, it will be interesting to discover if Shawn's bragging about his ancestry is true. He's not a bad guy, but he likes to ride the celebrity wave."

Dirt track racing.

Maybe Suzanne was unhappy because she worried something might happen to Shawn before the baby was born. Katie knew from experience how hard it was to raise a child on your own. Thank heavens she'd had help from her mom.

They finished lunch by discussing everything from the cute bow pump shoes Sarah had recently bought, to favorite TV shows like *Dallas* and *Simon and Simon,* to the opening of the new Epcot center in Orlando, Florida. Anything and everything but the Mothman. Katie was tired of thinking about the creature, and apparently, Sarah was too. In the good news department, Jerome had been released from the hospital and was resting at home. Katie made a mental note to visit him.

After work, she swung by the grocery store for a few boxed goods and some toiletries. She'd barely gotten home and deposited the groceries on the counter when someone banged on the front door.

"Just a minute." After dropping her purse on the table, she retraced her steps through the living room, then halted with her hand on the doorknob. There were so many strange people lurking around Point Pleasant lately, and according to Lach Evening, Lyle might be stalking her.

"Katie." It was him.

Another thud on the door as if he'd rolled up his fist and was battering it against the wood. How dare he try to threaten or frighten her? If he was the creep who'd been parked on the street, she'd put an end to his spying right now. She wouldn't subject Sam to potential tirades from a man who'd disowned him before he'd been born.

Furious, she wrenched open the door. "What do you want?"

Lyle stood on the stoop, looking momentarily confused. He blinked rapidly, then shoved past her, forcing his way inside. "Is he here? I want to know where he's hiding."

"Who?" She whirled to confront him, anger rising like a vice around her neck. He had no right to invade her home. "If you're talking about Sam—"

"Your kid?" Lyle shook his head as if trying to clear a fog. He hadn't changed much over the last twelve months, still lean and rugged looking with shoulder-length brown hair and a mustache. He'd always been a little stoop-shouldered, his gait like a flat-footed bird when he walked. "I'm looking for Flynn. I heard you're with him."

Ryan? Had he lost his head? "What are you talking about?"

"I want to settle things once and for all." He gripped her arm above the elbow, pressing hard. "Tell me where he is."

A sliver of fear twined with the anger in her blood. He'd never raised a hand against her, but he'd done his share of cussing and tossing verbal threats. "It's none of your business who I see."

Lyle barked with laughter. "You think I care who crawls between the sheets with you? Hell, woman, I don't give a flying fuck. But that bastard is going to pay for what he did."

He wasn't making sense. Lach Evening said his mind was messed up, and these insane ramblings were proof. "Look, Lyle, you need to leave." She tried to pull away, but he held fast. "There's a man in town who's looking for you. You need to talk to Lach Evening."

He recoiled as if she'd said something repugnant. Tromping backward, he ripped a hand through his hair. "I'm not going anywhere. Flynn took her from me. Nothing to change that." He mumbled the words, a flurry of nonsense tumbling out in an eerily repetitive string. "Told her he was no good...out of her league...should have listened to me...not going anywhere...took her from me..."

Gooseflesh pimpled her arms.

Katie backed toward the door. Lyle babbled, pacing off tighter and tighter circles. Another few inches and she would be free. She'd left her car keys on the table with her purse, but she was a fast runner. Had always been faster than him.

Spurred by a burst of panic, she sprinted through the front door and onto the lawn. Never slowing to see if he followed, she raced for the street. She'd reached the end of her driveway when she spied a battered white T-bird across the road. In the second it took for her to register the vehicle, Lyle caught her. Grasping her firmly on the arm, he wrenched her around to face him.

"Don't think this is over." He shook her hard, his gaze feverish in the glare of the sun. "Tell your boyfriend I'm going to even the score. Tell him he shouldn't have treated her like he did."

Fear bubbled up in her throat. "Lyle—"

Grunting something unintelligible, he shoved her to the ground.

She scrambled to her hands and knees, ignoring the sting in her palms. "Lyle!"

Ignoring her, he bolted for the T-bird. Seconds later, the battered car disappeared down the street, its exhaust coughing black smoke.

A Thunderbird, not a van. He wasn't the one who'd been staking out her house, but he was after Ryan. She raced inside for the phone, never bothering to close the door. Quickly, she dialed the sheriff's office.

"I'm sorry, Ms. Lynch," the deputy who answered told her. "Sergeant Flynn is out right now."

Her stomach plummeted. "What about Caden?"

"He's out too. Do you want me to have Ryan call you when he gets back?"

"Yes, please." She clutched the phone cord tightly in her hand, trying to still the erratic beat of her heart. "Tell him it's urgent."

"I'll radio him for you."

She breathed a sigh of relief. "Thank you."

After hanging up, she tented both hands over her mouth and counted to ten, breathing deeply. He would call soon. He had to call.

"Excuse me." A man said behind her.

She whirled to find Lach Evening standing in the open doorway.

"Forgive me for intruding, but I noticed the door was open."

"Why are you here?" The question came out far blunter than she'd intended. Her nerves were shot and her heart danced a chaotic rhythm. The man annoyed her, too proper and calm, as if he'd simply been out for an afternoon stroll.

"I was hoping to learn more about Lyle."

"Such as he's driving a white Thunderbird and left here under five minutes ago?" Her voice dripped acid as she strode toward him, hands on her hips.

Evening appeared taken aback. "Did you get a license plate number?"

"No, I didn't." She practically screamed in his face. "He was out of control, talking like a mad man."

"I'm sorry. He came to hurt you."

"No. You have it all wrong." She shook her head empathically, exasperated the man who'd caused Lyle's meltdown was clueless as to his real intent. "He wasn't looking for me. He's after Ryan."

"Sergeant Flynn?" Evening's brows pinched together. "I don't understand."

"I don't, either, but he seems to think Ryan did something to him. He kept talking about a girl." She wet her lips, her mind doing cartwheels as she sorted the possibilities. "Maybe someone Ryan dated in the past." While she doubted Lyle posed any true threat to an experienced lawman like Ryan, she couldn't help worrying her ex was capable of doing something crazy. All it took was a moment of surprise with a gun or a knife to tip the balance in Lyle's favor.

"Very well, Ms. Lynch. I'm sorry if the situation has distressed you in any way." Evening stepped onto the front porch.

"*Distressed* me?" She followed and watched as he walked down the driveway to a sleek black car. "You need to find Lyle and *fix* whatever you did to him." She jabbed a finger at his back. "Whether it's me or someone else, Lyle was acting crazy."

"I'm well aware of that. Good day, Ms. Lynch." Evening ducked into the car and closed the door.

Flabbergasted, she watched the vehicle back out of the drive and wind down the road. Her frustration melted into relief when the phone rang. Praying it was Ryan, she raced into the house.

* * * *

"Katie, I don't know what he's talking about." Ryan listened as his new girlfriend spilled a confusing tale about Lyle Mason over the phone. "I barely even bumped elbows with the guy before he left town."

He turned his back on a squabble happening behind him. After three days of Mothman terror, sightings had started to dwindle. But that didn't stop residents from inundating the sheriff's office, demanding to know what steps were being taken to assure the winged cryptid didn't return. At present, Wayne Rosling was getting an earful from a thick-waisted man waving a map of the TNT under his nose.

Ryan clamped a hand over his ear to block the noise. "Are you sure Mason is gone?" Despite the sheriff's office and local Point Pleasant police being on the lookout for Mason's van, nothing had surfaced. Not surprising, given he'd just learned Mason was driving a T-bird. Nothing like a false trail to stall in a dead end. Worse, it meant someone else had been staking out Katie's house. Maybe Jerome had spilled his guts to the mysterious Deputy Brown while under hypnosis and relayed how he'd passed along Parker's coded message. The jumble of numbers seemed to be the brass ring everyone wanted. "I think you should go stay with your mom for a few days."

Several seconds of tense silence passed before she unloaded her frustration. "I am *not* going to let that creep force me out of my house."

"Listen, Katie, it isn't just Lyle I'm worried about. If he showed up in a T-bird, it means someone else was in the van. They could be connected to Parker and Jerome. We don't know who we're dealing with, or what measures they might take to get the message."

A pause. "I've considered that." Grudging acknowledgement indicated a step in the right direction.

"I'm glad you're thinking clearly. The van aside, Lyle is a loose cannon. Now that we know he's in town for sure, he'll probably hook up with his cousin. I'll check with Darrell and see what I can find out."

"Aren't you the least bit concerned Lyle threatened you?" Katie's voice rose in disbelief. "There must have been someone you dated in the past who—"

"Katie."

"I don't care who you saw before me." Her words came quickly now. "I don't want him blindsiding you. If you'd seen him, heard him... I can see why Lach Evening said he's messed up in the head. He came here looking for you because he heard we're together."

"Which is why he could return again." Ryan clenched his jaw, frustrated by his limitations. "Stay with your mom for a few days, Katie. I'm sure Sam misses you too. You can keep an eye on them." He didn't add in the event Lyle decided to snoop around Doreen Sue's place, but it was a fair possibility. He'd see what he could do about sending a patrol that way.

After a few more minutes of coercion, she finally agreed, and he hung up the phone. Ryan blew out a breath. The man who'd been complaining to Rosling had left, but the older deputy looked no less harried for the grumbler's departure. Standing, he shook his head and randomly stacked files on his desk.

"What was that all about?" Ryan pushed from his chair and walked closer.

"Ready for this one?" Rosling picked up several loose sheets of paper and added them to the stack. "The guy drove here overnight from some place in Delaware because he'd heard the Mothman was back. Spent all day in the TNT but didn't catch so much as a glimmer of that winged freak. He complained because he thinks we scared it away. While most everyone in the county is telling us to get rid of the thing, this idiot is ticked because we might have done the job."

"Sounds like he'd be a good match for Duncan and Donnie." Ryan grinned." Hey, I'm headed out. I'm going to go pay Darrell Mason a visit. Looks like Lyle finally surfaced." He gave Rosling a rundown of his phone call with Katie. "When Weston gets back, can you bring him up to speed?"

"Will do." Rosling gave him a thumbs-up. "Sure beats getting my butt chewed out for keeping the public safe."

* * * *

Ryan caught up with Darrell as he was getting home from work, but the visit turned into a dead end. Darrell insisted he hadn't heard from his cousin, although he'd had several people tell him they'd seen Lyle around town. A co-worker thought they'd seen him driving an old white T-bird, which supported Katie's description. And while that helped target Lyle, the information did nothing to narrow down the owner of a dark green van, or why the driver would be stalking Katie. More and more, Ryan found himself thinking of the coded message Jerome passed to her. If there really was some shadow organization intent on recovering the code, Ryan had to find a way of turning that attention from Katie.

After ending his shift at five, he headed to the Parrish Hotel, hoping to catch Lach Evening. As luck would have it, the impeccably dressed man occupied a rocker on the front porch. Most would have considered it too cold to linger outdoors, but Evening didn't appear to mind. He wore an overcoat and his black fedora, but the coat was open and he hadn't bothered with gloves.

Probably wouldn't be able to find any to fit.

Ryan considered offering a "good evening" as he stepped onto the porch but the greeting seemed too much of a pun, and far from true. "I was hoping I'd catch you here." Turning his back to the street, he braced a hip against the railing. He had no idea how long the man had been sitting there, but his skin showed no signs of reddening due to the brisk weather. He seemed comfortably content, one leg draped over the other, his hands resting on the broad arms of the rocking chair.

"I gather this isn't a social visit." Evening's gaze remained on the street, the look on his face like a cat intently waiting for a mouse to appear.

A ragged scarecrow slouched in the chair beside him, a Halloween caricature out of place beside Evening's crisp attire. Or maybe it was the other way around. Sitting among cornstalks and pumpkins, the man in black might have easily passed for a fairy-tale king.

"Katie told me what happened today with Lyle." Ryan crossed his arms over his chest.

"I expected as much. Mr. Mason seems to have fixated on you."

"I have no idea why."

Evening's lips curled faintly. "Perhaps because of your attachment to his ex. Word has a way of getting around, Sergeant Flynn." He tapped one bubble-tipped finger against the rocker. "Remember that Lyle is living in the past."

Head-shrink double talk. "And that's important, because?"

Dark eyes flashed to Ryan's face. "Because in the past, he and Ms. Lynch were a couple. You have intruded upon that memory."

Ryan grunted and looked down the street. More psychological bullshit. "So why are you sitting here instead of trying to round him up?"

Two cars drove past, their headlights bright yellow in the murky gray of twilight. Three doors to the right, the owner of the drycleaner removed his Open sign and closed up shop. Point Pleasant was winding down for the night.

"I'm observing." Evening looked back to the road. "The more time that passes, the more likely Mr. Mason will surface. It's been several days since he left Pennsylvania."

Several days and still nothing. Lyle's memory might be short-circuited, but he'd grown adept at keeping a low profile. It was even possible he'd stocked his car with supplies and was living out of the vehicle. If that were the case, he could be holed up in the TNT. With all the patrols and circus of Mothman hunters scouring the area, it was odd someone hadn't spotted him, but he'd grown up here and knew the region well. The guy was proving every bit as elusive as the damn cryptid.

"You appear frustrated, Sergeant." Evening's tone was wry.

Smart ass. "I wish you knew why the hell Mason came back here in the first place. Saying he's ticked about something doesn't cut it."

"Perhaps you need to figure it out. Mr. Mason grew up in Point Pleasant, not Austin. He has history here."

That damn accent. It made Evening come across as superior. It was also maddeningly hard to place, as if the inflection was the offshoot of more than one dialect. He had a point about Mason, but the guy had been a loner with only a smattering of friends, and a handful of girls after Katie, none of whom Ryan knew. He could ask around and try to pinpoint connections to Lyle's past, but the whole thing felt like a crapshoot. It didn't make sense Katie was the catalyst of Lyle's rage, given their relationship ended before Sam was born.

"The people of this town are more likely to remember something unsettling in Mr. Mason's past than I am," Evening continued as if Ryan was too dense to make the connection.

"Point taken." The admission came grudgingly, Ryan's voice nearly as biting as the air. Evening might not be bothered by the cold, but Ryan had reached the end of his tolerance for standing outside. Time to wrap the conversation. "You're not from Pennsylvania."

"That much should be obvious." Evening stood, unwinding with the smooth agility of a cat. Before Ryan could press the issue, Evening tipped his hat in an antiquated parting gesture. "I believe I'm through observing. Good day, Sergeant."

Rather than head indoors, he preceded down the street—a tall man in a long black coat, as out of sync with the decade as he was with Point Pleasant. Ryan scowled after him, feeling something had slipped through his grasp. Something important he'd overlooked in their conversation.

Jamming his hands into his pockets, he headed in the opposite direction.

* * * *

It was nearing eleven-thirty at night when Doreen Sue walked into her living room to find Katie sitting on the couch, absorbed in a paperback. Nestled into the corner of the sofa, her daughter was dressed in comfortable-looking blue sweat pants, a dark blue pullover, and heavy pink robe. Legs curled to the side, she sat with one elbow propped on the armrest as she pored over the book.

"I thought you'd be in bed by now."

"What?" Katie flinched at her abrupt presence, placing a hand over her heart. She'd clearly been engrossed in reading to the point of tuning out her surroundings.

"Sorry. I didn't mean to scare you." Doreen Sue switched on a lamp by the front window. "How can you see with just one light?"

"I'm fine." Katie wedged a finger between the pages to mark her place. "Did you have a nice time with Martin?"

"Wonderful." Doreen Sue plopped her purse onto a chair, then peeled off her jacket. It was nice of her daughter to ask. Katie hadn't liked most of the men she'd dated, but she appeared genuinely fond of Martin. "We went for dinner, then headed back to his place so I could visit with Rex. I took him a nice new chew toy. He seems like his old self."

"That's what Sam said too."

Doreen Sue plopped into a chair across from her daughter. "I guess Sam's in bed. Is he sleeping okay?" She was glad to have Katie and her grandson as houseguests for a few days, but the reason for their stay troubled her. If Katie hadn't agreed to come of her own free will, Doreen Sue would have put her foot down and insisted they get out of the house. The sooner Ryan

Flynn and the sheriff's department rounded up Lyle Mason the better. "I worry about him having nightmares."

Katie hugged the paperback to her chest. "That's part of it, isn't it?"

"What?"

"Nightmares. It says so in here." Katie tapped the book.

Doreen Sue had seen her with the pulp piece before, a study of UFO sightings that had belonged to Jerome. She'd also noted all the handwritten notes in the margins. More than a casual observer of the unexplained, Jerome appeared obsessed with anything mysterious.

Shifting her feet to the floor, Katie leaned forward, elbows on her knees. "Did I have bad dreams too? After that night coming home from Ravenswood?"

"Oh, dear." Doreen Sue tucked a strand of hair behind her ear. Back to that again. "Yes, you had nightmares. But they went beyond dreams. You would see things in your room. Imagine a presence looming over you."

Katie's knuckles turned white as she tightened her grip on the book. "Sam thought the same thing…that there was a man in his room."

"It's just the confusion of his mind." Doreen Sue wasn't an expert, but she'd read up on the subject. She'd even sought out mediums and psychics after Ravenswood, hoping they could make sense of her encounter. "He saw something he can't explain, and his mind is processing it the only way he knows how. Turning all that mess into nightmares. They'll pass."

Katie's expression softened with relief. "They seem to be already." Hesitating, she wet her lips. "At the hospital, you said Wendy and I had pinkeye as kids. You made it sound like I should remember. Because of that night?"

Doreen Sue nodded. "Wendy's was just the routine stuff all kids get, but yours started that night and lasted for three days. I had it, too, but not as bad." She chuckled softly. "It was awful having to go without makeup."

Katie laughed. "That must have been traumatic for you."

"And bad for business. I wouldn't go near the salon. Wanda had to take all my customers." The sliver of humor faded as an ugly thought robbed its place. "A few people didn't think I was sick…told Wanda I was sleeping off a hangover."

Katie recoiled, glancing away. "Those weren't the best times."

"No." Maybe she'd flubbed talking about the past, but Katie's unsettled childhood had always been the elephant in the room. "You used to call me 'Mama' when you were little." What she wouldn't give to hear that name again. Just once. To know that beneath Katie's cool, unemotional exterior lingered a daughter who still needed her.

"That was a long time ago." Katie's words were crisp, her demeanor every bit as bristling. She stood, gathering her robe close. "I think I'll go to bed now."

Of course. Running, shutting down any avenue that might pry awake a measure of vulnerability. When had she become so self-sufficient, walled in a corner others couldn't reach?

Unwilling to cave so easily, Doreen Sue ignored the comment. "You and Wendy used to talk a blue streak."

"That was Wendy. She understood me." Katie's gaze was flat.

"And I don't?" Doreen Sue rose to her feet. The elephant grew bigger, pushing between them. "I know I wasn't the best mama, but I tried for both you girls. I could have done better. I know that, but are you going to resent me forever?"

Katie's eyes widened in surprise. "Resent you? How could you—where would you get such a horrid idea?"

Had she been wrong? "You disapprove of me. Always have."

"No." Closing her eyes, Katie pressed three fingertips to her forehead. Drawing a deep breath, she exhaled slowly as if curbing an impulsive reaction. "I disapproved of your lifestyle when you were running around with Amos or guys like him. What daughter wants to see her mother with a black eye?"

Doreen Sue blanched, shamed by the ugly memory. She wasn't sure what she'd ever seen in Amos Carter or why she'd stayed with him after he slapped her and cheated on her. Even when he'd died, she bawled like a woman who'd lost a spouse of twenty years. They'd been together less than two. She had no one to blame but herself. Her taste in men had never been good. Even the girls' father had left when Katie was two. Thank Heaven for Martin Ward, who treated her like gold and asked nothing in return.

"I made mistakes." It wasn't simply an admission, but a nasty reality that cut deep. "You think I don't know why Wendy wanted to run away? Why she got involved with a creep like Roger Layton?" She blinked hard, fighting the sting of tears. "Every time I think of her dead at the hands of that horrible man, I've got no one to blame but me. If I'd been a better mother, she wouldn't have run wild." Tears spilled down her cheeks. She had always been at fault. Her baby, strangled and tossed into an unmarked grave after that bastard had used her for pleasure. Unable to bear the shame, she covered her face with her hands and crumpled into the chair. "She'd still be alive if it weren't for me."

"No, Mom. Wendy had a wildness in her, but it didn't come from you."

A hesitant touch settled on Doreen Sue's shoulder as Katie crouched next to her. "Her recklessness came from Daddy, not you."

Doreen Sue raised her head searching for hope through a watery gaze. "How can you be so sure?"

"Because Wendy told me. I don't remember Daddy, but she did. She said she was exactly like him. I didn't understand it then, but she had a self-destructive streak. As much as I loved her, Wendy created her own grief. She knew better than to get involved with Roger. He was married and twice her age. That's probably what attracted her to him in the first place. The element of danger and something forbidden."

Doreen Sue sniffled. She'd never talked to her daughter like this before, her insecurities and emotions bare. Maybe that's what had kept Katie's walls in place all these years. Not an unwillingness to share, but a craving to be needed in return. "How did you ever get so smart?"

Katie smiled tenderly. "Don't you remember? I always had my nose in a book. At least that's what you used to say. 'Kathryn Eloise, what book do you have your nose buried in now?'"

It was her turn to smile. Wendy had loved makeup and clothes, Katie books. "You were the serious one."

"I used to think you disapproved. As much as you and Wendy fought, I used to think you wanted me to be like her. You doted on her."

"Oh, honey, you don't understand." An imaginary fist pummeled Doreen Sue's stomach. Half sick, she rooted through her purse for a tissue. "I never wanted to give that impression." She'd loved both her girls, but there'd never been a question Wendy was headed for trouble from a young age. "If I fussed over Wendy more, it was because she needed someone to keep her in line. You were so self-sufficient and focused. I always knew you'd turn into a woman I could be proud of, but I worried Wendy would end up like—" She bit off the word, unable to admit the truth.

"Who?" Katie pressed.

Bowing her head, Doreen Sue worked the tissue between her hands. "Like me."

"Don't say that. Don't even think it." Katie touched her cheek, drawing her head up. "You have so much to be proud of. You kept us going after Daddy walked out. You run your own business and have kept it solvent all these years. You helped me when Sam was born and made it possible for me to keep my son when I barely had two dimes to rub together. You still help me. Every day. You are the most unselfish person I know."

Fresh tears flooded Doreen Sue's eyes. "You never said anything like that before."

Katie squeezed her shoulder. "I should have. It's long overdue."

Doreen Sue smiled a watery smile, her heart wedged in her throat. For all its emotional upheaval, the night had been good to her. First a wonderful evening with Martin, now a heart-to-heart with her daughter. There was only one thing that would make it better. "Sometimes at night, I pray Wendy's forgiven me. Do you think she hates me?"

"No, Mama." Katie dropped to her knees and hugged her close. "I think she loves you. Just like I do."

Chapter 13

Ryan was at home the following morning when he got a call from Pete Weston. He'd just finished polishing off a ham and cheese omelet with a side of bacon when the sheriff phoned.

"Thought I'd save you a trip in...another out." The line crackled with static. "...called."

"I missed that." Ryan stretched the phone cord toward the kitchen sink, setting his empty plate on the bottom. Behind him at the table, his mother listened to the morning news on a local AM radio station. "We've got a bad connection."

"Yeah. Happening...over town." Another burst of white noise. "Darrell Mason called...go see..."

"Mason?"

Weston said something Ryan couldn't understand. Just his luck the phone lines would act up when Mason was involved. "Pete, I'm going drive out to Darrell's place before I head in."

More static. "Thought you...like a plan."

Whatever Weston said was lost in a jumble of mechanical interference. Assuming he'd been given the green light, Ryan hung up and swallowed the last of his coffee.

"I'm heading out, Mom."

"I thought you would." His mother glanced up from her plate of scrambled eggs with grits. The morning update had ended, the radio spitting out an old Glenn Miller tune. "I heard on the news there's a problem with the phones." She slathered butter on a piece of rye toast.

"Yeah. That was Pete." Ryan rinsed his cup at the sink. "We had a bad connection."

"The report said lines were down most of the night." Strawberry jam followed the butter. "People are blaming it on interference from UFOs. Apparently, there were a lot of lights spotted near the TNT last night."

"Probably low-flying planes." He was too focused on Darrell Mason to worry about green men in silver saucers. Bending, he kissed her cheek, catching the familiar scent of lavender bath soap and rose water. "Gotta run."

"Be careful, dear. And tell Caden and Eve we're due for a family dinner soon."

"Will do."

Outside, he dropped behind the wheel of his Camaro and cranked the ignition. The drive to Mason's trailer off Route 2 took no more than ten minutes. Darrell owned a double-wide with a flat roof, brown siding, and white skirting. An ornamental lamppost surrounded by red mums stood sentry in the yard, and a few brick steps led to a forest green door.

Ryan parked in a pull-off area, then sprinted up the steps and rang the bell. The ding set off a round of exuberant barking from a large dog.

"Quiet, Bailey." Darrell shushed the animal. Seconds later, he answered the door, his hand hooked through the animal's collar.

"Morning, Darrell." Ryan had been to the trailer before and knew Bailey, a boxer/lab mix, was friendly but vocal. He offered his hand for the dog to sniff. "I heard you called the sheriff's office."

"Yeah. Come on in." Darrell held the door with one hand as Ryan stepped inside. "You said to get in touch if I heard from Lyle."

"That's right." He tempered his restlessness as Bailey trotted over to greet him. Bending, he scratched the dog around the collar, then gave it a pat on the side. It snuffled around his feet, tail thumping against his leg in a welcoming back-and-forth wag. "Have you seen him?"

"Last night." Darrell had the same brown hair as his cousin, but his eyes were blue instead of hazel, his nose prominently hooked. He wasn't nearly as tall as Lyle or as broad-shouldered. Absently, he clicked his thumbnail against his teeth. It was a habit Ryan remembered well, having gone through twelve years of school with him.

"Want some coffee or something?" Darrell motioned to the kitchen. The front of the trailer was one big room with a living area and kitchen divided by a breakfast bar. Except for a rawhide chew bone on the floor by the TV, and an open newspaper on the couch, the place was whistle-clean. Darrell had always been a neat freak.

"No thanks." All Ryan cared about were the details concerning Lyle. "Just tell me about your cousin."

Darrell pulled out a stool from the breakfast bar and sat down. Behind him, a Mr. Coffee dripped dark brown liquid into a clear pot. The place smelled of Columbian beans and Pine-Sol. "He was here last night. Didn't stay long."

How many hours had they lost before Darrell got around to reporting the incident? "You should have called."

"I tried. A bunch of times." Darrell spread his hands and shrugged. "Phones haven't worked all night. Just got passable this morning. I heard most of the town was on the fritz."

"Yeah, all right." He'd forgotten about the stupid phones. "What did Lyle say and where did he go?"

"I don't know where he went." Darrell turned his head, watching as Bailey flopped down by his chew toy. The dog wedged the bone between his front paws and set to work, gnawing on the end. "Lyle was wired, acting bizarre. He stayed long enough to wolf down a meal and bum some cash. I told him I was short on funds, but could tell he didn't buy it. I was worried he might go ape on me, so I gave him a few tens. He kept talking about getting even."

"With me, right?" Aside from the money and the meal, Darrell's account was similar to Katie's

"Heck no. Where'd you get that idea?"

Ryan balked, caught off guard. "From Katie Lynch. He confronted her because he heard we're together."

"No, you got it all wrong." Darrell shook his head like a dog casting off fleas. "Lyle thinks *Caden* is with Katie. It's your brother he wants to get even with."

"Huh?" Ryan stepped back as if physically slapped. All the ideas he'd tucked into a tidy package flopped belly upright. "What's his beef with Caden?"

"Don't know. All I could figure is that it's got something to do with a girl they knew in high school."

Great. His brother had dated a lot of girls. Trying to pin down one that Lyle liked was going to be a lost cause. It didn't make sense the guy would hold a grudge over something for so long. "Where'd he go?"

Darrell worked his bony shoulders into a shrug. "Didn't say. He's pretty much living out of his car, an old white T-bird. I never thought he'd part with his Bronco, but he said it bit the dust in Pennsylvania."

Pennsylvania.

Something Lach Evening said clicked abruptly into place. A vital piece of information Ryan had overlooked from their discussion the previous night.

Mr. Mason grew up here, not in Austin.

Austin, Pennsylvania was the postmark on the envelope Caden had received nearly two weeks ago. Ryan should have caught the comment immediately. The note inside had been cryptic, referencing a girl. Apparently *the* girl for Lyle. Hell, the guy really was unhinged.

With the phone lines down, he wasn't going to be able to warn his brother by dialing. "All right, tell me everything Lyle said. It might not make sense to you or me, but it could trigger something for Caden."

He stayed another five minutes, jotting notes. Lyle had rambled on about "Flynn" and his need to right a wrong from the past. He mentioned a girl several times, but no name. Only that Flynn had taken her from him and had to pay. Darrell had gotten his plate number when he burned rubber out of the drive, one small victory for Ryan to add to an APB.

If Lyle figured out his mistake—that Caden wasn't with Katie—he might try to track him down at home. That could potentially place Eve in danger, or even Ryan and Caden's mother.

Maybe there was more in his yearbook than Caden thought.

Thanking Darrell for his time, Ryan returned to his car, then headed for town.

* * * *

The phones were still wonky by the time Ryan reached the sheriff's office. Joy and another clerk traded rumors about odd lights at the TNT, a few of the glowing objects supposedly spotted in the early dawn hours. The spacemen no longer limited their travel to nighttime. There'd been another sighting of the Mothman, too, but the report turned out to be a teenage prank.

Ryan stopped by Pete's office and gave him an update on the news he'd gotten from Darrell, including the plate number of Lyle's Thunderbird. Weston ordered him to share all relevant information with Lach Evening, confirming the guy's story, though sketchy, appeared to check out. Ryan mumbled an agreement but was more concerned with tracing Caden's connection to Lyle. Returning to the main office area, Ryan grabbed a cup of coffee, then stationed himself at Caden's desk. Intent on one item only, he fished through the drawers, locating what he sought in the bottom right.

"Bingo!" His brother hadn't bothered to take his high school yearbook home. Right now the old tome could prove a goldmine. Before, Ryan had been interested in photos, now all he cared about were autographs. Odds were the girl who'd meant so much to Lyle had probably penned a love note inside Caden's yearbook.

Moving back to his own desk, Ryan settled down for a trip into the past. Most of the messages were filled with the elation of graduating. Exclamations like *"we made it," "I want a copy of your first gold record,"* or *"time to party hardy and pig out"* were common. A couple referenced Vietnam, peace protests, or the assassination of Martin Luther King, Jr. Sadly, Bobby Kennedy would be dead two days after Caden's graduation. Ryan still remembered seeing news footage, glued to the television like everyone else in the country, hoping and praying the senator would pull through. It had been a dreadful time. Even at thirteen, he'd felt the horror of the tragedy.

Shoving the distressing memories aside, he kept reading.

Comments from close friends filled the pages of Caden's yearbook, along with lengthy notes from plenty of girls. The girls gushed about Caden's music and his "dreamy" singing voice, adorning their signatures with smiley faces, peace signs, and hearts.

Ryan paid most attention to the hearts. The first one was from someone named Becky:

I'll never forget that night at the Fairgrounds when you sang "Nowhere Man." I felt like you were singing just for me, trying to tell me something. We had good times and bad times, but I'll never forget any of them. Even when I'm old and gray, I'll keep you in my heart.

As if to prove the point, she signed her message with two intertwined hearts.

Ryan jotted her name on a tablet.

He flipped the page and found a message from Charlotte. The bad thing about yearbooks was that no one bothered writing last names, assuming they would live forever in your memory.

I hope you never forget me, even if you move away and become famous with your music (I know you will!). Smiley face. *I'll never forget you or how much fun we had at Homecoming. I know Maggie will be smiling down on you when they hand out diplomas. I miss her, too, but I miss the "old" Caden more (don't be angry I said that). Love you always.* Two hearts with a string of xoxo's.

Ryan remembered Charlotte, last name Wills, or something similar. She and Caden had been exclusive in the fall of '67, but when the bridge fell their relationship crumbled in the aftermath. Caden had cut himself off from a lot of people when Maggie died, and Charlotte had been one of them. From what Ryan could remember, she'd left for college and never bothered coming back. It was unlikely she'd been the object of Lyle's love struck adoration, but he jotted her name on the tablet, anyway.

The names of a few other girls followed. He was in the midst of reading a sappy message from Marian when someone loomed over his shoulder.

"What do you think you're doing?"

Ryan glanced up with a guilty start to find his brother hovering over him. "Uh…reading about your love life?" He tagged the question with an innocent grin.

"Those are private." Caden took the book and flipped it closed with one hand. Dropping it on his desk, he sat in his chair, facing Ryan. "I thought you'd already snooped through everything of interest. Without my permission." The last three words carried a sting.

Ryan shrugged aside the rebuke. "Don't get your feathers ruffled. When you hear what I have to say, you're going to be re-reading that sappy shit yourself."

"What does that mean?"

Ryan relayed his visit with Darrell, then pointedly folded his arms across his chest. "Now what do you think?"

Caden scowled. "That it doesn't make a scrap of sense." He flipped open the yearbook, staring down at the scribbled passages decorating the pages. "Lyle and I didn't run in the same crowd. He's got no reason to hold a grudge against me."

"He does if you were hot and heavy with a girl he liked." Ryan tossed him the tablet. He'd written eight names and had been ready to add Marian's. "Any of those a possibility?"

Caden gave them a quick glance. "No."

"Why so sure?"

"Because they just aren't. I wasn't serious with any of them."

"Which means you broke a few hearts. What about Marian?"

"Who?"

Ryan made a tsking sound. "I don't think she'd like your answer given she wrote two whole paragraphs about the Saturday night you spent by the river."

"Jackass." Caden ripped the paper from the tablet. "Marian Dosler." He wadded the sheet into a ball and shot it at Ryan. His brother dodged, then picked it up from the floor with a grin.

"We went out three or four times." Caden closed the yearbook and shoved it to the center of the desk. "That was it."

"Well, somehow, some way, you made an enemy of Lyle."

"Fine." Caden batted the observation aside. "We've got enough on our plate with the Mothman and UFOs. Katie's safe at her mom's place, so Lyle can take a backseat. If he's got a grudge, I'll be happy to hammer it out when I run into him."

"What about Eve and Mom? He might look for you at either place."

"He thinks I'm with Katie, so he doesn't know about Eve. I'll put Mom on alert to be on the safe side. You're there most of the time, anyway." He paused a beat. "I guess you heard about the phones?"

"Yeah." Ryan picked up his handset and listened for a second before returning the receiver to its cradle. "Still static-y. Popular opinion blames our returning spacemen. I heard they were busy at the TNT again."

Caden nodded thoughtfully. "Out-of-towners are starting to camp out on Conway Road, waiting for fly-bys. I heard a guy say you could set your watch by them."

"I wonder what he was smoking."

"It gets better." Caden gave a grim smile. "I stopped at the gas station on the way in and ran into Shawn Preech getting a fill up. He said he saw three red lights pass over his house last night. Within two hours, a guy dressed in black showed up at the door and told him he should forget what he'd seen."

Ryan grunted. "I bet that went over well. Knowing Shawn, he'll be telling everyone from here to Gallipolis what happened for sheer spite." The Men in Black hadn't been as visible lately, but still made occasional appearances according to town gossip. A few had given names when pressed—Smith, Jones, Williams—common surnames coupled with hastily produced credentials witnesses were never allowed to view for long. "Did Shawn get anything out of the guy? Figure out who he was?"

Caden shook his head. "Probably a friend of Evening's." His expression soured at the mention of the blond-haired man. "Speaking of him, think we should bring him up to speed with the latest news on Lyle?"

"Pete's orders."

"Yeah, I'm just soured on the whole deal. I'd bet money there's something that guy isn't telling us."

"You're right. I almost forgot." Ryan cursed himself for overlooking one of the most important pieces of information he'd discovered that morning. "Do you still have that envelope from Austin?"

"Yeah." Caden opened his center desk drawer. "Why?"

"Because the last time I talked to Evening, he let it slip that Lyle had been in Austin. I think that's where Evening's facility is. It all fits. That message you got in the mail had to be from Lyle. He must have sent it while he was still there. After he had the flicker episode, or whatever the hell Evening called it."

Caden located the envelope and removed the note.

"Anything?" Given recent discoveries, Ryan hoped there would be some clue Caden could decipherer from the terse message.

"I remember her. You should too." Caden read the words aloud, then tossed the envelope and note to Ryan. "That means absolutely nothing to me."

"Don't be so quick." Ryan glanced down at the note. Plain paper, nothing really distinctive about the handwriting. They could dust it for prints to cement Lyle as the sender, but the envelope had been through postage, and both he and Caden had handled the letter. Even without prints there was little doubt Lyle was the author. Circumstantial or not, too much added up. "Think about it, Caden. Whoever this girl is, he has a feeling you've forgotten her."

"Ryan, I'd forgotten Marian until you mentioned her. There are a lot of people I went to school with I've probably forgotten. It's not like I make a habit of thinking about high school every day."

"No, but a lot of those people still live here, and if you ran into them, you'd know them. You'd remember." Once again the nagging sense he'd overlooked something rose to haunt him. "He seems to think you won't remember *her.* Why? What makes her different than everyone else?"

Exhaling, Caden dragged a hand over his face. "I don't know. If I come up with anything, you'll be the first person I tell."

"You're not taking this seriously."

"As seriously as I can. I've got other things on my mind."

"Like what?"

Caden was quiet for a moment, idly bouncing a thumb against his desk. He looked right, then left, as if judging who was within earshot. Lowering his voice, he leaned forward. "Halloween is less than a week from now."

Ryan was still hung-up on the note. "And?"

"Jerome's code." Caden raised an eyebrow. "The thirty-first of October. Remember?"

He did now. According to Parker Kline, Indrid Cold was supposed to visit Earth at some time after eleven in the evening. "What are you going to do? Drive around the TNT and look for some alien named Cold on Halloween?"

"I'm thinking about it."

"Be serious."

"I am."

"Caden—"

"Listen to me." His brother's voice was sharp and gruff. "I'm not saying I buy into all the extraterrestrial bullshit, but Parker did. He's still out there. It's anyone's guess how he's surviving, because he's not capable of functioning on his own for long."

"Floyd's got to be helping him." It was the only thing that made sense. "He has to know where Parker is."

"Maybe, but Pete's had deputies watching Floyd since Parker escaped, and the guy hasn't gone anywhere."

"So you're going to scout out the TNT on Halloween hoping to come across Parker?" The idea was mind-boggling. It would be easier finding a needle in a haystack.

"I owe him that much. I put him in West Central."

"He put himself there. He shot Hank point blank."

Caden winced. "I know that. But I can't ignore the chance of catching up with Parker."

"Uh-huh." Ryan pursed his lips, realizing nothing he said would make a difference. "You do know the TNT is thirty-six hundred acres of wilderness? *If* I believed Parker's code and *if* I thought there was a chance in hell of finding him, you're still missing the location. Parker's code was down to the second. Yeah, he might be wandering around out there afterward or even before, but if you're not at the exact place at the exact time, he could be gone."

"I've got that covered." Caden leaned back in his chair, shutting down the conversation. "I know where he'll be."

"Where?"

"I'd rather not say. This is something I need to do on my own."

Ryan scowled. "Want to explain why?"

"No." A tight answer followed by an equally tight grin. "Rank aside, I've still got older brother privilege." Yanking open the top desk drawer, he picked up the yearbook, then shoved it inside. "By the way, Eve wants to know if you and Katie are interested in hooking up for dinner."

And just that quick, the topic of Parker was closed.

* * * *

The next night Ryan picked up Katie and Sam and took them to his mom's house for dinner. Sometimes he thought it odd that he still lived there while Caden had left as soon as he was able, enlisting in the army following graduation. His brother had spent the next four years in Vietnam, then snagged his own place and a job with the sheriff's office when he returned. The war hadn't changed him, but the time away had done nothing to erase the burden of Maggie's death. Thank God, that trauma was finally behind them.

Caden and Eve joined them for dinner with much of the talk centering around their upcoming wedding. They'd settled on June eighteenth as the date for the ceremony. Eve announced she'd already booked the church for two o'clock in the afternoon, and reserved the ballroom at the hotel for the reception. Ryan was happy for both of them. His mother positively beamed, overjoyed by the prospect of having a daughter-in-law.

It was nearing seven-thirty when Ryan took Katie and Sam home. The house was empty, but cozy. Doreen Sue had left a note on the kitchen table saying she'd gone to visit Martin and probably wouldn't be back until late. Katie brewed a pot of coffee while Sam took a bath and Ryan made himself comfortable in the living room.

He flipped on the TV while she fussed with Sam and helped him get ready for bed. The show options were minimal. *Tales of the Gold Monkey, Real People,* or *Seven Brides for Seven Brothers.* He decided on the first, but turned the volume down since his mind was elsewhere. They hadn't discussed Lyle in front of Sam, but it was time he brought her up to speed about Mason's true target, Caden.

A half hour later, Katie joined him on the sofa.

"That's mind-boggling," she said when he was through with his tale. "I bet it came as a surprise to Caden too."

"Yeah, I don't think he's taking the whole thing seriously, but my brother has his own way of doing things." Time to change the subject. It had been several days since he'd seen her, and he didn't want to spend the entire time talking about Caden. "My mom really enjoyed seeing you and Sam tonight."

"She doted on him. It was like having a second grandmother."

"Do you think he had fun?"

"Are you kidding?" Katie smiled and curled her legs onto the sofa. "Between your mom insisting he have more dessert, and you and Caden tossing a football with him in the backyard, I probably won't hear about anything else for days." Her smile faded slightly, but warmth lingered in her gaze. "Thanks for making the night special for him. He's had a rough time lately."

"I know." Ryan slid a hand onto her shoulder. "Is he still having nightmares?" She'd told him about those, along with the green cloud, and Sam's compulsive sketching.

"Rarely. And he's not drawing as much." She gave a half shrug. "Whatever was troubling him is starting to fade."

"The 'noise'?" He brushed his fingers against her cheek.

She nodded. "I think all the stability he's had with everyone around him—my mom, Martin, and you"—she lowered her gaze, a blush rising to her face—"has made a difference. He's not afraid anymore."

"What about you?" Lyle Mason was a supreme ass for having treated her with anything less than tenderness and respect. He tilted her chin up. "Are you done with UFOs?"

Jerome's paperback copy of *UFO Sightings and Stories* occupied a spot on the coffee table. Ryan nodded toward the book. "I should probably give that back to him."

"You don't need to. I called him yesterday to see how he was feeling and mentioned I had it. He told me to keep it, that it was the least he could do after I'd helped him. He wants to get together and chat UFOs over coffee."

Ryan narrowed his eyes. "Are you going to?"

"Would it bother you?" She leaned closer, her grin mischievous.

"Hell, yes. I mean—" He fumbled and drew back. "The guy's just a friend, right?"

"Of course." Her smile grew broader, lighting the depths of her eyes. Green like her son's, they were flecked with gold in the lamplight. "But you sound…jealous?"

Ryan's face grew warm. "Katie, I thought I made it clear how I feel about you. I'm tired of being casual friends. I thought we'd moved past that."

"We have." Turning, she nestled into his arms, her back to his chest. Snuggling closer, she drew his hands around her waist. "I like that you're jealous."

He grunted. "I never said I was."

"Then you won't mind if I have coffee with Jerome?"

It was a losing argument. "I've got something better in mind." He bent his head and kissed her—after which there was no further discussion of UFOs.

Or Jerome.

Chapter 14

The next night Katie helped Sam into his Luke Skywalker outfit and she and Ryan took him trick-or-treating. They started in her mom's neighborhood, going house to house as Sam collected candy bars, caramels, and gummy worms. After that, it was over to Ryan's home where Mrs. Flynn and Eve lavished him with homemade popcorn balls and individually wrapped blocks of peanut butter fudge. Neighborhoods were overrun with ghosts and witches waving flashlights, parents trailing behind younger children. No one spoke the name of Point Pleasant's notorious cryptid, but the Mothman undoubtedly lurked in the back of everyone's mind. Even Katie couldn't help shooting an occasional glance to the cloud-streaked sky, fearful the monster might materialize. After its recent rampage, the Mothman had taken to lying low as it had in the past, but a shadow of fear still hung over the town.

Eventually, she was able to tuck Sam safely into bed, dreams of candy corn and jack-o'-lanterns dancing in his head. It was nice staying with her mom, especially as they grew closer, but she was starting to feel displaced and wanted to get back to her own home. She'd shared the thoughts with her mom that morning over breakfast, and while her mother was reluctant, she'd understood Katie's need for independence.

Sam was a different story. He was having fun staying with his Grammie, a situation that worked well given Lyle and the driver of the green van were still at large. Katie agreed to leave Sam with her mom a few more days. When she kissed Ryan good night later that evening and shared her plans, he scowled as expected.

"Why can't you stay too? Wait a while longer. We're getting close on Lyle."

"Are you?" She raised a brow. They stood in her mother's driveway, leaning against Ryan's Camaro. The earlier cloud cover had given way to a star-strewn sky with a full moon, more orange than gold. If there was anyone still roaming the streets, the revelers would be older kids high on the fun of the holiday or dreaming up pranks. Her mom's house had been the target of egging and toilet-papering more than once, but Katie wasn't entirely convinced kids were the culprits. More than a few adults—male and female—weren't overly fond of Doreen Sue Lynch.

Ryan gripped her arms, turning her to face him. "We've got vehicle ID and a plate number. We know Lyle's running low on cash. Darrell said as much. He's got to surface sooner or later."

"I'm tired of waiting."

"I know you are." Ryan tugged her against him. Slipping a finger beneath her chin, he gave her a light kiss. When he drew back, he brushed a thumb down her cheek. "I think he's going to zero in on Caden, not you, but I can't help worrying. Humor me, okay?"

It was hard to say no when he was so attentive. She tugged her jacket closer. "A few more days."

"Till after Halloween."

She dissected the thought. "Why then?"

"It's the magic date. Don't you remember?" The corner of his mouth lifted in a crooked grin. "According to Parker, Indrid Cold is coming back. Maybe Lyle will too."

She'd have to make another trip to her house to pick up more clothes and other items she and Sam needed, but it wasn't as if he'd asked her to wait a week. "All right, and then I'm done." She wouldn't budge on that. "Agreed?"

He smiled, gloating a little that he'd won. "Agreed."

Score another for the sergeant. "Good night, Ryan. I'll see you tomorrow." She gave him a kiss, then turned and headed back up the drive toward the house.

"Tomorrow?" he called behind her.

It never hurt to do a little gloating of her own. He couldn't see her expression, but mischief bloomed in her smile. "We're having coffee with Jerome."

* * * *

Jerome.

Ryan blew out a breath as he followed Katie up the sidewalk to Jerome's front door. The morning had dawned clear and bright with the sun burning off a thin layer of clouds. He'd had breakfast at home, chatted with his mom, then swung by Doreen Sue's place to pick up Katie. Sam was in school, and Ryan's work shift didn't start until noon. He wasn't exactly looking forward to filling the intervening time talking to Jerome, but the guy wasn't without a unique perspective on recent events.

And he was clearly infatuated with Katie. Best to put an end to those fantasies before they mushroomed larger.

Jerome greeted them at the door, surprised and plainly disappointed to find Ryan hovering at Katie's side. Apparently, she hadn't told him Ryan would be joining their get-together.

"I hope you don't mind I tagged along." Ryan offered what he hoped passed for a friendly smile. "With everything going on in town, I thought you might have some insights to help us at the sheriff's office." With luck, the offhand comment would bolster Jerome's confidence and offset the letdown. Nothing like putting a damper on the party.

Jerome's smile faltered but he motioned them inside. "Always glad to have an audience."

Ryan wasn't certain if he was being facetious, but followed Katie into the living room. The house had undergone a makeover since the last time he was here. Newspapers and magazines still occupied a spot by the window, but they were tidily arranged and pushed back from the main walking area. Everything from the end tables, to the coffee table, and furniture looked recently cleaned. Pine air freshener replaced the odor of stale cigarette smoke and greasy fast food. Clearly, Jerome had taken the time to make his house look as appealing as possible for Katie. Ryan almost felt bad for the guy, given the trouble he'd gone to.

"How about some coffee?" Jerome directed them to have a seat. "I've got donuts, too, and picked up a few cinnamon muffins from Early Start." He twined his hands together, a nervous bird unmistakably out of his element. "They're fresh."

"Just coffee for me, thanks." Ryan took a seat on the sofa, conscious of the cushions sagging like a swayback horse beneath his weight. "Black is fine."

"Same for me." Katie's smile lit up the room. "Can I help you, Jerome?"

"No, I've got it." He shook his head, nearly tripping over his feet as he trekked backward.

Ryan waited until he'd disappeared into the kitchen, before taking Katie's hand and tugging her down beside him. "You're going to give him a coronary, smiling at him like that. The guy's besotted with you."

"He's being friendly. I think he's lonely."

"Of course he is. He's got a room in the back that's looks like a shrine to the Mothman and little green men from outer space. Not exactly hot date material for most women."

Katie cast a sideways glance. "How would you know?"

He held up a hand. "Just saying."

"Well, try to be nice. I like him."

"As long as you don't *like* like him."

"That territory's already been claimed." She leaned forward and kissed him.

The sound of Jerome clearing his throat pulled them apart. Ryan glanced up to find the scrawny man holding a tray with three mugs of steaming black coffee. Jerome's face flushed red as if he realized how foolish he was to think Katie might be interested in him.

She recovered quickly and patted the coffee table in front of her. "Here, Jerome, why don't you set that down?"

"Yeah." His voice spiraled lower, matching the misery on his face. He grabbed a cup with a bug-eyed alien on the front, then retreated to a chair across from the couch.

Ryan guessed he'd hoped to sit beside Katie, but the kiss he'd witnessed had naturally dispelled those ideas. "Smells good." Ryan picked up a mug with a silhouette of Bigfoot. He took a sip of coffee. "Hot too."

Katie's cup read MOTHMAN HUNTER in big red letters, but she merely retrieved it and cradled it in her lap. "It was nice of you to ask me to visit, Jerome. How have you been feeling?"

He worked a skinny shoulder into a shrug. "Good, I guess." His lips squashed into a sour line as he looked down at his mug. "It irks me to think someone played around inside my head and I can't remember any of it."

"You mean Deputy Brown?" Ryan took another sip of coffee. Aside from being hot, the stuff was strong enough to peel rust from metal. No wonder Jerome was a rail. If Ryan drank this junk on a regular basis, he'd be bouncing off the walls. He set the cup back on the table. "Katie's been reading that book you gave her, and I glanced at it too." He'd taken a peek, nothing too serious, honing in mostly on Jerome's scribbled notes. "You've heard about the dogs we found in the TNT, and about Wilson's cows?"

Jerome nodded, his earlier dejection replaced by a flicker of interest. "What about them?"

"Do you have any idea what could have caused their deaths?"

Jerome hesitated, narrowing his eyes. "I thought you had Doc Holden check them out?"

"I did." Ryan spread his hands. "All the reports came back the same... That an outside source exerted barometric pressure strong to make the animals' brains explode." It felt freaky sharing the details of Holden's report, but he was talking to a guy who believed in Martians and Sasquatch. If anyone was going to take the veterinarian's findings seriously, it was Jerome.

"That makes sense." Jerome took a gulp of coffee, then set the mug aside. "See... A UFO could do that. We don't know what kind of frequencies they operate at...sound that might not affect us, but could be a siren song to an animal." Standing, he hunched his shoulders and began to pace. "When I heard about the dogs, my first thought was that something lured them to that clearing. Probably not intentionally. It could have been an extraterrestrial craft transitioning through dimensions."

"What does that mean?" Katie hadn't taken a single sip of coffee, and probably had no intention of drinking the bitter brew. She set her mug beside Ryan's and leaned forward, lacing her hands on her lap. "Are you saying UFOs just appear, randomly popping in and out of space?"

"Exactly." Jerome beamed at her as if he'd discovered a star pupil. "That's why it's so hard for the government to track them. It's not like they fly into our air space. They appear and disappear at whim through layers between worlds. When people think of UFOs, they tend to think of them as existing in our universe, but the reality is most exist in parallel, even temporal universes. The Men in Black know that. I'm not even sure all of them come from Earth."

Ryan let out a slow breath. He'd seen enough strange shit lately to keep an open mind, but it was tricky navigating Jerome's rapid-fire delivery. "You're saying the Men in Black are aliens?"

"I'm saying some of them could be." Jerome stopped pacing and shoved his hands into his pockets. His shoulders were still hunched in an awkward posture, but his voice had grown stronger, fueled by confidence in a subject he knew well. "UFOnauts don't want to be discovered. They want to observe our world for whatever reason, and move on. That's why you've got all these guys running around, warning people who've seen flying saucers to keep the stories to themselves. In that respect, our government and alien visitors are on the same page. Big Brother isn't limited to our world alone."

Ryan's gaze drifted across the room to the stack of newspapers below the window. How many hours, days, weeks, even years had Jerome spent reading about stuff like this? His life seemed to revolve around little else. Katie was definitely off the radar, but it was a shame the guy didn't crawl out of his shell and try to be more social. He was clearly intelligent, but unquestionably most people would find his choice of topics odd.

"Okay, put that aside for now." Ryan chose not to go down the path of Big Brother and parallel worlds. "If I read you right, you think the pressure from a UFO caused the dogs and Wilson's cows to die the way they did?"

Jerome bobbed his head. "Rex was lucky. He was probably drawn to the clearing like the other dogs, but must have gotten there after the saucer left. That's why he was spared."

"But what about the green cloud my son saw the night Rex ran away?" Katie asked.

"Another dimension traveler, passing through on a different plane. Not all would have the same effect or cause the damage. It was probably unusual enough to lure Rex away, but didn't operate on a frequency that would harm him."

"And the star shit?" Ryan used Wilson's term for the silvery goop scattered throughout the farmer's pasture and the clearing in the TNT.

"Residue left behind by the UFO's passing. If you tried to get a sample of the stuff, it probably evaporated before a lab could examine it."

Katie squeezed Ryan's leg. "That's exactly what you said happened."

"Yeah." A few weeks ago he'd have thought Jerome had a screw loose. Now he was starting to think the guy was the only one who knew what was going on. "The first cow Wilson lost was in a pasture a good distance from the barn. We couldn't find any tracks in the field, animal or human."

"Probably transported there by whatever craft drew her outside."

Ryan webbed a hand over his face. The discussion was starting to sound like something out of *Star Trek*. Remaining seated was too confining. He stood and paced to the window. Jerome had opened the blinds before they arrived, the view outside a vista of browning grass and autumn-colored trees. "Hank Jeffries always said strange things happened around his house." The observation came out of the blue, a memory tugged awake by their unusual conversation.

Jerome stepped closer, halting halfway between the window and the sofa. "I think this house is on a ley line. I think it's where Indrid Cold is going to meet Parker on the thirty-first."

Ryan spun. "Here?" The idea made a warped kind of sense. Parker had watched his brother die at Hank's hands, then killed the drunken man in a blind rage. Caden had hinted he knew where Cold might appear and Caden was directly tied to the Jeffries house, now Jerome's. Ryan should have pieced it together.

Katie stood and placed a hand on Jerome's arm. "So you're going to wait for him at the appointed time?"

He flushed with a visible start, obviously pleased by her touch. "I am."

"And if he doesn't show?"

"I'll be no worse off than before." He sucked on his bottom lip. Somewhat reluctantly, he glanced back to Ryan. "Parker told me he heard a lot of radio chatter. That's how they communicate, you know. It's just static to us…noise that shouldn't even be there. But Parker understood it. He knew what they were saying when they talked to each other. The only message he wanted was from Cold. He did that drawing-thing as homage to him, waiting for the contact." His eyes grew large, rounded by a hint of awe. "And then it came."

Cold must return. Evening will follow.

"Yeah." Ryan wasn't sure what he was agreeing with, but knew the conversation had reached its usable end. If he'd gleaned nothing else from Point Pleasant's prime conspiracy theorist, at least he'd learned where his brother planned to be on Halloween night.

"Thanks for the coffee, Jerome. Sorry we've got to leave so soon." He extended his hand to Katie, who stepped to his side and clasped her fingers with his. "You've been a big help."

"That's good." Jerome sounded anything but pleased. His shoulders slumped lower, and a look of dejection crossed his face.

Katie tugged on Ryan's hand. "Do something," she whispered. Her meaning was clear, backed up by a pointed glance only a female could deliver.

Ryan sighed, committed to the extra mile. "Hey, um…sometime you should join us at the River Café. Maybe the three of us could hook up for a few beers and a burger."

"Really?" Jerome went from staring at his toes to grinning broadly. "That'd be great—I mean… I'd be into that. I don't get out that much."

"You should." Katie stepped to his side and gave him a kiss on the cheek. "Six o'clock tomorrow night. How's that?"

The kiss left Jerome blinking like a deer in the headlights. He gulped and swallowed. "S-sure."

Katie waved good-bye, and they stepped outside. As Ryan led her to the car, he hooked an arm around her shoulders. "I wasn't planning on anything that soon, you know."

She smiled up at him. "I know. But Jerome needs friends."

"He's not a stray cat or a dog you can take in."

"But I can help him be a little more social." She nudged him in the ribs. "You can too."

"Yeah." It wasn't hard to temper his enthusiasm. "Looks like I've already got a date for tomorrow night."

* * * *

Caden wasn't certain why he hadn't thought of it before. Three days before Halloween, he drove to the property Lyle Mason's parents had farmed when Caden was in high school. He'd known of Jerry and Joan Mason the way people in small towns are sometimes aware of others. He'd gone to Lottie's funeral, along with some other kids from school, when she'd died. Wanting to pay his respects to the shy girl he'd barely known, but unwilling to intrude on the family's grief, he'd kept to the back of the church.

The Masons had moved years ago, and another family had taken over the farm. Caden thought their name was Gardner or Gander. He recognized the man to offer a nod when they passed on the street, but that was all. With a property nestled several miles out of town, they kept mostly to themselves. Weston had interviewed them personally after learning about Lyle from Lach Evening, but neither the husband nor wife had seen Mason snooping around.

Still, it was worth a try. Especially considering Lyle was growing reckless.

Caden drove past fields filled with brown cornstalks, others dotted with baled blocks of hay. A three-story house jutted in the distance, black against a twilight sky. Night fell fast, evident by the messy ebb of the sun into the horizon. Caden pulled off the road several hundred yards from the house and silenced the car's motor.

Ever since Ryan had told him about Lyle's grievance against him, he'd racked his brain, trying to unearth a source. He'd gone through his yearbook privately, studying faces of long ago friends, girls he'd dated, and notes written by people he thought he'd remember forever. Nothing jarred his memory.

Stepping from the car, he closed the door behind him. A short stretch of road and fields wound like a ribbon to the house in the distance. Would Lyle have come back? Was there a secret place tucked among the sprawling grounds and outbuildings surrounding the house? An area where he could hole up and remain hidden until he chose to be seen? He'd grown up on the farm. He'd know every inch of it.

Stuffing his hands into his pockets, Caden walked to the front of his car and leaned against the hood. He didn't know how long he stayed watching the house, only that the air grew colder, the quiet of the night heavier. After a time, light footsteps sounded behind him, jarring him from the peaceful solitude.

"You won't find him here." Lach Evening strolled closer. No overcoat, no gloves, not even the black fedora to crown his platinum hair. Beneath an emerging moon, his white shirt gleamed with a spectral sheen, contrasting his midnight-dark suit.

Momentarily speechless, Caden glanced around trying to pinpoint where he'd come from. He couldn't spy a car anywhere in sight, or a single trail that would have led to the road. Evening would have had to trek through the cornfields, clearly not the case given the impeccable condition of his clothing. "Where did you come from?"

"I've already spoken to the family that owns the farm." Evening stepped closer. "A charming, if reserved couple. They haven't seen Mr. Mason, but I've advised them he might materialize at some point." There was nothing haughty in the words, but they rolled from Evening's tongue with a superior lilt regardless.

"That's the sheriff's job."

Evening made a V of his index finger and thumb, thoughtfully rubbing his chin. "Perhaps I have overstepped my boundaries. Surely, you took care of the matter yourself."

Caden fought a scowl. "Not personally. Weston interviewed them."

"And yet here you are, waiting for Lyle."

He couldn't deny the obvious. "It was worth a shot. What about you?" He eyed Evening critically. "What are you doing here?"

"Perhaps the same as you. In any event, I think it's a pleasant hour for a stroll. Good evening, Sergeant." He started past Caden, walking casually as if soaking up the pleasant surroundings of a balmy summer night.

Caden let him go several feet without challenge. "Mr. Evening," he called at last.

The man stopped without turning.

"Do you know Indrid Cold?"

A pulse beat, then two. Slowly, deliberately, Evening twisted to face him. "Where did you hear that name?" Three brusque strides brought him face-to-face with Caden. His expression, frequently bordering on bland or disinterested, had turned icy with resolve. "How do you know Cold?"

The sudden crispness of his accent set off a red flag in Caden's mind. The inflection wasn't an exact match for the being in the igloo, but with an edge of anger coloring Evening's voice, the nuance was close. He narrowed his eyes. "Who the hell are you? *Really.*"

Evening stiffened, then drew back slightly. "I asked you a question."

"And I did the same. Do you want to talk about Parker Kline? Jerome Kelly? Deputy Brown? Do any of those names ring a bell?" The anger and frustration he'd harbored for weeks bulldozed to the surface. He was sick of games, sick of spitting out questions and getting nowhere. "What about the Mothman?" Fisting his hand in the pristine fabric of Evening's shirt, he yanked him closer. "You aren't getting *shit* out of me, until you deliver something in return."

Evening's gaze dropped.

The sleeve of Caden's jacket had been wrenched backward by his aggression, exposing the brands on his forearm. Evening remained perfectly still, his face impassive. It took several seconds for him to find his voice. When he spoke, his tone had lost its terseness.

"Those are interesting marks you carry, Sergeant." He glanced up, his dark eyes probing. "I believe it's time you and I had a serious discussion."

Chapter 15

Caden wished Evening would sit. It wasn't that he paced. Rather, he walked a short distance, stopped to examine a knick-knack or photograph as if discovering a new peculiarity, then moved on to another trinket in Eve's living room and repeated the procedure over again. Unsure where to hold a frank discussion, Caden ended up bringing him home. The sheriff's office was out of the question with too many people on duty, and the River Café would only draw attention. Fortunately, Katie and Ryan had coerced Eve into joining them for dinner and drinks with Jerome so the guy wouldn't feel like a third wheel. His fiancée's absence gave Caden the opportunity to talk to Evening alone.

"You appear to like plants." Evening fingered the browning leaves of Eve's latest acquisition. Caden had no idea what the potted lump was called, only that it had been added to her growing collection near the end of summer. She'd fussed, watered, fed, and talked to it, but unlike the rest of the jungle scattered through the house, the sickly looking thing had withered to a few twigs with shrunken leaves. Caden wanted her to toss it, but she wouldn't hear of parting with the plant.

"They belong to my fiancée. Eve."

"Yes. I met her at the hotel." Evening strolled to another plant, this one much healthier. He stroked a finger over the leaves in a light caress. The hint of a smile touched his lips.

Damn, the guy was strange.

"Look, I've had enough of the niceties." Caden sat on the couch, his legs braced apart, hands locked between them. "We both know there's a lot more to you than you've told us. Shit has hit the fan in Point Pleasant. Lyle's running around with a screwed up head, I've got a kid who escaped from a mental institution, dead dogs and cows, UFOs, the Mothman wreaking havoc, and some disembodied oracle in a World War II bunker. If you know anything about *anything*, now's the time to tell me."

Evening straightened his cufflinks. "So, you've met Indrid Cold?"

"Huh?" Caden felt the floor shift beneath him.

"In the bunker." Evening spoke as if the connection should be obvious. "If you spoke to the being inside, then you spoke with Cold."

"Are you telling me that Indrid Cold—an alien from Lanulos, according to Parker Kline—is the thing...the oracle, or whatever it is, inside that igloo? The legend of that thing is as old as the original Mothman sightings."

Evening clasped his hands behind his back. "Cold has been here longer. Much longer, though not in the physical sense. Corporeal occurrences are structured for certain moments in time. You might say Indrid Cold is a Watchman, much as I, though his obligation is driven by regret more than duty. On that plane we are different."

Caden stood, trying to follow the twisting logic of the conversation. It was absurd to put stock in mind-blowing revelations, yet difficult to scoff after all he'd experienced. "You have the same accent." Did that mean Evening was from Lanulos too?

"Similar, but separated by a generation." Evening tilted his head to acknowledge the observation. "My race doesn't age in the same manner as yours. The names we take on your planet are a means of accommodating your native languages. You would be unable to pronounce my name or that of my father."

"Father?"

Evening's smile was sharp. "Indrid Cold."

Caden was suddenly conscious of the quiet. A grandfather's clock in the corner ticked the hour, but other than the steady *tock-tock,* a heavy pall settled over the room. Nothing looked out of place, Eve's latest mystery novel resting on the coffee table, his guitar case standing upright in the corner by the TV. A collection of plants sprouted from containers on the floor and ceramic crocks positioned on end tables. It could have been any family living room, an average setting for an average home, yet he was *talking to an alien.*

Swearing softly, he dragged a hand over his face. "Cold is your father?" He needed a beer, would have sunk back to the sofa, but was too wired to sit.

"Does that surprise you?"

"Nothing surprises me anymore. Are you going to abduct me or something?"

Evening grinned. "I assure you, Sergeant, you are safe. So is your town. My purpose here isn't one of hostility."

"Thank God for that." Caden started for the kitchen. "I need a Coors. Want one?"

"No, thank you." Evening followed as far as the kitchen doorway, waiting patiently while Caden grabbed a can from the refrigerator and popped the top. "I don't make a habit of revealing myself to most people, or discussing my intentions when I visit a town," he said after a moment, "but in your case, Sergeant, I believe it would benefit us to pool our information."

"Agreed." Caden shouldered back into the dining room and waved him to a seat at the table. "Who starts?"

Evening eyed the red welts peeking from beneath the cuff of Caden's shirt. "The Mothman made those." It was not a question. "Perhaps you should start there."

"Fair enough." For the next few minutes, Caden dumped every bit of information he had. He started by sharing how he'd helped the Mothman when he was eighteen, then explained how the creature had saved his life when the Silver Bridge fell, and again when Roger Layton would have killed him and Eve. He talked about Hank Jeffries and Parker Kline, Jerome and the coded message Parker had given him, even the mysterious Deputy Brown and the UFO sightings plaguing Point Pleasant from one side to the other. When he was through, he took a long swig of beer to wet his throat. Evening had let him ramble without question or comment, the man's expression unreadable through Caden's longwinded speech.

A cool cucumber, but one who could be rattled when pushed. He'd already seen that.

Caden set his beer down. "Your turn."

"So it would seem." Evening tapped a slender hand against the table. "What would you like to know?"

The squat tips of Evening's fingers recalled the suction-cup like grip that clutched Caden's jaw in the igloo. What had Cold said? *Parker is my mistake to fix.*

"How is your father connected to Parker Kline?"

"I can't answer that."

A prickle of anger crept up Caden's spine. He tightened his hand on the beer can, one step from crushing the pliable aluminum. "I thought the idea was to share information."

"Information I have. If my father is connected to Mr. Kline, I am unaware of a personal relationship."

"What about Deputy Brown and the Men in Black?"

"Those you term Men in Black are Watchmen like myself." Evening appeared at ease, his voice as casually modulated as if he discussed the weather. If he lied about anything, then he did a remarkable job of masking the falsehoods. "You've mentioned the abundance of UFO sightings. Dimension activity is at a high right now. You've no doubt heard the rumors that your town and much of this county are intersected by ley lines, creating thin spots between worlds. Throughout your centuries, there have been numerous occasions when the veils that separate those realms are more easily breached than others. That produces an excess of UFO activity. It happened in Point Pleasant in nineteen sixty-six and sixty-seven."

A flap.

The guy sounded exactly like Jerome.

"So you're saying the Men in Black are aliens too?" Thank God Nurse Brenner wasn't around to eavesdrop on their discussion or she'd want to lock them in West Central.

"Their intent is not to harm anyone, Sergeant. Call it a cover-up if you will. It's best your world doesn't become fixated on dimensional travel, at least not at your present rate of advancement. Perhaps in time."

"So when there's a flap, the Men in Black show up to warn everyone silent?" He could buy that. From what he'd heard, warnings were the extent of what they'd done.

With the exception of one.

"Brown did more than that. He had the wherewithal to duplicate a Mason County patrol car and uniform. He posed as an officer and accosted a citizen." The anger slithered back, hotter this time. Point Pleasant was his town, Jerome one of the people he was sworn to protect. Evening and Cold might look down their alien noses, considering Earth an inferior planet, but the residents of his town were not specimens to be placed under a microscope or manipulated. "Brown messed with Jerome Kelly's mind, then dumped him outside the hospital when he'd gotten all he could from him."

"I'm aware of that. A regrettable circumstance." Evening bowed his head, appearing momentarily contrite.

Maybe the guy really did have a conscience underneath that cool exterior.

Evening waited a moment, then drew a slow breath. "Water if you please, Sergeant."

Caden pulled back. "Huh?"

"You offered me a beverage when I arrived. I'd like water."

A stalling tactic? Frowning, Caden stood. "Sure, okay." After retreating to the kitchen, he poured a glass of water and grabbed a second beer for himself. By the time he returned to the dining room, Evening was sitting comfortably at the table, Eve's withered plant stationed in the center.

Caden passed the water to him before sitting. "What's that for?" he nodded to the plant.

"It's withering."

Newsflash there. "Dying is more like it."

"Exactly." Evening didn't touch the water. Crossing his legs, he laced his hands on his lap. "All things die eventually, but not all linger in a declining stage of death."

Double talk. Evening was reverting to his head-shrink mode, and Caden had no intention of playing along. "We were talking about Deputy Brown and what he did to Jerome."

"Deputy Brown is human."

Caden tensed. "What?"

"Your government is every bit as interested in silencing rumors of UFOs as are my people. From what you've told me, Brown must have been assigned to monitor Parker Kline. The organization that employs him is no doubt clandestine, and would have been aware of Mr. Kline's gift for interpreting radio static."

"So they wanted the coded message?"

"Unquestionably. Even if Mr. Kelly wasn't physically carrying the written text when apprehended, Brown would have been able to retrieve the sequence through hypnosis. A single glance is all it takes for information to root in the subconscious."

Caden tripped over the logic, his mind doing cartwheels as he digested the facts. "If Brown already had the code, and learned through hypnosis that Jerome passed it to Katie, why stake out her house?"

"A precaution, perhaps." Evening palmed the water glass, turning it slowly. "Likely to determine if she shared the information with someone else, or quite possibly to scare her. Intimidation often makes people rethink what they've seen."

Caden clenched his jaw. No doubt Jerome would find Evening's revelations exhilarating, but trying to stay on top of the twists and turns was giving him a headache.

"I believe Mr. Kline was able to decipher a precise time when my father would appear in physical form," Evening continued. "That is the information he passed to Mr. Kelly."

"Yeah, I know about that." Caden rolled a hand, wanting to move the conversation along. "Cold is supposed to rendezvous with Parker on Halloween."

"No." Evening's black eyes glinted. "My father intends to meet with someone he abandoned centuries ago. A creature, who like this plant"—he motioned to the spindly cluster of dried leaves in the center of the table—"is dying."

Dying.

The word echoed in Caden's head. Pushing his sleeve back, he dropped his gaze to the brand on his arm. He'd experienced the creature's melancholy and fatigue, been battered by its crushing sense of depression. It *wanted* to die.

But like Eve's plant, it was trapped in some agonizing state of limbo.

"The Mothman is the last of his kind." Evening caressed the side of the water glass with a finger. "Eons ago, my father arrived on your planet with others from Lanulos. Our atmospheres are much the same, and our planet was undergoing volcanic changes that made the terrain unstable."

"So you were looking for a new world to inhabit?" It sounded like the plot of a science-fiction movie.

"Precisely. Earth was unlike it is now, the landmasses and oceans structured differently, your dinosaurs the only true predators. My people stayed for a time, studying, paving the way for others of our kind to follow. My father, however, returned to Lanulos with news that Earth had proven habitable. As it turned out, our own planet stabilized and an exodus wasn't necessary."

Caden took a swig of beer. Bully for Earth. He wasn't sure he liked the idea of Evenings and Colds running around in number. "The Mothman doesn't look anything like you."

"Your atmosphere changed my people, warped their physical form, even their minds. They chose to remain rather than return to Lanulos where they would have been outcasts. Those who stayed became like the being you call the Mothman."

It was a lot to absorb. "Damn."

"As the leader of the expedition who brought our people here, my father feels responsible. He has returned to Earth time and again, offering what comfort he could to those he abandoned. But the eons have weakened his connection." Evening dipped a slender finger into the glass. Retracting his hand, he rolled a bead of water around the bulbous tip below his nail. "All of those he left behind have died—with the exception of one."

Caden wet his lips. "The Mothman."

"The creature yearns to pass on." Evening's gaze flashed to his face, steady and hard. "You've felt that. But his time isn't now. Unlike this fragile plant, which can be revived, his death will come in a desolate hour when a tear in time renders past and present as one."

Stretching out his hand, Evening brushed his wet fingertip lightly across Eve's plant. One stroke, then two, the touch as gentle as a father caressing a sick child. As if spelled by magic, the wilted stalk stretched upright. Buds sprouted, opened, and grew. Withered leaves unfurled into glistening fronds, fresh and green with new life.

Caden sucked down a breath. For a moment he couldn't move, mesmerized by the sight. "How did you do that?" His voice came out a strained whisper.

Evening's smile was thin. "I'm not without power. Unfortunately, I can't do the same for the Mothman, nor can my father. Do we understand each other now, Sergeant?"

"Yeah." The admission came freely, twined up with admiration he hadn't expected. "There's only one thing I'm still not clear about."

"Lyle Mason."

Caden nodded.

"Everything I told you in Sheriff Weston's office is true. Unlike my father who travels between dimensions, I exist solely in your world. My people have since found ways to adapt our body chemistry to your planet, unlike our forebears who arrived in a time when Earth was primal. We may not blend perfectly, but for the most part we're able to fade into your society as needed."

"Except you don't age. Katie Lynch said you were here before…in '67 before the bridge fell. You were looking for her mother."

"Ah. Yes." Another tight smile. "Word reached me that Mrs. Lynch had witnessed an interdimensional UFO crossing. I arrived to warn her not to speak of the event, but the tragedy of your Silver Bridge overshadowed my mission. Even I was emotionally affected by that catastrophe." He dropped his gaze momentarily, a pained expression crossing his face.

Caden was surprised by the glimpse of feeling. From the moment he'd met Lach Evening, he'd considered the man detached, possessed of a patronizing attitude. Tonight's discussion had proven many of his perceptions wrong. "You left."

"Yes. I didn't feel the need to intrude afterward, given the misery plaguing your town." Evening sat straighter, recovering his usual control. "You have, however, hit upon the one characteristic of my people that remains problematic. Because of our slow progression in aging, I am frequently forced to relocate. Others like me—those you call Men in Black—also staff the facility I operate."

Caden narrowed his eyes. "I thought you were some kind of subcontractor or employee?"

Evening offered a shrug as apology. "A slight, but necessary, distortion of the truth to gain your aid, and that of your sheriff. I did not lie when I said I use flicker phenomena on contactees who claim encounters with supernatural creatures. There are some who have no desire to remain silent, but are extremely vocal in spreading their stories. Many of what your people call monsters are simply dimension travelers. We work to sort true encounters from perceived fantasy, and do our best to erase those memories. You might frown on our methods, but the results are necessary to maintain the security of our separate populations."

Caden's head was spinning. At the same time, he believed everything Evening said. The rumors of Point Pleasant and the TNT existing on a ley line were true, which explained the area's unusual degree of otherworldly activity. At least now he knew what he was dealing with.

"If Lyle surfaces, I can handle him." He had no qualms about Mason. Tracking him down would bring one problem to a conclusion, and the guy couldn't stay hidden forever. "Lyle's head might be screwed up, but he's human." He leaned forward, forearms on the table as he met Evening's steady gaze. "What do I do about the Mothman?"

Evening pushed the water glass away. "There's nothing you can do. Let my father arrive—"

"But this bond I've got—"

"I understand." A flicker of distaste twisted Evening's mouth in a downward curl. Evidently, he was not used to being interrupted. "If there is any benevolence or morality that still lingers within the creature, he has chosen you as the conduit for that compassion." Appearing thoughtful, he glanced to the side. "I am unclear why. Perhaps it is nothing more than the mercy you showed at your first meeting, when—perceived as a monster—he expected antagonism, fear or aggression." Evening's gaze snapped back to Caden. "Our conversation is over now, Sergeant."

"Huh?" The abruptness of the statement made Caden wrench physically backward.

"Your fiancée is home."

The words no sooner passed Evening's lips, than the front door burst open and Eve hurried in, slightly out of breath. "Caden, you won't believe what happened at the café." She dumped her purse on the couch, then slipped from her coat and tossed the garment over the bag. "I met Ryan, Katie, and Jerome for dinner like we planned, and things exploded. Shawn Preech was out of control." It took her a second to realize she spoke to an empty room, a second longer to spy the two men through the arched opening into the dining room. "Oh!" She crossed the distance to the table. "I didn't realize you had company."

Evening stood and Caden followed suit.

"A pleasure to see you again, Ms. Parrish." Evening inclined his head in an old-fashioned greeting. "May I extend my congratulations? I understand you are recently engaged to Sergeant Flynn." Taking her hand, he kissed her fingertips lightly, a courtly gesture resurrected from another time.

Eve flushed in delight. "Why...why, thank you." When he released her, she placed the hand over her heart, an entranced smile warming her face.

Caden raised a brow. Evening might be odd, but he oozed genteel charm when it came to women, an inborn charisma further enhanced by his bearing and accent. "Lach was just leaving."

Eve deflated. "You can't stay?" She looked directly at their guest.

"I'm afraid not. Other matters demand my attention. But it was good to see you again. I can find my own way to the door." Another tilt of his head as parting. His gaze shifted to Caden. "Sergeant."

"I'll be in touch."

"What a charming man," Eve said after he'd left. "I didn't see a car outside. How will he get back to the hotel?"

Caden hadn't considered that, but given the man's peculiarities and abilities, he didn't think traveling would be an issue. "I don't think that will be a problem." He pulled her close and kissed her. "What happened at the River?"

"You're not going to believe it." Just that quickly, Eve refocused. "Everything was going fine until Suzanne came in, looking for Shawn. She's pregnant, you know?"

He'd heard the news somewhere before, probably from Eve when she was sharing town gossip with him. People tended to talk about anything and everything when they camped out at her café.

"Even Jerome was doing okay. We had him talking about stuff other than UFOs and spacemen, and then—" She stopped suddenly, her attention shifting to the healthy plant in the center of the table. "Caden, did you throw away my Dumb Cane and get a new one?"

"Your dumb what?"

"You did, didn't you?" Indignation cracked in her voice. "I told you I was going to nurse it to health." She motioned to the leafy plant in its bright ceramic container. "That's the pot it was in, but that is *not* my plant."

"Oh. Yeah. About that..." How did he explain what Evening had done? "I didn't get rid of it."

A COLD TOMORROW

She knuckled her hands against her hips, jutting her chin to stare up at him. "Then where is it?"

"Um... Can we talk about this later? It involves Lach, and it's complicated." Taking her arm, he steered her toward the living room. "I promise I didn't get rid of your plant, but at the moment I'd rather hear about what happened at the River."

She pressed her lips together and eyed him as if measuring how truthful he was being. Finally, she exhaled, clearly having a hard time holding back whatever news she'd originally wanted to share. When he pulled her to a seat on the sofa, she pivoted to face him.

"Shawn had too much to drink. Nancy overheard him mumbling that he was unhappy about Suzanne's pregnancy."

Caden didn't make a habit of sticking his nose in other people's business, but ever since the domestic dispute he'd responded to last summer, he'd thought the couple a disaster waiting to happen. Both were volatile and self-centered, two people who didn't know how to share a spotlight. And at twenty-four, three years younger than Suzanne, Shawn was still grossly immature, more interested in his growing fame on the dirt track than in maintaining a healthy marriage. Caden didn't see how a child was going to change any of that.

"Anyway," Eve picked up the thread of her story. "Suzanne came in and started screaming at Shawn. He was at the bar with Floyd and the Bradley brothers when she unloaded on him. Telling him she was sick of him going out every night and coming home in a stupor. That he had a child on the way and needed to shape up. I've never seen her so angry."

"Ryan saw all this?" He couldn't imagine his brother not intervening.

"Yeah, but before he could do anything, Shawn stood up and pushed her." Eve's eyes widened with the memory. "I mean *really* pushed her. She fell back against one of the tables and ended up on the floor. A pregnant woman!"

Caden swore. "I hope Ryan threw Shawn across the bar."

Eve shook her head, flapping her hands in the air like a bird. "Jerome beat him to it."

"*Kelly?*" He must have heard wrong. "Jerome Kelly?"

"I couldn't believe." Eve gulped for air. "He flew across the room and punched Shawn straight in the face. I think the poor guy bruised his hand, and all Shawn did was stagger—probably because he was drunk. He shook it off and clobbered Jerome. Suzanne was screaming and sobbing, the whole time he was whaling on Jerome. Ryan and the Bradley boys finally got them separated, and Ryan turned Shawn over to the Point Pleasant police."

"What happened to Jerome?"

"Katie and I iced his hand, then got him a steak to put on his eye. It was already turning black when I left. He's pretty banged up, but I think he's going to be okay. People at the café went out of their way to treat him like a hero. He was actually still there and smiling when I headed home."

Caden released a quiet exhale. It could have been worse. "What about Suzanne? Is she okay?"

"Hopefully. Donnie volunteered to take her to the hospital to be checked out, and make sure the baby's okay. She took a hard fall, and I think she banged her head." Eve fisted her hands on her laps, her expression hardening with determination. "I am *not* going to serve Shawn at my café. He either gets his act together or he can find someplace else to socialize."

"I'll back you on that one." Although he had a feeling after tonight's episode and the way gossip spread through town, it would be some time before Shawn Preech grew bold enough to show his face again. A man who abused a pregnant woman had nothing to look forward to but shame and scorn.

Hooking an arm around Eve's neck, he tugged her close and kissed her temple. "You've had a chaotic evening and so have I. What do you say we call it a night and start over again tomorrow?"

She flattened her palm against his chest, searching his face as she gazed up into his eyes. "You still haven't told me about my Dumb Cane."

He sighed. She would be fixated on the plant. Each of the leafy greens scattered through the house held a special place in her heart. Thank God they didn't have a dog.

"Honestly?" He raised a brow. "It had a growth spurt. Other than that you'll have to ask Lach."

Chapter 16

On Halloween night Katie joined Eve and Sarah Sherman to watch the town's Halloween Parade from the front porch of the Parrish hotel. Earlier, she and Eve had positioned extra rockers outside, and made sure hot cider and cocoa was available for a small fee in the lobby. Residents lined the streets with lawn chairs and stools, others gathering under the awnings of local businesses to watch the colorful procession. Overhead, the sky was clear, a cauldron of black jeweled by the glittering pinprick of starlight. A nip of cold underscored the air, but an atmosphere of excitement kept the worst of the chill at bay.

Katie had allowed Sam to accompany her mom and Martin Ward down the road, the three of them claiming a prime spot in front of Doreen Sue's salon. The location was perfect for Sam, giving him an up-close view of the costumed skeletons and ghouls strutting down Main Street. The high school marching band followed, decked out in hooded black capes and stark white face paint. There were scarecrows, zombies, and ghosts.

"Look at that." Katie motioned down the street where the top of a green glowing head was visible. Given the recent UFO activity and the flap that occurred in the sixties, it was only natural that extraterrestrials would make an appearance in the parade. From experience, she knew the Mothman would be last, several people costumed in gray, white, or black to represent Point Pleasant's infamous monster. "I think the parade is bigger this year." She liked the addition of several women dressed in fairy costumes passing out candy to the children in the crowd.

Eve moved beside her, a cup of cocoa cradled in her hands. They had a corner of the porch to themselves. "Too bad Caden and Ryan couldn't be here."

"Where are they, anyway?" Bundled into a coat that looked too big on her small frame, Sarah hunched her shoulders. She'd never liked the cold.

"Where else?" Eve sipped her cocoa. "Working late shift. At least with most everyone here for the parade, they should have a quiet night." A wagon loaded with mammoth pumpkins rolled past. The cart was driven by a man wearing the flowing robes and coiffed white wig of an old-fashioned judge.

"Maybe they'll get lucky and find Lyle." Katie bit her lip. She and Sam planned to move home tomorrow, but it bothered her to know her ex was still out there. She also worried about the driver of the green van and whether he might return for a repeat visit. Ryan seemed to think she was in the clear. With Jerome out of the hospital and Parker still missing, Deputy Brown, or whoever he might be, would be focused solely on Indrid Cold and the Mothman.

"Let's hope so." Sarah tugged the collar of her coat closer.

Across the street, Katie caught sight of Jerome as he waved to her over a throng of teens with spiked fluorescent hair. The extravagant styles were most likely the work of her mom's salon. Smiling, she waved back.

"I think he has a crush on you." Eve elbowed her side.

"We're just friends. He knows I'm with Ryan."

"So I guess the Ouija board was right." Sarah's eyes danced with amusement. "You did get involved with him."

Only several weeks old, the memory of that night seemed an eternity of the past. The board wasn't something she liked to think about, but the eerie game had served a purpose. "It indicated I was going to be involved with someone named Cold." She shivered, disturbed the prediction had come to pass. "In a roundabout way, through Parker's message, I guess that came true." She and Eve had told Sarah about Cold's message.

Katie eyed her friend. "Did you ever find out who Q.M. is?"

Sarah exhaled a breath that sent her bangs fluffing from her forehead. A quartet of baton twirlers dressed as jesters danced past. "No luck. I wish the silly thing had spelled out L.E. instead."

"L.E.?" Eve's brows knit together.

"Lach Evening." Sarah rubbed her gloved hands to circulate warmth. "I haven't seen him tonight. I thought he'd want to watch the parade."

Eve shook her head. "I don't think he's the frivolous type."

"Or much for flirting." Sarah sounded disappointed. "I tried to strike up a conversation with him and all he did was respond politely, then excuse himself. If he hadn't been so courtly about the whole thing, I would have thought he was snubbing me."

Katie laughed. There was something undeniably magnetic about Lach. Unquestionably attractive, his accent and the aura of mystery he projected had most of the women in town twittering like besotted hens. "I wouldn't worry about Lach." She leaned closer to Sarah. "You still have Q.M. waiting for you. You just have to figure out who he is."

"Great. The love of my life is a phantom." Sarah rubbed her nose. "I'm getting cold. I'm going inside for cider. Anyone want to join me?"

Katie glanced back to the street. "Jerome is headed over. I think I'll stay here and say hello."

"And that's the unfairness of life." Sarah tapped Katie's arm. "You've got Ryan Flynn wrapped around your finger and Jerome following you around like a love-sick dog." She chuckled lightly, her tone one of warm affection. "Lucky girl. The next time we consult a Ouija board, I'm going to insist on more than initials."

* * * *

Halloween night was a prime time for vandalism, especially with kids and teens high on the excitement of the annual parade. Point Pleasant police held jurisdiction over the town, while Caden had the broader scope of the TNT and Mason County. He still had every intention of visiting the old munitions site when 11:00 PM rolled around, but for now it was enough to vanish for a short time, doing a random patrol in his car. He'd already told Eve not to expect him until after midnight.

The parade had long passed the sheriff's station and progressed farther down Main. A few streamers littered the sidewalks, pieces of orange crepe paper scattered with black confetti. Several people folded up lawn chairs or lingered in small groups, talking among themselves. Jack-o'-lanterns glowed in the windows of most local businesses, and farther down the road, the sound of music and applause floated on the air.

Caden rounded the corner of the sheriff's office and headed for the parking lot. He walked briskly, hands in his pockets, head down as he concentrated on the night ahead. After everything Evening had told him, he had a thin chance of connecting with Cold. Even if Lach's father wasn't returning for Parker, there was still a connection between the two. Caden owed the kid whatever help he could offer.

He was almost to his patrol car when he heard footsteps behind him.

"Trick or treat."

Caden pivoted, coming face-to-face with a leering skeletal head—a black mask overlaid with fluorescent white bones. The person who stood before him wore a form-fitting dark top and jeans.

Exhaling, he shook off the surprise. "Hey, the parade's that way." He pointed down the street. The moment he glanced aside, a blunt object cracked across his cheek, driving him to his knees. Instinctively, he groped for his revolver. The second blow battered the back of his neck. His gun was half out of the holster when he crumpled to the ground unconscious.

* * * *

The first sensation Caden became aware of was the pull of dried blood on his split cheek, the taste of dirt in his mouth. Someone muttered in the background, a low string of words that ping-ponged inside his skull. Face down, he'd been deposited on bumpy ground, his arms stretched behind his back and bound at the wrists. It took a while for him to process his surroundings. The crude concave walls splattered with graffiti and the rusting containers that had once contained chemicals could only mean his captor had taken him to the TNT.

Lyle?

Whoever it was, the guy had kindled a fire. Shadows leaped and danced on the stone walls, distorted and exaggerated by the bowl-shaped dome of the igloo. The memory of a grinning skeleton mask floated up from the quagmire fogging Caden's brain. He didn't have to look to know his gun, cuffs, and radio were gone.

Closing his eyes, he tried to roll onto his back. A sharp sting knifed down his neck, wrenching a groan from his lips.

"Let me help." A hard kick to his ribs flipped him over and left him gasping for air.

Lyle Mason bent close, the mask gone, his face a maniacal blend of firelight and shadow. "Been waiting for you to wake up. Gotta have a talk with you, Flynn. It's long overdue."

Gripping Caden under the arms, he dragged him backward. Caden kicked out, trying to snag his legs, but the movement was sluggish, hampered by his stupor. Mason flung him against the stone wall. His shoulder hit with an audible smack, igniting a burst of pain.

He spat blood from his mouth. "What do you want?"

"You forgot her, didn't you?"

Caden's head spun. "Who?"

"Not the right answer!" Lyle cracked him across the face. "I knew you forgot. I knew she meant nothing to you." Fisting his hands in his hair, he yanked frantically, as if trying to rip the dirty strands from his skull. He paced in a tight circle, bent his head back, then screamed at the ceiling.

Definitely unstable, a prime candidate for West Central.

Had Lyle tossed his gun, or was the revolver somewhere in the igloo? Even with the small fire Lyle had kindled, the interior of the bunker was festooned with shadow. Strewn among the old chemical containers Caden spied a few crumbled packages—crackers, chips, and jerky—along with a raggedy blanket and a six-pack of beer. Lyle must have been living in this place. It wasn't the same bunker where Caden had conversed with Cold, but there were numerous igloos scattered throughout the warren of the TNT.

"Lyle, stop and listen." Caden wet his lips, his mouth dry. He tried to ignore the incessant pounding in his head, splinters of pain taking root behind his eyes. "You're confused. There was a man. Lach Evening—"

"No." Whirling, Lyle stabbed a finger in his direction. His eyes blazed with fury. "I have nothing to say about him. Only her."

Caden hedged, fearful of setting off another explosion of anger by questioning who "she" was.

Lyle bent forward, hands locked on his knees. Behind him, the fire crackled and hissed, spitting embers into the air. He sucked on his lips, then blew out like a fish. "I want you to say her name."

"She..." Caden racked his memory. Someone from the past. Someone from high school who'd mattered in a way no other girl had.

"You're not answering me." Lyle's fingers twitched.

Shit.

The name struck Caden in the same instant he met Lyle's demented gaze head-on. "Lottie." He should have realized sooner.

Lyle blinked, the fall and rise of his eyelids mimicking the slow wink-stare of an owl. He recoiled as if slapped. For a split second, the deranged fire dimmed in his gaze. "You do remember." Rubbing his palms against his jeans, he squatted on his haunches, a grotesque hobgoblin backlit by firelight. "She loved you." His face hardened, carved by hate. "She died because of you."

Caden swallowed. Behind his back, he flexed his hands, trying to force circulation through his bound wrists. Needles pinged up his arms. "Lyle, I never did anything to Lottie."

"That's the problem. You ignored her." Tugging on his shirt, he squeezed the soiled fabric repeatedly, a nervous tick. "Except once. You gave her a ride home from school."

Caden clenched his jaw, struggling to remember. He'd barely spoken to Lottie. She was backward and shy, a plump girl shunned by the more popular kids in school. His crowd. If he'd given her a ride, it would have been in kindness, not to take advantage of her.

"Yeah. I remember now." He forced himself straighter, drawing his knees to his chest. He scraped his wrists against the rock behind him. With enough friction he might be able to fray the binding. Lyle didn't seem to notice the effort, focused somewhere in the past.

Damn Evening. The guy had really fucked up Mason's head.

"There were some girls giving her a hard time after school." The memory was spotty, but piecemeal enough to stitch together. "Three or four of them, surrounding her. She looked scared."

Lyle bobbed his head.

"I was driving by and stopped." If he could get Lyle close enough, he might be able to scissor his legs around Mason's neck. Render him unconscious. He kept his gaze pinned on Lyle's face as he scraped his wrists against the rough stone. A trickle of blood sluiced into his palm. "I asked Lottie if she wanted a ride, then drove her to your house." An innocent offer, an innocent ride. How could Lyle possibly connect that to his sister's death?

"That was all it took." Lyle sat on his heels and dragged his fingers across his cheek. In the limited light, his nails looked green, packed with dirt beneath the tips. "You rescued her, and from that moment on, all she did was talk about how she wanted to be with you. I told her you were out of her league, that you'd never be interested in a girl like her. I tried my best to make her see reason, but she'd come out of her shell. It took weeks to work up her nerve, and what did she do?"

Caden's gut plummeted. *Oh, fuck.* "She asked me to the spring dance."

Lyle's lip curled in a snarl. "And you turned her down."

"I already had a date."

"It didn't matter!" Lyle bellowed the accusation, spittle flying from his mouth. "You wouldn't have taken my sister, anyway. You crushed her." He scrambled to his feet, his chest rising with the whistling hiss of his breath. "I found her at home…on the flat roof outside her bedroom. It's where we'd go to talk. She was sobbing, crying her eyes out. You made her feel ugly, like a fool. Silly Lottie thinking Caden Flynn would want to be seen with her."

"Lyle, I never—"

"Shut your fucking mouth!" Lyle balled his hands into fists and screamed at the top of his lungs. Whirling, he spun in a circle and clutched his hair again. "I tried to talk to her, but she shut me out. I was angry. She'd made a fool of herself rather than listen to me. We argued, and I pushed her. Oh, God! Oh, God!" He buckled to his knees. "I pushed her and she fell."

Curling in on himself, he locked both arms over his head. Deep sobs ripped from his throat, punishing his body with convulsions.

Caden used his heels to brace himself against the wall. Awkwardly, he manipulated his shoulders to scramble upright, all the while sawing the rope across the stone. It wouldn't take Mason long to become completely unhinged after his meltdown.

"It was an accident, Lyle."

"No. No." The sobs were tortuous, gut-wrenching. A primal weeping that bore little resemblance to anything human. "Someone has to pay for her death." He looked up, his face streaked by dirt and tears, spittle clinging to his cracked lips. "I'm sorry, Caden." He reached behind his back and pulled a black object from his waistband.

The rope snapped on Caden's wrists. He dove to the side as the crack of a bullet struck the wall behind him.

* * * *

The parade had ended and Main Street was quiet. His shift over, Ryan walked to the parking lot, debating the wisdom of heading to the TNT. In a little over an hour, Jerome would be camped out near his house waiting for Indrid Cold to appear, like Linus anticipating the arrival of the Great Pumpkin. He could play Sally Brown and stake out the pumpkin patch too, but the whole thing was probably a waste of time. Even after everything Caden had told him about Lach Evening, Ryan still believed the coded message was a fool's errand. Without a precise location—

He came to an abrupt stop, noticing Caden's patrol car in its usual spot. Odd.

His brother had left while the parade was winding down. He would have been on duty, so it would have been unusual for him to leave in his own car, but not out of the question. Especially since he planned to visit the TNT later that night. Ryan sprinted to the back of the building where the sight of Caden's red Capri clamped a fist around his gut.

His mind kicked into overdrive. Maybe Caden had returned and Ryan hadn't noticed.

No, he would have picked up on that.

Scrubbing a hand over his jaw, he crushed a stab of alarm. Could be Caden had left, come back, then headed down the street to the hotel or the café. That made the most sense.

Spurred into motion, he jogged toward the road. Halfway there, he drew up short, spying a smattering of dark circles on the asphalt near Caden's patrol car. He'd seen enough dried blood to recognize the stains.

His sense of foreboding grew as he squatted and brushed his fingertips over the dime-sized splotches.

Ryan spun, a single hasty step bringing him smack up against Lach Evening. "Oof!" He expelled a grunt of air. "What the hell? Get out of my way. I've got to alert the station Caden is missing." He ducked to the side, but Evening snagged his forearm, his grip surprisingly strong. Not a muscle of effort twitched on Evening's face, but his grasp formed an unbreakable iron band.

"It would be better if we went alone."

"Went?" Ryan spat the word.

"To find your brother." Evening released him. "I noticed the same thing you did. Blood near Caden's patrol car. It stands to reason Lyle has abducted him."

*It stands to reason...*Ryan wanted to smack the lilting accent and overly proper words from his mouth. "All the more reason to sound the alarm."

"All the more reason to proceed with as little commotion as possible." Evening took a step backward, putting space between them. He wore black again, but his button-down shirt and tailored jacket had been replaced with a turtleneck and long leather coat. His slacks and shoes were equally dark in color. But for his white-blond hair, he would have blended into the shadows. "Mr. Mason is my problem. I can't have others apprehending him. I'm sure your brother told you of my background and my true nature."

"Yeah." A sour admission. If the guy really was some kind of alien, then he'd want Lyle handled as quietly as possible. Buried in that ugly dilemma was an ethical question of whether or not Mason should be handed over to someone like Evening. At the moment, Ryan didn't give a rat's ass about the morality one way or another. "I need to find my brother. I'm going to do whatever's best for him."

Evening raised a single eyebrow. "Would it not be safe to say I am your best resource for accomplishing that goal?"

"Hell, Evening, you can't even find Lyle."

"We don't need Mr. Mason. All we have to do is locate your brother."

"No shit. And how are we going to do that?"

Evening overlooked the vulgarity. "Your brother shares a bond with a creature who can manage it for us."

Ryan hesitated as the logic sank in. "The Mothman."

"Precisely."

Easier said than done. "And how do you plan on summoning a creature that has eluded hunters for decades?"

Evening smiled thinly. "I'm afraid you'll have to trust me."

* * * *

Caden dove to his knees as the bullet ricocheted off the wall. His teeth clacked together and he lunged forward, plowing into Lyle. Matched in height, Mason still outweighed him by a good twenty pounds. The heavy man fell backward, arms cartwheeling. He barely missed the fire as they struck the ground together. Grasping his wrist, Caden slammed his arm against the hard-packed soil to break his hold on the gun. Lyle grunted, but clung to the weapon.

"*No, no no!*" Stretching his free arm toward the fire, he fumbled to clasp one of the blazing sticks.

Caden caught the movement from the corner of his eye a second before the burning rod crashed into his shoulder. Heat and pain exploded in his arm. He released Lyle on reflex and rolled to the side. With effort, he got his feet under him.

Mason snarled something unintelligible and jerked the gun into motion. Caden bolted for the doorway and ducked through the opening as the crack of the .38 reverberated through the bunker. The bullet sliced open his arm, the graze sharp enough to double him over. A messy splatter of blood soaked his sleeve. Clamping a hand over the tear, he ran unsteadily for the trees.

"You can't hide." Lyle's voice bounced among the tangled nest of birch and pine. Heavy footfalls, snapping twigs, and a rustle of trampled leaves followed.

Caden ducked behind an oak, fighting to hold his breathing in check. He'd trained for situations like this. Lyle might know the TNT, even how to track an animal in the woods, but he wasn't thinking rationally and his quarry was a skilled law-enforcement officer who'd also served in Vietnam.

Mason had shot two rounds. Four remained. Caden pressed his back to the tree and listened to his pursuer stumble around in the dark.

Several yards away, a flashlight burst to life. The narrow beam swept back and forth, cutting a path through the shadows. Lyle moved in the opposite direction.

Caden waited until he couldn't see the bobbing flashlight any longer, then shoved from the trunk and lurched into the darkness.

Chapter 17

Ryan eyed the small clearing. There was no trace of the dead dogs he'd found over a week ago, or the silvery globs of "star shit."

"Why here?" He turned to face Evening, who stood in the center of the exposed area. They'd left Ryan's patrol car tucked into a weedy strip of grass off Potters Creek Road, then hiked the rest of the distance. Even with the aid of a flashlight, Ryan had blundered his way. By contrast, Evening had walked unassisted, never once floundering. He'd stepped easily, almost soundlessly, among knots of briars and matted overgrowth.

"Why not here? As you can see it is open." Evening extended a hand to indicate the unusual baldness of the terrain. "An ideal spot to summon the winged cryptid we seek."

The cryptid.

Ryan had never actually seen the Mothman. Up until last summer he'd considered the thing more fantasy than fact, a local legend to be told around campfires and debated over beers at the River Café. He wasn't entirely sure what to expect.

"Fine. Just get busy with whatever tricks you've got up your sleeve." Shifting restlessly, he angled the beam of his flashlight onto his watch. "It's after eleven-thirty. Caden's been missing for hours. Who knows what Lyle could have done?"

"I understand your impatience, but I require silence while I concentrate. Whatever comes of my efforts, do not interfere."

Ryan exhaled, his only reply a curt nod. On the drive to the TNT, Evening had explained how he intended to summon the Mothman using a form of telepathy shared among his people. Ryan might have placed more confidence in the idea if Caden hadn't told him there was little of the original "person" remaining in the Mothman. That entity had become a mutation, a thing as far removed from his original race as Ryan was from Evening.

Clenching his jaw, he narrowed his gaze on the blond-haired man.

Freaking alien.

The guy was supposed to be some kind of ultra psychic with advanced cognitive and extrasensory powers. Or so Evening had told him in his lightly accented voice. No boasting or ego stroking in the straightforward revelation, but a blunt statement of fact. If anyone had the power to breach the chaos of the creature's mind, Evening was the best candidate. Not even his father, Cold, could claim his particular skills.

Right. Ryan puffed out his cheeks.

Evening wasn't doing much of anything except standing with his eyes closed. His arms hung at his sides, his head tilted slightly back. Moonlight gilded his hair with a coin-bright polish, but otherwise, he appeared as a murky stain concealed by heavier darkness.

Ryan resisted the urge to look at his watch again, crushing a stronger impulse to pace. Halloween night, and he was standing in a slaughter-pen for dogs, placing his faith in a self-purported space invader—who might just as easily be whacked in the head—hoping to summon a bogeyman from folklore. If anyone had told him last spring he and his brother would be mixed up in a hotbed of unexplained hocus-pocus, he would have laughed in the idiot's face.

"Get on with it already," he mumbled under his breath.

Whether his words triggered the results, or the timing was coincidental, a burst of silver-blue shot upward from the ground engulfing Evening in a geyser of flickering light.

Ryan wobbled back a step. Flashes of argent and pearl twined with flames of cold sapphire, outlining Evening's form. The snarl of trees encircling the clearing appeared to dance, grotesquely animated by a nightmarish blend of light and shadow.

Transfixed, Ryan stared.

A metallic sheen seeped over the grass, inching forward with the speed of slowly oozing blood. Evening hadn't moved, his posture a mirror image of before. His eyes remained closed, arms limps at his sides. The only outward clues to betray his tension were the rapid tapping of a single index finger against his leg, and a noticeable tightness at the corners of his mouth.

Ryan fidgeted. Evening didn't appear in any outward distress, yet the sense of strain rolling off the man was palpable. Hell, maybe that kind of conflict was normal for an alien, part of the everyday gig. For all Ryan knew, he could be plotting an invasion of Earth, communicating with a mothership instead of calling the Mothman.

Minutes passed, Evening's toll in maintaining the trance growing more apparent. The eerie light flared brighter, a white sun, threatening nova. Evening's face contorted, his expression bordering on agony. The tremor in his hand crept into his arm and traveled down his leg.

"Evening." Ryan lurched forward, drawing up sharply when an earlier warning echoed in his head.

Do not interfere.

Shit.

A whirring hum started at the back of Ryan's head, the gradually building drone like a drill boring into his skull.

Evening grunted and dropped to his knees.

"Evening." No response. The light flickered and dimmed, but the buzzing intensified. Ryan ground his teeth . "Lach, what the hell is happening?"

The man swayed forward, planting his palms against the ground to keep from crumpling altogether.

So much for not interfering. Ryan gripped him under the armpits and tried to haul him upright. The whine whistled higher, then exploded with a roar. A strong wind ripped through the clearing, blowing the hair back from his face. The light died abruptly, snuffed by an invisible hand.

Ryan glanced to the sky.

He had the presence of mind not to scream when the Mothman winged into the clearing.

* * * *

Caden's eyes had adjusted to the darkness, but exhaustion and cold crippled his movements. A smattering of moonlight penetrated the tree canopy, barely enough to illuminate the ground. The arm wound left him disoriented. Bleeding freely at first, it had finally begun to slow, the sleeve of his jacket stuck fast to his skin by coagulated blood. At least the bullet hadn't ripped through muscle and tissue. The damage would be minimal if he could get to a hospital.

Drained, he leaned his good arm against the scarred trunk of an elm in an effort to stay upright. A few minutes. That's all he needed to gather his strength. A few moments of rest and he'd move on.

"Can't hide forever, Flynn."

Lyle was close. Caden had lost track of how long he'd been running, dodging and hiding among the trees. He was starting to think Mason was part bloodhound. Wearily, he pushed forward. The beam of a flashlight swept across his path. A bullet blasted into the elm, splintering the bark.

Caden crashed to the side, tucking and rolling through a snarl of brush. He grunted when his injured arm struck the ground, the pain bringing him close to blacking out. Another bullet whistled over his head.

"Nowhere to go." Lyle's heavy footsteps crunched through the leaves, drawing nearer.

Caden froze.

"Come out of there." The light found his hiding place.

He blinked against the beam. How pathetic to be hunted and penned like an animal. "Lyle, we can talk about this."

"Out here. Where I can see you."

He stood slowly, the pain of gaining his feet drawing his jaw into a clench. He slogged through the thistles, a bloody hand clamped over his wounded arm. Lyle had used four bullets but two remained in the gun. This time there was no chance of Caden running or dodging. He played the only card he had left. "Lottie wouldn't want this."

Lyle faced him, one hand gripping the .38 at waist level, the other slanting the flashlight from his shoulder. All he had to do was pull the trigger for a gut shot.

"You didn't know her. You wouldn't know what she'd want."

"I know she wouldn't want you wasting your life in a jail cell, and that's what's going to happen if you shoot me."

"Shoot you?" Lyle guffawed, his laugh tweaked with sarcasm. "Nah, I'm not gonna shoot you. I got better things planned." He motioned Caden ahead of him, back the direction they had come. "Start walking."

Biding his time, Caden did as instructed. He glanced over his shoulder, gauging the distance between them. Too far away to make a play for the gun, too close to miss being shot if Lyle pulled the trigger. "Where are we going?"

"Back to the igloo."

"Why there?"

"Because that's where I have everything I need to finish the job." Lyle's face was implacable, an unforgiving mask, twisted by tentacles of insanity. "I lost my heart the day my sister died. I'm gonna cut yours out as payment."

* * * *

Ryan ground his teeth and clamped his hands over his ears, trying to block the incessant droning. The damn sound was going to drive him insane if it didn't ease up. He whirled away from the creature, stumbling beneath a wave of terror. What had Caden told him? The Mothman projected emotion, wielding fear as a weapon. Nightmare images plundered his mind—his body, broken and discarded in the clearing, his intestines leaking from his gut in a pulpy, blood-soaked string.

Stop!

He squeezed his eyes shut and gulped for air.

Lach Evening touched his arm. Immediately, the droning ceased and the images vanished. As if an invisible hand had been squeezing the life out of him, then abruptly released its hold.

Breathing heavily, he straightened. Fear fired along his nerves, but without the same mind-numbing constriction as before. Enormous red eyes met his gaze head-on when he turned. He'd never seen a color like that—a chaotic fusion of blood, crimson, and char.

It has no face.

Beside him, Evening said something in a language he didn't understand. Lach had recovered most of his poise. A measure of strain still showed in his black eyes, but otherwise he appeared composed.

Immune to the bombardment of projected fear.

Ryan chanced another glance at the creature. Made his gaze travel from its eyes to its wings, then the bony structure of its mid-section. It towered over them, its upper body hunched slightly forward. Its flesh—if flesh it could be called—appeared rubbery and pliant. Half bird, half man, it was hard to believe the monster had once resembled someone as striking as Evening. Time and Earth's prehistoric atmosphere had warped it into the nightmare that stood before him. Too bad Evening's people hadn't figured out a solution for the problem until after it was too late for the Mothman.

Something foreign touched his mind. An inquisitive exploration that lasted only a second. A flicker of sorrow for the creature's fate passed through him. The last of his fear melted with the fading probe.

"It accepts you," Evening said.

Ryan jerked in response. "What?" Had he been tested in some manner?

"It also understands you and Caden are family. It is impatient, angered. It has sensed your brother's pain." He frowned, noticeably troubled. "Their bond is much stronger than I anticipated."

Ryan looked from the cryptid to Evening. The thing was already retreating, its gait a strange shuffle-lope as it took three steps backward. "It knows where Caden is?"

A gust of wind buffeted Ryan as the Mothman launched straight upward. The thunder of its wings was almost as punishing as the droning buzz, both sounds amplified throughout the clearing. Not as sharp this time, or as piercing, but enough to make him grit his teeth. He grasped Evening by the arm. "What the hell's going on?"

"Hurry. Back to the car." Evening wrenched away, striding crisply in the direction of the road. "It will lead us to Sergeant Flynn."

"Then you did communicate?' Ryan ran to catch up. He switched on his flashlight, irked that Evening was able to dash so agilely, never faltering or stumbling. The guy wasn't even breathing hard. He also didn't bother to answer.

By the time they reached the road, any strain Evening had experienced during his telepathic communication with the Mothman was no longer evident. The tension lines on his face had vanished, his black eyes sharpened by preternatural intelligence. Ryan still had no idea how they were going to find Caden when the Mothman abruptly materialized several yards down the road. The thing had been daunting when standing, but far more intimidating soaring in flight, its wing span large enough to rival a pterodactyl.

"Holy shit." He froze with his fingers wrapped around the door handle of his patrol car. Backlit by moonlight, on a cloud-streaked sky, the creature looked like a demon from the Netherworld. A ripple of fear crept down his spine.

"Get in the car, Sergeant." Evening opened the door on the passenger's side and ducked into the seat. "The creature will stay within range, at least until we reach the area where Mr. Mason has your brother."

Ryan did as instructed, firing the ignition and shifting into gear. He hit the gas, his gaze traveling to the mic on the dashboard. It wouldn't hurt to have backup, but he'd committed to Evening that he'd keep the sheriff's department out of their plan. Stupid. Then again, there was no logical way to explain getting help from an alien and a monster rooted in folklore. All he needed was a witch on her broom to make the Halloween night complete.

"You said it sensed Caden's pain." He craned his neck, leaning forward to peer upward through the windshield. The Mothman was still there, a giant black bird blotting out the stars. "Does that mean he's hurt?"

"Most likely."

"Fuck."

Evening sent him an arched glance. "I have never understood the attachment for that particular vulgarity."

"Yeah?" Ryan tightened his hands on the steering wheel. "You might want to try broadening your vocabulary. When you talk, you sound like some aristocratic duke from the 1800s."

"Ah. Perhaps my favorite period of Earth's timeline." Evening tapped one finger restlessly against the dashboard. He didn't extend his gaze upward, but tension was evident in his rigid posture, impatience in the fidgety beat of his fingertips.

In Ryan's opinion, the edginess made him more human. "You've lived on Earth that long?"

"Longer. I remember when Fort Randolph was all that existed of Point Pleasant."

Ryan nearly choked. "You were here in the days of Chief Cornstalk?"

"Yes, a great leader to his people. His murder was a tragedy."

Ryan would have said more, much more—Cornstalk supposedly cursed Point Pleasant with his dying breath—but the Mothman veered abruptly into the woods on his right, vanishing from sight. He stomped on the brake, bringing the car to a screeching halt. "Damn. I can't see where it went. Now what?"

Evening opened the door and stepped outside. "Now we run." Without waiting, he leaped outside and sprinted for the trees.

Chapter 18

Lyle hadn't tied his hands. That much was good.

Caden squatted in the corner of the igloo, directed there by Mason. Two lousy bullets left in the gun and he couldn't get the damn thing away from the guy. The trek back had worn him out, his injured arm throbbing with each thudding beat of his heart. The wound had stopped bleeding, but it hurt like hell.

Mason was back to mumbling to himself. He kept the gun steadily pointed in Caden's direction as he snagged a duffle bag from his sleeping area and dumped its contents on the ground. Four iron stakes, coils of rope, and a thick-bladed butcher knife.

Crazy. Fanatical.

Lyle hadn't joked when he said he planned to cut out Caden's heart.

Caden gripped his forehead with one hand, pressing hard on his temples. Trying to reason was pretty much out the door. The moment Lyle tried to tie him, he was going to have to make a play for the gun. Even wounded, he stood a chance of taking Lyle down. If only his head wasn't pounding, his arm pulsing, his thoughts muddled by pain.

The fire still flickered, but it was sputtering, the shadows in the igloo growing heavier. Caden welcomed the darkness, the gloom better for concealing himself. With any luck the damn thing would die altogether. Unless—

A spark of hope shot through him. With Lyle's mind twisted the way it was, maybe he could use the dying flames to his advantage. Caden didn't have Evening's abilities, but if light had been a trigger in altering Mason's mind, there was a chance he could use it as a trigger again. At the very least, a delaying tactic to buy him time. He had nothing to lose.

"Lyle."

Mason halted what he was doing and straightened, two spikes clutched in one hand, the .38 in the other. "Need to stake you out before I can cut out your heart. That's how they do it on TV in the horror shows."

What a whack job. "Sure." Caden dragged his tongue across his lips, tasting dirt and blood. "But the fire's dying. You won't be able to see."

"Uh. Yeah." Lyle scrunched his brows together. "I guess you're right." He took a few steps toward the flames, then seemed to realize he couldn't stoke them while holding everything in his hands. Frowning, he glanced from the gun to the stakes, then back again, the decision plainly complicated in his present state. Finally, he dropped the stakes.

To Caden he looked like a kid whose mind had been pulped to mush. Lyle located a few sticks from a pile off to the side, then squatted to feed the fire. The moment his gaze settled on the flames, he froze.

Flicker phenomenon.

Caden launched himself across the igloo. The hard hit of collision ripped the breath from his lungs. He struck the ground with Lyle, rolling over in the dirt.

"Nooooo!" Lyle shrieked.

Caden straddled him, delivering a hard crack to his face. He hammered Mason's wrist into the ground, trying to loosen his grip on the gun. Lyle jerked the trigger and the .38 exploded. The discharge kicked back a deafening roar, the ricochet pinging off the walls twice before burrowing in the dirt near the entrance.

"Lyle, you asshole. You're going to kill us both." Caden drove Lyle's chin to the side, but the momentum sent him sprawling off balance. Mason pistol-whipped the revolver against his wound, sending pain boomeranging the length of his arm.

Caden clenched his jaw, his vision swimming.

"You're outta luck, Flynn." Lyle knocked him to the side. Scrambling quickly to his knees, he shoved the barrel of the gun beneath Caden's chin. "One bullet left." His breath dispelled in a hot, fetid whoosh. "Yeah, I know you've been counting. You're a cop. It only makes sense. I wanted to cut out your heart, but I'll settle for blowing your head off all the same."

Caden tensed, his Adam's apple bobbing as he swallowed. "Lyle—"

The humming started as a low drone, but built swiftly, a thousand angry bees. An audible vibration of vengeance and wrath.

Lyle jerked backward. "What the hell is that?"

A roundhouse kick to the head sent him sprawling facedown in the dirt. Caden wrenched the gun from his slack grip, then staggered backward. The kick had knocked Lyle out cold.

Closing his eyes, Caden pressed his back to the rough stone of the bunker. He wanted nothing more than to sink to the ground and rest, but his predicament had summoned something far more dangerous than Lyle.

You don't have to come. There's no need.

How had he ever bonded with such a creature? For a moment, discordant noise threatened to overwhelm him, the harshness nearly as painful as the ache in his arm. Gradually, it receded. A tempest of wind blew into the bunker, swirling dirt and debris into a funnel from the ground. The fire was extinguished in a single, powerful gust, plunging the interior into impenetrable darkness.

Using his hands to guide him along the wall, Caden fumbled his way outside.

The Mothman waited, a demon from folklore, wings arched high above its back. The sight of the alien no longer inspired fear, but as always, its presence filled him with awe. The welts on his forearm burned as fiercely as they had on the day the monster had placed them there.

It had come. To save him. Again.

Exhaustion, weakness, and pain rolled off him in waves, sensations he had no desire to telegraph. The Mothman cast emotion effortlessly, but consumed the same with equal ease. Now that he understood it better, the last thing he wanted to do was add to the being's misery.

Safe.

He tried to share the concept mentally, hoping the creature would grasp he was no longer in danger. Stepping closer, he was surprised to have no qualms about its proximity. Despite their connection, there had always been a sliver of uncertainty on his part. Bumping against a fallen log, he slumped to a seat three feet from the cryptid.

Immediately a barrage of sensation struck him—indignation, anger, a hunger to hurt and punish, a primal need to terrify. The feelings were not meant for him but for Lyle.

Wearily, Caden scrubbed a hand across his cheek, flecking dried blood to the ground. "It wasn't his fault. Someone from your planet altered his mind." He spoke aloud, uncertain if the creature understood him.

It made a hissing noise.

He wondered how far away Lyle had parked. How long he'd have to flounder in the dark before he discovered Mason's car.

The Mothman hissed again.

He lifted his head and looked into its eyes. Its wingtips rustled.

"I don't know what you want from me."

The thing shrieked.

Caden jerked to his feet, the creature's scream like the razor cut of a sharp knife. Ryan and Lach Evening burst from the trees on his right, Ryan trailing behind.

"Caden." His brother raced to his side, gripped him tightly by his good arm. Ryan swept the beam of his flashlight from his cut check to his blood-soaked jacket. "Oh, man, brother, you look a mess. How bad?"

"It's a graze. Looks worse than it is."

"Where's Mason?" Evening asked.

Caden jerked his head toward the igloo. The blond-haired man dashed toward the opening and disappeared inside.

Ryan used the flashlight to examine Caden's arm. "You were lucky."

"Yeah. Hurts like hell, though."

"My patrol car is back that way." Ryan hooked a thumb over his shoulder. "I can radio ahead to have triage ready at the hospital." He paused, searching Caden's face. "Are you injured anywhere else?"

"Just battered and bruised, and I took a whack to the back of the head." He glanced to the side, starting abruptly when he realized the Mothman had disappeared. "Hey, where'd it go?" Somehow the cryptid had vanished without the usual fanfare of droning and wing-buffeting. He spun on his heel, nearly stumbling in his haste to look behind him.

Ryan gripped him under the arm to hold him steady. "Would you believe the damn thing led us here? Evening summoned it somehow and communicated with it. We followed in my car."

"How'd you know I was missing in the first place?"

"Cop's intuition." Ryan looked around at the cluster of trees penning in the igloo. "It must have walked away, Caden. I got the impression it was, um…ticked off, that Lyle might have hurt you. There is some really weird protective thing going on there."

"I don't want to think about it now." Caden's head was pounding.

Evening stepped from the igloo, leading a docile-looking Lyle by the arm. He stationed Mason to the left of the doorway, then quietly instructed him to remain there until summoned. Lyle's eyes were glazed, his face slack and expressionless.

"What'd you do to him?" Ryan asked as Evening approached. "Put him in some kind of trance?"

"That's exactly what I did, Sergeant Flynn. It's necessary until I can return him to Austin. At that point, I'll repair his mind and wipe everything that has happened from his memory since he returned to Point Pleasant."

Caden frowned. "How are you going to explain that to the people he interacted with here? Lyle might forget, but they'll remember."

Evening tilted his head to the side, his expression complacent. "I'll tell your sheriff I was mistaken about the identity of the man who escaped, and place a post-suggestion in his mind that he accepts my account as factual."

Ryan looked appalled. "You can do that?"

"And more. Sheriff Weston will relay the information to the rest of the men under his jurisdiction. The only people Mr. Mason interacted with are his cousin, Darrell, who I already saw and addressed earlier today, and Ms. Lynch."

Ryan stepped in front of him. "You *will not* mess with her head."

"You want her to retain her memory, as the two of you?"

"Absolutely."

Evening seemed to consider.

"Lach," Caden said quietly. "You owe us that much."

"Perhaps I do. Very well. You and your brother"—his gaze shifted to Ryan—"as well as Ms. Lynch, are the only ones who will retain any memory of the events. In time, word will spread through the town that Mr. Mason was never here, and that the reports were merely rumors in error."

"Eve retains her memories too." Caden had no intention of relenting on that point.

Evening frowned his displeasure. "More loose ends."

"Eve is my fiancée and knows your true identity. We're in this together."

"You told her?"

"I did."

A flicker of displeasure passed through Evening's eyes, but after a pause, he consented. "Very well."

Caden nodded his appreciation. As tired as he was, something else struck him. "Hey. It's got to be after eleven."

"Eleven fifty-six to be precise." Evening did not glance at a watch or explain how he knew.

Regardless, Caden believed him. "That means we missed Indrid Cold's passage into this world." Exhaling in defeat, he rubbed the back of his neck. "I wonder if Jerome sat outside waiting for your father to show up." He looked meaningfully at Evening.

"He would have been wasting his time."

"Why?" Ryan asked.

"Because it was not the correct location."

"You knew that?" A twinge of irritation rippled through Caden. "Why didn't you tell us where he'd be if you knew?"

"I didn't know."

"You're not making sense," Ryan snapped.

Evening drew a breath to explain, but there was nothing self-centered in the pause, as Caden would have determined when they first met. "There was never a location in the code, because the site was not up to my father. He planned to appear wherever the Mothman was at that precise moment."

Caden exchanged a glance with his brother. "But that would have placed him somewhere with—"

"Us." Ryan finished the thought. He looked at Evening. "My best guess puts the time close to when you and I were in the clearing."

Evening nodded. "I summoned the Mothman, and by answering that call, he placed himself out of my father's reach for those few seconds. I do not know when, or if ever, my father will physically be able to materialize on Earth again. As I explained before, he does not have my abilities, and thus must rely on transitioning layers between dimensions. Right now those layers are interlocked, which is why there is an unusual amount of UFO activity. "

"All of which has been steadily increasing," Caden noted. Not only had the frequency of the sightings been escalating, but the craft had also started to appear during daylight hours, no longer limited strictly to nighttime.

"Precisely." Evening's black eyes appeared without pupil in the darkness. "Tonight signaled the peak of activity. Dimension travel will dwindle and cease in the next few days as filaments break apart."

And there went Caden's chance of finding Parker. "When that happens, do you have any means of communicating with your father?"

"No more than you."

"Look, Lach. I need to find out what happened to Parker Kline."

"Then go back to the igloo. Ask again. You've proven yourself worthy of the answer."

"What makes now any different than before?" Ryan chimed in.

"Because the Mothman chose your brother over my father."

The gravity of the situation was not lost on Caden, but it was too much to absorb with his head pounding and his arm bathed in fire. Grimacing, he rubbed his jaw. "It's not that I'm not grateful, but I don't understand what the thing wants from me." It had shrieked and hissed, attempting to communicate vocally for the first time.

"Only the Mothman can answer that." Evening turned and walked back to Lyle. "In the meantime, Sergeant, I suggest you allow your brother to drive you to the hospital. I'll escort Mr. Mason to his car and take care of him from there."

Caden glanced to the sky. "And the creature?"

"As I told you before." Gripping Lyle beneath the arm, Evening led the docile man from the igloo toward the intertwined mesh of trees. "His demise will come in a desolate hour. Be vigilant, for that time is not far."

* * * *

It took a week before Caden felt good enough to drive to the TNT and wend his way through the overgrowth. As Lach Evening predicted, the sightings of UFOs had dwindled. Now or then a sporadic rumor cropped up, but for the most part, reports had ceased.

He'd been out of commission for several days, the graze deeper than he'd originally thought. The wound had required stitching, with a few sessions of physical therapy waiting in the wings. At least he'd kicked the prescribed pain meds early and had finally finished the last of his antibiotics. Because he couldn't blame Lyle for the injury, he'd attributed the stray bullet to a Mothman hunter. That put a clampdown on the TNT with the sheriff's office stepping up patrols again.

Caden often wondered what had become of Lyle, but had heard nothing from Evening. Parker Kline was still listed as missing, but there was no longer a concentrated effort to find him. Caden had a strange feeling he'd never see the kid again.

Ten minutes in, he stumbled over the bunker where he'd communicated with Indrid Cold. The igloo stood still and silent, bathed in afternoon sunlight. The last time he'd been here, Cold had turned belligerent, Caden's questions about Parker the catalyst to provoke his hostility. If Parker had really met Cold on the night he'd killed Hank Jeffries, it was possible the alien was partially responsible for Hank's death.

Parker is my mistake to fix.

The memory of Cold's words swirled in Caden's head as he stepped inside the bunker. With the door ajar, a shaft of sunlight penetrated the murky interior. He switched on his flashlight, sweeping the beam to the darkened corners. The place looked much as it had the last time he was here, the old metal canisters undisturbed, the walls marred by graffiti. He turned slowly in a circle, wondering how Cold existed here, a disembodied presence, but couldn't cross boundaries and appear in the flesh.

"Indrid Cold." The last time he'd been here, he'd felt foolish addressing the empty dome. Much had changed since then. "Can you hear me?"

Yes.

As before, the voice echoed in Caden's head. The air temperature plummeted, noticeably colder and heavier. A sense of presence swelled around him, an invisible aura that made the hair prickle on the back of his neck. Unlike his son, or even the Mothman, Cold presented something dangerous. An entity not to be trifled with.

"I met your son."

No response.

Were they going to play the yes/no word game again?

"He sent me here to ask you about Parker Kline."

Still nothing.

Caden exhaled. Flicking off the flashlight, he stood in darkness, the only illumination a small shaft of sunlight angled through the open door. Counting the seconds, he waited until they stretched into minutes. Around him the air grew icier, a physical weight that carried the sting of winter. Tension corded his muscles, drawing his body ramrod straight. An ache started in his wounded arm and splintered to his fingertips. Still he didn't move.

Something wrapped around his wrist. A touch like suction cups pushed beneath his sleeve and fingered the brand left by the Mothman. Caden fought the urge to recoil. He withstood the probing with no more aversion than the slight tightening of his jaw.

Finally the touch withdrew and the air warmed a few degrees. He breathed easier, sensing he had passed a test. A weight lifted from his chest.

Parker is with me. Cold's voice spoke in his head. *He is safe in my world, where I can care for him.*

"You took him from the hospital." Caden thought of the strange life-sized puzzle Parker had taped to his wall. Nurse Brenner said the drawing of Cold had erupted with light, opening a crevice. "From his room. He's been gone all this time?"

Yes.

"Why?"

I will show you.

The interior of the igloo vanished. Suddenly Caden was on the porch of Hank Jeffries' house, the lifeless body of Parker's brother, Tim, cradled in Hank's lap. But he wasn't there as an officer arriving on the scene of a murder. This time he saw the grisly night through Parker's eyes, felt the clutch of red-veined horror at the sight of his brother's ruined face. Bone, blood, and brain matter soiled the ground in a macabre halo. An eye dangled from one empty socket, a string of connective tissue holding the gruesome orb in place. Hank sat in a puddle of blood, chunks of flesh clinging to his chest and arms where he clasped Tim close.

"No!" Parker screamed.

Hank wailed something in reply, but between his hysterical sobbing and drunken, slurred speech, Caden had no idea what he babbled. He remained inside Parker's body feeling the thudding beat of his heart, the choking hand of horror as it squeezed the air from his lungs.

Can't breathe.

He had to get help.

Tim wasn't dead. Couldn't be.

It was all a bad dream, a prank gone wrong. He needed to find help. Someone to get Tim to the hospital where they'd piece his face back together.

Stop playing dead, Tim. It isn't funny.

Parker ran for the road, half crying, half gasping for breath, his legs pumping beneath him. His dad's truck wasn't far. They'd left it a half mile down the road.

He was a distance runner. Ran track in school.

Piece of cake.

He'd drive to town and have help back in no time.

Oh, shit, oh, shit.

Why hadn't he just used the damn phone in Hank's house?

What a stupid ass.

Turn around. Turn around, you idiot.

He'd have to look at Tim again. Hear Hank blubbering.

Could he do it?

Your brother is dying. Your brother is dead.

No, no, no!

It was just a stupid prank.

He pivoted. Would race to the house. Find the phone. Call for help.

Yes, yes! A plan.

Run like you're running for a trophy. For the finish line.

Parker drew up short, blinded by a bright light. Raising an arm, he tried to shield himself from the glare. Something large and cylindrical hovered a few feet above the ground, covering the entire expanse of road. It made a hollow beeping noise, blue and green lights winking rapidly across its surface.

Dumbfounded, he lowered his arm. The light was dazzling, beautiful. It held him enthralled, filled his mind with words he couldn't understand. Languages that tumbled one upon the other, peeling back his brain like the skin of a grape. The music was intoxicating, painful. It ripped through him, tore something vital inside. Chaos and wonder filled his head with marvels so exquisite, he was left hollow and broken when the visions withdrew.

"No!" He fell to his knees.

The craft was gone. All the beautiful lights and musical voices gone too. How could he live without them? Without that foreign language constantly chattering in his brain? Something had to fill the void.

He clambered to his feet, wondering how much time had passed. It seemed like mere seconds, but something told him it was much longer. He'd been headed back to Jeffries' house because Hank had killed his brother.

Tim was dead. No help for him now, his face gone, pulverized by a shotgun blast.

Parker's head hurt. Hurt so badly. No more voices or music.

Everything was wrong, nothing left to fix.

All he could do was run to his dad's truck. Get the handgun his father kept tucked under the seat.

Why wouldn't the voices come back? The otherworldly noise?

Panting, he raced for the truck and the gun. Tears rolled down his face. He reached the Ford and wrenched open the door. Blindly, he groped beneath the seat until his fingers encountered the cold grip of the Smith and Wesson.

No more voices, no more music.

Parker flipped open the chamber of the pistol to check for ammo. He counted the bullets.

The music had vanished. All that remained was death.

Caden staggered and drew a breath, fighting to orient as he was wrenched into the present.

I don't think you need to see the rest, Cold spoke inside his head.

"No." He'd arrived on the scene almost simultaneously with Parker, unaware the boy was armed. He'd watched helplessly as Parker had walked up behind Hank and shot him in the head. He'd been forced to shoot in retaliation.

"Were you in the craft that night?"

Yes. Parker was caught in a type of flicker phenomenon. It happens sometimes with UFO witnesses. His mind couldn't absorb being trapped like that. It damaged him. Changed him.

"He'd been going for help. He had no intention of killing Hank."

No. Something similar to remorse underscored Cold's voice. *Now do you understand why Parker was my mistake to fix? Our brief encounter made him a killer and destroyed his mind.*

"You said he's safe."

Yes. On my world, he hears only the music and voices he craves. He is happy. I will care for him the remainder of his days.

"He has a father on Earth."

Unfortunate, but I cannot reverse the damage to Parker's mind. Would you rather he lives the remainder of his life in a mental institution?

"No." Floyd had already lost his wife and Tim. Parker's father held nothing but animosity for Caden, but it wasn't fair for him to constantly wonder what had become of his son. "You have to give Parker's father closure."

How?

"I don't know, but you owe him that much."

I don't owe humans. I do what I do by choice. Stiff anger lingered in the declaration.

"But you owe the Mothman."

Silence.

Caden pushed further. "According to your son, you abandoned him and others like him. The Mothman is the last of the original group you left on Earth."

The air grew icier, frigid.

Why mention the creature?

"Because I will take your burden." Hopefully, his sanity was intact and the idea sprang from rational thought, not madness. "The cryptid and I are already bonded."

Yes. The word was curt, almost hostile. *His failure to rendezvous with me on Halloween is proof of that.*

"Give Parker's father some kind of closure, and I will make sure the Mothman is protected for the duration of my life. I'll find a way to communicate and do whatever I can to ensure his safety and well-being."

He is not an animal.

"He's not human, either."

But he once looked as you do. As my son does. And he possessed the same, if not greater, intelligence and compassion. That part of him is almost gone. It exists only in spurts now, brief moments of clarity. It will not be easy to communicate.

"I told you I'd find a way." He had no idea how. Part of him regretted making the offer, but he owed Parker. Even if that boiled down to something as simple as bringing Floyd closure, he intended to fulfill the debt.

If you proceed with this offer, the price will be steep.

Caden frowned. "What does that mean?"

The day will arrive when you will be required to do something that won't come easily.

He'd done a lot of things in his lifetime that hadn't come easily. From losing his sister to a murderer, to nightmare memories of Vietnam and shooting Parker, he held plenty of regrets. He was also running out of patience. "Do we have a deal or not?"

Cold considered for the span of several heartbeats.

Fair enough. I will arrange closure for Parker's father, and my debt to the Mothman is thus transferred to you. I will not return to your planet again.

"What about here? In the igloo?"

The air thinned, growing warmer. Caden could almost pinpoint the second when Cold withdrew. A light breeze scuttled through the open doorway and sent a handful of dried leaves swirling around his shoes.

Epilogue

July 6, 1983

"Whew!" Katie flipped the registration book closed and sank onto a stool behind the reception counter. The Parrish Hotel had been busy the last several days with guests checking in and out over the long holiday weekend. Boat rides, fireworks over the river, a town parade, and plenty of cookouts had filled the past three days. "That's the last of our weekend guests to check out."

"That's nice." Seated in a chair by the window, Eve sounded dreamy and far away.

The tone was typical of Katie's friend lately, Eve still floating on the glow of being a newlywed. Her wedding to Caden had been beautiful, with the groom singing a love song to the bride in church. Afterward, the reception had carried well into the evening, a good portion of the town invited to the festivities. Everyone had enjoyed themselves, especially the happy couple, who later honeymooned in Key West, soaking up the tropical weather.

Not that it didn't border on tropical now. The temperature was already in the low 80s and it was only eleven in the morning. The air conditioner kept the lobby pleasant, but the moment she stepped outside, sticky heat would plaster her from head to toe.

"Ryan told me about the letter Floyd got from Parker." Abandoning the counter, Katie circled the desk, then dropped into a seat across from her friend.

How Indrid Cold had managed the feat, Katie had no idea, but she sensed Lach Evening was involved. The man parading as a human apparently had a number of abilities he hadn't shared. After leaving Point Pleasant, Evening had followed through as promised, restoring Lyle's mind while wiping his memory about his visit to the river town. The last Katie had heard, her ex had been in Pittsburg looking for work.

"I wonder why Cold waited so long to follow through with his promise to Caden?" Nine months after the fact seemed a long interval to Katie.

Shrugging, Eve plucked at a seam on her shorts. "I guess he wanted to make it seem believable Parker could have really left the country. Give everyone else time to forget. Caden was beginning to doubt he'd live up to his part of the bargain."

Rumor had it the postmark had been from somewhere in South America, the penmanship and wording a dead ringer for Parker's style. Floyd was convinced his son was safe and starting life over. He'd destroyed the message immediately, preventing anyone from tracing the source. The Mason County Sheriff's Department kept Parker on the missing list, but otherwise looked the other way. If not for Shawn Preech, who Floyd made the mistake of confiding in, news likely never would have leaked.

Shawn had been a popular topic of town gossip after Suzanne announced she'd filed for divorce. A miscarriage over the winter, followed by rumors of Shawn's infidelity, had destroyed any chance the feuding couple would ever repair their relationship. Suzanne had kicked Shawn out of the house immediately after filing, and he'd promptly moved in with his girlfriend. According to Sarah, she'd found some troubling things in Shawn's family tree that left her shaken. She'd yet to tell Katie and Eve what they were, but apparently the Preech ancestry wasn't as noble as Shawn had led others to believe.

"At least we haven't been troubled by UFO sightings or visits from Men in Black," Katie commented.

"Life is returning to normal," Eve agreed.

The sightings had dwindled, then stopped altogether within the first weeks of November. Jerome had been disappointed, but explained flaps were limited to periods of time when the layers between dimensions were unusually weak. It had taken fifteen years from Point Pleasant's last flap to the most recent. He fully expected a reoccurrence in the future, but kept himself busy by delving deeper into Mothman research in the interim.

Katie was tempted to ask Eve about the cryptid and if Caden had made progress in communicating with the creature, but had the impression it wasn't something her friend liked to discuss. Caden made it a habit to venture into the TNT once every few weeks, but was usually tight-lipped about what he encountered there. Or so Ryan had told her.

Like the UFOs, Mothman sightings had dwindled. There were still occasional reports that cropped up, one as recent as last week when Chester Wilson swore he saw the monster soar over his barn. Old timers gathered to debate "the bird" over drinks in the River Café, and hotel guests often lounged on the porch rockers, eagerly reading through information on the TNT and anything else they could get their hands on.

Eve yawned and stretched. "I don't know why I feel so lazy today."

Katie smiled. "Maybe it's being blissfully married. I think it agrees with you. Caden too."

"No arguments on that front. What about you and Ryan?"

"What about us?"

Eve nodded toward the diamond engagement ring on Katie's left hand. "Have you picked a date yet?"

"Aren't you rushing things a little? He only proposed last week." She was still floating on her own high, the idea of being happily married something that had seemed an improbability last year. "We have a lot to sort through, including living arrangements."

"It's wonderful he plans to adopt Sam."

Warmth spread through Katie's stomach. It had been important to Ryan that Sam was onboard with their marriage. A lot of guys wouldn't have cared, but Ryan not only wanted her for his wife, he wanted Sam as his son. The evening Ryan sat down to chat with Sam had left the boy so overjoyed he hadn't been able to sleep that night. He was finally going to have a father like other kids.

"We might do a fall wedding." Katie had always loved autumn with its colorful bounty of pumpkins and brightly hued leaves. "Either that or wait until spring. It depends on how long the adoption process takes."

The trill of the phone interrupted her. Eve started to stand but Katie shooed her back into her seat. "I'll get it."

Leaning over the counter, she snatched up the receiver. "Good morning. You've reached the Parrish Hotel."

"Yeah. I'd like to book a room." The man's voice on the other end was even, without accent. "I need something within the next month. Can you accommodate me?"

"What type of room would you like, and what dates did you have in mind?"

The man rattled off a few requirements, the oddest being that he wanted to book his stay open-ended. Katie stretched the phone cord, moving behind the counter to grab the registration book. Rates were reasonable, in line with the accommodations they offered, but most guests couldn't afford an open-end reservation. After looking over availability, she suggested a second floor suite. "Given you don't know how long you'll be staying, you might want the extra living space."

"That's fine." No hesitation.

Katie's comment had caught Eve's attention. Her friend stood, raising her eyebrows. The hotel only had three suites, the others all double or queen rooms with baths.

"I'll need a credit card to hold your reservation." Katie relayed the nightly rate, pen poised to jot down the information. The caller supplied a MasterCard number and expiration date.

"And the name on the card?

Katie nearly dropped the phone when the man answered. "Thank you." She recovered quickly. "I believe I have everything I need. We'll see you on Friday the twenty-third for check-in."

"What was that about?" Eve asked after she'd hung up.

"A suite reservation for someone who booked an open-end stay."

"I figured that much. Unusual, but not completely unheard of." Eve stepped closer to the counter. "I was talking about your not-so-subtle look of shock when you asked for a name."

Katie bit her lip. "I know who Q.M. is."

"Q.M.?"

"From the Ouija board. Remember?"

"Oh. I'd forgotten." Eve plainly conjured the memory from last autumn. "What does that have to do with the reservation?"

"Because the man who booked it is named Quentin Marsh." Her gaze dropped to the entry she'd penned in the reservation book, her handwriting noticeably wobbly. Not surprising, given she had an inexplicable feeling something disastrous waited in the wings.

Biting her lip, she slammed the book shut.

Without a doubt, the Mothman would be at the heart of that unknown tragedy.

In case you missed it, keep reading for an excerpt from the first book in the Point Pleasant series,

A THOUSAND YESTERYEARS

Behind a legend lies the truth...

As a child, Eve Parrish lost her father and her best friend, Maggie Flynn, in a tragic bridge collapse. Fifteen years later, she returns to Point Pleasant to settle her deceased aunt's estate. Though much has changed about the once thriving river community, the ghost of tragedy still weighs heavily on the town, as do rumors and sightings of the Mothman, a local legend. When Eve uncovers startling information about her aunt's death, that legend is in danger of becoming all too real . . .

Caden Flynn is one of the few lucky survivors of the bridge collapse but blames himself for coercing his younger sister out that night. He's carried that guilt for fifteen years, unaware of darker currents haunting the town. It isn't long before Eve's arrival unravels an old secret—one that places her and Caden in the crosshairs of a deadly killer . . .

A Lyrical e-book on sale now.

Learn more about Mae at
http://www.kensingtonbooks.com/author.aspx/29541

Prologue

December 15, 1967
Point Pleasant, West Virginia

"Do you think Caden Flynn will go?" Eve Parrish kept pace with her friend, Sarah, as a brisk December wind pushed them down Main Street toward the Crowne Theatre. Eager for a glimpse of the movie poster that had everyone in the tiny river town of Point Pleasant, West Virginia talking, she barely felt the sting on her cheeks. Her mother would box her ears if she knew what Eve was up to, but all the boys at school said the poster hung in the window, plain as day for anyone to see. That had to mean she could sneak a peek. She was twelve now, practically a teenager.

Her parents had called *The Graduate* racy, and Mrs. Quiggly, who sold brown eggs and fresh milk from her farm outside town, said the poster was shameless. She wanted to bring a petition against the theater and make them take the "vile thing" down.

"Silly, busybody," Aunt Rosie had chided behind her back. Never one to get hung up on proper behavior, Aunt Rosie did artsy things like taking photographs and hosting moonlight picnics for friends. She even had a darkroom in her home and occasionally sold shots to the local paper who proudly displayed them with the byline *Photo courtesy of Rosalind Parrish.*

"I heard Caden tell Wyatt Fisher they should take their girlfriends to see it," Sarah said, interrupting her thoughts.

Eve gasped. It was bad enough the boys might see a movie as shocking as *The Graduate,* but more appalling that girls would go, too.

"Maybe they'll chicken out." She had a hopeless crush on Caden, an awkward situation given he was eighteen and the brother of her friend,

Maggie. Although careful not to make a fool of herself whenever Caden was around, she usually ended up tongue-tied.

Sarah shrugged and tugged the collar of her coat higher against the wind. Several cars drove by in the pre-holiday rush, the glow of headlights holding the night at bay. Sunset was still a half hour away, plenty of time for Eve and Sarah to reach the theater and ogle the poster. The movie didn't open until next week, but the buzz it generated had already swept through their school.

"I wish Maggie was with us," Eve said with a touch of melancholy.

Sarah rubbed her reddening nose. "Me, too."

The walk to the Crowne was only a few blocks from the Parrish Hotel, owned by Eve's parents and Aunt Rosie. Despite the short distance, it was cold enough to make her wish she'd brought a scarf. At least she'd have something titillating to share with Maggie once she saw the poster. Maybe her gushing about how improper the advertisement looked would make her friend smile.

"Do you think she really saw the Mothman?" Sarah's voice was barely audible. Nervously, she glanced over her shoulder as if fearing the giant birdlike humanoid would sweep from the sky. "Was she near the TNT?"

Eve shook her head.

A remote area of dense woods and small ponds, the TNT had once been used to store ammunition during World War II. Eve's father had taken her there on a few occasions, allowing her to explore the abandoned weapons "igloos." But ever since the Mothman was first spied in the region, she hadn't been back. Her father said bad things happened there, and Mrs. Quiggly insisted the place was a haven for UFOs.

"She was visiting Nana and followed Mischief into the Witch Wood."

A fat orange tabby, Mischief belonged to Maggie's grandmother, an elderly woman who everyone called Nana. She lived in a sprawling house snuggled up to a thicket of woods at the farthest end of town. Eve and Maggie had dubbed the thicket the "Witch Wood" after discovering a sycamore tree that resembled an old woman with legs.

"But it's too cold to go into the Witch Wood now," Sarah protested.

Eve nodded. She, Maggie, and Sara occasionally played there, but usually in the spring and summer when the trees were green with leaves, making it easy to catch caterpillars and grasshoppers.

"Maggie was afraid Mischief would get lost."

Sarah made a *pffing* sound. "As if! He's always getting into trouble and always finds his way home. I wish she hadn't followed him."

"Me, too." Eve bit her bottom lip, worrying it between her teeth. She'd visited her friend for a brief time yesterday, finding Maggie huddled beneath the blankets in her bedroom. She hadn't been to school for three days. "She's afraid to go outside."

They had almost reached the theater. Farther down the street, traffic was lined up at the red light that led to the Silver Bridge. Her father would be home soon, returning from Gallipolis, a neighboring city nestled on the Ohio side of the river. He'd headed there earlier in the afternoon to meet a friend, and like everyone else, would need to cross the Silver Bridge.

"I heard the Mothman's eyes are red," Sarah said.

"Maggie thought so. She told me when she couldn't find Mischief, she got an odd feeling, like something bad had happened. Her skin broke out in goose bumps."

Sarah's eyes widened. She rubbed her nose again. "My mom says people get a weird sensation when they see the Mothman. I've heard her talking about it to my dad when she thinks I'm not around."

"My parents do the same thing." How strange to be focused on something scary when everything around them reflected the festive mood of the coming Christmas holiday. The streetlights on Main were decorated with cheerful ribbons, wreaths, and pinecones, and a lighted Christmas tree brightened the display window of G. C. Murphy, the local five-and-dime. At the store entrance, a man in a Santa Claus suit called out holiday greetings and beckoned shoppers inside. A sense of excitement and seasonal cheer hung in the air.

"Maggie was scared." Eve wet her lips, remembering what her friend had told her. "She thought she heard a noise. Like scraping, or someone digging."

"What did she do?"

"She crept closer, but stayed hidden behind the trees. At least, she thought she was."

There was no mistaking Sarah's nervousness as she squeezed her mittened hands together. "But she wasn't?"

Eve shook her head, only then realizing how frightened she was for her friend. A lot of people thought the Mothman was trying to warn the town about something terrible, like a looming disaster, and that's why it kept reappearing. But Maggie said the creature was awful. A hideous monster with hateful eyes that bored into her soul. Those who'd seen it said its eyes were so ghastly, they couldn't recall any other feature of its face. Rumored to be at least seven feet tall, it had large wings that allowed it to fly vertically like a helicopter. Most said it was gray in color, and the Mothman's terrifying eyes glowed scarlet even in the daylight.

"She got close and peered through the trees," Eve explained. They stopped in front of the theater, but the poster they'd come to see no longer felt important. Someone blew a horn as the light for the Silver Bridge turned green, but traffic remained at a standstill. "That's when she saw it, crouched on the ground."

"What was it doing?" Sarah's eyes filled with fear.

"Maggie didn't know. It was hunkered down with its wings draped around it like a cape. Then it turned and saw her, and she screamed."

Sarah looked like she wanted to do the same.

A chorus of horns blared from the stalled traffic, causing Eve to knit her brows. "Why do you think all the cars are backed up like that?"

Sarah appeared too focused on the story to pay attention to the vehicles bottled up at the entrance to the Silver Bridge. "Did she run? Did it chase her?"

"Of course she ran. Wouldn't you?"

"I would have screamed my head off."

"Me, too." Her heart kicked into a prickly rhythm. Was it because of her fear for Maggie, or the cold sensation that crept over her as she stared at the unmoving traffic two blocks away? Instinctively, she headed for the backup, Sarah keeping pace beside her. "Maggie heard it chasing her, but she managed to get away and run to Nana's home. She didn't tell anyone about it until two days later. She pretended to be sick so she wouldn't have to go to school."

"But Dr. Pullman couldn't find anything wrong with her." Sarah's observation was half question, half statement.

"Nope. And that's when she had to tell the truth."

"How awful." Sarah soaked in the story as they continued walking, seemingly unconcerned they hadn't stopped to gawk at the poster for *The Graduate* as planned. The sidewalk was busy with Christmas shoppers heading in and out of G. C. Murphy and the local bank.

Any other time, Eve would have delighted in the festive mood, but something didn't feel right. Was she the only one who sensed the ominous undercurrent in the air? And why were there so many birds flitting around overhead, as if they couldn't find a place to rest?

"What happened to Mischief?" Sarah asked.

"He came back later. I heard he was fine."

"He's such a bad cat." Sarah shook her head. "I feel just awful for Maggie. Do you think anyone believes she saw the Mothman?"

"Her parents didn't. They tried to convince her she saw a large bird or something."

"What about Ryan and Caden?"

Ryan was Maggie's other brother. Only a year older than the three of them, they often hung out with him and his friends. Fun and kind of goofy, he was unlike Caden, who Eve thought as dreamy and mysterious as an ancient knight.

"She said Ryan believes her, but Caden thinks she's overreacting."

"Well, he is eighteen." Sarah shrugged. "He's one of them. An adult."

How could she have a crush on an adult? "My mom was talking to Mrs. Flynn earlier, and she said Caden was going to try to get Maggie to go Christmas shopping tonight. You know how she's wanted to visit that new department store in Gallipolis? He thought that might get her out of the house."

"I hope it worked."

"Me, too." Eve's stomach did a queasy flip-flop. Did she really hope so? It would mean Caden and Maggie would be on the Silver Bridge. "It's getting near dinner time. If it worked, they're probably headed back right now." *Like my dad.* "Do you notice all the birds?"

Sarah eyed the sky. "Yeah. Weird, isn't it?"

More horns from the stalled traffic.

"Something's wrong." She started walking faster, bypassing the Santa who waved shoppers into the five-and-dime with a hearty "ho-ho-ho." As the doors opened and closed, the cheerful notes of "Jingle Bells" carried onto the street, spurring her into a jog.

"Eve, wait." Sarah hurried to catch up. "What's wrong with you?"

"The traffic." Goose bumps broke out on the back of her neck. "Look." She'd never seen it stacked up like this before. Friday nights were always busy, especially around rush hour, but even with the addition of Christmas shoppers, there were far too many cars.

The pungent tang of exhaust snarled with the rumble of idling motors as they neared the entrance for the bridge. From her vantage point on the sidewalk, she spied the tall rocker towers erected against the sky. The sun had yet to set, the fiery ball ebbing toward the horizon, painting the silver framework with splashes of tangerine and copper.

"The light's green," Sarah said at her side. "Why aren't they moving?"

Eve glanced at the traffic signal just as it cycled to yellow, then red. Not a single car had inched forward. "The light must be out on the Ohio side. Everything's backed up."

"So people are going to be stuck on the bridge."

Like her father. Like Maggie and Caden.

It shouldn't have bothered her, but an unsettled feeling gnawed at the pit of her stomach. The Silver Bridge defined Point Pleasant, much like the Parrish Hotel. Eve had been on the bridge once when the rocker towers swayed slightly, but her dad had told her they were designed to be flexible, and she shouldn't be afraid. The towers moved with suspension chains to help reduce strain on the bridge piers. She didn't understand the construction, but knew the people of Point Pleasant were inordinately proud of their beloved Silver Bridge.

Sarah shook her head, apparently deciding they'd seen all there was of interest. "Hey, we missed the poster for *The Graduate*. Let's go back."

Eve nodded, trying to mask her uneasiness. "Okay. If my dad's on the bridge, he's going to be stuck in traffic anyway."

She started to turn from the sight when a deafening boom split the air like thunder. A woman's shrill scream knifed deeply into her bones. Within seconds, the terrified shriek was echoed by a dozen more voices raised in horror. Those stalled in traffic poured from their vehicles. On the ramp for the Silver Bridge, reverse lights flashed as cars tried to back away from the traffic signal amid a mad chorus of blaring horns.

"Oh!" Sarah shrieked. "Oh, no. No, no, no!"

Her friend lurched forward, rushing toward the bridge, and Eve jerked in her wake as if pulled by an invisible string. A sob built in her chest. It wasn't happening, couldn't be happening! But even before her gaze fell on the rocker towers looming above the Silver Bridge, she understood the horrified screams, the frenzied bleat of car horns, the chaotic cries of starlings wheeling overhead.

As if trapped in a slow motion bubble, the solid framework twisted sickeningly above a bridge crippled with stalled traffic. Christmas shoppers, truckers, workers returning at the end of the day, even visitors crossing from state to state. How many lives were clustered in that frozen string of cars? Her father. Her friend. Caden.

"Daddy." The name was a pitiful squeak, pushed past the lump in her throat. She lurched another step, vaguely conscious of people swarming past her. They came from cars and stores, from traffic that had stopped haphazardly on Main Street. Screams and voices that made no sense. Birds shrieked above her. Somewhere in the background "Jingle Bells" still played through the open doors of the five-and-dime. Even the suited Santa raced past, waving and hollering for people to get off the entrance ramp.

A scream built in her lungs. Someone yelled for police, someone else for an ambulance. Three steps ahead of her, a woman huddled on the street, hugging a small child to her chest. From the look of the open car door behind her, she had been on the ramp but managed to scramble free, abandoning a brown station wagon. Both the woman and the child were sobbing.

No more than thirty seconds had passed, Eve was sure. Why couldn't she scream? Why couldn't she look away from the twisting rocker towers? In the span of a single heartbeat, they collapsed, the entire bridge folding like a mammoth deck of cards. A heap of metal, steel, and headlights plummeted into the Ohio River.

Eve stumbled to her knees, the scream in her chest ripped lose in a mournful wail.

In little more than sixty seconds, the Silver Bridge was gone, claiming the lives of those she loved.

Chapter 1

June, 1982
Point Pleasant, West Virginia

Eve Parrish stared through the windshield of her Toyota Corolla at the two-story house her aunt had bequeathed to her in her will. A house she remembered fondly from childhood, it had been in her family for four generations, just like the old hotel in downtown Point Pleasant.

Tightening her grip on the steering wheel of the parked car, she vowed to worry about the hotel later. *One problem at a time.*

At twenty-seven, it was staggering to find herself the sole owner of her family's homestead *and* the Parrish Hotel. She'd inherited the latter after her father died, and Eve's mother had signed her ownership of the property over to Aunt Rosie. Not long afterward, her mother had uprooted them, determined to put the tragedy of the Silver Bridge in the past. It had always been Aunt Rosie who came to visit Eve and her mom in Pennsylvania.

But Aunt Rosie was gone.

Why couldn't she have told them about the cancer? Eve would have done something, anything to help. Insisted she get treatment.

"She didn't want treatment," Adam Barnett, Rosie's lawyer had explained as he'd passed her the keys for the hotel and the house earlier that day. "She went quickly, which is how she wanted it."

Eve swiped a tear from her cheek. Aunt Rosie had planned to marry in the summer of '68, but the Silver Bridge altered those plans. Shaken by the tragedy, Eve's aunt had called off her engagement to Roger Layton and never married. Was that why she'd allowed herself to go so quickly once diagnosed with breast cancer? Did she think no one loved her?

A spasm of guilt twisted Eve's stomach. Her small apartment was only six hours away in Harrisburg, but her mom had drilled a steady dislike of Point Pleasant into her head from the time they moved away. It was the place where her father had met his end in the icy waters of the Ohio River only weeks before Christmas and a hotspot for bizarre Mothman and UFO sightings. Was it any wonder her mother had insisted on burying the town in their past?

Right or wrong, Eve hadn't returned in fifteen years. She barely recognized the sparse streets now, so changed from the thriving river community she remembered. She'd been glad to see the Crowne Theater still in operation, but saddened to know G. C. Murphy's had closed its doors. How she, Maggie, and Sarah had loved their soda fountain.

Taking a deep breath, she popped the door on the Corolla and stepped onto the street. Aunt Rosie's house—the same house in which her father and his sister had grown up—was located several miles from downtown Point Pleasant. Every bit as imposing as she remembered, the large two story was offset by a covered porch and a towering chestnut tree in the front yard. Her father had once hung a tire from the lowest branch at Aunt Rosie's behest so Eve and her friends would have a swing when they visited.

Reluctantly, Eve glanced to the house next door. Not quite as large, the cheerful colonial looked in far better condition than the imposing structure Eve had inherited. The paint appeared fresh, the shrubs neatly trimmed. Colorful blooms had already sprouted in the flowerbeds, and a pot of pansies welcomed guests to the front porch.

She'd spent countless afternoons playing in Maggie's home. Countless Friday night sleepovers when they'd stayed up late eating Mrs. Flynn's peanut butter cookies and giggling about boys. She'd never told her friend about the crush she'd had on Caden, but Maggie had known. Best friends always did. Unlike his sister, Caden had survived that fatal night on the Silver Bridge.

With an inhale of determination, Eve hooked her purse onto her shoulder. She would leave her overnight bag and suitcase in the car for the time being. She'd packed light, hoping to finalize plans for the house and hotel within two weeks. Hopefully, Adam Barnett could recommend a real estate company capable of handling residential and commercial sales.

He'd warned her about the break-in. "Nothing taken, it appears. Just vandalism. It happens sometimes when a house sits empty. Probably teenagers looking for a thrill. I had all of the damaged items removed and disposed of as you requested."

The key turned easily in the lock. According to Mr. Barnett, the vandals had gained entrance through the screened porch in the rear, and then busted the kitchen door. Both doors would require reinforcing. With any luck, the rest of the damage would be minimal.

As she stepped inside, a swarm of memories assaulted her. The house smelled stale, closed up for too long, but a trace of Aunt Rosie's signature scent lingered beneath the mustiness. A light bouquet that whispered of spring flowers and clover. On the heels of having visited her aunt's grave at the cemetery, the fragrance brought tears to Eve's eyes. Hugging her arms close to her chest, she blinked them away.

Mr. Barnett had made sure all of the utilities were working, but it was stuffy in the house. She'd have to set the ceiling fans to circulate the air. At least no one had covered Aunt Rosie's pretty furniture with those dreadful white sheets people used when closing an estate.

Her aunt had kept most of the furniture Eve remembered from childhood. The gold and crystal lamps on the end tables were new, but the heavy-footed couch and easy chairs upholstered in crimson brocade were as she remembered, if faded from time. Black walnut tables and thick butternut drapes covered with climbing grapevines accentuated the décor. Surprisingly, there was little damage to the room.

Tracing her fingers along a chair rail, she headed for the dining room. Whoever bought the old monstrosity would have to crave a home with character. It certainly had that. From its wide windowsills to arched openings and massive moldings, it echoed the detailing of a different time.

In the kitchen, she found the door leading to the screened porch reinforced with plywood to prevent further break-ins. The upstairs fared worse. The room her talented aunt had employed as a dark room had been completely ransacked. Mr. Barnett had been hesitant to volunteer the information but said there were chemical spills, and many of her aunt's beloved photos had been found torn and littered on the floor. Looking at the damage, Eve felt a slow burn of anger that someone would destroy her aunt's work. They had no right! As if in mockery of the act, the vandals had used black spray paint to leave a large squiggle on the wall like a brand. Stupid, stupid kids.

Two of the bedrooms had barely been touched, but the last—her aunt's room—had suffered nearly as badly as the dark room. The contents had been dumped from the dresser and closet. At least Mr. Barnett had seen to it that her aunt's lovely clothing had been piled on the bed for her to sort through and replace. Someone had obviously overturned the bureau— the mirror was shattered— and the bedspread had been ripped off and thrown on the floor. This time when the tears welled, she couldn't stop them. It wasn't fair. Her aunt had been taken prematurely at forty-nine by an ugly disease, and this is how her memory was honored? Lifting a soft terry robe from the bed, she inhaled her aunt's scent and pressed the fabric to her cheek.

"I'm sorry, Aunt Rosie. I'm sorry I wasn't there for you when you needed me."

Eve jerked reflexively when a sharp pounding interrupted her thoughts. Given the vandalism she'd witnessed, her heart lurched frightfully, sending a flutter through her stomach. It took a few seconds before she placed the sound as someone banging on the front door. Mr. Barnett had indicated someone from the sheriff's office would likely stop by to talk to her about the damage. She hadn't expected them so soon, but was eager to learn the details of the report. Tucking a stray strand of hair behind her ears, she hurried down the steps, then yanked open the door.

"Why hello there." The petite woman standing on her front porch offered a friendly smile.

"I..." Eve mentally stumbled, her mind doing cartwheels. Something about the woman was familiar. The appearance was off—there was gray in the woman's hair that hadn't been there before, and her eyes looked watery, not bright like Eve remembered—but the inflection of her voice was the same. She swallowed hard. "Mrs. Flynn?"

"I saw your car. Maggie said you were coming."

"Excuse me?"

Her dead friend's mother smiled indulgently and patted her hand. "It's all right. I realize things are different now." Turning, she roamed to the edge of the covered porch and rested her hands lightly on the railing as she gazed over the front yard. "Maggie has waited a long time for you, Eve."

Flummoxed by her unexpected arrival and the strange comments, Eve trailed after her. "Mrs. Flynn? I...don't understand what you mean." Surely, her best friend's mother wasn't discussing Maggie as if she were still alive. Perhaps the woman was ill. Her odd behavior made the whole scenario seem like a dream.

A car passed in front of the house, sending a flutter of leaves into the yard on a puff of air. The breeze smelled of honeysuckle and exhaust, and a clingy kiss of sunlight warmed Eve's face. She couldn't be dreaming.

"Did you know they didn't find her body until June of '68?"

Eve bit her lip, uncertain how to respond. When her mother had uprooted them the spring after the bridge collapse, the bodies of three victims were still missing. She'd later learned that Maggie's remains had been located during the summer, but there was no talk of returning for the funeral. Her mother wouldn't hear of it.

"I'm so sorry." At least her father's body had been discovered in the debris pile on the Ohio side of the river, allowing him the dignity of a proper burial. Not Maggie. For nearly six months, her remains had been battered and misshapen by the cold currents of the river. If the knowledge ripped at Eve's heart, how much more the heart of her friend's mother?

"Would you...would you like to come inside?"

"No thank you, dear." Mrs. Flynn turned to face her. "I just wanted to welcome you back. Maggie asked me to."

Oh, God. The woman was certifiably crazy.

She might have contemplated the thought further but for the arrival of a police car in front of Aunt Rosie's house. Mrs. Flynn shook her head at the sight, then quietly left the porch without so much as a goodbye. She was halfway across the yard when the man in the car stepped onto the street.

"Mom," he called.

Mom?

Eve felt her eyebrows launch into her bangs as she watched the man dart around the rear of his car to greet Mrs. Flynn on the grass. They exchanged a few soft words before the woman continued her path back to her home and the man jogged toward the porch. As he hustled up the steps, Eve got the shock of her life.

"Ryan?"

"Hey, you remembered." Maggie's brother grinned and extended his hand.

When she slid her fingers into his, he yanked her close, hugging her tightly. In no time, she found herself laughing breathlessly.

"It's so good to see you, Ryan." She hugged him back, delighted by the warmth his unexpected presence brought. "Mr. Barnett never said you worked for the sheriff's department."

"Yep. A sergeant." He tapped the badge pinned to his neatly pressed uniform, then held her at arm's length, his smile igniting a sparkle in his blue eyes.

It was hard to believe the skinny thirteen-year-old she remembered had matured into such a tall, broad-shouldered man. His black hair, no longer curly but wavy, lay tousled over his brow, his grin as infectious as always.

"God, it's good to see you after all these years." Ryan seemed reluctant to release her. "I ran into Adam Barnett at the bank, and he told me he'd given you the keys. I can't believe you're really here."

"I can't either." She hugged him again, then laughed. "You got so tall."

"And you got so…" He paused and wiggled his eyebrows, molding his hands in the shape of an hourglass. "Curvy."

She swatted his arm. "You always were a trouble-maker. Do you want to come in for a while? The house is a wreck, but—"

"Actually, that's why I'm here. I wanted to go over the vandalism report with you." He sobered abruptly and stepped away. "And I'm sorry about my mother. I hope she didn't say anything to upset you."

"No, I…" How did she explain the odd conversation? She'd only been in Point Pleasant a short while. The last thing she wanted to do was offend a childhood friend by pointing out that his mother was off her rocker.

Ryan shook his head, clearly conscious of what may have been said. "Sometimes she gets confused and gets caught up in the past."

Eve let the remark slide without comment. "I was just going to get my bags out of my car." She steered the conversation elsewhere. "Maybe you could give me a hand?"

"Sure."

Together, they trudged to her Corolla. Ryan grabbed her suitcase and overnight bag while Eve snatched a jacket from the backseat along with a few boxed goods she'd brought for the trip. Later, she'd hit the grocery store and stock up on perishable items. At least the refrigerator was in working order.

In the house, Ryan carried her luggage upstairs while she detoured to the kitchen with her small parcel of crackers, instant rice, and peanut butter. She wished she had something to offer him, but the best she could manage was peanut butter and crackers. Mentally, she bumped the grocery store higher on her to-do list.

"I put everything in the spare bedroom for you," Ryan announced, entering the kitchen. "I guess you saw Rosie's room is a mess."

Eve added her box of instant rice to the nearest cupboard, nudging aside several cans of Campbell's soup left behind by Aunt Rosie. A vivid memory flashed through her mind as she recalled her aunt feeding her tomato soup and a grilled cheese for lunch on a brisk autumn day.

"Her dark room, too." Eve shut the cupboard and turned, bracing her back against the counter. "The vandals hit the upstairs hard. Do you have any idea who would have done such a thing?"

"Afraid not." Ryan motioned her toward the dining room. "Let's sit down."

At the dining room table, he withdrew a folded sheaf of papers from his breast pocket. "I thought you should have a copy of the vandalism report."

Eve eyed the papers he handed her. It was standard stuff—date, time, damage done. "Who reported it?"

"No one. I still live next door with my mom. It's um…complicated." He cleared his throat awkwardly. "After Rosie died, I kept an eye on the place. Several days after her death, I was walking around the house when I noticed the door on the screened porch had been busted. I guess the vandals chose it because it was hidden from the street. Easy entry."

"Did they take anything?"

"Not that I could tell, but Rosie isn't here to answer that question. I should have said it before, Eve, but you have my sympathies." He covered her hand with his where it rested on the table.

She managed a wan smile and nodded a thank you. It was good to see him again, a familiar face that made the shock of returning to her childhood home less traumatic. Even if he was grown, no longer the thirteen-year-old boy she remembered, he was still the brother of her one-time best friend.

"So you think it was just kids out for some fun?" She winced, unable to comprehend how anyone could view destroying the home of the recently deceased as entertaining.

He hesitated. "It looks that way."

"Is there something you're not telling me?"

"Nothing of importance." He patted her hand again and stood, then paced a short distance away. "What are you going to do with the place?"

The million-dollar question. "Sell it, of course." It hurt to say, as if she was turning her back on Aunt Rosie and all her aunt held dear. "Vandalism aside, the home needs work to make it desirable. I'm no expert, but it looks like it could use a new roof and several of the rooms should be repainted. If I want to put it on the market, I'm going to have to fix it up first." It was a sobering thought. "I don't suppose you could recommend someone?"

He surprised her with a quick answer. "Do you remember Caden?"

"Your brother?" Her heart lurched again. How could she forget her childhood crush?

"He has a contracting business. Home remodeling, repairs. That sort of thing."

"It sounds ideal." For some reason she hadn't considered encountering him when she'd returned to Point Pleasant. "Do you have a phone number for him? I'd like to talk to him about taking on the repairs."

"How about if I have him stop by tomorrow? Will that work?"

"Perfect." She was planning on addressing the hotel tomorrow, something that would probably take most of the day. "Do you think he can stop early? Around nine? I was planning on visiting the hotel later."

"It shouldn't be a problem." He shot her a sideways glance as if measuring her reaction. "The hotel is still the center of town."

"I thought as much." Eve glanced at her hands, thinking back to the years when her parents and Aunt Rosie had made the hotel the focus of their lives. It had been her family's defining legacy long before she was born. Her great grandfather Clarence had paid for its construction in 1922, then quickly turned the establishment into a thriving operation, bolstered in part by Point Pleasant's blossoming river trade. It hadn't taken her more than a few hours in town to realize those days were nothing more than a memory. "I noticed things are different."

A shadow crossed Ryan's face. "A lot's changed since you left."

"The Silver Bridge affected everything."

He nodded, shoulders slumping as he stuffed his hands in his pockets. "It wasn't just the catastrophe. Bruce Mechanical closed up shop shortly afterward. That dried up half the employment in town. Point Pleasant isn't the thriving river community it used to be."

How sad. Eve had fond memories of watching riverboats and tugs traverse the waters of the Ohio and Kanawha Rivers, ushering barges loaded with coal from Ohio to West Virginia and vice-versa. When Bruce Mechanical launched a new boat, the event was guaranteed to draw a crowd. She, Maggie, and Sarah had eagerly raced to the docks as the newly built ships slid sideways into the water, tilting so far she feared they would capsize before righting themselves.

Ryan returned to his seat at the table, then reclined comfortably, crossing an ankle over his knee. "Main Street is pretty much a ghost town these days. I'm sure you noticed."

She nodded. "They moved the Silver Bridge."

"We call it the Silver Memorial Bridge now, but you're right." A frown flitted across his mouth. "The new bridge diverts the flow of traffic out of town, bypassing Main. As much as we appreciate the Silver Memorial Bridge, it's partially responsible for sapping Point Pleasant's lifeblood."

"What about the hotel?" She had to know.

"It holds its own." Ryan gave a one-shouldered shrug. "It may not pull the traffic it did in its heyday, but according to Rosie, it was solvent. I'm sure you've seen the books."

"Enough of them." The hotel was a juggernaut she needed to tackle.

"So you really want to sell it?" Ryan asked.

She glanced at her hands. The Parrish Hotel was as much a part of Point Pleasant as the historic Silver Bridge. Her family had invested decades in its growth. The idea of fluffing it off for financial gain was nothing short of sacrilege.

"I'm still undecided." It wasn't an entire lie. Part of her resisted the idea of unloading an institution that had been her family's legacy. "Right now I'm using two weeks of my vacation time from Labor and Industry. I do clerical work, not the most exciting thing, but it's a Commonwealth job, and the benefits are good. I don't know the first thing about overseeing a hotel."

"That's what a manager is for."

"I'm not sure I want to go that route." The thought of entrusting so much to someone she didn't know left her uneasy.

"You've got a lot on you," Ryan conceded. "Half of the businesses on Main Street were forced to close."

"But the hotel survived."

"Along with the Crowne Theater. At least for now. Your aunt saw to the hotel's prosperity. The Parrish name still has enough clout to draw visitors from neighboring states."

She nodded and laced her hands on her lap. "I'll look into it tomorrow." Wrapping her head around the house was enough for the day. Suddenly, she didn't want to think about the past or the pressing matters looming over her head. She simply wanted to bask in the warmth of seeing an old friend. "Thanks for bringing the vandalism report. I never would have pegged you as a cop. You always got into so much trouble as a kid."

He laughed. "Odd how things turn out. What about you? Did you marry?"

"No."

"I didn't either. No luck yet, or just not ready to settle down. I can't figure out which."

"That doesn't surprise me." He'd always been a free spirit, much like Rosie, playful and prone to trouble. "What about Caden?" She hoped the query appeared as nothing more than the innocent probing of an old friend trying to catch up on the present. Her heart gave a little flutter when she thought of him. Amazing her long-buried attraction was still there.

"Caden's single, too." Ryan shook his head. "He'll probably end up an old man living alone unless he moves past his guilt."

"What do you mean?"

Ryan waved a hand as if brushing away the thought. "He hasn't forgiven himself for taking Maggie shopping that night. Most of us have moved on. Caden hasn't."

She thought of herself, her mother. Their world had come to a crashing halt that cold December night when her father's car fell into the Ohio River. And yet somehow they'd rummaged up the strength to continue. It had taken uprooting, leaving the shadow of the disaster behind in Point Pleasant, but somehow her mother had managed to put the pieces together for herself and her twelve-year-old daughter. Eventually, her mother had remarried, and Eve found herself with a stepfather. As much as she loved the man, part of her understood Caden's refusal to relinquish the past.

"What about your parents?" She couldn't help venturing the question given the odd discussion she'd had with Mrs. Flynn. Should she tell Ryan what his mother had said about Maggie...talking about her as if she were still alive?

He shrugged, and she sensed his reluctance. "My father passed away a few years ago."

"I'm so sorry." She had fond memories of Mr. Flynn.

"It was his lungs. All those years spent working in a coal mine finally caught up with him."

"What about your mother?"

"She's accepted his death, but Maggie's..." Again a shrug that said far more than words. "A part of her died when that bridge went down."

Eve bit her lip. She could understand Mrs. Flynn's pain.

"Most of the time she's okay," Ryan continued. "But other times, she retreats into the past and insists Maggie is still alive. She talks about her as if they share discussions. It's the reason I still live at home...to take care of her. She can be a handful when she's in the past."

Eve wasn't sure what to say. So much tragedy had happened when the Silver Bridge collapsed. The town had suffered, but more than that, the populace had crumpled under the blow of individual losses. Fifteen years later, splinters of that residual pain reached far and wide.

"I'm sorry." There were no words for the loss or the choking reach of its tentacles.

"We do the best we can." As if deciding he'd had enough gloom, Ryan stood. "It's good to have you back, Eve, even if only for a short while. I'll tell Caden to drop by tomorrow morning."

She walked him to the door, thankful to have encountered a familiar face. It had been a stroke of luck to learn Caden was a contractor. It would save her the trouble of looking for someone to do the repairs and speed the sale of the house that much more quickly.

"What about Sarah?" she asked as he stepped onto the front porch. Eve stayed inside on the threshold, a breeze scuttling past her like an uninvited guest. "Does she still live in town?"

He nodded. "She works in the records division at the courthouse. We had a bad situation there several years back. I'm not sure if Rosie told you about the bomb blast."

She had. A suicidal ex-convict had forced his way inside with a shotgun and a homemade explosive device. Despite attempts at negotiation, the bomber had leveled the entire first floor, killing three and injuring six others. After hearing about it, Eve had called her aunt to make sure she was safe.

"Another tragedy in a town plagued by them," Aunt Rosie had said. "Fools around here are saying it's the curse of Cornstalk come to blight us again."

"I saw it on the news when it happened," Eve told Ryan. At the time, she'd wondered if it was in some way connected to the Mothman. She didn't believe in the curse of Cornstalk, an Indian chief who'd been murdered in the days preceding the American Revolution. Local legend said he'd cursed the town with his dying breath. You couldn't grow up in Point Pleasant without having the shadow of that legend leech into every event that took place.

"Sarah wasn't hurt, was she?" Cold fear gripped her stomach as she thought of her childhood friend.

"No, she wasn't working then, but we lost a lot of good people. Strange how things keep happening in this town." He raised a hand in farewell. "Stay in touch, Eve. Don't leave without saying goodbye."

She stayed at the door, closing it only after he'd driven off in his police cruiser. The emptiness of the house settled over her with a marked hush, and she wondered how Aunt Rosie had managed living there on her own for so many years. Then again, like the hotel, the house was part of Parrish history.

Meet the Author

Mae Clair opened a Pandora's Box of characters when she was a child and never looked back. Her father, an artist who tinkered with writing, encouraged her to create make-believe worlds by spinning tales of far-off places on summer nights beneath the stars.

Mae loves creating character-driven fiction in settings that vary from contemporary to mythical. Wherever her pen takes her, she flavors her stories with mystery, suspense, and a hint of romance. Married to her high school sweetheart, she lives in Pennsylvania and is passionate about cryptozoology, old photographs, a good Maine lobster tail, and cats.

Discover more about Mae on her website and blog at MaeClair.net